PUSHKIN VERTIGO

LONDON
IN
BLACK

'A truly absorbing novel – an all-day-on-the-couch read if ever there was one. Its vision of the near future is plausible enough to be legitimately frightening… an unusually compelling thriller'

KEVIN BROCKMEIER, AUTHOR OF *THE BRIEF HISTORY OF THE DEAD*

'A taut and timely blend of crime and dystopia'

ALEX SCARROW, AUTHOR OF THE DCI BOYD THRILLERS

'A skilfully rendered homage to London, with a dystopian police procedural woven in… a protagonist you want to root for, and a fast-paced mystery at its heart'

GUY MORPUSS, AUTHOR OF *FIVE MINDS*

'[A] genre-bending whirlwind of a read… Read if you dare'

AMY LILWALL, AUTHOR OF *THE BIGGERERS*

'This dark dystopian thriller has the makings of being one of the best first novels out this year… powerful and unsettling… has the potential to become a cult classic'

SHOTS MAGAZINE

'Gripping, evocative and will keep you guessing'

PRESS ASSOCIATION

'A debut that's genuinely exciting, page-turning and frighteningly credible'

BUSINESS POST

JACK LUTZ lives in London with his wife and daughter. He is fascinated by the city he calls home and loves to read about and explore it. The idea for this book came to him while changing trains on the Tube. *London in Black* is his first novel.

JACK LUTZ

LONDON IN BLACK

PUSHKIN VERTIGO

Pushkin Vertigo
An imprint of Pushkin Press
Somerset House, Strand
London WC2R 1LA

The right of Jack Lutz to be identified as the author of this Work has been
asserted by him in accordance with the Copyright, Designs & Patents Act 1988

Copyright © Jack Lutz 2022

First published by Pushkin Press in 2022
This edition published 2023

3 5 7 9 8 6 4 2

ISBN 13: 978-1-78227-806-1

All rights reserved. No part of this publication may be reproduced,
stored in a retrieval system or transmitted in any form or by any
means, electronic, mechanical, photocopying, recording or otherwise,
without prior permission in writing from Pushkin Press

Designed and typeset by Tetragon, London
Printed and bound by Clays Ltd, Elcograf S.p.A.

www.pushkinpress.com

For my wife, my daughter and my mother

CHAPTER ONE

London, 2029

I just threw a fucking chair through Wilkes's window.

Lucy looked down at her shaking hands. The red tint was fading. *Breathe.* Looked back up, around the squad room. Six other cops, all men: cheap suits, stubble. All staring. She saw six, knew there were more, hidden in the dark edges of her tunnel vision.

Her thoughts came in bursts.

I just threw? A fucking chair? Through Wilkes's window?

She had.

She could see the chair. There it was, crumpled in the corridor, covered in bits of frosted glass. Black letters stood out against the flooring, and for a split second she thought of trying to fix it, trying to glue the thing back together like a giant puzzle. First, the big letters: LONDON METROPOLITAN POLICE—HOMICIDE COMMAND—MIT 19. Then the small type: Commanding Officer, DCI Marie Wilkes.

Wilkes.

Wilkes's brand-new window.

Fuck me.

She tried to think, to process what she'd done. *Why? Why would I...*

A rustle behind her. She spun around, saw DS Andy Sykes.

Oh.

Sykes.

She couldn't remember what he'd done, which button he'd pressed. *Touched my stomach? No. Trapped me? Can't have.* It was gone, vanished into the red. But he'd done something to set off an attack. Must have done. Sykes knew her triggers. Pretended not to, but most certainly fucking did. And now there he stood, shoulders shrugging, acting shocked. Playing the victim.

Bastard.

A young DC reached out a hand—*it's okay, Lucy*—but Lucy was too quick. She pushed it away, took off. Out of the bullpen, away from the stares, into the corridor, slamming the metal door behind her.

DI Lucy Stone, the Met's youngest homicide detective, was on fire.

Her hands shook as she stomped down the hallway. She jammed them into the pockets of her baggy black hoodie and focused on her breathing.

Inhale, exhale. Inhale, exhale.

Fuck me.

Lucy reached the end of the corridor, rounded the corner. Ahead, she could see the gleaming New Scotland Yard lobby. It was late, had been dark for hours, but the lobby still bustled. Two uniforms sauntered down the hall towards her. She split them, sending coffees flying.

Focus. Breathe.

Just an attack. It's now. It's now, not then, stay now…

Images from two years ago burst into her mind, rapid-fire. Heaps of bodies, skin blistered, sloughing off. Green hazmat suits. A shrieking child, running naked. Drones.

The Scourge.

And then, she saw—*It.*

The Thing That Happened.

She held back a scream and willed herself forward, towards the exit.

Inhale, exhale.

Lucy wiped away a tear as she shot into the night.

‡ ‡ ‡

8

Outside, the chilly November air felt soothing on her face.

The panic faded as she passed the New Scotland Yard sign and turned down the Embankment. Big Ben loomed ahead, a giant hypodermic pricking the night sky. She pulled a hand from her hoodie and held it out as she walked. *Better.* It trembled, but she could at least read the tattooed script curving round the inside of her right wrist: JACK. She rubbed it and thought of her older brother.

Oh Jack, help me. I fucked up.

Would Wilkes take it personally? Hard not to. Twenty-five years on the job, no kids, whole life given to the job. Finally made up to DCI, finally *her* name on the window. *Her* window. And then, in an instant: *smash.*

Lucy's stomach twisted.

I didn't mean it, Ma'am. Truly.

Just, Sykes did something, set me off, an attack. Fucking Sykes…

The Tube roundel came into view and, next to it, the yellow lights of the Carpenters' Arms: MIT19's local. Lucy slowed, took a breath. Checked her mobile. *Eleven. An hour. Fine. Plenty of time for a quick one.* She threaded through the punters smoking on the pavement and ducked inside.

The Carpenters was a shit pub. Grim, threadbare carpets. Whiffy. A coach party of tourists in matching red anoraks clogged the entrance. She pushed through them easily, arms strong from years of boxing. Past the blinking fruities, straight for the empty rear of the bar. She sat down on a stool.

Harry the bartender came over.

"The usual, Lucy?"

She said nothing, just gave a final exhale.

"Right." He poured a Coke from the gun, fiddled with the coffee machine, sunk two shots of espresso into the glass. Pushed it across to Lucy. "The usual."

She took it without looking up.

Good bartender, Harry. Deserves a better pub.

Across the room, the tourists laughed at something. Lucy glanced over, saw they had discovered the poppy box. A cardboard box filled with black paper poppies stood next to the till, and the tourists were taking turns plunking in a pound coin and pinning a poppy to their Gore-Tex. She caught snippets of the coach guide's commentary: "...second anniversary...worst terror attacks in...drones, all releasing London Black. Yes, yes, precisely, a nerve agent, no antidote..."

One of the tourists fished a black rubber wristband from the box.

She squinted. *London Strong* was printed in white on one side of the band. On the other was a number. It was too far away for her to read the digits, but she knew it all the same: 32,956. Every Londoner knew that number.

Christ. A fucking death-count band. What sick fuck—

Her mobile phone began to vibrate. She pulled it from the pocket of her faded black jeans, glanced at the screen: Incoming call, DCI Marie Wilkes. Lucy mashed the red button and thumped the phone down on the bar. *Not in the mood for a lecture, Ma'am.* She took a sip from her glass. After a moment, texts began to bubble up.

Suspended.

A pause.

Unofficially.

A longer pause.

Lucy...please. For me. Try the Counsellor. Just once.

More ellipses appeared, but Lucy ignored them. She shoved the phone back into her jeans pocket and put her head down on her forearms. Took a deep breath. *Fuck. Fuck fuck fuck. Suspended.* She felt like vomiting. *Wilkes can't. I need to work. She knows I need to work. Else, what am I? If I can't work, if I'm not a cop, how can I ever pay the Debt? How can I—*

A squeak, as someone sat down on the stool next to her.

"Long day?"

Man's voice. Unfamiliar. She didn't bother to look up.

"Lot of things flying around," she said into her bicep.

Do I look like I'm up for it? Really?

He paused, then tried again.

"Saw you just now as you came in. Haven't we met before?"

Christ. Of all the lines to pick. Well, Romeo, let's see. She raised her head, sighed, then stared up at his face. Squinted. Felt the gears turn, her little Party Trick working its magic.

And...nope.

"No," she said. "No, we've never met."

Out the corner of her eye, she noticed Harry grin. *Wait. Harry knows I'm a Super Recognizer?* She filed this away. Meant to be private, a goddamn medical condition, but some other MIT19 regular must've let it slip. *Probably Sykes. Wanker.*

"Oh," said the man. "Right. Course. Sorry."

She watched him scan her face. *Inspecting the goods, yeah?* Lucy had a broad, square jaw tapering to a pointy chin. A cute chin, men told her. *Which, fuck that, it's a strong chin. Chin that can take an uppercut.* Espresso hair, chopped short. Big almond eyes, bigger purple bags beneath. Thin nose, hard mouth. Twenty-nine years old. *Like what you see, buddy? Too bad. Not on offer. Item out of stock.*

His eyes lit up.

"Oh, sorry...but it's just, I think I know..."

She saw where he was headed. *For fuck's sake. Not the Actor now.*

"I mean," he continued, "this is awkward, I know, but you aren't by any chance—"

"No. Not her."

People had made the comparison at least once a week for years. It annoyed her more and more each time. *Yes, flattering, yes, the Actor is pretty, really she is, but how can they not see how*

11

different we look? Apples and oranges, oranges and apples. And I'm the wormy fucking apple.

She stood, finished her drink, pushed the empty glass back towards Harry.

"Now if you'll excuse me…"

"Wait, wait. I didn't mean…" He rose from his stool, hands raised, but Lucy was already moving. She brushed past. Tried to avoid contact, slip him like a punch, but his arms were too long.

She felt his fingers graze her stomach.

Oh fuck.

Not again.

Images began to flash.

She put her head down and bolted for the door, crashing through the tourists with their poppies and their smiles and their ghastly fucking wristbands. It was raining now. Her black trainers squeaked as she fled down the steps into the Tube station.

‡ ‡ ‡

She was calm again by the time the train pulled into Barbican Station.

It was fully kitted out for London Strong Week now, Lucy noticed. Banners, signs, posters of sombre-looking Londoners holding hands. A programme of events: the Remembrance Wreath Procession, a London-wide moment of silence. Black poppies everywhere. As she rode the escalator upwards, she passed a poster with a bright red tag line across the top: CAN YOU SEE ME? But she couldn't—the man's head was completely defaced. Someone had stuck dozens of round stickers over the top, each with an image of a large double-barred cross. At the bottom she could still make out the poster's footer: THE SURVIVORS' RIGHTS ASSOCIATION SUPPORTS LONDON STRONG WEEK.

Heathens. She tried to peel off a sticker as the escalator carried her past.

At the top, she tapped through the ticket barrier, then stopped at the Cox gate for the London Black scan. An amber light flashed. The chem sniffers whirred as they passed over her body.

God bless Flinders Cox.

She tried to remember the last copycat attack. Up in Harringay, she thought, week ago now, but maybe she'd missed one? *Never know. No one announces them, no one claims them.* Not the same terrorists as the Scourge, the original attacks two years back. Couldn't be, those men were locked up, rotting away in Belmarsh. *But the copycats? Whoever they are, whatever they want, the attacks just keep fucking coming.* The station clock read 23:40, and she tapped her foot as the scan finished. A click, then green light. The Cox gate doors whooshed open. She walked through and headed out of the station, into the night.

It was raining harder now. Thick drops soaked her top. Lucy flipped up the hood. It muffled the street noise, tunnelled her vision. Like one of her attacks in a way, but there was no red, thank God, and she could still think, sort out the new problem. *So. Suspension. Fuck. But…unofficial. Which means…what, exactly?*

As she moved north on Goswell Road, the neighbourhood grew grittier. Betting shops, chicken shops. Metal shutters covered in graffiti. Teenagers' tags, mostly, but some bits still left from the Scourge, if you knew where to look. A few red X's. Evac arrows. And scrawled in silver on the side of a corner shop: *We aLL DeaD NoW, WoE, WoE.*

Lucy tugged on her hoodie drawstrings.

Reckon it's just a warning. Unwritten warning, those are a thing. Still feel pretty shit about it. Sorry, Ma'am. But…might not be so bad, yeah? If I can still work, still pay the Debt, that's what counts.

She passed a cash point alcove. A rough sleeper huddled inside, under a red tarp. His cardboard sign was soggy and the pen had run, but she could still read the words:

I SURVIVED † LONDON BLACK † GOD BLESS

She stopped, reached into her jeans pocket, dropped a pound coin into his battered Costa cup. The man stirred. A wheeze: "Bless." He pulled back the tarp. Lucy turned away, but not quickly enough. A thin gauze mask covered the man's face, but through a slit, she could still see his eyes.

Black.

His eyes were entirely black.

She kept walking. Sighed. Felt bad about looking away, knew it was rude and hurtful and cruel, but seeing Survivors' faces always made the guilt worse somehow. Made the Debt seem bigger. *As if it wasn't big enough already.*

Five minutes later, Lucy turned off Goswell Road and approached her building, an ugly block of flats. Barely affordable when she was a student at City; she'd only stopped worrying about making rent once Simon moved in, just before he proposed. She unlocked the lobby door—hard to call it a lobby, really, just a crap little stairwell landing with a few post cubbies—and climbed three flights to her hallway. Last door on the left: dented metal, its cherry red paint cracked and flaking.

Lucy stomped three times on the grubby doormat and entered.

The flat was tiny. Spartan. One small bedroom, nearly empty. She'd painted the walls black. Ceiling, too. A battered wooden desk shoved against the far wall was the only piece of proper furniture. One mirrored cupboard. Three floor lamps were spaced around the room, and Lucy made a quick circuit, switching them all on. A free-standing pull-up bar lurked in the corner.

There was no bed.

She kicked off her trainers, then removed the hoodie, revealing a black vest. A clothes hanger dangled from one of the lamps. She took it down, pulled the hoodie through and hung it back up, smoothing the damp material with her hands. With her finger, she traced the 'Jack' embroidered above the left breast. Thought about Jack. About Simon. How strange it was they never met.

Her phone alarm began to chirp.

Midnight. Perf.

Lucy padded through to the bathroom. It had no door. She'd taken it off the hinges, dragged it to a skip behind the building, left it to rot. It was her first task two years ago, once everything was over. Done it even before she'd removed the bed, before she'd painted the walls. Now she sat down on the toilet seat and pulled the vest over her head.

Every inch of her torso was covered with bruises.

Big, angry, purple bruises. Mean-looking, like she'd taken a full fight's worth of body blows straight on, one after another after another. In the middle of each one: a tiny needle mark. To the left of her belly button, a small ceramic disc with a Cox Labs logo was attached to her skin. She waved her phone in front of the disc, and a number appeared on the mobile screen: 7.4.

Right. Boost time.

A white cardboard box sat on the sink, beneath a cobweb-cracked mirror. Lucy reached inside. Pulled out a syringe. It was enormous, needle fit for a horse. The label running down the spine read: COX LABS — ELEMIDOX © — 30mL. She rotated it in her fingers.

God bless Flinders Cox, she thought again.

And then, mechanically: *I am thankful for this Boost.*

She dug back into the box. This time she pulled out a small white sachet. Tore it open with her teeth, extracted an alcohol swab and rubbed it on her stomach. The purple skin glistened. She removed the black circular cap from the syringe and tucked it into her jeans pocket. Primed the gigantic needle. Took a breath.

Now, think.

Think about what you did.

Lucy jabbed the needle directly into one of her bruises.

The liquid was viscous; the plunger moved slowly. Her hand trembled, then shook. *Christ.* The shaking spread to her arm. She stared at her cracked reflection. The plunger was still only halfway down. *Oh. Oh, Jesus, it fucking hurts.* As the last of the liquid disappeared into her body, she spoke out loud to the splintered Lucys in the mirror, each word coming out as a gasp:

"You. Deserve. This."

You deserve the pain.

She closed her eyes and sat for a minute, arm still twitching. Forced herself to picture what had happened back then, two years ago. What she'd done. Everything, all of it, start to finish, right up to The Thing. A tear plunked to the tile floor. Then she stood up, took a deep breath, tossed the empty syringe into a yellow sharps bin and swiped her mobile in front of the sensor disc once more.

8.7.

Lucy frowned. She tried again. *8.7.*

Not 9? Strange.

She shrugged—*must be a mistake*—then walked to the desk. *Right, back to it. Work time.* Her laptop sat square in the middle of the desk top. Lucy flipped it open and sat down. *Wilkes won't have thought of blocking remote access. Plus, unofficial suspension, right? Right. It'll work. Has to.* She clicked on the remote login icon, typed in her Met ID and password. Hit return. *Fingers crossed.*

A pop-up: Access denied.

God fucking bitch shit fuck wanker.

"Rats," she said out loud.

She tried a second time. Same result.

Lucy pushed her chair back from the desk, ran unvarnished nails through her hair. *Now what the fuck do I do? Now how do I pay the Debt?*

The Debt was awful. Horrible. She felt it always. Not a financial debt, not money, but a jet-black, deep-down guilt that crushed her, overwhelmed her, threatened to obliterate her. The Debt felt like a weight she dragged wherever she went. Had done for two years now, ever since the Thing happened and the Debt was born. The worst part about the Debt was that she didn't know how much she owed, when the guilt would lift. *If* it would lift. Working helped, that much she knew. Each murder she solved felt like a tiny payment. But no work meant she couldn't pay. And then the guilt would mount, rise to the skies, a giant black mountain that would tumble down and flatten her, once and for all.

Fuck me.

And then there was the time.

She checked her phone. It was barely half midnight.

So what do I do for the next four hours?

Each night, Lucy's tiny flat hosted a prize fight, a knock-down-drag-out ten-rounder. Lucy Stone in one corner, ladies and gents, squaring off against her perpetual opponent: sleep. She hated sleep. Feared it. Sleep brought the dreams, the Screamers, the ones that made her wake up shaking, cheeks wet with tears. Work helped her fight the sleep off. She could last until four most nights, poring over case files, planning next steps. Trips to the kitchen, where she mixed her drink of choice: a canned espresso double shot cracked open and dumped into a bottle of Coke. *A Lucy Stone,* Harry called it sometimes when he mixed it at the Carpenters. *One Lucy Stone, coming up.* She might drink three, four a night. With no bed to tempt her—she'd dragged that out to the skip, too, the mattress and bits of frame left next to the bathroom door—she worked until she passed out at her desk.

But now there was no work.

And books, films, TV—those were all things for old Lucy. Not for her, not with the Debt.

So…

She looked over to the pull-up bar.

Only one left thing to do.

Lucy put her phone down and walked to the bar. Looked up.

Before the Scourge, she had struggled to do a single pull-up on Simon's bar. Now she could do a hundred. Two hundred, maybe. She didn't keep track. Couldn't. Too painful. Just did them, over and over and over, until the tears streamed down and her mind burned with the memory of The Thing That Happened and she finally slid down and crumpled to the floor, gasping and shaking but somehow, the tiniest bit lighter. The pull-ups paid the Debt, too.

She took a breath, then leapt up and grabbed the bar.

On the desk, her mobile buzzed.

Wilkes? Could be. Fine, okay, Ma'am. You can have your lecture.

Lucy dropped down, walked over to the desk. Looked at the screen: Incoming Call, Annoying Reporter 2. *Not Wilkes then.* She frowned. Hit the green button.

"DI Stone."

"On suspension, Lucy?" The reporter's accent was cut-glass. She always wondered why they assigned toffs to the crime beat. *Chasing thrills, down with us plebs?* She kept a few as contacts in her phone, in case she needed a favour with the press. Didn't bother learning the names. They changed out quickly anyway.

"It's not a suspension—"

"Not what I hear." An annoying singsong.

"Then you hear wrong."

She could make out noises in the background. Chatter. A quick blast of siren.

Fuck is all this about, then?

"Right," he said. "Sure. If you say. Bit surprised not to see you here, is all. Asked around. Heard the goss. Just thought you'd appreciate a heads-up. But if you already know, then hey-ho…"

You're looking to bank a favour. But for what?

What could you possibly know?

"Wait," she said. "Wait. Where are you?"

"So you *haven't* heard, then?"

She sighed, sick of his game. "Heard *what?*" *Spill it, Nigel or Basil or whatever the fuck your name is.*

"Well…" He paused, suddenly coy. "Not sure if I should be saying, really…"

"Want me to say it? Fine. I owe you. Now talk."

Silence.

And then:

"Flinders Cox was murdered tonight."

CHAPTER TWO

Lucy pressed the door buzzer a third time.

It was pouring. Small, hard drops struck the cobblestones, bounced, returned to the ground. Lucy's hair was plastered to her head. She hadn't bothered with her hood on the walk from the Overground station. Hardly even noticed the rain. Hardly noticed anything, really, not the cold, not the dark, not the drunken lads catcalling as she marched past. She only had one thought: *I need this fucking case.*

Need it more than anything. And I can't let you stand in my way, Ma'am.

As she reached for a fourth press of the buzzer, the lock clicked. The door inched open. A woman's head appeared above the chain. Late forties, tall, well-groomed. Wavy chestnut hair, up for the night. A handsome woman.

"Lucy?" DCI Marie Wilkes stared down at her rain-soaked protégé.

Lucy said nothing, stared right back. Her eyes blazed. *How could you? Yes, chair, smash, right, fine. Bad Lucy. But...Flinders Cox? Flinders fucking Cox? Of all the people in the world, Ma'am, Flinders Cox is murdered and you keep me off the case?*

Wilkes tried again. "Lucy, what on earth are you—"

"Flinders Cox, Ma'am."

Silence, save for the steady patter of rain.

How could you do it?

A rustle as Wilkes unfastened the chain and pushed the door wide.

"Well, suppose you'd better come in, then. Can't just *stand* out there, can we?"

Lucy wiped her feet on the mat and entered.

Inside, the flat was elegant. A converted warehouse: clean lines, high ceilings. Wilkes's silk dressing gown swished on the hardwood floor as she led Lucy halfway down the hallway, then stopped next to a side table. Pink carnations stood in a shabby chic vase.

She looked uncertain.

What's the matter, Ma'am? Scared I'll break something? Tear up your posh new digs?

"Can I get you something, Lucy? Tea, coffee?"

Lucy shook her head. Water dripped from her hoodie. It began to pool on the wood. Expensive-looking wood—beech, maybe, Lucy wasn't sure, had only half-listened all those times Wilkes tried to talk interior design. *Please give me what I want and then I'll stop dripping all over your vintage distressed whatever fucking flooring.*

Wilkes sighed. "I was going to tell you in the morning," she said. "Hoped you'd be sleeping."

Oh, Ma'am. Please. You know better.

"The call came in just after you made your little exit," Wilkes said. "You know how it is. Madhouse. Everyone scrambling." She fingered her gold watch. "And it doesn't matter, anyway. You're suspended. By rights, you should be here grovelling for your job. Destruction of Met property? You could be sacked. Done. So if you think I'll change my mind just because some new case comes through…"

Lucy glared. *Some new case? What, just "some" case, then?*

"Flinders Cox," she said. A long pause. Then, icily: "Ma'am."

Wilkes threw up her hands.

"Lucy, it's one in the bloody morning. You can't just swing by, buzz me up out of my blessed slumbers and then just say 'Flinders Cox' over and over like a raving lunatic."

Fine. Let's get into it. Lucy squared her shoulders, set her jaw.

Drew herself up to her full five foot four. *I'm up for a fight.* "I need to work this case," she said. "Truly. *Need* to."

"Well, perhaps you should've thought of that before you started redecorating."

"But Sykes—"

Wilkes snorted. "Yes. Sykes is an ass. Believe me, I know. I had ten years of him before you arrived. And if I thought for a second that he really understood what he said to you…"

A fleeting thought: *So it was something he said then?*

"…what it *meant*, he'd be suspended, too. Officially. But Sykes isn't the point, is he?"

"Well, he *is*, Ma'am, sort of…"

"He *isn't*. You know that. It's more than that. And I'm sorry, but the answer's no."

You're sorry? Really? That's it? Lucy frowned. Reached into her hoodie, into the special padded pocket she'd had custom sewn inside the left arm, and pulled out a syringe: her emergency Boost. Placed it next to the vase, label facing up: Cox Labs. Looked at Wilkes.

"Yes," Wilkes said, "I know."

Not enough?

She stuck her hand under her vest and grabbed the monitoring disc. *How about this, then?* Pulled it slowly away from her skin, then took it out, put it down next to the syringe. Tiny drops of blood glistened on the ends of three sensor needles. She rotated it until the Cox Labs logo faced Wilkes. Crossed her arms.

A sigh. "I know, Lucy. I was there, remember? I know. You're a Vulnerable. And you're one of the Sixty-Two. Without Cox's Boosts, you'd have been dead two years ago—or a Survivor, anyway. Believe me, I do know what this means to you."

No. No, you don't. Because you don't know what I've done. No one does.

No one still alive.

"Please, Ma'am. As a favour. I'm asking."

"Lucy—"

"Ma'am, I—"

Wilkes's voice grew louder. "No, Lucy, listen to me—"

"I need it, truly, I do, and you can't just—"

"*DI Stone, be quiet.*"

Silence. The two women locked eyes.

"Listen to me," Wilkes said. Her voice was stern. "You know I think highly of you. Promoted you three times, haven't I? DI at twenty-nine, that's unheard of. You have a gift. A unique talent."

Leave the Party Trick out of it.

"And you're more than that. Clever. Good intuition. Hard-working—and I don't just mean now, these past two years, your insane hours. You *always* were. Not like Sykes and his lot, ready to piss off down the pub the moment I look away." A sneer at the thought. "I saw it back then. Helped you. You *know* that."

Lucy looked away. Her eyes rested on the carnations. Memories flashed up, snippets from a shopping trip: Marie Wilkes leading an eager young Constable Stone into clothing stores. Upmarket stuff, the sort Lucy had always given a wide berth. Jigsaw, Hobbs, Max Mara. Late-night chats about the importance of presentation, of professionalism. How hard it could be.

"But this case…" Wilkes sighed. Her voice softened. "It's too important. I'm sorry, but it is. Everyone's watching. Not just the top brass. The whole world. And I can't take the risk."

The risk? Fuck risk. If I solve this…

"Ma'am—"

"You say you need this, Lucy? No. *No.*" A pause. "You *know* what you need."

Lucy said nothing. Just stared.

Don't say it, Ma'am.

Don't say therapy.

That's for people who deserve to get better. Not me, not yet. I owe a Debt.

"You should go home now," said Wilkes. "Get some sleep."

And then she fingered her watch again.

Lucy frowned.

Wait.

I've seen that before.

A memory: Simon, fiddling with his mobile phone. Years back, before he'd proposed. He'd moved in, but still had his old place, still crashed there on nights he worked late. They were on the bed at Lucy's, eating dinner, sprawled across the big fluffy duvet. Takeaway curry, his favourite. But he was ignoring his veg korma, playing with the phone, rotating it in his hands. Frowning, like Wilkes was doing now. She'd had a hunch. Asked. And he'd broken down. Confessed straight away. His ex, Melanie, they were drunk, it was just once. Never again, Luce. Promise. Never let you down again. Die first. I swear.

And now here was Wilkes, toying with her watch in just the same way.

Guilty.

She feels guilty.

Lucy started to connect the dots.

Guilty because…? Watch is new. New watch, new flat. Promotion money. So, guilt about the promotion. Her thoughts sped up as she saw the light. *Guilt about the promotion, because of me. Because of how much my cases helped her, because she got credit as my superior.*

And—

She ran her fingers through her wet hair and thought of the leaflets. All those fucking leaflets, the ones Wilkes left on her crap desk when she wasn't looking. Titles like *PTSD: Signs and Symptoms* and *You're Not Alone* and *Understanding Reactions to Trauma*. The ones Lucy crumpled up, binned, because those were for other people, not for her, not yet.

24

And she thinks she should do even more than drop leaflets. Scared she's taking advantage.

She feels guilty.

Oh, Ma'am.

She stared at her mentor. The track lighting shone harshly on Wilkes's worry lines. Lucy thought about it, weighed it all up, then decided.

I'm sorry. I am. It's unfair.

But I need this.

So…

"That's a lovely watch, Ma'am," she said slowly. "What is it? Gucci?"

"Mmm." Wilkes didn't look up. Tried to push the watch up beneath the sleeve of her dressing gown.

"New?"

A nod.

"Nice. Truly. Well, reason to celebrate, yeah? Congratulations again, by the way. Well-earned." Her voice was hard beneath the compliment. "And this flat…" She made a show of looking around. Up at the high ceilings, down at the flooring, where the hoodie puddle was now the size of a handprint. "It's lovely. Like from one of your magazines."

Wilkes said nothing. Shifted uncomfortably.

"And you always wanted to be here in Wapping, right? Down by the river? Know you mentioned it. Bet you've got a smashing river view. So sort of a dream come true for you, yeah?" Lucy ran her finger down the shabby chic vase. "Everything you always wanted…"

So you owe me this, Ma'am.

Wilkes gave a deep sigh. Looked at her with disappointed eyes. Lucy stared right back.

You owe me Flinders Cox.

A pause, then: "Fine, Lucy."

Lucy said nothing, just nodded.

I'm sorry. Guilt trip, not fair, know it. But needs must.

"DI King is taking the lead on Cox."

"King?"

"New bloke. Down from Birmingham. You skipped his welcome drinks, of course. Seems a good chap." Hesitated, then said it: "Not bad on the eyes, either."

"Right." *Long as he's not Sykes, Part Two.*

"I'll call him. Let him know. You can work the case, but you need to work *with* him."

I'm a shadow now? Fine. Whatevs. "Yes, Ma'am."

"Please don't make me regret this, DI Stone."

"No, Ma'am. And thank you."

A slight nod.

Lucy nodded back, then turned and walked down the hallway. Opened the door.

"Lucy?"

She stopped. Turned around. Looked at Wilkes. Watched as the older woman's eyes travelled over her baggy hoodie and faded jeans, down to the grimy, waterlogged trainers.

"Just wondered. Do you still have it?" Her voice was wistful. "The suit? The Max Mara?"

Outside the door, rain beat down on the cobbles.

"No," said Lucy softly. "I burned it, Ma'am."

CHAPTER THREE

Posh place for a murder.

Lucy looked up at Flinders Cox's imposing Mayfair townhouse. The red carpet was still out, she noticed, but the top-hatted doormen—*Had to be top-hatted doormen, right? Big do, place like this? Must have been*—were gone, replaced by a uniform wearing a high-vis waterproof. He yawned as she trotted up the steps.

"It's only half two," she told him.

She walked through the front door and into the entrance hall. It was dazzling. Mirrors, chandeliers, parquet flooring. A staircase rose up at the back. Lucy looked around, impressed. *Christ. Wilkes needs to check this place out. She'd love it.* The hall was packed with police: half of MIT19, plus forensics, photographers, press officers. To her right, open double doors gave a view of a ballroom dotted with round tables. She stuck her head in, saw the aftermath of a gala drinks reception. Leftover canapés. Half-empty champagne flutes. Remains of a full bar at one end, a raised lectern at the other. Three forensics flitted about taking samples. *No body, no tape. Not the murder scene.*

She turned back to the entrance hall, grabbed a uniform as he shuffled past.

"Where's the scene?"

He pointed upstairs. She nodded and wove through the crush of cops. At the foot of the staircase, she spotted Sykes. He was talking to a tall man in an olive rain jacket. Their backs were to Lucy, but there was no mistaking Sykes's grey fedora. Wore it smashed down over his thinning hair to any scene where there might be a female news reporter. *Like he's Humphrey Bogart. What a knob.* She enjoyed watching the reporters ignore him.

He was miming throwing something as she walked up behind them.

"…crazy fucking bint," he finished.

"I can hear you, Sykes."

He flinched. Turned. "Stone." A cough. "Well. Heard Wilkes let you off easy. Figures."

The tall man took a slight step away from Sykes. He was easily six foot three. Big. Not fat, burly. The navy suit jacket beneath the rain jacket struggled to contain his chest, and his tie was loosened below his bull neck. A heavyweight. Lucy glanced at his face. Strong chin, stubble. Broad, flat nose. Striking green eyes.

Oh. You. I recognize you.

"Ed King," said the burly man. He smiled at her, extended a paw. "Don't think we've met."

"Think you're wrong about that," said Sykes. He gave Lucy a quick sneer.

Sykes, don't.

"Sorry?" King looked confused.

"Nothing," she said. Shook his hand. "Stone. Lucy. Scene's upstairs, yeah?" She stepped around Sykes and began to climb the stairs. "I'll just go up…"

"Oh, don't be modest, Stone," said Sykes. To King: "Didn't you catch it just now? When she looked at you? She recognized you. It's her little gift. Stone's…'special'."

A freak, his tone suggested.

Lucy stopped. Shot Sykes a dirty look. He knew she hated talking about the Party Trick, especially with someone she didn't know. It was there, yes. A gift. Fine. But so incredibly awkward. Made everyone paranoid. *Plus, I'm more than just the Party Trick. I'm a damn good cop, Sykes. And you're a bone-idle crap bastard.*

King looked from Lucy to Sykes and back. "I don't understand…"

Sykes kept talking. "Stone here is what's called a 'Super Recognizer'. Met started recruiting them a few years back, after some Oxford toff realized there was such a thing."

"Okay…" King shrugged.

"Something to do with their brains. Abnormal."

"The fusiform face area," Lucy said. "Forget it. More important things right now." *Much more important. Come on, Ed. Let's get to it.*

But Sykes was enjoying her embarrassment. "It's like this," he continued. "Normal bloke remembers maybe five per cent of the faces he's seen. Good cop, with training? A few more. But one of her lot?" He wrinkled his nose at Lucy. "Eighty. And Stone, she's like their queen. Remembers…what's the number again, Stone?"

"You know."

"Ninety-three per cent. Ninety-three per cent of the faces she's seen. Ever."

King stared at her. It was a good stare, though, she decided. Not jealous or intimidated. Just interested.

He really does look a little like Jack.

"So we've met before? Really?"

She nodded.

"Where?"

A sigh. *Well, if you really must know…*

"Bristol," she said. "Three years ago. Training event. Anti-discrimination, I think." She watched as he frowned, tried to think back. "One of the breakout sessions. You were two ahead of me in the coffee queue. I remember you from there."

"Good lord." He gave a little laugh, showing straight white teeth. "Really?"

"Yep."

"You saw me for ten seconds, three years ago, and you still remember? That's amazing."

"It's freaky, is what it is," said Sykes. He looked annoyed that King wasn't more put off.

"And you really just *keep* them in your mind? You don't forget them over time?"

"Honestly? Some I wish I could." Stared hard at Sykes. "Now, please can I get cracking?" She tugged on her hoodie drawstrings. *Enough of this bullshit. I have a murder to solve.* "Up here, yeah?"

"I'll show you," said King. "Andy, go check on the daughter." He began to climb the steps after her, moving nimbly despite his size. "He's in a little room off the master bedroom. Like a study. And Lucy...brace yourself."

‡ ‡ ‡

Flinders Cox lay on his back on the floor of his study.

Blood from the jagged hole in his neck pooled around his head, matting the silver hair. His long beard was crimson-streaked. He looked surprised: mouth open, arms spread.

A wooden crucifix was jammed into his right eye socket.

"Jesus," said Lucy.

King stood beside her. "Actually," he said, "that wasn't the murder weapon."

She looked up. "No?"

He shook his head. "Forensics made a first pass. Killer used a knife. Hunting. Combat maybe. Not quite certain yet. But a proper blade. This was done just after."

She bent down, stared into the open left eye. Sighed.

Always wanted to say thank you, Mr Cox.

"The crucifix came from there," King continued. He pointed to a nail head protruding from the far wall. "Only bit of decoration in the room."

Lucy stood. Glanced around. The tiny study was windowless

and nearly bare. Whitewashed walls. A small writing desk, thick red books and a picture frame on top. Chequerboard tile floor. No rug. An uncomfortable-looking camp bed was pushed up against a wall.

"Odd, right?" King asked. "Middle of all this luxury?" His nose wrinkled in disgust. "Makes me a bit sick, if I'm honest, massive house like this. His missus has a room larger than this for her shoes. And then he spends all his time in *here*." A shake of his head. "Like a little monastic cell."

She nodded. Cox was religious, she knew. Catholic. Everyone knew that. Gave three mil to repair Westminster Cathedral two years ago, after it was damaged in the body removal riots. Lucy wasn't religious herself, not beyond ticking C of E on forms and loving Christmas carols, but she admired the gesture. *All that good he did… Chemistry, philanthropy. Survivors' rights. All for this. Fucking awful.* A deep breath. *I need to solve this. Not just for me, Mr Cox. Not just for the Debt. For you.*

"Right," she said. "So where are we, then?"

"Full rundown?" King pulled a small blue notebook from his rain jacket, flipped it open. "You saw downstairs? Little get-to-gether. Come round and have a few, Mayfair style. Champers, canapés. Cox was meant to give a little speech at the end." A tech with a camera stuck his head in the doorway; Lucy waved him away. "Closing remarks, sounds like. Guests all fed and watered, Flinders comes down, says a few chipper words, sends them out smiling into the night."

"That was the plan?"

"That was the plan. Bit of a snag, though."

"So I see." Lucy was slowly circling the room, checking angles, sizing up the scene. *What do we have to work with here? Must be something.* She pulled on her hoodie strings.

"Cox spent the evening upstairs, practising his speech. Wife and daughter left to entertain the masses. Nervous speaker, apparently." He shrugged. "Hate pressers myself. Feel like a monkey, grinning for the camera." He looked across the room at Lucy. "You?"

God, pressers. She'd loved them, actually. Felt strong, in control. Ready for all comers. But Wilkes hadn't let her near one in over a year. Scared she might explode on camera. *Plus, can't have me on telly in a hoodie, can we, Ma'am?*

"Don't do many these days," she told him.

"Lucky you. Anyway, he never came down. Daughter went up to check on him. Found this mess, poor woman."

Poor woman? Or a suspect? "Have you spoken with her?"

He shook his head. "Looked in, but Doc says no. Not yet. Shock. Sykes will let us know."

Fucking Sykes. "He's family liaison, then, is he?"

King nodded. "You two seem close, by the way."

She frowned. Said nothing.

"Well, just remember, I'm the new guy. Goodwill to all. Totally neutral. Switzerland." A twinkle. "Bit of a wanker, though, isn't he?"

For the first time she could remember, Lucy laughed. Looked over at King, at his strong chin, wide smile. *Like this King chappie,* she thought. And then: a surge of guilt, like a blow to the gut. She turned away. Shut her eyes, hoped King wouldn't notice.

He didn't. Kept talking. "But what you really want to know is, any leads? Answer, fuck all. Have the guest list. Wife, daughter. Two dozen guests, mostly Cox Labs employees. Geoffrey Hurst, the CEO. A few Survivors' rights activists sprinkled in. Couple of reporters. Dozen catering staff, all Survivors."

"All of them?"

"Yep. Survivor-owned business. That's Cox's thing, right? Doormen both Survivors as well."

"Hmm." *Knew there'd be doormen. Fiver says top hats.*

"No blood on anyone, not to the naked eye at least. Forensics will confirm. No weapon. No one remembers seeing anything. And there was a back door, so someone could've just strolled in off the street for all we know."

"Right." She knelt, checked under the camp bed. Nothing.

"Full interviews tomorrow—in the morning. Three DCs lined up. Hicks, Evans. Forget the third."

She walked up to the desk, stepping carefully over the edge of the blood pool. "Salford, I expect. Bit up himself, but he works hard." Looked at the book titles, at the framed photo: a smiling man in his twenties. A Cox Labs paper pad, full of doodles. Three cheap biros, all tooth-marked. *Strange. Think a billionaire could spring for a decent pen.*

"Salford. That's the one. Crap taste in ties, Wilkes said?"

Lucy shrugged. *Whatever. Better than Sykes's fedora.* A small stack of pink record cards stood in the corner of the desk. "Ed?" She pointed at them. "What are these?"

"Speech notes. No prints besides his. We checked. Have a squiz if you like."

She picked the cards up, turned them over in her hands. Cox's handwriting was awful.

"'Two years ago,'" she read out loud, "'death rained down upon the London streets. The Scourge. Days…horrors…forever carved into our memories.'"

"Like I said. Chipper." A uniform came in, handed King a duty roster on a clipboard, left.

Lucy flipped to the next card. Kept reading, "'Survival, genetic roulette. For nine in ten of us, exposure to London Black meant nothing. Touch of nausea. Itchy eyes." Her husky voice rang off the bare walls. "But for that unlucky tenth, for the Vulnerable…without a Boost to protect them, exposure meant death. Horrible, agonizing death. Or, for a few, a new life. A changed life. Full of challenges, full of pain. A Survivor.'"

A scribble: *Mention the 62?*

Her voice caught and she stopped reading.

That's me. The Sixty-Two.

Flinders Cox was thinking about me.

She took a breath. Continued onto the next card, reading silently now.

'But tonight, my friends, is a new beginning. A new era. One without fear.'

And then, at the bottom of the card, a note:

'(show syringe of U)'

A jolt of electricity ran up Lucy's spine.

"Ed?"

He looked up from the duty roster. "Hmm?"

"Did anyone check what the speech was meant to be about?"

"Course. Did it myself. Cox made it out to be a big secret, but everyone knew. All the Cox Labs employees did, at any rate. Next-gen Boost. Just started clinical trials, meant to be ready in a year. Calling it Elemidox Ultra."

"Ultra? With a 'U'?"

"How else?"

"So, just an updated Boost? Same basic thing, London Black prophylactic for Vulnerables? Twenty-four hours' protection against copycat attacks, must jab before exposure?"

"Sounds like it. The two blokes I spoke with were pretty blasé. One of them mentioned something about helping with…" He checked his notebook. "Reduced enzymatic uptake." A shrug. "Meant to be painless, too. But yeah, basically a slightly better Boost. Why?"

"Well…" She crossed the room to him. Held out a card, pointed. "What's that letter? That one, there. Show syringe of…what?"

He studied it. "Looks like a lower-case 'A' to me. Why?"

34

"Not a 'U', then?"

A slow head shake. "I mean...couldn't swear to it. Handwriting's crap. But it almost touches there at the top. I'd say 'A'."

Lucy ran her fingers through her hair. Thought of Cox. Of watching his speech, just after the all-clear from the final attack. Thought about what he'd promised. Sworn it, looking into the cameras, looking into the face of a city reeling from the greatest tragedy it had faced in centuries. Her left thumb crept to her tattoo. *Please let it be. It has to be. Has to.*

Antidote.

A is for Antidote.

‡ ‡ ‡

"I don't know, Lucy," King said.

They stood on the first landing of the staircase. Lucy stared down at the hallway floor. She felt giddy. Dizzy, almost, like when she was a little girl and Jack would push her on the playground roundabout, round and round for what felt like hours, just because she loved it and he wanted to make her happy and if he didn't who else fucking would?

She took a breath. Focused.

An antidote.

If there's an antidote, if Cox really did it...and it was stolen, and I find it...

It felt like something from a dream. A good dream, not the Screamers.

If I recover an antidote for London Black, that's it. Debt's paid. Clean slate. Has to be.

Which means, I need this more than anything. Not just want.

Need.

King looked over at her. Frowned. "It's just, no one's mentioned an antidote, right?" He spread his huge hands wide.

"No one. None of the Cox Labs guys. Not even Hurst, and he's the bloody CEO."

"Maybe they're trying to keep it from the media."

"But if Cox was about to announce it…?"

"Maybe it's a secret. Maybe they don't know." She frowned, thought of the scene upstairs, the tiny study. *So, why the crucifix? Who would do that? And to Flinders Cox, of all people? Man's practically a fucking saint. But still, has to be about an antidote. Know it.*

King shrugged. "It just seems unlikely, is all. Occam's razor. Probably just a 'U'."

Lucy glanced at him. He looked tired.

Need you on board, Ed.

"Think about it," she said. "Techs searched the study, yeah? And no one found a syringe? A vial, nothing like that?"

He shook his head. "Just normal stuff. Wallet, keys. Phone."

"Certain?"

"Signed the log. Watched the bags leave for the station myself."

"Right. So then what about the card? It said 'show syringe'. Must have been *something* there for him to hold up, right? But if so, where'd it go?" A quick tug on her hoodie drawstrings. "No one would kill Cox to steal something that's already in clinical trials. But a secret antidote…"

Another shrug. "Perhaps someone would've handed him a syringe of the Ultra stuff before he went on? Dunno. We can ask in the interviews. Full slate lined up." He pulled up the sleeve of his jacket, checked his watch. A cheap watch, Lucy noticed. Scratched face, flaking metal. "Getting on three. Shall we call it? Regroup in the morning?" Without waiting for an answer, he began trotting down the stairs. "We'll get forensics back," he said over his shoulder. "Start looking into Cox properly. Enemies. Business, personal, all that."

Lucy watched him for a moment—*moves smoothly, light on his feet for such a big bloke*—and then followed. Down to the hallway, past the ballroom. The techs were gone, but half-full glasses still studded the tables.

She caught up to him as they reached the front door.

"Ed, I need you to take this angle seriously."

King stopped. Sighed. "When I spoke with Wilkes…"

Oh, Christ. God knows what she told him.

"Yes, stick close, right, I know—"

"No, listen." He paused. "Shouldn't tell you this, but I believe in transparency. Openness. Communication. So…" A deep breath. "Yes, Wilkes said to keep an eye on you. She's worried. But she also said I'd be a fool if I didn't follow any hunch you had. Said a lot of things about you, Wilkes. And d'you know what? Think she might be right." He flashed a smile. "You're an interesting one, DI Stone."

She looked at him, then away. Simon's face flickered through her mind.

"So," he continued, "shall we say, meet at eight?"

Five hours? She thought about next steps, then nodded. "Fine. Have a vehicle?"

"Yep. Toyota. Perk."

"Right." She pulled out her mobile, sent him a text. "Meet me here."

He checked it. "You live in Brompton?"

Part of me does. "Eight o'clock," she said. Pushed open the front door, stepped outside. Still raining. The yawning uniform had bunked off, she noticed. As they reached the pavement, a shrill voice rang out.

"DI Stone? Lucy?" Annoying Reporter 2 materialized from behind a phone box.

For fuck's sake. Now?

He moved towards them, the heels of his brogues slapping on the wet pavement.

"What's all this, then?" asked King.

"It's nothing," she said. To the reporter: "I'll put in a word with the press liaison. Okay?"

"Well, I was hoping—"

She turned away, kept walking. King followed suit. The reporter sped up and headed them off. "I was hoping for some time with you, actually."

"No." She sidestepped him neatly. "Liaison."

"But, Lucy…" He raised his voice. "I want your angle, actually. It's brilliant. Can't you see? Just think. One of the Sixty-Two, on the hunt for Cox's killer."

King stopped walking. Turned around.

"*What* did you say?"

The reporter shrugged. "What? I don't—"

King looked at Lucy, then back at the reporter. Scowled. "You," he said, pointing a meaty forefinger at him, "piss off. Right fucking now. Else I swear fucking *Time Out* will get tips before you."

The reporter gaped at him. Thought about it for a second, then turned, pissed off.

"And you." King took a step towards Lucy. "Did he just say you're one of the Sixty-Two?"

Lucy said nothing, just stuck out her jaw. *What of it?*

"Wow," he said. Gave a little chuckle. "*Wow*. Right. Didn't see *that* coming. So what is it, then? Rich daddy? Put on a little Mockney accent, come muck around with real life for a bit? Suppose that's why you're working Mayfair? Feel right at home? Probably got your fucking Maybach parked around the corner."

"It's not like that." Shook her head. *Slow your roll, Ed.*

"Oh, it's not?" A sarcastic laugh, but she sensed injury beneath it. A loss. "So how'd you do it, then? Huh? Tell me." His voice rose. "How the fuck were *you*, a *not*-filthy-rich cop from a *not*-filthy-rich family, one of the sixty-two Vulnerables who made it through the attacks alive and unscarred?" Voice echoing off the luxury townhouses now. "The Sixty-Two *all* had black-market Boosts. Every fucking one of them. So how'd you do it? When Boosts were gold dust, ten thousand quid a jab? Tell me *that*."

Lucy stared at him. Her fiercest stare, the one she'd used on her dad when he was at his worst. King stared back, and for a moment, she thought of two wounded fighters in the late rounds, eyeing each other through cut lids: pain recognizing pain.

Sorry, Ed. You don't get to know what happened.

You just get to help me find this antidote.

"Eight o'clock," she said. Turned on her heel. Marched away. As she turned the corner, she heard him calling after her: "How the *fuck* did you survive, Lucy Stone?"

CHAPTER FOUR
London, 2027

I did it!

Lucy felt a surge of pride as her chin scraped the pull-up bar. She beamed and lowered herself down to the carpet. *Wait 'til I tell Si.* She'd been trying to do a pull-up—a proper one, not jumping into it, no cheating—ever since he'd dumped the unassembled bar on the floor a month ago. It was the grand finale of a day's worth of trips back and forth to the van he'd hired for his move-in, and since then she'd been dying to show him that her boxing muscles could be pull-up muscles, too.

He won't believe it.

She flexed her arms in front of the mirrored cupboard—*hench!*—and grinned.

Right. Now, time to get ready.

Jack's old black boxing hoodie lay on the blue duvet cover. She grabbed it and pulled it over her sports bra, then looked around.

The flat was a mess. It always was these days. What could she expect, two of them crammed into a tiny place like this? But it didn't matter, she couldn't care less about crumpled T-shirts on the floor or the books for Simon's tour guide course piling up beside the desk. This was their home and she loved it. *Our place. The two of us.*

Her eyes roamed the framed snapshots that filled the crisp white walls. The subjects were all the same: Lucy and Simon, Simon and Lucy. Random selfies. A few holiday snaps from the week in Barcelona. Some new photos, too, from the cheeky Paris weekend break just ten days ago. Under an umbrella at the Eiffel Tower, laughing in the rain. Strolling the Champs Élysées. And the best photo of all, the one he'd secretly tipped a waiter ten euro to take: Simon, on bended knee, holding out the ring box as Lucy nearly fainted into her *soupe à l'oignon*.

She looked down at her finger. The ring sparkled. Lucy smiled again.

So happy.

Now—where'd my gloves go? Time for spar night, haven't been in donkey's…

She knelt and checked under the bed. Two black boxing gloves were half-hidden behind a stack of books about London history. *More bloody London books, Si? You're lucky you're cute.* As she pushed the stack aside, she heard the front-door lock click.

"Si?"

She grabbed the nearer of the gloves, then popped up and looked across the room.

Simon stood in the doorway. He was still wearing his white pharmacist's coat, she noticed, the monogrammed one she'd given him for Christmas. She shot him a quick smile, then ducked back down. "Just heading off to spar night," she told him, as she reached for the second glove. "Thought you were working late tonight?" Her fingertip grazed the cuff. *Stupid bloody thing.* She tried again, then gave up for the moment and resurfaced. "Anyway… never guess what your badass fiancée just did?"

He stared blankly at her.

Simon was a handsome man. Tall, lean. Roman nose, high cheekbones, sky blue eyes. But just now, the eyes were wider than usual, and the Windsor knot of his orange silk tie was loosened in an un-Simon-like way.

"You okay, babe?" she asked.

"I…erm, can I see your finger, Luce?"

She frowned. *Something up with the ring?*

"Why? Anything wrong?"

41

He shook his head. "Just want a quick look."

Odd. Looks…stressed. Scared, almost. But why? He'd sworn he could afford it. And the jeweller was a family friend, old mate of Jack's actually, so she knew it wasn't a fake. *So then, what?* She tossed her glove onto the duvet and faked a smile. "Can't take it back now, Romeo," she said, as she padded across the carpet. "Don't want to take it off, not even for spar night. But reckon I'll allow a quick look…" She kissed him. Held out her ring finger.

He took it in his hand, then looked up. His eyes focused on something over her shoulder.

"Lucy…what the fuck's *that*?"

He pointed.

"What? I don't…"

As she turned, he pulled a tiny needle from his coat pocket and pricked her finger.

"*Hey!*"

A drop of blood appeared. Lucy watched, shocked, as Simon drew a blue plastic testing stick from his pocket. It reminded her of a pregnancy test. *Like that time after Barcelona. But…blood? Is this for…what, then? HIV? Can't be. Right?* She frowned as he touched the end of the stick to the blood.

"Si? What on earth…?"

"Sorry," he said, as he shook the stick. "You and needles. You know. Nearly fainted when you got that." Pointed to her wrist tattoo. "Reckoned this would be easier."

"Could've just *said*." She pulled her finger back, sucked it angrily. "I'm fine if I look away. But what's it *for*?" A pause. "Is there something you need to tell me?"

"Shh. Wait a tick…"

Her eyes flashed—*did you just* SHUSH *me, Simon Baker?*—but she said nothing. His silence scared her. Simon was never silent. He was the brash Aussie, the one that wouldn't leave off about the Ashes and how shit London coffee was. A man who dreamt of moonlighting as a tour guide, the centre of attention at every drinks. A joker. *Where's the little joke, Si? What's wrong?*

He stared down at the testing strip. He was holding his breath, she noticed.

The rectangle in the middle of the strip turned from white to yellow.

"Okay," he whispered. "Okay, now stop."

Silence.

Yellow changed to black.

"*Fuck.* Fuck fuck fuck." He put his hand over his mouth, frowned, then looked at her. "We have to go. Right now." He reached for the doorknob. "Ready? Come on."

"Wait. Where are we—"

"Back to work. My work. The pharmacy. St Thomas'. Explain on the way."

She looked down at her white cotton socks. "I need shoes…"

"Oh, right…fine. Okay. You have your warrant card, right? Good. Meet me outside. I'll just…"

His voice trailed off as he disappeared into the hallway.

Lucy watched the door close. Ran fingers through her hair. *I don't like this.* She grabbed her new black trainers from the corner and pulled them on. For a split second she thought of the lone boxing glove hidden beneath the bed—*never did like me going to spar night, did you, Si?*—and then she was out the door after him.

‡ ‡ ‡

Dark, she thought as she stepped outside.

It was only half four, but already the winter sky overhead was black. Headlights whizzed by. Simon stood on the pavement, staring out into the Goswell Road traffic.

"Well, come on, then," she said, grabbing his elbow. "Tube's this way, remember?"

He shook his head. "Cab."

"Black cab? Really?" She frowned. "Bit spend-y…"

"No Tube. Not now. Trust me." He spotted a taxi with an amber light. Plunged into the street, arm extended, blocking its path. The driver slowed and rolled down his window. "St Thomas' Hospital," Simon said.

A nod. "Hop in, mate."

Lucy opened the door and scooted across. Simon followed her.

"Waterloo's a nightmare," said the driver. He was grey-bearded and fat. Lucy didn't recognize him—*not one of Dad's cabbie friends from down the pub, no one I've ridden with before*—but she immediately knew the type. A talker. "Telling you now, mate. Bloody disaster area."

"Fine," said Simon. He slammed the door. The taxi edged back into traffic.

"Really, though, can you believe it? Block off traffic around Waterloo Station for two days because of bloody *tear gas*? I mean…"

Lucy ignored the cabbie's banter. "Seriously, Si—what's going on?"

Simon looked towards the front of the taxi. The Perspex partition between the driver and the passenger compartment was covered with taped-up notices—*Cash Preferred, No Food Allowed, Support Our Veterans*—but the sliding privacy door was missing.

"Later," he whispered.

"You ask me," continued the cabbie, "Mayor's worse than the bloody terrorist." A Union Jack air-freshener dangled from his rear-view mirror. "I mean, right, I was gassed in a demo once, no bloody picnic, but when it comes to creating total fucking gridlock, pardon my French, I mean…"

The taxi swept past Smithfield Market.

Out the corner of her eye, she saw the giant arches of the Victorian meat market buildings, the ones Dad roamed before sunrise, wandering among the hanging carcasses and pig heads and blood-spattered aprons, searching for a deal. She'd never been. He'd taken Jack, never her. Not even after, when it was just the two of them, chained together, staring in grim silence over dinner before he cracked another can and settled into his ratty orange armchair to watch *Fight Night*.

The meat market disappeared from view.

She fixed her fiancé with a hard stare. "Tell me what's going on, or I stop the cab."

I'll do it, too. You know I will.

A sigh. "Fine. Okay." He leaned in, lowered his voice. "Listen. Something odd came into the pharmacy this morning. Huge lot of some drug. Elemidox, it's called. All headed up to the iso wing. Where they're keeping everyone from Waterloo."

"What—you mean, the tear gas victims? They're still in hospital?"

He ignored her, kept talking. "I went up to have a look. No one stopped me. Should've, I reckon. Anyway. Most of the people from the attack, seems they're fine. Just a bit of nausea. But the others, maybe a dozen of them, they're calling them 'Vulnerables'…"

He took a deep breath.

"Luce, it's *horrible*."

She saw terror in his pale blue eyes.

"I don't understand. What? What's horrible, the tear gas?"

Simon said nothing. Shook his head. She realized the cabbie had stopped talking, too. His eyes were on her in the rear-view; he looked away as she glanced up. Silence. The taxi sped over Blackfriars Bridge. Neon lettering blazed from the sides of darkened buildings: Sea Containers, the OXO Tower.

"Well?" *Come on, Si, out with it. I want to know. You're scaring me.*

He pulled his prescription pad and pen from his breast pocket. Scribbled something. Showed her. She could just make it out in the dark:

IT WASN'T TEAR GAS.

"Rubbish." She pushed the note away. "We had a briefing. Straight from the Chief Super. Man in a red gas mask sprayed tear gas on commuters from the retail balcony. Caught him hiding in WHSmith's. Precautionary treatment for victims. That's it. End of."

The cabbie was watching her again, she noticed.

More scribbling. Another note, underscored twice: LATER.

No, Si. Now. As she started to tell him off, the taxi pulled to a stop at a red light.

"See, look at this nonsense," said the driver.

To their left, a street was blocked off. Yellow tape, empty police vans. Three different media trucks, cameramen and reporters milling about. Lucy squinted. In the background, standing in front of the Waterloo Station entrance, she saw a soldier. He was holding a sub-machine gun.

A chill ran up her spine.

"I reckon it's a plot," said the cabbie. He nodded knowingly. "You watch." The light changed and they sped forward. "Week from now, they lift the tape and presto—more bloody cycle lanes…"

She turned back to look at Waterloo through the rear window. Something felt wrong. The Chief Super hadn't mentioned the army. And where were the cops? An AFO could carry a sub-machine gun. Did it all the time, she knew. Airports, escort duty, trial protection. *So why the bloke in a camo smock?*

The taxi slowed again. "For fuck's sake." The cabbie waved at the road ahead. Two black vans were parked in the middle of the street, blocking the way. "Look at this mess. Hang on."

The air-freshener swung as he turned down a side street, pulled to a stop in front of the London Eye. "Mind if I set you down here? Quicker. Just along the river there, two minutes." He eyed Simon's white coat. "You know the way, I reckon. Oh, any chance you've got cash?"

As Simon paid, Lucy opened the door and got out. The air was cold. She shoved her hands into her hoodie pockets, looked up at the Eye. The rotating ring of capsules cut a perfect circle into the night sky: a staring, jet-black pupil.

Don't like this. Not one bit. But now I want to know what's going on...

Simon pocketed his change and they started to walk.

"Here," he said. Dug into his pocket, pulled out two pairs of blue nitrile gloves. Handed her a pair. "Nicked these from the stockroom." He tugged his on. Looked at her. "Go on, then. Do yours."

Really? She shrugged, pulled the gloves on. Her ring stretched the rubber.

"So now, tell me," she said. "What's up with the tear gas?"

He put his arm around her waist. Leaned close.

"It's *not* tear gas, Luce. They're just avoiding panic."

He took a deep breath, paused, then spat it out:

"It's a nerve agent."

What?

"And," he added, "they reckon there could be more attacks."

"Blimey," she said. *Nerve gas? Here?* Images from a television programme she'd seen on BBC Four: a terror attack in the Tokyo metro, schoolgirls in respirators staring mournfully at the camera. "So...what, then? Antidotes? They have stockpiles, I think. Is that what we're—"

He cut her off. "There is no antidote."

A man brushed past. Simon stopped talking, waited for him to move out of earshot.

"It's a new agent," he said. "Novel. Antidotes do fuck all. Tried all the normal ones: atropine, pralidoxime, obidoxime. Nothing. May as well burn some incense or wear a lucky charm round your neck."

Jesus. She frowned at him. *Okay, so then…?*

"And it gets *everywhere*. Hangs in the air for hours, floats, sticks on surfaces. Anyone at Waterloo yesterday, it's on their clothes still. Might even be some here, close enough, so…" He raised a gloved hand. "Poor sods in iso are actually toxic now. Exhaling bits of it every time they breathe, exposing the doctors. Horrible. It's like they took the most awful thing possible, weapons-grade stuff cooked up in some nightmare-fuel Cold War military project, and then took away its toys until it got *really* fucked off at us." A pause. "Luce…what it *does* to people…"

He stopped talking as they climbed the steps up onto Westminster Bridge. It was crowded. Tourist hordes, watching scammers with three cups and a ball. Bus tour touts, carts selling nuts. They fought through the current of selfie sticks and puffer jackets, reached the kerb, crossed the street. The North Wing of St Thomas' Hospital loomed ahead.

Lucy frowned. "Babe? Si?" Her mind was racing now. "You said *most* people aren't vulnerable…" Thought of the testing strip, of the rectangle turning from yellow to black. Of the look in his eyes. Connected the dots. "So then…me?"

He looked away.

Oh.

I see.

They arrived at the hospital entrance.

"And you?" she asked.

He stopped, dug back into his pocket. Pulled out two testing strips. Held them out in the palm of his gloved hand.

Both rectangles were black.

‡ ‡ ‡

Inside, the hospital throbbed with people.

Lucy followed Simon down a brightly lit corridor, threading through children in pushchairs and patients wheeling suitcases. The air reeked of bleach.

"So," she said, as she dodged an orderly pushing a theatre trolley towards the fracture clinic, "what are we doing *here*, then?"

"Elemidox." They rounded a corner. A sign for the hospital's internal pharmacy pointed dead ahead. "The stuff that showed up this morning. Meant for pesticide poisonings, but some genius realized it does the trick, as long as you inject it *before* you're exposed. Must be before. Prophylactic. Anyway, I'm getting us some. Might need your warrant card for yours."

He slowed as they reached the double doors that led to the pharmacy.

"Erm, better if you wait here for now. May need you in a tick, but let's see."

Lucy nodded. Watched as he tapped his wallet on a card reader, disappeared through the doors. *Right. I'll just…stay here.* She looked around. Images from the television programme kept creeping back into her mind: men wearing orange hazmat suits, makeshift hospital tents. She tried to shove them away, calm herself. *Si's got this. He knows what to do. Prescribing pharmacist now, practically a doctor.* She looked down, realized she was rubbing her tattoo. *Don't worry, Jack. I'll be fine.*

A wiry woman with tight red curls hobbled past on sticks. Lucy smiled at her. *From the pizza shop next to Barmy Park. Works the till.* The woman looked puzzled, then suspicious. Kept moving. Lucy watched her as she turned the corner.

Must be nice to forget a face.

As she checked her phone—*anything from work?*—the double doors swung open. Two junior pharmacists with matching green hospital lanyards came out. In the distance, Lucy could hear Simon's raised voice: "For fuck's sake, Mel…"

Melanie?

Hang on…

She ducked through the doors, marched down the hallway. A sliding window on her left gave a partial view into the pharmacy. Blue plastic bins in storage units covered the far wall. A television screen flashed order numbers. Simon stood in the middle, his back to Lucy, arguing with a thin platinum blonde.

Lucy rapped at the window. The blonde saw her, looked away.

That's right, Melanie. Hide.

Simon turned around. His face was flushed. He mouthed a swear, then walked to the window, slid it open.

"Luce…"

"*That's* why you wanted me to stand outside?" She crossed her arms.

He sighed. "I can't help it. I can write the script, but someone else needs to fill it, right? Rules. And she's on shift now. Just my luck."

Lucy said nothing, just frowned.

He reached through the window and put his hand on her forearm. "Look at me." His blue eyes pleaded. "It was just that once. I swear on all that's holy. Besides—we were *arguing*, right?"

True. And right now, there are bigger things to worry about.

But still, Si, you know how I feel about her…

"Just wait here," he said. "I'm going to go get the meds." He patted her arm, walked away.

Across the room, Melanie leaned on the countertop. *You look all done up*, Lucy thought. Thick Scouse brows, coral lipstick.

Giant shiny earrings, dangling from stretched earlobes. *Did you know he was coming back in tonight? Making another play?*

Melanie mustered her courage, stared out at Lucy.

Lucy stared right back. Pulled off her glove, raised her hand. *Ring.*

Simon reappeared, carrying six white cardboard boxes in his arms. He put them down on the counter next to a roll of labels and began to scan the barcodes.

"One each," Melanie told him.

He stopped scanning. Looked at her.

"*What?*"

"One box each," she repeated. Smirked at Lucy over his shoulder.

"No, Mel. She's a first responder. Luce, you've got your warrant card…"

Oh, she knows. Just one of her games. Really, Si, how could you ever?

"Doesn't matter," said Melanie. "Rationed. See?" She picked up a piece of paper from a nearby counter, put it down in front of him. Tapped it with a pink fingernail.

Simon picked up the paper. He frowned as he read.

"*Rationed*? What the fuck is this, World War II? Coupons for soap?"

"It's the rule. Someone on high called the Deputy GM. We have the entire stock. Takes the manufacturer three weeks to make more."

Another smirk at Lucy.

"Fine," said Simon. A sigh. "It's fine. Two boxes is plenty." He pushed the paper away, finished scanning the barcodes, scribbled on a clipboard. "Here," he said, handing the boxes to Lucy through the window, "take these. Be right back. Don't worry, Luce, it's fine. Promise."

She looked down at the boxes. Read the lettering: COX LABS — ELEMIDOX ©—30mL. Opened one. The needles were

51

huge, like something from a cartoon. Her stomach hurt. She thought about the soldier and the black vans and Melanie's pink nail tapping the rationing memo.

Don't worry, Luce.

Right.

She should trust him, she knew. Simon was clever, resourceful. Top of his class at uni. Knew his meds, knew the system. The perfect guy to have in her corner for something like this.

So...

She tugged her hoodie drawstrings.

Why am I fucking terrified?

CHAPTER FIVE

London, 2029

Don't look up.

The bell on the Brompton caff door tinkled. Lucy stared down at her plate. Same as always: egg, beans, tomato, mushrooms, white toast. She knew without looking up it was King. Had to be. It was eight. They'd agreed, he hadn't cancelled. She heard his footsteps on the black-and-white tile. *Don't look,* she thought. *Ignore him. You look up, he sees weakness. Sykes would. And even if he's not a Sykes, not a complete and utter fucking wanker, anyway he can fucking well apologize after acting like a total shit and—*

"I'm sorry," King said.

He sat down across from her. Sighed.

"Out of line. It's just…I get worked up. About that. I…" His voice trailed off. "Well, another time. Point is, not my business. Sorry. Truly. Won't happen again."

Better fucking not. She forked a mushroom, popped it in her mouth. Finally glanced up at him. He looked tired, she thought. Stubble heavier. His eyes were still green, still striking.

"I promise, Lucy."

Lucy nodded. Finished chewing. Considered. *Okay. You lost someone. I get it.*

Fine.

She said: "A butcher."

King looked confused. "Sorry, what?"

"Dad. My father. He was a butcher. Up Bethnal Green Road." She took a bite of toast. "You asked last night. 'Rich daddy?' Remember? Well, that's what he was."

I didn't buy my way through the Scourge, Ed. Not like the rest of the Sixty-Two.

53

So now you know.

"Okay. I see." Kept his face neutral, but she could tell he was secretly pleased. "Well, like I said, not my business." He watched her eat a tomato. Smiled at something. Tried to hold it back, but couldn't. "Veggie fry-up, huh? Funny sort of breakfast for a butcher's daughter."

Oh?

She thought of Dad. Joe Stone, Jr, standing behind his counter, staring grimly out at the world in his bloody apron. The old shop, his father's before him. Sawdust on the floor, the Queen on the wall. His frown. What can I get you then? Right, whack whack whack, sling it on the scale, that do?, here's your change, now piss off. No time for nonsense. Not from him, not from his customers. And certainly not from his damn leftover of a daughter. His words.

"Depends on the butcher," she said.

And now enough of this shit. We have work to do.

She laid down her fork, pushed the half-full plate aside. "Ready to go?"

He nodded. "I'm parked outside."

"Right." She stood, then looked down at her empty glass. Her head felt light. *Maybe one more for the road.* "Hang on a tick," she told King. Walked to the till. To the man with the greasy apron: "One more. Just the bits. I'll mix it myself, yeah?" Took the Coke. As the espresso brewed, she nodded to the dapper old gent eating a bacon butty in the corner. *Seen him in before. Won't remember me.* Grabbed the paper beaker from the counter, then followed King out the door.

Outside, the light was still dim. It was misty.

"Fucking winter," said King. "Least it's not raining." He led the way to a grey unmarked Toyota.

"Yet," Lucy said. She slid into her seat. Unscrewed the Coke, drank it down to the middle of the label. As King watched, she poured the espresso slowly into the bottle. "Have to mind the fizz or it bubbles over," she told him. Took a sip.

He stared at her, nose wrinkled.

What? Good advice, Ed.

A bit of the foam bubbled over the edge of the bottle.

"Rats," she said. Frowned, wiped her hand.

King chuckled. "Did you just say 'rats'? Come on, Stone. You're a cop. Cops fucking swear."

"I don't."

Mum taught Jack not to swear, and Jack taught me.

So fuck you, Ed.

"Hmm," he said. Blinked. "Right. Well, next steps. Team's doing interviews all day. We can join as and when. I'd like to be in with the daughter, no question. Last to see him, all that. Wife, too." He buckled up. She didn't, just stared out the window as he talked. "Have someone check the caterers, rule them out. Then, start breaking down guest alibis, see if we can spot anything there while we wait for forensics." He put his key in the ignition. "Make sense?"

"No," she said. Took another sip of her drink. "We should focus on the antidote."

A tired smile. "Right, yes, the antidote. Well, I've told everyone to ask in the interviews. Haven't forgotten. Promise. But I think if we focus on who saw who when, we can start—"

She shook her head. "It was a drinks. Alibis'll be rubbish. Who remembers every second of drinks?"

"Fine. So then in the interviews, we ask about the antidote."

Lucy sighed. This was tiring. She thought about Wilkes. *Should've known better, Ma'am. He's treating me like I'm a fucking DC.* "We already have prelims from last night, yeah? CEO, COO, the big shots. Antidote for London Black's not the sort of thing that slips your mind. Either they don't know, or else they're lying and will just lie again."

"Or there's no antidote," King said.

She stared at him.

Of course there's an antidote. Has to be, please God. So get on board, Ed.

"What we *need* to do," she said, "is find *where* the antidote was made. We do that, we can work out who else knew about it. Go from there." Took one more sip, then capped the bottle.

"Cox Labs is out in Stepney—"

Not there.

Anywhere but there, don't want to go there.

Memories from two years ago began to bubble up but she took a breath, pushed them away. Shook her head. "Can't be there. Everyone would know. We'd know. Someplace else. Another lab. Secret."

He laughed. Not sarcastic, just exhausted. "Okay, right. So then how exactly do you propose—"

"Reckon I've found it."

"You *what*?" He took his hand off the key. "Already? How?"

Lucy reached into the pocket of her hoodie, pulled out something small. Placed it on the console: a paperclip, its end bent straight. "With this." She sat back, looked at King. Watched him frown, his gears turn. *Will he get it?*

"His phone?"

Well done, Ed.

"But…it's in evidence," he said. "Wait. Hang on. You went back to the station? At four in the morning? Took the SIM card out of his phone, stayed up all night with the geotracking data?" He pointed to her bottle. Chuckled. "No fucking wonder you're drinking that mess."

Hey, leave the drink out of it.

She pulled her mobile from her jeans pocket. Tapped a few times, then put it down next to the paperclip. A map of London showed on the screen. "Watch," she said. Pushed a button. Red dots began to pop up, pimples on the face of the city. "This is the past two months. Everywhere Cox went."

King squinted.

A pattern emerged. The dots clustered in three places: a triangle.

Lucy pointed to one of the clusters. "Home." To the second, further east. "Cox Labs."

"So what's that one?" asked King. He put his finger on a cluster of dots in Southwark, just south of the Thames.

"That," she said, "is what we're going to find out."

‡ ‡ ‡

She was on Goswell Road.

It was back then. Scourge times. The road was empty. Metal shutters, doors with red X's. Mist. Flinders Cox was up ahead, one street away. Bloody-bearded, hair matted, crucifix in his right hand. In his left—a syringe, glowing golden, and she knew it, knew what it had to be: A for Antidote. She walked faster. Must catch him, need to. Turned a corner. A removal team: green hazmat suits, sprayer truck, body wagon. Searchers with white test wands, fresh X on the door. From a window, a woman, shrieking: Oh! Dead, dead, dead.

She started to run.

Ran towards Cox, past the soldiers and the body wagon and the shrieking woman. He was holding the syringe up, waving it, a beacon. She needed it. Must get it. Sped up, faster, sprinting, but she was back on the bridge now, Westminster Bridge, Big Ben pricking the sky and it was crowded, full of people, and they were all exposed, all of them, red eyes, black eyes, skin blistered and she pushed, fucking pushed, but they held her back, hands grabbing, faces peeling and the skin came off in sheets and she couldn't get past and then oh God oh Jesus her face in the mirror, screaming, screaming, it was The Thing, The Thing That Happened, she saw it and—

"Lucy!"

Her eyes opened and she shoved King away.

Oh Christ oh what the fuck where—

"It's okay," he said. "It's okay, Lucy." His voice was deep, soothing. "You're all right."

Lucy blinked. Looked around. *The car. King. Right.* Took a breath. *Fell asleep. A Screamer.*

"We're there," he said. "In Southwark. Cox's triangle, remember? Your secret lab?"

She nodded. Felt around for her phone, pulled it from the seat crack. Checked the time.

"Half nine? Already?" Grogginess made her voice even huskier.

"Bit of traffic coming in. Survivors' rights march this morning, up to New Monument. They've blocked off the Embankment, closed London Bridge." He watched as she took a sip of her drink, smoothed down the hoodie with her hand. "And once we got here, I had to phone Wilkes back anyway so I got out. Let you sleep for a few. I was over there, on the phone." Pointed to a spot thirty feet away. "Lucy…" Paused, then came out with it. "I could hear you screaming from *there*."

Welcome to my world, Ed.

"Yeah," she said. Wiped tears from under her eyes. "Well. Happens sometimes."

All the time.

"If you ever want to talk…I mean, I know it helps me…"

She glared.

"Right," he said. "Point taken. Well, offer's open."

Lucy took a deep breath, ran fingers through her hair. She wished he hadn't seen that, not a full-on Screamer. Not because it was awkward—who cares really, fuck it—just that it was private. Sharing was therapy, sort of, and therapy wasn't for her, not yet. *My Debt. My fucking cross to bear.* She opened the door. "Let's go."

King nodded.

He'd parked one street back from the address she'd given him. A quiet road. Crumbling yellow-brick warehouses on one side, long iron railing on the other. Part of the railing was covered in ribbons, dried flowers, sun-bleached notes. He glanced at it as they passed.

"That's not…is that a…?" His voice trailed off.

Burn site? It's okay, you can say it.

"No." She shook her head. "Those were further out. Mostly old biscuit factories." Biscuit factories, because of their giant ovens. She'd seen it on the telly back then: body wagons backed up on Newham Way, smokestacks puffing in the background. Hadn't eaten a single biscuit since.

"Ah."

"This is older. Much, much." Simon had shown her this place, years ago, on one of their walks. "Graveyard. Unconsecrated. For sex workers." *Different sort of tragedy, really.* "People leave ribbons. Used to, anyway. Council keep trying to turn it into a car park."

They passed a pub, still closed. She caught a whiff of stale beer and piss as they walked past. Pulled her mobile from her hoodie pocket. She'd loaded Cox's geotracking data into her map app; their blue dot was almost on top of his third cluster. "Up there," she said. Pointed ahead, to a brick arch where the railway ran over the road.

"Where? *In* the railway arch?"

She shrugged. "Looks it, yeah?"

It was dark under the bridge. Clammy. The *chunk-chunk* of an overhead train echoed off brick walls. A rusted door was built right into the railway arch. No signage, not even a number. Someone had wedged a piece of scrap metal between the frame and the door, jamming it open.

"Here?" King looked doubtful.

Another glance at her phone. The blue dot was directly on top of the geotracking cluster.

Lucy nodded.

This is it.

The third point of Cox's triangle.

"Someone's here," she said, pointing to the makeshift door-stop. Her skin prickled. *If I'm right—if this is Cox's secret lab, if he was making an antidote—then anyone who knows about this place could be the killer...*

She knocked on the door. No response. Knocked again.

"Police," she called out.

Silence.

Right. Let's do this.

"Come on," she told King. Eased the door open, entered.

Inside was windowless. Pitch black, except for the tiny stream of daylight coming from behind her. She felt around for a light switch. As her eyes adjusted, she recognized a familiar shape: a Cox gate, unplugged, up against a wall.

Promising.

Her fingers found the switch and she flicked it on. Fluorescent lights hummed. They were in a large vaulted room. Ceiling and walls were grimy, blackened brick: the underside of the railway arch itself, uncleaned, unfaced. The back wall was blank, but steel doors cut into the sloping walls on the left and right.

"Police," she said again, voice raised. "Anyone here?"

Nothing.

She sniffed the air. Smelt bleach.

A train rumbled above.

"Right, then." Lucy walked to the right-hand door, King following close behind. She tried the handle: locked. Looked through the window. A small room, empty wooden shelves on the walls, empty wooden table in the middle. Black leather sofa at one end. At the other, a sink and something that looked like a large free-standing fireplace.

"Pottery kiln," said King, towering over her shoulder.

She turned, surprised. *Random thing for you to know...*

"My wife was a potter," he explained.

Wife? She glanced at his finger but already knew: no ring. Must have checked without thinking when they met. Purely as info, of course. *So, a wife? That who you lost, then, Ed? Was she visiting London? Or just the same old story, cops and their shit marriages? I wonder...* But she pushed the thought away. *Stop. Someone could be here. Focus.*

You need this.

The other door was windowless but unlocked. It led directly into a small room, scarcely larger than a wardrobe. Against the far wall stood what looked like a bright yellow phone booth with silver tubing running from its top up to the ceiling. Lucy recognized it immediately. She'd seen these before. Been in one, once. Her skin tingled at the memory. Chemical disinfectants raining down, burning her bare shoulders, arms, back; then water, washing her body, mixing with her tears.

"You know what that is, right?" she asked.

King nodded. "Decon shower."

"Yeah. A decon shower." She looked around. A pair of black wellies stood beneath a small wooden bench. On it sat a plastic face shield and a box of surgical gloves. In the corner, a green hazmat suit hung from a free-standing clothes rack. Well-worn. Duct tape covered tears in the seat. She walked to it, felt the fabric: dry. *Not used recently...*

"Drain's dry," said King, from inside the shower. He stepped back out. "But it would dry quickly. Might've been used recently, might not. Either way, you'll want a look at this." He pulled back the shower door, showed her. A steel door. Bolted to the door was a bright yellow sign, and on the sign, an emblem in black: four circles and a ring. The letters *LB* were stamped in the centre.

Chemical weapons. London Black.

The door was open.

Fuck. She turned away, backed up to the wall. *Oh fuck. What if my levels dropped…?* Pulled her mobile from her pocket. Shoved it under her hoodie. Tapped the hidden ceramic disc on her stomach, pulled the phone back out. A number appeared: *7.8*.

Phew.

"All good?" asked King.

She nodded. Took a breath. "Seven point eight. Just need to be above five." Simon's voice in her head: *Five alive, Luce. Remember that. Five alive.* "That's the threshold, five. So all good."

But at half nine in the morning, really ought to be well above 8…

King looked unconvinced. "Well, maybe I do a quick solo recce. Just to make dead certain…"

Lucy frowned at him. *Like fuck I'm not going in, Ed.* Pushed him aside, walked through the shower. Went in. And—

Bingo.

There was no question.

She was standing in a chemical weapons lab.

‡ ‡ ‡

"Lucy," King said, "we need to make some calls."

He stood next to her, both of them staring in awe at the set-up in front of them. The lab was large, larger than her entire flat. In the middle was a room-within-a-room: a sealed-off workspace with glass walls on three sides. Warning signs everywhere. A loud hum filled the air.

This is it. Where Cox created the antidote.

"It's brilliant," she said.

"There's no fucking way this is legal."

So? She moved closer, eyes wide. The inner workspace had one door, an airlock with another decon shower attached. It was filled with equipment. Microscopes, sharps bins, boxy grey machines with blinking digital displays. Coiled red air hoses hung down from a ceiling vent like giant Slinkys. At the back, a fume hood was built into the wall, and through its glass window she could see blue plastic stands filled with test tubes, vials, bottles.

"Look," she said, pointing to the ceiling vent. "Negative pressure. Like an iso ward." She'd seen that before, too. Memories of grim nurses, frowning doctors with clipboards. An orderly pushing her back, thick arms, raspy voice: *Time to go, Miss, don't make me...* She tugged on her hoodie drawstrings, took a breath. Focused.

Smiled.

This is good. Good? Better than good. Fucking brilliant. Adrenaline surged through her as she processed what it all meant. *Could even be more antidote in there, yeah? What if it wasn't just one syringe? Need to get techs in asap, find out. Or could be notes, just as good. God, what if? Can you imagine? No more Boosts, no more copycat attacks, no sniffers or gates or—*

"What the fuck is all this doing *here*?" asked King.

She looked at him. Shrugged. Fair question.

Why do this here, Mr Cox? Why in secret?

Who were you scared of?

Lucy took one last admiring glance at the lab—*so fucking brilliant*—then started to think practically. *Next steps.* "Someone was here," she said. "So someone knows. Perf. We pull CCTV, check that. Door-to-doors if we have to. We find that person, then..."

"Shh," said King.

She stared at him. *Did you just SHUSH me, Ed King? I'll give you—*

"Listen," he whispered. "Hear that?"

Lucy frowned. Listened.

Heard the hum of the air vents, but nothing else. *Oh, wait. That?* Inside the workspace, two chest freezers were fixed to the back wall with heavy chains. One was open, and she could hear a tiny alarm chirping.

"Erm, yeah. Freezer door?"

"No, no. Something else." He walked back towards the door, started to open it. "Sounded like maybe—"

CRACK!

A fist crunched King's jaw, knocking him flat.

The fuck—

She saw the man for a split second—black jumper, Survivor mask—and then he was gone.

"Hey!"

She took off after him. Leapt over King. Flew through the shower, the small room, the entrance. Popped out into dim daylight.

Fucking mist.

Looked left. Right.

Now where the fuck…

In the corner of her eye: a black blur.

There.

Shot down the road. Hit a cross street, didn't stop, right over, dodged a cab—*watch it*—kept going. *Don't stop don't stop don't stop…*

He had orange trainers. Focused on them. Only them. Pushed. Harder. Gasping.

Get…the fuck…back here…

But he was fast. Faster than her. Tore down an alleyway but she was losing ground now, he was quick, too quick, getting away…

God fucking dammit…

Around a bend. Signs blurred people cars shit fucking faster run *faster…*

And then:

Oh fuck.

Borough.

The great green arches of Borough Market rose up ahead. London's biggest food market, mobbed with people on a Monday morning. He dove into the crowd. She followed, pushing people aside. Tourists taking snaps, locals buying veg. Bulled straight through.

"*Police,*" she screamed. "Move, move, move…"

Keep him in sight.

She took little jumps, bobbing up above the sea of shoppers. *There.* Saw him turn left, down a row of stalls. *And there.* As she ran, she pulled out her phone, hit the Code Zero button on the side. Gasping: "Backup. Stone. Location Borough Market. Suspect thirties male masked…"

She skidded around a corner, bang into a man carrying a basket of dairy. Cheeses flew, hit the ground, rolled.

"Hey!" he shouted. "What the fuck?"

Lucy bounced off, stumbled. Kept running. *Fuck your fucking cheeses.* Looked around, panting. *He gone? I lose him? Where…*

…fuck…

…FUCK…

…there! Spotted him moving towards a flight of stairs, stuck behind a food cart. Lowered her shoulder, ploughed through the crowd. *Closer.* Her mind raced. *Those steps…they lead to London Bridge…*

Realized: *He's headed for the march.*

Thousands of people.

All in masks.

She looked ahead. He was still trapped, trying to squeeze past, arms flailing.

Almost…

He reached the stairs an instant before her but she had momentum now. Flew up behind him, grabbed his jumper. He kicked. She let go, dodged it, kept coming. Reached the top together. *Got you, you shit.* Grabbed his wrist.

Saw the knife.

Oh fuck…

He swivelled. The blade flashed. Hit her square in the chest. *Ugh…*

The blow knocked her back, and she stumbled, tumbled back down the steps, thump, thump, the sky spinning above and pain and she watched, helpless, as his orange trainers melted into the crowd.

CHAPTER SIX

I let him get away.

"…the knife *would've* been a bit of a surprise, to be fair," King was saying. He'd arrived two minutes after the fight, found Lucy sitting by a salt-beef bagel stand. Dazed, frowning, rubbing her tattoo. He checked her but she said she was fine, stab vest blocked the blade, just a bump on the head from the fall. They listened to the radio chatter for a few minutes until hope died. Orange Trainers was gone. Vanished. Poof.

Now she was tuning King out as they walked back to the Toyota, skirting the edge of the Borough crowd.

I let him go. A surge of guilt at her fuck-up. *Had him. His wrist. Just take the blow, roll with it, but for fuck's sake, hold on. Could've solved it, then and there. Paid the Debt. Everything. Now? Now he'll be on the lookout. Knows we know.*

God fucking dammit.

"I mean," King continued, "punch, run…then, blam, a knife? Pulled it out that quick?"

Lucy shrugged. Fingered the tear in her hoodie. *Leave it? Sew it?* Tried to remember if she'd ever actually sewn anything before.

"I'd've been fucked," King said. "In this?" Tugged at his olive rain jacket. "Would've been a chicken shish. Cop pincushion."

"Mmm." She pulled the zip on her hoodie, inspected the damage beneath. *Now I need a new stab vest.* It was her own, not Met-issued. Bought online specially. Ultra-lightweight. Fit beneath the hoodie, didn't block the Cox sensor. *And now it's trashed. Fucking orange-shoe wanker.*

"And you always wear a stabby under that?"

She nodded. *Thanks, Jack.*

The market was even more crowded now. They stuck to the outside, away from the stalls flogging posh bread, imported sausages, tiny yellow-green bottles of truffle oil. As they walked, Lucy replayed the fight in her head. Kept thinking how she had him, fucking *had* him, just needed to…

Wait.

A twinge of memory. *Something useful?* Tried to focus, but her head still hurt from the fall. Dull ache, like the time she forgot her gum shield and sparred anyway. She pulled her drawstrings in frustration.

Come on. Think.

"We should check CCTV," she told King. Dodged a tourist snapping pics of macaroons. "He was in a mask, but maybe we get lucky. Or a vehicle?" Thought back. "That open freezer… if he took something, must have put it somewhere. Reckon a car. Van maybe." She reached for her mobile. "I'll call Salford. Get it going."

He grinned. "Already in the works."

Oh? "Right, fine. Well, we also need a team in that lab. There could still be antidote—"

"Still not sure that actually exists, though, right?"

She stopped walking, stared. *Really, Ed? For fuck's sake.* "You saw that lab—"

A shrug. "Well, there's a Public Health team inbound, so we'll see. We're to keep away for now. Safety. Wilkes."

Dammit, Ma'am…

"And forensics are still working their magic," he continued. "Results tonight, hopefully. We can head back to the interviews in a few, but given your little ordeal…" Checked his battered watch, grinned. "Thought perhaps a cheeky pint?" He looked around, towering over the scrum, hoping to spot a pub. "That is, if any of these places open this early?"

Lucy cleared her throat.

"What, too early for…oh. *Fuck*. Sorry." He sounded genuine. "Forgot. Can't drink, right?"

She shook her head. "The Elemidox. Does bad things. But maybe…" Noticed a wooden cart selling coffee. Pointed. "Yeah?" She rocked up, ordered a double, frowned when she realized they didn't sell Coke. *Just not the same without. Get on that, posh Borough coffee cart.*

King ordered a filter coffee, black. Tried to pay for hers— "C'mon, you deserve it, took one for the team"—but gave in when Lucy slapped a fiver down.

No one buys for me, Ed. Got enough debt as it is.

She led him out a side entrance and they walked back towards the car in silence. The coffee helped her head. King slurped his, and she noticed that the left side of his face was swelling. *Forgot about that. He got dropped. Cheap shot. Fucking Orange Trainers.*

"How's the jaw, then?"

He rubbed his stubble. Grimaced. "Be okay. Clicking a bit. Mainly embarrassed I didn't dodge it." A chuckle. "Actually was a bit of a boxer once."

Knew it!

"Me, too," she said, eyes shining above the dark bags. "See?" Gestured with her thumb to the back of her hoodie, the letters *BGBC* arcing across the top. "Bethnal Green Boxing Club. My brother, too. He was for real, though. Won cups." A note of pride.

"Your brother, huh?"

"Yep." She tossed the espresso beaker into a bin as they passed. "Brill with his left."

King pondered for a moment.

"So…" He pointed to the embroidery on the hoodie. "Is *he* the mysterious Jack, then?" Bit of tension in his voice, she thought. Like he was hoping she wouldn't say, Oh, no, boyfriend, actually. *Or am I just making that up? Hmm. Well, he is actually quite—*

Stopped. Pushed it away. *Mustn't.*

Just said: "Yep. His hoodie."

"I see." Green eyes twinkled. "Does he still fight?"

Oh, right.

She looked away.

You don't know.

Lucy took a deep breath. *Okay. It's fine. We can talk about Jack. That's all before. Not the Debt, nothing to do with it. So yeah, fuck it, let's talk about Jack.*

Exhaled.

"He's dead."

Said it simply. A fact. A fact that her older brother, her idol, the gentle giant who let her tag along after and taught her things and was the one person who actually gave the slightest fuck about little Lucy, that he was dead now. Buried. Had been. One night, outside a chicken shop, three boys, two knives. And why? There was no *why*, no fucking reason. Nothing. Just *whack, whack, whack*. All gone, Jack.

A fucking fact.

"I'm so sorry," King said.

"Jack was stabbed when I was fifteen."

He was silent. She could feel his eyes on her. *Kind eyes.*

Finally: "Truly, Lucy. Really sorry to hear it."

She sighed. "Well. Knife crime island, yeah?"

"Mmm." He finished his coffee, crumpled the cup in his huge hand. "And so, the vest."

"Yep." *Thanks again, Jack.*

They turned the corner, crossed a side street. She could see the railway arch ahead. Two yellow chequered vans marked *Incident Response Vehicle* were parked outside. A man in a green hazmat suit fiddled with equipment on the kerbside.

She sped up. "Just a quick squiz." Reached into her hoodie for her warrant card.

"Lucy." He reached for her, grabbed her shoulder. "Wilkes was clear. We stay out. You especially." Cheeky grin. "Or else she'll kill us both, and your mate Sykes will work it."

She stopped.

Stood staring through the yellow tape across the door. Frowned, ran fingers through her hair. *Want to do something. Actually fucking* DO *something. Not just fuck around, waiting for forensics, grilling the bartender at Cox's who didn't see anything, course he didn't, he was busy making fucking Manhattans, wasn't he? Want to go, sort this out, solve it. Killer, antidote, everything, because if I do that, then just maybe—*

And then, in a flash, she remembered.

Remembered the thing her fall had jarred loose, what she'd seen when she grabbed Orange Trainers. In the split second before the knife blade hit her, she'd noticed: he had a tattoo.

One she'd seen before: a double-barred cross.

Fucking brilliant.

She turned to King. Smiled.

"I know where to go," Lucy said.

‡ ‡ ‡

Lucy stared up at the largest of the three skulls.

"Bit macabre," said King.

The churchyard entrance was certainly grim. Three leering stone skulls above the arch, crossbones, a thick row of iron spikes bristling above it all. And two more spike-impaled skulls in the corners, Lucy noticed. *Just for shits and giggles.*

"How'd you like to walk under *that* every Sunday?" he asked.

She shrugged, said nothing. *Seen worse things, Ed.*

"Suppose it was all the rage in…" He eyed the gate's inscription. "1652?"

Another shrug. *Whenever.* Dates were more a Simon thing. Opened the iron gate, walked into the churchyard. He followed. The church in front of them was tiny. Squat, stone, impossibly medieval here in the shadow of the Gherkin and the Scalpel and the rest of modern London. She'd been to this place before, too. Simon's voice in her head: "Know what you're walking on, Luce?"

Hope they're still inside.

Checked her mobile. It was already one. Light drizzle, gloomy. Lucy frowned as she marched towards the church's heavy wooden doors.

Be crap if I've missed them.

It had taken her three calls and a favour to pin down the exact spot. The Hand of God didn't exactly advertise their meeting locations. Hope you're bringing plenty of backup, her last contact told her. Word is, they're dangerous. Fanatics. Serious shit.

Lucy looked up at King. "Told these things get a bit iffy," she said. "So stick close, yeah?"

Pushed open the doors. Went in.

Inside, the church was heaving. People in flowing white gowns were packed from one side of the church to the other, filling the pews, clogging the aisles. Women shrieked. Men groaned. Everyone was swaying, shaking, writhing. Lucy and King stood in the rear; him with beefy arms crossed, her on tiptoe. At the front, a skeletal man in a white cassock with a double-barred cross up the middle preached into a microphone.

"And so, my children," the preacher cried, "the Great Father of Nations sent us the Scourge! His divine arrows, falling from the heavens! The ancient stroke of Deber and Resheph, the noisome affliction that torments the sinners, but spares His beloved. He that is our shield and buckler, my children, our refuge and fortress…"

"That's our boy," she told King. Pointed to the skeletal man. "Enoch Clapham."

"Hmm. Don't like him."

He was whipping the crowd into a pure frenzy now, screaming out questions, basking in the chanted replies echoing off medieval stone walls.

CLAPHAM: *Can there be doubt? Did we not see? Have we not eyes in our heads, my children?*
CROWD: *We do we do we do...*

Lucy looked at the women swaying in front of her, then frowned. *Wait. Hold on a tick.* Walked to the back corner, climbed up on the base of a column. *Could it really be...?* Felt her gears turn as she scanned the frenzied crowd. *Yes. Christ.* Hopped down, returned to King.

"Come on," she said. "Enough of this."

She plunged into the middle of the writhing crowd.

CLAPHAM: *The skin of the damned—blistered, peeling! The very scorch of Hellfire! Satan, marking his own for all to see! Did we not witness? Tell me now, my children! Did we not all see?*
CROWD: *We did we did we did...*

Lucy elbowed past wailing women. Pushed aside quaking men. *This is some serious bullshit.*
King struggled to keep up.

CLAPHAM: *And their eyes? Black, loathsome, God's own tokens of damnation, were they not?*
CROWD: *They were they were they were...*

She reached the front row. A massive man, taller than King and two stone heavier, blocked her way. Lucy gritted her teeth, shoved the man aside and stood, staring up at the preacher.

73

He was screeching to his followers, hands outstretched, eyes blazing.

CLAPHAM: *And then—those they would have you call by the name "Survivors"—oh, no, not Survivors, never that, but—devils! See their faces, oh my children, know them for what they are! Devils on earth, walking amongst us! They are the damned! They are...the guilty!*
CROWD: *They are they are they are they are they are...*

Lucy turned around and looked up, into the mezzanine.

Saw exactly what she was expecting to see.

I so do not have time for this shit.

Lucy left the crowd. Marched straight up to Clapham. Put her hand over the mic.

"Stop this rubbish," she said.

Behind her, the white-robed mob wailed. Clapham glared at her. His eyes burned with fury. "Who are *you*," he screamed, "to tell the sacred emissary of our Father of—"

She pulled out her warrant card, held it inches from his nose. "Now."

King grabbed her elbow. "It's a religious service, Lucy..."

"No, it isn't." To the preacher: "Stop the filming now." Turned back to King. Nodded to the mezzanine. "See the camera up there? This crowd—they're *actors*. All bloody actors. Recognized half of them from that column in the back. Look." Pointed to a lean redhead with double-barred crosses painted on his cheeks. "Volvo advert, few years back." To a small blonde, still shrieking and writhing. "Bit part on *Spooks*. And *that* one..." Waved her hand at the giant in the front row. He snarled back. "That one... well, here. See for yourself."

She tapped her phone, handed it over. On the screen: the giant, his hair crisply parted, beaming as he held up a bottle of salad dressing for the camera.

"Yeah," she said. "He's the face of a bloody organic condiment company."

Clapham began to speak, but she cut him off again.

"You have a licence to film? Bet you don't."

Wanna get nicked? Fucking try me.

In the front row, the giant stopped snarling. "Hey," he called, voice high-pitched, "hey, what *is* all this? This wasn't in the casting note…"

Lucy grabbed the mic.

"You. Salad Cream." Glared at him. "Simmer." To the crowd, who were now murmuring in confusion: "You lot. All of you. Take five. Do it."

She turned back to Clapham.

"And *you.*" *You horrid fucking wanker.* "We're about to have us a chat."

‡ ‡ ‡

They stood in the corner of the mossy church graveyard.

The drizzle had stopped, but the lone wooden bench was still wet. Clapham leaned against an old tombstone. He was short, an inch or two taller than Lucy at most. Pale, waxy skin. Thinning brown hair. Wore a suit under the cassock, she noticed. Looked expensive. Tassel loafers, croc leather. Seemed a different man away from his pulpit: quiet, controlled. A cross medallion hung from his neck, double-barred like the one on his cassock, and he stroked it with his fingertips.

"How can I assist, Officers?" To Lucy: "Of course, if only I'd known who you were…"

If you knew who I was? What I've done?

You'd be fucking running.

"So," she said. Voice hard. "Everyone's an actor, then."

Clapham shrugged. "A necessary charade." Without the

microphone, his voice sounded faint. "The Hand of God is an *online* ministry. My church is wherever my children are. In their homes and cars, their laptops, tablets, phones. This…" He waved a thin hand at the church. "This is just a tool, a device to spread God's truth."

God's truth. Christ.

She shook her head. "Don't just mean *those* actors. You. You're an actor, too." Pulled the mobile from her hoodie pocket. Read off the screen. "Enoch Clapham. Real name, Gavin Morley. Born '67, Ealing. Former letting agent. Stretch in the Ville for corporate tax evasion. And now playing at this nonsense." She snorted. "The Hand of God."

"Oh," said Clapham, "the Hand of God is hardly a game, Officer…?"

She said nothing, just stared. *Not finishing your fucking sentences. Want my name? Ask.*

He didn't seem to mind. "Our streaming channel has over thirty-five thousand followers and a quarter-million views." A little smile. "My flock is multiplying."

King stood nearby, elbow resting on a statue. His eyes were narrowed, head tilted to one side. Lucy got the sense that he hadn't paid attention to the sermon and was trying to catch up. *He's awful, Ed. End of.*

"In fact," Clapham continued, "the Lord God revealed His message to me in prison. And some of your police brethren were among the Hand of God's earliest believers."

She thought of Sykes. *Yeah, I can see it.*

The rain began again, a cold mizzle. Clapham straightened up, started to move back to the church. Lucy froze him with her eyes. *Not done with you yet.* Leaned closer, looked at the double-barred cross sewn on his cassock. Embroidered on its top bar were groups of letters, separated by miniature crosses:

Brilliant. Exactly like the tattoo.

"That cross." Gestured with her mobile. "Those letters…"

"Saint Zacharias's Blessing."

Whatever. "It's your symbol, yeah?"

"It's a very old symbol. An amulet of sorts. But, yes, the Hand of God have adopted it."

"Right. And you all wear it around? T-shirts, hats?" Thought of the defaced Survivors' rights poster she'd seen in the Tube station. "Little round stickers?"

"We have an online shopping portal, yes."

I bet you do. "How about tattoos?"

Clapham shrugged. "Perhaps. That I wouldn't know. As I said, I am always with my children spiritually, but physically, it is difficult. My children are spread across—"

"Show me your wrists."

A look of surprise, then another shrug. He pushed up his sleeves. His wrists were bare.

Well, knew you weren't Orange Trainers. But one of your little children is. That I know.

He looked at her, eyes mild.

Lucy stared back, searching. *I can't tell. Truly. Can't. Are you just a fraud? Scam artist, working an angle, playing on the worst in people? Or do you actually believe all this vile rubbish?* She ran her fingers through her hair. *Honestly, don't even know which is worse…*

The rain picked up. Clapham shivered. "If I may suggest…" he began.

She shook her head.

Whatever you are, you're the key to what I want. So let's see what you know.

"Flinders Cox was murdered last night."

She watched his face. No response. *Expecting that, then? Or just don't give a fuck?*

Finally: "A God-fearing man, I understand. I'm saddened."

"Are you?" She paused. Frowned at him. "I know what you preach, Clapham. The people who died from London Black, they deserved it. It was their fault. Right?"

Out the corner of her eye, she saw King's swollen jaw clench. *Now you see, Ed? Repulsive, yeah?*

Clapham nodded. "London Black touches those whom God would have it touch. It is God's arrow, and He directs it against the sinner. Against the corrupted." Smiled a smile that made Lucy want to say fuck it and just drop him on the spot. *Almost be worth it.* She took a deep breath. Exhaled.

But I need to pay the Debt.

"Thing is," she said, "Flinders Cox was working on an antidote. And if he found one, then that's you all done, yeah? Copycat attacks stop. No more arrows for your precious children to fear. No need to buy Hand of God T-shirts. You had every reason in the world to want him gone."

And I want it to be you. You, with your disgusting, victim-blaming little cult. I want it to be you, so I can shut you down, Enoch Clapham or Gavin Morley or whatever the fuck you want to call yourself.

He chuckled softly. Maddeningly.

"There will never be an antidote for London Black, Officer. It is God's will, made manifest. Go where you please, His hand will find you out. Why kill a man for something I know he can never do? No, you should be looking to *them*."

Clapham pointed out to the street beyond. Three men wearing Survivor masks walked past. One carried a home-made Survivors' Rights Association banner.

"Who do you think is behind the copycat attacks?" he continued. "Their goal is to make others in their image, to create an entire race of devils. Don't you remember the stories from the Scourge? The dying who were breathing on the faces of the well, hoping to expose them?"

Lucy glared at him.

Don't believe those stories. Didn't then. And you're wrong. The dead didn't deserve to die. And the ones who lived? They sure as fuck didn't all deserve that, either.

Just look at me.

"But," he said, "God protects His children. Only the sinners, the corrupted creatures—"

"Hey, Clapham."

For the first time, King spoke. Voice low, a growl. He walked towards the preacher. Took his large hands out of his rain jacket pockets, began to crack his knuckles. A tiny voice in Lucy's head: *No ring.*

"I learned something about London Black two years ago," he said.

A knuckle cracked.

Clapham watched him come. His foot had started to tap, Lucy noticed.

"Most nerve agents—sarin, VX, whatever—when they kill you, they kill you quickly. Minutes. Seconds. Over in a flash."

Crack.

"But London Black? Oh, no. It takes days. And you're alert. *Conscious.* You don't even lose your fucking appetite." King was directly in front of the preacher now, towering over him. "You know *exactly* what's happening. All the effects. The spasms, the convulsions. Skin coming off in sheets, blood filling your eyes, your mouth fucking *disintegrating*. Everything."

Crack. Crack.

"You see yourself in a living nightmare. Trapped, right until the last fucking second. And now you're telling me all those people, they *deserved* that?"

"Sinners must pay for their sins."

King bent down until his face was inches from Clapham. Stared in his eyes. Said:

"My. Nine-year-old. *Daughter*?"

Silence.

Christ, thought Lucy. *Oh, Ed.*

For a second, she thought he was going to kill him. Take the preacher by the neck, shake him like a dog with a toy, snap him in two with his bare, muscular hands.

But he turned away.

Jammed his hands back into his pockets. Walked over to the sculpture. Stood, staring down at the ground, down to an ancient grave marker buried in the wet grass.

No one spoke.

And then, from beneath Lucy's hoodie: a soft triple beep.

Now?

She looked at Clapham, frowned. "We'll speak again," she said. Dismissed him with a tiny nod of her chin. Watched him for a moment as he shuffled towards the church, then turned away and swiped her phone beneath the hoodie.

7.0.

Lucy felt the hairs on the back of her neck stand up.

Seven? Really? This early?

Oh fuck.

"Everything okay?" King had collected himself and was standing next to her.

She nodded. Noticed his eyes were glistening. "Ed…"

He waved his hand. "Look, it's…not just that she died, or even how. It's more than that." He sighed. Checked his watch. "Half one. We should be getting back. Maybe later on, if you've got a few minutes, I'll tell you about it?"

"I don't want to bother…"

"No. No bother. It helps, actually. Truly. I started talking a year ago. Told everyone, started therapy. Without that…"

Nodded towards Clapham. "*That* would have ended differently. Much worse. For him, and for me."

Lucy looked at him. Thought of Wilkes's leaflets.

Maybe someday, Ma'am.

"Anyway," he said, "I ordered the surveillance. We'll see what he does. What do you think about our new pal?"

She thought for a moment.

"The crucifix," she said. "It fits. Forget this meek and mild rubbish. When Clapham was up in front of the crowd, I saw his eyes." A firm nod. "Eyes of a man who would jam a crucifix into a dying man's skull."

Which means, I'm on the right track. Now I just need to keep on it.

It began to pour.

"Right," she said. Flipped up her hood. "I'll ring you in an hour. Something I need to do."

King looked at her, surprised, but she was already on the move. Turning away, walking through the old churchyard, out beneath the skull-studded gate.

I need to go stay alive.

CHAPTER SEVEN

Lucy stared into the eyes of the terrified child.

Horrible thing to put up. Even at a doctor's.

The poster hung on the wall across from the exam table where she sat. Bright red title at the top:

EARLY STAGE SYMPTOMS OF EXPOSURE TO AGENT A-267 (LONDON BLACK)

Arrows with thick bold type captions pointed to different parts of the girl's body—to her stomach (NAUSEA), her eyes (PINPOINT PUPILS), her mouth (DROOLING). A Cox Labs logo was printed in the lower right corner. Lucy tugged on her hoodie drawstrings. Felt nauseous. *That child died. Three days after that photo. Two, if she was lucky. And now she's hung on a wall forever. Staring. Scared. Alone.*

She took a breath.

Thought about her monitor beeping. Her resistance levels, oddly low.

The fuck is going on with me?

"So. Lucy." Doctor Hodges finished typing. Turned to her, pushed his specs up. "Seven point 0 after, what, thirteen hours, you said?"

"Thirteen and a half."

"Hmm."

She smelt the alcohol on his breath from ten feet away.

Can't really blame him, though, can I? What he's been through? She'd seen Hodges in action back then, on duty in the worst part of an Iso Centre, right smack in the thick of the blood and the skin and the death. Remembered his face: oval, hooked nose, wide-set eyes. His frustration. Looked him up after, once it was all over, when she needed a doctor. Never mentioned she'd seen him before.

"And immediately post-injection?" he asked. "What was the reading?"

"Eight point seven."

"Hmm. Mind lifting your shirt up, just at the bottom there? Want to check the sensor."

Hodges leaned close.

Wine. Sweet. Smells like Nan did at Christmas.

He pressed directly on the sensor. Frowned. Carefully avoided touching her stomach. He knew better. One of her first attacks was right here, in this very exam room. Her first visit. Hodges had touched her skin—just brushed it, a little graze, but it was enough. No red, thank Christ, she hadn't thrown anything, flipped over a table, nothing like that. Just staggered to a corner, collapsed. Crying. Terrified.

"It's not the sensor," he said. Another frown. Sat back in his swivel chair, crossed his legs. "I'm worried. I think Elemidox is becoming less effective. I've heard about this. Haven't seen it. Would make sense, though, that it would show up first in patients who have been using the drug the longest." Tented his fingers. "Lucy, this is not good."

Not good how? Not good like I have to do two Boosts a day? Fine, fuck it, just write me a script, then. I'll get back to work, you get back to that bottle of cream sherry in your desk drawer. "So I just, what? Boost more often? That'll sort it?"

He shook his head. "Doesn't work that way, I'm afraid. Won't clear your system. Once, twice, ten times a day—doesn't make a blind bit of difference. Anything beyond the first Boost of the day is meaningless."

Wait. What?

83

"Cox Labs is working on a product," he continued. "Calling it Elemidox Ultra."

Ultra. With a U, not an A.

"Heard of it," she said.

Hodges looked surprised. "Really? Well, thing is, they've started clinicals, but it won't be rolled out commercially for, I'd say, a year. Perhaps nine months, best case."

"And how long do I have? Until the Boosts stop working?"

A shrug. "No way to tell. Could be weeks. Could be tomorrow."

Oh.

Her fingers crept to her tattoo.

"So until the new drug's ready, you're in danger. All these copycat attacks. One every other day, seems like. And you know how easily the agent spreads in the air."

She nodded.

A memory from two years ago: in bed with Simon, curled under the fluffy blue duvet, watching a history doc on their crap little telly. Something about Charles the First. Maybe the Second, who can keep them straight, honestly? She wasn't into it, rather watch *Fight Night*, but it didn't matter. She was happy enough. The world outside was scary, yes: more attacks, more men in red gas masks spraying aerosols. But they still had a box of Boosts left between them. Should be plenty, and there'd be more Boosts available soon. It was all going to be okay, everything was going to be okay...

And then suddenly it wasn't a history doc any more.

It was a special announcement, a serious-looking man with a Welsh accent and yellow tie. He was coming live from the studio, telling them that the terrorists were using drones now. Two spotted in the air above Brixton, private residences there can no longer be considered safe, repeat residences not safe. Please stay tuned for information on Isolation Centres or visit our website at...

Lucy frowned at Hodges.

Yeah. Yeah, I do know how easily it spreads.

Hodges uncrossed his legs, leaned forward. Best bedside manner now.

"So for the time being, you need to leave. I'd say cities are right out, too many attacks. Beyond that? Tricky to say, if I'm honest. There are some good iso camps these days. One up in Lapland, I hear raves. Beautiful country up there, Lapland. Ever tried Nordic skiing? Camp's pricey, but maybe for a few months…"

Lucy stared at him.

You don't understand, Doc.

I need to pay off the Debt. I need to solve this case. Cox. The antidote. Clapham. All of it. Can't solve a homicide from the fucking Arctic Circle, can I?

She shook her head.

"Need to be in London."

"I would strongly advise against that."

Then agree to disagree. She shrugged, hopped down from the exam table, started towards the door. *No time to waste, best get back to the Station…*

"Lucy."

She turned, looked back.

"If you're exposed…" He paused. "You know how it ends."

Of course I know.

"Reckon I'll have to take my chances."

Her mind raced as she walked out of the exam room, down a corridor, past reception. Tried to keep calm, but felt scared. Helpless. Wondered whether this was it, whether it was finally all catching up to her now and wasn't this just the perfect fucking ending, make her suffer for two years and then just as the end was in sight, blam, pull the rug out. Really thought you'd get away from London Black, Lucy? *What I deserve, only fitting and…*

...no.

No.

A different voice inside her. Stronger. She stopped walking. Took a deep breath. Exhaled.

No, no, no. I'm not fucking dying now. Not before I've paid off the Debt.

Then maybe we'll see.

She looked around. She'd wound up in the waiting room. Horrid taupe wallpaper, fake palm trees. It was empty. *Okay, right.* She pulled her mobile from her jeans pocket. Typed in King's name, pushed the call button.

He answered on the third ring. "Lucy?" Sounded stressed.

"Are you at the Station? Just on my way. Be there in twenty, tops."

"Nope. Back at the railway arch. Cox's secret lab."

Oh?

A burst of background noise: someone shouting directions, beeps as a vehicle backed up.

"PHE team are leaving," he said. "They've finished their exam."

So soon? She felt her pulse speed up.

"And? The antidote? Did they find it?"

Tell me yes. Please God, yes—

"No."

The word hit her like a blow. *Fuck.* But she rolled with it, came back swinging. "Okay, right, but something was missing, yeah? Something from the freezer, for starters. Anything else? Papers, a laptop? Orange Trainers must've nicked it all, stashed it someplace before we arrived..."

King sighed. "They found traces of Elemidox Ultra. They think Cox was working on it in his spare time. But listen, Lucy." His voice sounded strange. "That's not all they found."

A surge of hope. *Knew it. Fucking knew it.*

"Something *like* an antidote? Or a permanent Boost? Maybe some form of—"

He cut her off.

"Lucy, they found a human foot."

CHAPTER EIGHT

Lucy stuck her head into the kiln.

"I wouldn't do that," said King. "May still be some human ash in there."

Yeah, well, you're not a Londoner, Ed. She pulled her head out, coughed. Remembered the end of the Scourge, when even the biscuit factories were overwhelmed and the dead were just burned where they fell. *Bet you never had corpses burning in the street up in Brum.*

She wiped her hands on her faded black jeans, looked around.

King stood in the middle of the pottery studio, arms crossed, rubbing his swollen jaw. *Looks stressed.* The PHE man next to him was still wearing his blue hazmat suit, but the face shield was up. Big black beard, high cheekbones, hazel eyes. Lucy didn't recognize him. Wondered whether he'd been on a removal team back then. Rumour was, they were all on the take. Few thousand quid and the body went quietly, middle of the night, no red X on the door, no muss no fuss.

"It was in the back," the PHE man said. "Beneath a pile of ash. Fragment of a metatarsal."

"Surprised you checked," said Lucy.

"Secret London Black lab in the middle of metropolitan London?" He chuckled. "We check everything."

Fair.

"How long was it there?" she asked.

The man shrugged. "Question for Forensics, really. But that kiln hasn't been fired for at least a year. More likely, two." Pointed his rubber-gloved hand towards a box in the corner. "Wood fired. And the wood's gone rotten."

She nodded. *Right. Two years ago. Scourge time. So question is, is there a connection?* Looked at the kiln. It was the size of a kitchen oven. *Little thing. No fucking way a corpse fits in there, not in one piece. Must've chopped it up.* Pictured Cox's body, crucifix sticking out of his eye socket. Ran her fingers through her hair. *Don't know. This feels cold-blooded. Cox felt hot. But maybe it's a lead.*

She walked back towards the studio door. Glanced around again at the bare floors, the empty shelves. Frowned. Thought about art classes at school, her manky primary, the one with stubby Crayolas and damp on all the ceilings. They'd done clay for a bit. She'd made a tiny cup for Jack, boxing glove carved into the clay with a paperclip end. Wobbly little thing, could barely tell what it was, but he'd loved it, hugged her, *brilliant, Luce*, put it on his shelf next to the cologne and the photo of Mum.

Clay was messy. Buckets of water and slip and that. None of that here.

Hmm.

"It wasn't all body parts," King said. "Someone had fun." He picked an evidence bag up from the coffee table, handed it to her. Inside were rubber tubing, a dirty spoon and a syringe. "Not exactly Elemidox."

"Blimey," she said.

"And the sofa is heavily stained," he added. Glanced at her, then away. "Semen."

"Slathered," said the PHE man.

You're shitting me. She thought of Cox's monastic Mayfair study. Of the Survivors' rights advocate, the man who donated his money to cathedrals and church groups. *Doesn't much sound like you, Mr Cox, does it?*

"Did Cox own the studio?" she asked.

King nodded. "Studio, lab, whole thing. Checked the land registry. He bought the freehold ten years ago."

"Anyone else use it?"

A shrug.

Out the corner of her eye, through the window in the studio's door, she caught a flash of orange. Across the hallway, a man in a dayglow hazmat suit was closing the heavy steel door to the lab. He pulled a roll of yellow tape from his pocket, sealed the door shut. A ring of bold type warnings: **TOXIC—LETHAL—TOXIC**. Job complete, he turned to the exit.

"Just a tick," she said. Left the studio, ran after the man in the suit. Caught up to him as he reached the incident response van outside. It was cold, still raining, but the arch kept them dry. "A freezer was open," she told him. "Did you swab inside?"

He looked annoyed. Reached down, tugged off one orange wellie, then the other. They were wet, she noticed. Unhooked a respirator, then yanked off his face shield. A thin face. Squinty. Grey hair, cropped close.

"Stone, right?" Yorkshire accent.

She frowned. *Who's asking?* Gave him the faintest of nods.

"Thought so." He opened the van's rear door, began placing his equipment inside yellow plastic bins. "Yes, DI Stone. Of course. We swabbed everything. Needed to make sure you hadn't kicked off a mini-Scourge by running out of there without using the decon shower."

Oh. Fuck.

"Whoops…"

"And everything we found was relayed to DI King." He unzipped his suit. "As per protocol. Which," he added pointedly, "we actually follow."

Lucy frowned at him. *I said, "whoops".*

He stepped out of the suit. Just pants and a sweaty vest underneath. Didn't seem to care that she was watching. Moved slowly, painstakingly. Done this thousands of times, she could tell, but still took each step seriously. *Bet you never took a bribe. Or if you did, you regret it.*

"So," she said, "the only thing anyone was working on inside that lab was Elemidox Ultra?"

"Didn't say that." He folded the orange suit. "Not what we told King. Said that's the only thing we *found.* Difference. Beyond that, can't say. Half the lab was wiped."

"Wiped?"

"Last twenty-four hours. Sodium hydroxide solution. Effective."

Fucking Orange Trainers. I'll wipe you. But that means…

"There *could've* been something else in there, then? Say… an antidote?"

He stopped folding. Looked at her.

"Anything's possible, DI Stone. Even a miracle." She nodded, turned to leave, but he kept speaking, "Word of advice. King mentioned that you're a Vulnerable."

Oh he did, did he?

"You're lucky," he continued. "Going in there? Incredibly dangerous. Might have been a new compound, something that would blow right through your Boost like a bullet through a wet kitchen towel." Placed the suit inside the bin, slammed the van door shut. "Trust me. If you start seeing hazmat suits, get the hell out of there."

She stared at him. "I'll be fine." *Now put some clothes on before you catch something.*

As she walked back into the arch, she smiled to herself.

Wiped. Didn't mention that, Ed.

Could be an antidote after all.

And whoever was doing all that shagging? Reckon they might have seen. Which means I need to find them. Right fucking now.

She opened the door to the studio, stepped inside. King stood alone by the coffee table. He was holding a dusty piece of pottery, a dish, turning it over in his giant hands. Looked away as she entered, but not quickly enough: she saw the tear.

Wife was a potter. Poor Ed. Did she die, too? Like your little girl… For a second, she thought of just walking up, giving him a hug. Noticed there was no surge of guilt. *Good. Just sympathy, then. Best keep it that way.*

"Found it at the back on a cooling rack," he said. He put the dish down. It was beautiful. Ring of blue and yellow flowers around the edge, blossoming nosegay in the centre. "Tin glaze. Unusual."

She nodded. Thought about it.

Tin glaze. Sounds specific. Wonder if…

Pulled out her mobile, began to type. After a moment, she looked back up.

"Cox's daughter. The one who found him. What's her name?"

He answered without hesitation, "Veronica."

She smiled. Showed him. A gallery listing from five years ago, some posh place in Chelsea. And there, hidden towards the back: *Traditional tin-glazed earthenware.*

By Veronica Cox.

‡ ‡ ‡

I won't want to look. Know I won't. But I need to.

They were standing in the gleaming lobby of a Fitzrovia office building. It was pitch black outside. Had been when they'd left the railway arch at half four, and now it was well past five. The ride over had been quiet; King silent when he wasn't muttering at pedestrians, Lucy staring out the window. *Should be excited,* she told herself, *antidote's still in play, Clapham's a lead, now this…* But her stomach hadn't stopped twisting since King told her what Veronica Cox did for a living, where she worked. Where they were headed.

"Makes sense, really," he said, as he pressed the lift button. "What with her father, everything he's done for them. Only natural she'd end up a Survivors' rights activist, right?" He waved a paw at the marble floor, the leather chairs. "Expect this was all paid for with Cox money."

She nodded. Looked at the sign on the wall. It was small. Cryptic. No glossy posters, no bright red triangles. Just plain black letters: SRA Charitable Trust Pty Ltd.

"Low key," he said, reading her mind. "Security, I reckon. Not everyone finds Survivors so inspiring. Enoch Clapham's nutters find this place? Could get ugly."

The lift beeped.

As they entered, King looked down at her. Frowned.

"You all right, Lucy?"

Am I ever?

She pulled on her hoodie drawstrings, exhaled. Thought about seeing Survivors, why she dreaded it. Not because it was gross, not it at all. *Face is a face, we're all of us different.* And not a real trigger, thank God. Shouldn't cause a full-on attack, not like touching her stomach or whatever the fuck Sykes had said. But seeing them brought back memories. Painful ones. Reminded her of what she'd done. Of the Debt.

"I just…" A sigh. *Don't want to talk about it.* "It's hard. Seeing them."

He nodded.

"I can imagine. Sort of, there but for the grace of God, right?"

God? God had fuck all to do with it, Ed.

The lift slowed. Stopped. Lucy braced herself. The doors slid open and there, on the reception desk, sat—DC Andy Sykes.

Fucking Sykes.

"Evening," said King.

Ugh. Forgot. Sykes is the family liaison officer. Course he's here.

She frowned at him.

"'Bout time you lot showed up," Sykes said. Hopped off the desk, oozed over. "Fucking tragic. Expecting to spend the afternoon chatting to Veronica Cox." Winked at King. He had his crap fedora, she noticed. "Instead, she's holed up in her office, door closed, doing fuck knows what, and I spend all my time listening to some disgusting Meat—"

In an instant, Lucy was in his face. Fists balled, staring up into his eyes.

"We don't use that word, Sykes."

The M word? Really? The fuck is wrong with you?

He grinned, pleased at winding her up. "Didn't realize we were all so very PC. Just a *word*, Stone. Don't throw a chair."

She reached for him but King was too quick. He grabbed her shoulder, pulled her back.

"Easy, Lucy."

I'll fucking drop you, Sykes. Kept staring, but took a deep breath. Let it out slowly. Not worth it, she knew. Not now, not with the antidote and the Debt and everything else on the line.

But Christ, it would feel good.

She took another breath, turned away, looked around the lobby. Modern, stylish. Scandinavian, she thought. *Like a really posh Ikea.* London Strong banners hung from the ceiling. Box of black poppies on the desk, metal pins, not paper. No death-count bands, she noticed.

King changed the subject. "Did the caterer come through? Meant to, I thought."

"Had a word with him," said Sykes. "Seemed properly torn up. Course, I would be, too. Cox probably his only customer. Serving staff all checked, yeah?"

King nodded. "Checked. Cleared. All twelve. No ties to Cox, no sniff of a motive."

"Were they wearing masks?" Lucy asked.

He shook his head. "No. Already checked. Point of pride. They don't cover up."

"Huh." *Okay, fine. Just a thought.*

"Christ," said Sykes. "Can you imagine? One of *them* rocking up with a tray of finger foods? 'Steak tartare, sir? Perhaps a Beef Wellington?'" A snicker. Looked to King for approval, but the big detective frowned, shook his head.

Thank you, Ed. To Sykes: "You're disgusting."

"And you're fucking crazy." He sneered. "And whatever suction you have with Wilkes? It won't last forever." Smashed on his fedora, leaned against the desk. "Go on back there if you want. Her mother's in with her now, but she's got a little helper out front you can chat to. Can't miss him. Just your type, Stone."

Just you wait. One day.

"Come on," said King.

Lucy nodded. Glared at Sykes, then turned, followed. Her stomach tensed as they rounded the corner. She stayed behind King, letting his body block her line of sight. After a few steps, she heard the squeak of a chair being pushed back.

"Evening, Officers."

The man's voice was scratchy, the telltale vocal fry of a London Black-damaged larynx.

"Marv Clarke," he continued. "Veronica's PA."

"Evening," said King.

You need to look, Lucy told herself. *Do it. Don't be rude.*

It's okay, just look.

She did.

His face was a mass of scar tissue. Nose, cheeks, chin, scalp—everything was mottled red and pink, seamy and ridged. Shiny, almost glossy. She tried not to think about it, not to see the resemblance, but it was too hard to ignore. She couldn't not see it.

Mince. His face looked like raw minced beef.

Two jet-black eyes stared at her, waiting.

She felt the guilt surge, but she attacked it, shoved it away. *Not now. Yes, I owe, yes, believe me, I know it, but not fucking now. You're not like Sykes, not rude and cruel and hurtful, and besides you need this, could be useful in the case and just for fuck's sake, be okay for once.*

The surge passed.

"Nice to meet you," she said. Smiled. Shook his hand.

You did it.

"It's a tragedy," Clarke said. "Mr Cox. The entire Survivor community is in shock."

"A great man," said King.

Clarke pointed to the closed office door. "She's devastated, Veronica. But brave. Keeping on. Flat out, actually." He smiled to himself. "Always is. In here around the clock, first in, last out. *If* she leaves. Found her sleeping on the lobby sofa once or twice. Really, just a clever, dedicated, motivated, truly *wonderful* human being."

Lucy caught King's eye.

In her head, the PHE man's voice: *Slathered.*

Reckon she needs a release every now and again?

"She must associate all of this with her father, though," King said. "Must've steered her towards SRA work…"

Clarke shook his head. "Actually, Flinders had nothing to do with it. No one believes it, but it's true. Veronica was a paramedic before. See?" Pointed to a framed certificate on the wall. "Pressed into service in the Iso Centres. Saw the worst of it. The dark wards." His hands shook, Lucy noticed. "Couldn't even get doctors in there half the time, but there was Veronica, walking the halls."

Lucy nodded. She'd seen one of those wards. *Like being in hell.*

"She kept working after the Scourge, but one day…" He shrugged. "She'd just seen too much. One tragedy too many.

96

So she followed her heart, moved to social reform. To us." He nodded. "We're very lucky."

"I'm sure," said King.

Lucy smiled. Felt good. *Wasn't so awful. You sorted it. And now you'll sort the case.* She started thinking through leads. *Fingers crossed, Veronica gives us something on the lab. Or the foot. Then after, I can pull CCTV and try to track Orange Trainers, and then there's someone watching Clapham, that should pay off...then maybe forensics...*

Cox's door flew open.

A middle-aged woman burst out. Fur coat, sable. Looked real. Black hat, gloves, thick strand of pearls above a black dress. Giant designer sunglasses. Lucy watched her walk towards them. *Seriously posh.*

"Goodnight, Ma'am," said Clarke.

"Evening, Mrs Cox," said King.

Helen Cox glanced at them, sniffed, kept walking. Heels clicked on marble as she turned the corner and vanished.

Nice to meet you, too.

From inside the office, a tired voice: "Send 'em in, Clarkey."

Right. Here we go. Let's see what you can tell us, Veronica.

They walked inside. Veronica Cox rose from her chair, smiled at them. She was pretty. Blonde hair, high cheekbones, long neck—

Lucy's eyes opened wide.

Oh fuck.

Her.

‡ ‡ ‡

Lucy turned. Ran.

Oh fuck oh fuck oh fuck...

King, from behind her: "Lucy...hey, are you—"

97

And then sound went. Just a hum.

Inhale. Exhale.

Out the door, past the desk, down the hall.

Clarke, on his feet. Lips moving, saying something.

Oh fuck.

She kept going.

Looked down. Hands shaking. Tasted ash.

Images flashed: pop, pop, pop, blows in a fight. Horrible things, bodies burning, skin crackling, mothers shrieking.

Veronica Cox, pretty blonde, long neck.

Her, it was her, she was there, at The Thing—

And in a flash it was then. A film in her head but no, it was real, she was there, running now but running then, down the street, dodging cars, running hard, fucking *hard* and she knew it was wrong and how the *fuck* could she do it and please God and—

Breathe, Lucy. Breathe.

Inhale. Exhale.

But she couldn't stop it. It kept playing. She was still running, running, turned the corner and saw her, oh God oh Jesus a paramedic, pretty blonde long neck—

No, no, NO. Shook her head. Cried out.

Stop it. Fucking stop it. Control it.

The film stopped.

Breathe.

Need to go back. Back to the office.

But she couldn't. Wanted to, needed to, but it was too much.

Her.

She blazed through the lobby, trainers on marble. Under the banners, past the sofa.

"Lucy? Toilets, Lucy?"

King. Muffled but she heard him. He caught up, was beside her now, guiding her, big hand on her shoulder. Trying to help. Strong chin, green eyes. *Looks like Jack.* "Lucy? Lucy, can I—"

No. Shook her head. Pushed him away. Flipped her hood. Kept moving. "Fine. I'm fine. Just…" *Leave me. Fucking leave me. Go back. Finish the job.* "Veronica. Go…"

Toilet sign. Crashed through the door.

Stood. Panting. Staring.

Saw her face in the mirror.

An image flashed: Her face in a mirror, screaming, screaming…

Lucy screamed.

And she was screaming now and screaming then, and it was then and now and she cried out, *oh God oh Jesus*, saw it, it was The Thing, The Thing That Happened, is Happening, and she fell, cold floor, hard, crawled to the cubicle, elbows and knees. Pulled the door. Dragged herself in. Closed it.

Make it stop.

On the floor, curled up, rocking. Shaking. Rubbing her tattoo.

Then her monitor: *beep beep beep.*

And she was crying.

Crying because it was too much, all too much, the Debt and the Thing and the Boosts, and she just wanted it to be over, just *all over for fuck's sake Jack please help me Jack please make it stop…*

beep beep beep

Lucy wept, all alone.

CHAPTER NINE

Get up, Champ.

Her eyes were shut.

She was back at her first fight, age thirteen. Ratty gym, crap lighting. Strip-club bouncers sweated out shit booze as they worked tattered bags, thwack, thwack. Smelt like socks. Onions. The other girl was older, fitter than Lucy. Longer reach. Dropped Lucy with a hook one minute in, left her dazed, flat, staring at the worn blue canvas inches from her eyes. Thought about staying down, maybe Dad was right, not for her. And then she heard Jack calling from the corner: Get up, Champ. Get up.

Get the fuck up.

Lucy opened an eye.

You have work to do.

She pulled herself up off the loo floor. Stood, swaying. Took a breath, then pushed open the cubicle door, walked to the mirror. *Look. Now. Fucking do it.* Stared at her reflection. *No screaming. See? It's now. Not then.* Splashed water on her face, evened her hoodie drawstrings. Exhaled. *Get back in there, Champ.*

And you won that fight, remember?

She remembered.

Strode out of the lav. Chin down, eyes up, like bring it fucking on. King was sitting on the arm of the sofa. Said nothing, just handed her a bright-red plastic water bottle. Printed in black on the side: *Can You See Me?*

"Thanks," she said. Took the bottle, drank.

"Clarke found me a Coke. Only had filter coffee, though."

She nodded, took another sip. *Works.* "Brill."

"And this is from Veronica." Handed her a sandwich: cheese and pickle, malted bread. Lucy noticed he spoke the name softly, scared it might trigger another attack. "Said you might want it. Told her you had an eyelash in your contact lens, but..." Hint of a smile. "She's seen a lot, that one."

Lucy looked at him.

So that's it, then? No complaints from the victim's daughter, no "lunatic DI freaked the fuck out in our toilets, press'll hear about this"? Just a sandwich? That's...amazing. Turned the packet over in her hands. "Waitrose, huh? Posh." A tiny grin.

He jerked his thumb towards the door. "Let's?"

She nodded.

The lift down was silent. Lucy watched him out the corner of her eye, hoping he wouldn't ask questions, give advice. But he just stared at the lift doors. Rubbed his stubbly jaw. Still swollen, she saw. *Get some ice on that, Ed.*

Outside, they had the street almost to themselves, just the odd office worker heading towards Goodge Street Tube. It was nearly seven. The rain had begun again. King pulled up the hood of his olive rain jacket. She ignored it, let the drizzle wet her hair. Gave it a few steps until they were clear of the building, then started in on him.

"So, anything? Tell me."

"Not her drugs. She hasn't been to that studio since before the Scourge."

"Hmm." She tried not to think of Veronica Cox's face. *Nothing to do with the case, nothing to do with now. Just a coincidence.* Conjured up a random face from her childhood: square jaw, drooping jowls, narrow eyes, that'll do, perf. Her old school nurse, couldn't even remember the name. A replacement. *Nurse Jowlsey, I hereby pronounce you Veronica Cox.*

"Think I believe her," King said.

"Why?"

They turned a corner and the grey Toyota came into view, parked flush to the kerb. Lucy took a sip from the water bottle. She was saving the sandwich for later.

"For starters, she was wearing short sleeves. I could see her wrists. No track marks."

Seriously? Come on, Ed. "More than one place to stick a needle, though, yeah?"

"True, but it's not just that. Took some pushing, but she told me who it was."

A shrug. "Could be lying."

"Could be. Be a hell of a lie, though."

Oh? She glanced over. *Spill it.* "Who?"

An office worker skittered past, newspaper over his head to keep dry. King waited for him to disappear around the corner, then: "Her mother."

Lucy stared at him.

Get the fuck out.

Helen Cox? Mink-wearing, posh-as-fuck society hostess? Under a railway arch, slamming H?

Are you fucking shitting me?

"Blimey," she said.

"Veronica swears it. Like I said, it'd be one hell of a lie."

That it would.

"And the sex?" she asked. "Her and Flinders, then? Between experiments he'd just, what, pop over, have a quickie?"

King shook his head.

"Affair. Expect that's why Veronica was willing to talk. Angry at Mum for doing Dad dirty."

Think you're taking the piss, Ed. Or Veronica Cox is. "Across the hall from her husband's lab? Why? Why not a hotel? Or his?" Took a sip of her drink. "And who's the bloke, then?"

King shrugged.

"Wouldn't say who with. Not sure she even knows. But she was positive. *Not* her father."

They arrived at the Toyota. Lucy wiped the rain from her hoodie, got in. Watched King buckle up, then stared out the window, thinking. *Her affair, not his. Right. So why kill him, then? He found out, threatened divorce? Lot of money. Maybe, but why cheat right under his nose? And why kill him last night? Why not any other time, an accident, poison? Row, perhaps?*

Why the crucifix?

And why would Helen Cox ever steal a London Black antidote?

The raindrops on her window blurred. She suddenly felt tired all over. Weary. A deep ache in her bones, happened after attacks sometimes. *Fight it off. Need to keep pushing.* As King started the engine, she finished her drink. Remembered that she'd left a half-full Coke bottle in the car that morning. Dug around, found it down by her feet.

None of this makes sense.

Unscrewed the bottle, took a big sip.

"Fuck of it is," said King, as he pulled away from the kerb, "you were right. Alibis *were* all shit. Everyone was floating around, all night long. Except for one person—Helen Cox. *She* was by the door all evening, greeting. Two doormen and a bartender confirmed."

Fine. Poor fit anyway. "But she may still know something."

"She may. Which is why we're headed to Mayfair."

He turned into Regent Street, steering wheel small in his hands. London Strong Week banners cut the sky above them. Black poppies everywhere: posters, bus grilles, shopping bags. Paper flowers filled store windows. Lucy stared out at the tastefully sombre sale signs. *Honour the dead, buy a jumper.*

Her monitor beeped again.

King glanced over. Said nothing, but looked alarmed.

"Just the battery." Turned in her seat, swiped her mobile, checked the results.

6.7.

Christ. Below 7 already.

"It's fine," she told him. Thought of Hodges, tenting his fingers. Tried to remember the last copycat attack. Been a week, she thought. Maybe longer. *But it's London Strong Week now. Last year's was bad, a dozen. This year, could be worse.*

As she tried to work out when she'd dip below 5, King's mobile rang.

He picked up. Listened. "Understood." Rang off.

Sighed.

"Change of plans," he said.

What? No, Ed. No fucking change of plans. The plan is good.

"We need to go see Helen Cox," she said. "Alibi or not, she knows something. She may know about the antidote. Or know who else might. Plus, there's the foot…" Her eyes blazed. "Ed, she needs to be interviewed again. Properly. Right now."

A slow nod. "She will be." He looked over at her. "By me."

And?

And what about me?

"You, Lucy, need to go have a word with DCI Wilkes."

‡ ‡ ‡

Lucy watched as Flinders Cox stroked his beard.

"Of course I remember what I was thinking at the time," he said. "I was thinking, oh, dear God, how could you allow this to happen?"

Across the MIT19 squad room, a young DC holding a chipped mug stared up at the television screen. He fiddled with his tea bag as the old interview played. Lucy felt bad for him. Media review was a proper fucking nightmare. No action, no rush. Just hours and hours of stare, slurp your PG Tips, repeat. *And no one ever kills anyone you'd want to watch on telly.*

She glanced over at Wilkes's door. Still closed. *For fuck's sake, Ma'am. Been an hour. Got things to do.* Ate a bite of Veronica Cox's sandwich, then looked back at the screen.

"…yes, thank you, Doctor Cox," the interviewer was saying. She had an American accent. Caption at the bottom of the screen: *Cox Interview_CNN_Feb2028.* "I think some background on the nerve agent used in the attacks would be *very* helpful for our viewers here in the States."

Cox leaned forward in his leather wingback chair. He looked uncomfortable, Lucy thought. Like his suit jacket was too tight, or his socks itched. "Right. Well. London Black is what we call an acetylcholinesterase inhibitor. Like sarin or VX. It prevents the body from breaking down an enzyme called acetylcholine, which…here, I'll show you." He balled his hands into fists. "Imagine this is a motor neuron." He raised his right fist. "And *this* is a muscle cell." Raised the left. "Now, when the neuron wants the muscle to work, it releases acetylcholine, and *that* crosses this gap and tells the muscle to contract." He began to open and close his left hand. "You follow?"

The interviewer nodded. The DC yawned. Lucy took another bite of cheese and pickle.

"Nerve agents prevent the body from breaking down the acetylcholine. So it builds up, and the muscles don't know to stop. They just keep contracting." His hand sped up: open, close; open, close. "The victim twitches, spasms, convulses." The hand was a blur. "Your body completely breaks down. Choke to death on your own mucus." He let his hands fall. Shifted in his chair. "Horrible."

"But the agent used in the London attacks was different, I thought, because—"

"Yes, right. With most nerve agents, the point is to kill people, as quickly as possible. Developed for battlefield use, after all. But not London Black. London Black was designed by terrorists, and terrorists want terror. Maximum terror. And so, the effects take days." A pause. "It's irreversible. No antidote. Ninety per cent of people die. But they have days to see it coming. Agonizing, terrifying days."

He sat back in the chair, stroked his beard again.

The DC slurped his tea.

Lucy frowned. Thought of Cox's body, soaked in blood, lying on the floor of his tiny study. *Wasn't just a study, though, was it? There was a bed. Slept in. Why? Why live like that, sleep there? What was going on?*

For a moment, she thought of her own flat. Black walls, black ceiling, no bed, no anything.

Did you feel guilt too, Mr Cox?

Something with your wife? Or the foot in the studio?

Did you owe a Debt?

"But that wasn't all," he was saying on the screen. "There's something called phosgene oxime. A vesicant, like mustard gas. Corrosive. Causes tissue damage, chemical burns. And the way London Black was designed, as the compound breaks down, phosgene oxime is released into the bloodstream and—"

"Lucy?"

Wilkes stood in her office doorway, hands on hips.

Crap. Lucy grabbed the half-eaten sandwich, marched into Wilkes's office. *Hands on hips? That's her properly fucked off, then. But why? The fuck did I do?*

"Sit."

She sat.

"Ma'am?"

"Heard about your attack."

Lucy stared. *How? Who told you?* Thought of Veronica Cox, now a middle-aged school nurse. *What the shit, Veronica? Give me a nice cheese and pickle, then stab me in the back? The hell kind of move is that?* She held up the sandwich carton. "But…she gave me a sarnie, Ma'am…"

"*Not* from Ms Cox. Thank God."

Well, if it wasn't Veronica, and of course it wasn't King, then who… Oh.

Of course. Fucking Sykes.

"It was Sykes, Ma'am, wasn't it?"

Thought he'd pissed off by then. Must've been there, laughing his fucking fedora off as I ran screaming past. If I'm off this case because of him, swear I'll—

"Doesn't matter who told me," Wilkes said. "Beside the point."

"Well, yes—"

"No, the point is—are you all right?"

Lucy lowered her sandwich.

What? That's all this is about? Just that?

"I care about your health, Lucy. Not just as your boss. Are you okay?"

Well no, but…

"Yes, Ma'am. Thank you." Forced a smile. *See?* "And if that's all, I'll just…" She stood up.

"Sit *down*, Lucy."

She sat. It was an annoyed sit.

"There's more. I was called into the Chief Super's office this afternoon. Most unpleasant." Wilkes leaned forward, elbows on her desk, fingers clasped. Waited for confession.

Lucy stared back.

"Ma'am?" Said it sort of, *I have no idea what the fuck is going on here, but I'd really quite like to get back to solving a high-priority murder and finding a life-saving antidote, thanks, so if you could stop faffing the fuck around already and just tell me whatever it is I'm meant to have done, it would be truly fucking lovely. Ma'am.*

Wilkes sighed. "It seems one of my DIs was fool enough to disrupt a religious service today."

Oh, Christ.

Clapham.

"No, Ma'am," she said. "*Not* a service. It was an advert. They were filming, and—"

"You terrified the worshippers…"

The worshippers? Who, Salad Cream?

"…got into a row with an ordained minister…"

Minister, con artist, murder suspect…

"…threatened him…"

The lecture dragged on. Hands unclasped, waved, clasped again. It became the usual: chain of command, department protocol, blah blah blah. Lucy tuned out, let her eyes roam Wilkes's new office. Stylish, she thought. Clean desk, vase of carnations. Noticed a photo pinned to the wallboard. Snap from a holiday party, three years back. One of those posed pics, everyone holding a prop. Wilkes in an elf hat, Salford in Groucho Marx glasses and a light-up tie, Salford's phenomenally pissed girlfriend snogging a fake plastic fish. Lucy, beaming. And there, in the back, with his Windsor knot and perfect smile: Simon. She stared at his face. For a moment she was back there, back at the dodgy pub they'd hired, looking on as he charmed everyone, life of the party, so interesting, so *cute*, and in the loo Wilkes saying, Definitely gorgeous I mean he knows it but still, well done you, Lucy…

"What do *you* think, Lucy?"

Wilkes leaned in.

I miss him.

A rap on the door.

King poked his head in. "Sorry, Marie," he said. Pointed at Lucy. "Mind if I have a quick word with Stone? Something's come up."

Wilkes frowned but nodded. Looked at Lucy. "Assume I've made my point, yes?"

"Yes, Ma'am." She took a last glance at Simon, then followed King to the empty kitchen.

Did you just try to save me, Ed? Don't need saving.

"Looked like a laugh," he said. A half-filled pot of filter coffee stood on a hot plate. King grabbed it, filled a paper beaker, pushed it over to her. "No Coke, but…"

"Ta." She took it. "Any luck with Helen Cox?"

He shrugged.

"Definitely her H. Pupils like pinpricks. Couldn't get much out of her. She'll be in tomorrow." Poured himself a beaker. "But listen. Our friend Enoch Clapham—"

"Mmm," said Lucy, mid-sip. Swallowed. "I know. Serious suction with someone. Leaned on the Chief Super." She waved towards Wilkes's office door. "Went mental."

King stared at her.

"That's just it," he said. "Enoch Clapham's disappeared."

‡ ‡ ‡

Lucy left for home an hour later.

King had headed out before her, jaw still swollen, looking exhausted. She thought about his news as she entered Westminster Station. Clapham had shaken his tail, he'd told her. Gone into a curry house, right out the back. Poof. Oldest fucking trick in the book, he couldn't believe it, the DC on obbo was dead to him. But there it was.

Knew it.

Dodgy as fuck.

Past ten now, but the Tube was still busy. Tourists, mostly. Few Whitehall types mixed in, black poppies threaded through buttonholes of long wool overcoats. Two Alsatians watched her step through the Cox gate. She frowned as she passed. *Odd. Never see sniffer dogs here. At events, maybe. Concerts and that. Not the Tube.* A dog's nose was better than the chem sniffer on a gate, she knew. Thousand times better, unless the counter-terrorism officer giving the briefing two years back was just taking the piss. Either way, LB-sniffing dogs were rare, special use only.

So why are they out tonight?

Two Transport Police AFOs in full body armour stood nearby, sub-machine guns slung across their chests. Lucy walked over, flashed her warrant card. Nodded towards the dogs.

"Something up?"

The taller AFO shook his head. "For show, mainly. London Strong Week, everyone's a bit on edge. Don't want any more copycats." No eye contact, just kept scanning the crowd over her shoulder. His foot was tapping, she noticed. "Nothing specific, don't worry."

"Right," Lucy said. Wondered if he was bullshitting her, if something was up and she should be turning around, getting the fuck out, back to the safety of New Scotland Yard. She could work there just as well. But late nights at MIT19 had a sort of trench camaraderie, a we're-all-in-this-shit-together-tomorrow-let's-grab-a-cheeky-one feel. She'd loved that once. Before. Now it felt wrong. *Not after what I've done.* Her place at night was in her flat, alone, bare black walls and the Debt for company.

She kept going.

Westminster Station always made her think of a film set for some grim dystopian thriller. Rough concrete walls. Giant escalators with sheer hundred-foot drops on each side, exposed steel girders slicing overhead. Gritty. Lucy liked it. Felt right. As she walked towards the top of the escalator bank, her thoughts went back to Clapham.

So was he the killer? One of his little children?

None of the guests had Hand of God ties, not that she knew. But that meant nothing. The service entrance at the rear was open all evening. No CCTV, no one paying attention.

Anyone willing to take a little risk could've walked in, killed Cox and left.

So many fucking questions, she thought. Stepped onto the escalator. *Orange Trainers knew about the secret lab. Was he working for Clapham? How did they find out about it? Through Helen Cox? Was she shagging one of them? Was that the affair? And oh yeah, who does Clapham know at the Met? Definitely someone senior, had to be, because Wilkes was scared and she doesn't scare easily and wha—*

A blow: hard. Got her from behind, back of the head, *the fuck?* and a man was grabbing her, had her, shoved her to the rail and she swiped at him but too late, she was over the railing, tumbling, *Jesus*, reaching back, *fuck fuck fuck…*

Caught the railing.

One hand.

Felt her legs dangle, hundred feet of air below her trainers. *Oh Jesus.*

Shoulder on fire. Her grip going. Slipping.

Must get…other hand up…

She swung her other arm. Fingertips scraped the railing, slipped off.

Come on…

Tried again. Just missed.

Pull-up, just a pull-up, one-hander, fucking do it…

She pulled. Searing pain shot through her shoulder. Her arm shook. Felt her grip weaken, *fuck*, tried to hang on but it was too much, she was slipping, starting to slide, *oh God oh Jack*, grip almost gone and she couldn't hold on, couldn't, *no no no FUCK—*

And then she had it.

Her other hand grabbed the railing and she gritted her teeth, pulled herself up, back onto the escalator. Heart pounding, shoulder burning, ready to vomit.

Alive.

A tourist in a London sweatshirt: "You okay, Miss?"

She ignored him. Looked down. Saw Orange Trainers at the bottom of the escalator, mask over his face, running for the Jubilee Line platform. *Get back here*. Shoved the tourist aside, bounded down the escalator, hair flying as she ran. Hit the landing. Sprinted towards the platform, screaming, *Police, Stop, Stop*, but the doors slid shut in her face and Lucy watched, panting, as the train pulled away.

CHAPTER TEN

I will fucking find you.

Seven computer monitors stood on a table in the corner of the MIT19 squad room. Grainy CCTV footage played on the screens. Lucy pressed a half-thawed bag of frozen chunky chips to her sore shoulder, watched the images flicker. Thought about Orange Trainers. *You're in there somewhere. One of those cameras caught you. Must have done. And I need to find you.*

I WILL *find you.*

Last night was a blur. She'd watched Orange Trainers's train disappear into the tunnel, then turned and marched straight back to New Scotland Yard. The squad room had been a graveyard. Wilkes gone, King gone. Not even Salford, just the lone DC on media review asleep in his tea mug. Lucy said fuck it, do it myself then, started grabbing wireless monitors from the Tech room down the hall. Took all they had, then began scrounging around conference rooms for more.

At midnight, her alarm beeped: Boost time. Pulled her emergency syringe from its special padded pocket, injected in a cubicle in the empty women's. No mirror to stare into, no alcohol swab. Just uncap, prime, jab, *oh Jesus it fucking hurts.*

And: *You deserve this, Lucy.*

You deserve the pain.

By one, she'd stopped hunting monitors. Seven would do. Let her shoulder burn for a bit, but when she couldn't lift her arm any more she dispatched Media Review to the 24-hour off-licence for a bag of frozen peas. He came back with a choice: skin-on chips or Yorkshires, DI Stone, Ma'am? Lucy told him to drop the "ma'am", only one of those in MIT19. Took the chips—*potato's veg, close enough*—and went back to setting everything up.

At three, she started calling DCs at home.

Salford arrived first, rubbing his eyes, tie the colour of tropical Lucozade. Now, at eight o'clock, she had six of them in. All men, all in suits. Everyone was staring at the monitors, had been for hours. Strict instructions from Lucy: no talking, no mucking about, just someone please spot the bloke with bright orange shoes and it's a hundred quid behind the bar at the Carpenters.

And when I find you, Orange Trainers, you fucking—

"Morning, Lucy."

She smelt aftershave. Turned around. King stood towering behind her.

"All right?" he asked. Eyed the frozen chips. "Just heard about last night."

She shrugged with her good shoulder. "Hanging in." Looked him over. Suit, fresh white shirt, but the knot of his navy tie was lopsided. Bloodshot eyes. Jaw still puffy, she noticed. *Got some frozen Yorkies for you, Ed.* Stubble almost a full beard now, probably hurt too much to shave. *But why the scent?* She sniffed. It smelt like something Jack would wear on a Friday night. *Don't read into it,* she decided. *Guy likes to smell like the men's aisle at Superdrug, his fucking business.*

"So what's all this, then?" King nodded at the half-dozen bleary-eyed DCs.

"CCTV. Spot him, track him back. Maybe he takes off his mask."

"Right." He squinted at the screens. "That's not the Tube station, is it?"

Lucy shook her head. "Railway arch. Tube cameras still in the works. BTP taking their sweet bloody time sending them. But we've got four cameras from near the secret lab, and he must have been there before and—*hey!*" She caught Media Review lowering his head. Glared at him. *Watching you, mate.* Back to King: "And soon as BTP pings over last night's footage, that goes up as well."

She took a sip from a red plastic cup with the Arsenal cannon on it.

"Fair enough," he said. Pointed to the cup. "Gooner, eh?"

Lucy snorted. *Sport where they fall down on purpose? Bollocks to that.* She'd needed a double to fight off the sleep. Nicked two Cokes from the kitchen fridge, gave Media Review a tenner to run to the Costa for the espresso. The faded Arsenal souvenir cup was the only thing large enough to hold it all. Each sip felt like she was swallowing battery acid, but fuck it, she was awake.

"What's that?" she asked. King was holding a thick folder.

"Forensics, mainly. Walk with me?"

She gave the DCs a warning glance—*I'll be back, don't you lot go anywhere*—and put the chips down on a desk, then followed him down the hallway. MIT19 was buzzing. Uniforms chatted. Phones chirped. Lucy spotted Sykes making tea, frowned at him as she passed. *Went running to Wilkes, yeah? Rat bastard.*

He sneered back.

"Nothing much from the scene," King said, as they turned a corner. "No blood on anyone. Stabbing like that, killer would've been drenched. Looks like someone crashed the party."

Lucy nodded. Pictured Enoch Clapham sneaking into Cox's flat. *Or was it Orange Trainers?*

"There *was* one interesting development, though," King continued.

"Tell me."

"The foot," he said. "From the pottery studio. Whoever it was, they'd been exposed to London Black. And they were Vulnerable."

Huh. That changes things.

"Forensics sure about that?"

He nodded. "Thinking it might be an old BYO."

A *BYO*. Her head felt light. She took another sip of her drink. Remembered first hearing about BYOs from Simon, late at night in their flat as they lay in bed. People are really doing it, he'd told her. Don't trust the government, not after the last few drone attacks. All the stories about what happens out at the biscuit factories? The vats, the mass ash-pits? Fucking horrible. They want the remains back. Want Nan scattered in the park she loved, Auntie Beatrice on the mantle in an urn. So they're doing it themselves, Luce. Fireplaces, garden fire-pits. Stealing oil drums from industrial estates, lighting matches. Call it a BYO, he said.

Burn Your Own.

"Well," she said, "it did happen."

"It did. But if the foot was from a BYO, probably doesn't tie to us. Still, need to bottom it out. Which reminds me." He squinted at the scratched surface of his watch. "Helen Cox is coming in. Due any minute. Shall we?"

She finished her drink as they walked to reception. Her shoulder still hurt.

"Helen Cox in yet?" King asked the blonde behind the desk. A nod. "In three."

"Quick squiz first," said Lucy. "See what we've got." Led King down the hallway to the interrogation wing. Pushed through an unmarked door into a dark observation room. Two computer monitors glowed. "Here we go."

On the other side of a one-way mirror, Helen Cox sat behind a tall metal table. Lucy stared at her through the glass. Same sable coat. Pearls again. Enormous sunglasses, Versace maybe, Wilkes would know. Dark red lipstick ringed a hard mouth. *Looks exhausted. About to fall asleep.*

"Hell of a coat," King said. "Must be roasting in there."

Covering up track marks, Mrs Cox?

116

Next to her, a man in a chalk-stripe suit tapped a gold pen on a leather portfolio.

"Name's Facer," said King, pointing at him. "Jeremy Facer. Cox family solicitor, I expect. Reckon he writes wills all day."

Lucy looked at the solicitor's face. Angular jaw, pointy nose, eyes a bit too close together. *Seen you before.* Shook her head. "Don't think so," she told King. "He's been around. Does crim work. Must do. Seen him at Old Bailey." *Looks different somehow, though…*

Helen Cox leaned towards Facer and whispered something. Lucy watched as he rested his hand on his client's thigh. As Helen put her hand on his. Squeezed.

"And, Ed," she said, "I think she's shagging him."

‡ ‡ ‡

King came in bombing.

No intros, no bullshit formalities. Not even a "Sorry about your husband, Ma'am, he was a great man, truly." Just walked into the room, pulled a photograph from his folder, slapped it down on the metal table. Another. A third. Pushed them all across to Facer. "Her gear," he said. Didn't even look at Helen Cox, just glared at the solicitor. "All hers. Tubing, spoon. Fingerprints all over the fucking syringe. Tell me I'm fucking wrong, Facer."

Whoa, thought Lucy. *Easy, Champ.*

She stood at the back of the interrogation room, leaning up against the grimy concrete wall, watching King fume. *The fuck got into you, Ed?* When she'd told him that she thought Facer and Helen were banging, he'd said nothing, just stuck out his swollen, stubbly jaw and stomped down the hall so fast she had to jog to keep up. Now he was towering over Facer, huge forearms crossed, sixteen stone of inexplicably fucked-off cop.

Facer picked up the photos. Muttered something, whipped out a pair of gold-framed specs from his breast pocket. Put them on. Squinted down, pointy nose wrinkled like he'd just stepped in dog shit with his £800 wingtips and was checking the damage. Finally said: "It's rubbish."

"It's heroin, is what." King's voice was a deep growl. "Black tar. Residue on the needle."

A shrug from Facer. "And?"

"And? And heroin's illegal. And your client needs to start fucking cooperating. Or else."

Facer snorted. "My client," he said, "may have once touched an empty syringe. *May* have. God knows where, God knows when. After that? Where it went? What went in it? Pfft." He tossed the photos back across the table. "Does this nonsense have a point?"

Lucy watched as King's thick neck strained his shirt collar. He was turning red.

"The point," he said, voice rising, "is that we have another body. Remains. A foot. Found it in your client's little crash pad. Asked her about it last night, but she was—"

"She was *grieving*."

"She was off her fucking head, is what she was."

Christ, Ed, thought Lucy. *Killing me here.* Frowned at King. *Be tactical, yeah? Pick your spots. Can't just go toe-to-toe, start throwing bombs. Not with a solicitor.* She looked over at Facer, at his slicked-back silver hair and sarky grin. *Not this one, anyway.* Didn't like him, she'd decided. She'd met plenty of defence attorneys, knew all the types. This wasn't some idealistic Legal Aid solicitor, or a prim-and-proper big firm lawyer. No, Facer was something else: dodgy. Dodgy as fuck, actually, could tell straight away by his smirk and his probably-fake specs and the way he tapped the table with his gold pen like he owned the fucking place. Sort of solicitor who would tell his client to do a runner, just make sure you pay me first. *But are you the one I want, Facer? Did you learn about the antidote when you were banging Helen Cox in the pottery studio? Did you tell someone? Enoch Clapham? Orange Trainers?*

Or are you just some sleazy chancer bonking your married client?

She took a sip from the topped-up Arsenal cup. Her shoulder hurt.

Meanwhile King had given up on Facer, turned to Helen. "Do *you* want to tell me about it?"

Helen said nothing, mute behind her giant black sunglasses.

"Help me here." King spread his huge hands, palms upturned. "Come on. Else we may need to do another search of that posh little townhouse, make sure we didn't miss anything, any little packets of black tucked away in your sock drawer." He paused. "Was it a BYO? That it? We're not Public Health, not looking to do you for a BYO—"

Facer jumped in. "A BYO? How old is this body, exactly?"

"Why?" King frowned.

"Because during the Scourge, my clients were living apart."

Interesting. Lucy filed the fact away.

But King wouldn't quit. "So?" He glared at Facer. "She had a key, right?"

"She gave it back."

"Bullshit."

Jesus, Ed. The fuck is with you? Calm down...

"This is ridiculous," said Facer. "Completely unprofessional."

"*You're* unprofessional, you sleazy fucking—"

"That's it," snapped Facer. "This is over. We're done." He stood, dusted off his suit, tucked the gold pen back into the leather portfolio. "Off we go, Helen. Come on." Motioned for her to follow him.

Lucy frowned.

Oh no you fucking don't.

My turn.

From her spot in the rear of the room: "You're shagging her, Facer."

He stopped dead.

That got your attention, yeah?

She left the wall, walked past King, over to the table where Facer stood frozen. "You," she said. Took a long drink from the Arsenal cup, eyes never leaving the solicitor's face. "Her." Nodded at Helen. "Shagging. Right?"

Facer frowned. A puffed-cheek, guilty-as-hell, politician-caught-with-a-hooker frown.

Yeah, you fucking are.

He began to bluster. "My client's personal life has no bearing whatsoever—"

"No," Lucy said. "Wrong." Another sip. "Husband murdered? An affair? Don't be daft. Course it's bloody relevant." She put the cup down on the table, leaned in close. "We know. Shagging her rotten. In the pottery studio, on the little black leather sofa."

They locked eyes.

And then she spotted it: surprise. A tiny flicker, behind Facer's gold specs.

Wait. Hold on.

Lucy stepped back. Tugged on her hoodie strings. She knew she was right, had to be banging, deffo. *But the sofa surprised him somehow. So then…what? Someone else with her in the studio? Two affairs?* She looked over at Helen Cox, all sable and pearls and stony silence. *That it, Mrs C? Someone else in the mix and Facer doesn't even know?*

Well, he's about to find out.

"As I said," Facer began, "this is personal, and the fact that we're even talking about it is frankly a load of—"

"Oh, found lots of those," Lucy said. "*Loads* of loads. Spunk all over the sofa. *Slathered.*"

Facer flinched. Glanced at Helen. The quickest of glances, but Lucy caught it.

Now you want to know, too. Perf. Let's find out together, shall we?

She grabbed an empty chair. Pulled it around the table, metal legs scratching on the concrete floor, until she was right next to the widow. Sat down. Stared at her, into the depths of her massive black sunglasses, Armani or Versace or whatever the fuck, Lucy still couldn't tell, the one with all the circles. "Who were you shagging in the studio, Mrs Cox?"

For the first time, Helen Cox spoke.

"Fuck off," she said. Slurred it, like she was punch-drunk.

Christ, thought Lucy. *She's high. At eight a.m.*

"I need to know. It matters."

"Why?" Helen's voice was raspy. Not the posh accent Lucy was expecting: Essex, maybe, couldn't say for certain with the heroin drawl. Facer reached out a protective arm but Helen pushed it away. "Flinders didn't care," she said. "Never did. Why d'you?"

King, from ringside: "Didn't care? What, he had another woman, then? That it?"

"Flinders?" A hollow laugh. "Flinders doesn't pay attention to humans. Just his precious little chemicals."

"It's relevant to our investigation," Lucy said. "Tell me. Who were you with?"

Helen shook her head.

"You aren't in trouble, forget the drugs, just tell me."

Another slow shake.

For fuck's sake...

Lucy looked over at King. *Any ideas?* He shrugged.

"Give us a moment," she told Helen. To Facer: "Stay."

She grabbed King and walked out of the room. Led him down the hallway, back to the squad room. Five DCs straightened up as they walked in. Media Review was down for the count, passed out on his desk next to a soggy pile of used tea bags. CCTV footage played in the background.

"Nothing yet," Salford reported. The knot of his awful tie was loosened, his sleeves rolled. "Still a few cameras to check, though. If nothing pops, I'll take a second pass, just to be certain. And I'll chase up BTP."

Lucy nodded. *Good work, Salford.* "Do." Turned to King. "The hell was all that?"

"What?"

"I need her to tell me who else was in that studio. Then you go off on the drugs. Scare her. Now she's keeping shtum."

"Yeah, well." A shrug. "Sorry."

Lucy frowned. Closed her eyes, sighed. She suddenly felt exhausted. Wobbly, like she might fall over, just crash right there on the squad-room floor. *Fuck. Fuck me.* Her shoulder burned, a fiery prodding and it was the Debt, tapping her, poking, *remember me?*, and she *had* to sort this, had to figure it out and find the antidote and...

Focus.

Opened her eyes. Exhaled. Forced herself to think.

We could hold her. Twenty-four hours in a cell, cold turkey? We'll know names, dates. Positions, probably. But Facer'll block that. Run to Wilkes, the brass. So then, what? What do we do? What can we do?

She ran her fingers through her hair. Looked around the squad room, at the dirty desks, the owl-jacketed chairs. At the DCs, eyes glued to the monitors. At the screens.

Saw something.

Wait...

Felt a jolt of adrenaline as the gears turned: the Party Trick working its magic. "Stop," she called out. "Stop it. Now. *Stop.*" Marched across the room, past the startled DCs, to the table of monitors. Pointed to a screen. "This one. Right here. Back it up."

Salford tapped on a laptop. The footage reversed.

"There," she said. "Stop. Look."

A blurry image of a man and a woman, walking together, one street back from the railway arch lab. Her face was hidden from view, but she wore a long fur coat. A sable. His arm was around her. Tall man, late middle age. Square jaw, bulbous nose, salt-and-pepper hair. *I know you*, she thought. Grainy, but she was sure. Knew him from the case files. Party Trick told her she'd seen him somewhere else before, too, ages ago, couldn't quite place it but it didn't matter now. Because:

"That's Geoffrey Hurst," she said.

King whistled. "Christ. The CEO of Cox Labs."

Lucy nodded.

"Helen Cox was shagging her husband's partner."

‡ ‡ ‡

"Well, this is a fucking shit-show," said King.

Traffic on the Embankment had hardly moved for twenty minutes. Lucy stared out the window of the grey Toyota. Sipped from her fresh Coke bottle, watched the protesters stream past on their way to the demo in Parliament Square. They spilled off the pavement and onto the road, an endless parade of Survivor masks. All shades: red, blue, black, rainbow. Customized, some of them. She spotted one with a Spurs logo, another with chemistry symbols on the cheeks. Thought of the days just after, when masks were all still hospital-issue: simple gauze things, crude slits for eyes and mouth. Meant for burn victims originally, but it was all they had, make do and mend, hey? White, only white. *Like ghosts. They looked like ghosts, wandering, restless. Angry. Scaring the living.*

Haunting us.

King honked his horn. "The fuck is the hold-up here?" Sighed. "Least we're headed east," he said. "Westminster'll be a

123

disaster. No way a bunch of Specials handle this mob." Checked his battered watch. "Half an hour to get to the Gherkin before Hurst moves again. Reckon we'll make it?"

Lucy shrugged, said nothing.

Welcome to London traffic, Ed. Told you. Should've taken the Tube.

"Christ." He frowned, rubbed his flat nose. "Hate to reschedule. Hurst's assistant…ugh. Painful. Banged on for ages about back-to-backs and media interviews and excuse *me*, Officer, but Mr Hurst is a very busy man." A snort. "Think we were scheduling an audience with the fucking Pope."

"Just bring him in, then," Lucy said.

King glanced at her. "You know Hurst went to school with the Chief Super, right? Old Something-or-others. Tread lightly."

Fuck do I care? Bring him in wearing bracelets if we need to. Just one more lecture.

A passing protester beat a marching bass drum with a black poppy decal on its head. Through the window glass, Lucy could hear chanting. Couldn't make out the words, just a steady rhythm of angry voices.

"Here we go," said King, as they pulled forward. "Finally."

A few car lengths ahead, they reached the source of the tailback: two groups of protesters, screaming bloody murder at one another over the shoulders of the uniformed cops keeping them apart. One group was Survivors. Looked hard-core: khaki and camo, SRA tattoos, banners. No masks. Their leader was waving a hand-lettered sign. Lucy squinted, read:

THE MLF IS COMING

She frowned.

MLF? Never heard of that…

"Look," King said. "Clapham's nutters." He pointed to the second group. They wore matching T-shirts, white with a double-barred cross on front and back. Mostly men, but a few women sprinkled in. Seemed even angrier than the Survivors. Faces red, twisted, screaming: pure hatred. "Load of wankers."

"Speaking of," said Lucy. "Any sign of him? Clapham?"

"Fuck all. Just gone. Poof." Glanced over at her, grinned. "Know what you're thinking, by the way. Promise I didn't kill him."

She thought of King staring down at Clapham in the church-yard, green eyes blazing, ready to snap. *Good to know, Ed. Glad I can count on you.* "He'll surface," she said. "Just wait."

"Hope so."

He will. Even if I have to track that skeleton fucker down myself…

Traffic sped up. As they dipped under the Embankment pedestrian bridge—Lucy could never remember the name, the one with the triangle beams on top that reminded her of sailboat sails—her mobile vibrated. She pulled it from her hoodie pocket. Checked. A text from Salford: "Still waiting." *For fuck's sake.* "Bloody BTP," she said. "Like pulling teeth. Just some CCTV…"

"Have their hands full, though, don't you think?"

She looked over at him, puzzled.

"What, didn't you hear? Last night?"

Lucy shook her head. *Last night? Last night was wireless monitors and chunky chips.*

"Another copycat," he said. "London Bridge station. Had an aerosol spray, done up to look like shave cream. Dog caught it, but not before a bit was released."

London Bridge? Thought of her commute home, the one Orange Trainers interrupted. *Would've changed trains there, London Bridge, Jubilee Line to Northern…*

"Attacker got away. Still cleaning it up. No one seriously ill, any rate. Everyone exposed was a non-Vulnerable or else fully boosted."

"Huh," she said. Thought: *Fuck. Fuck me.* She'd checked her monitor half an hour ago, as they were leaving New Scotland Yard. Not even noon, already down to 7.1. Doctor Hodges's voice in her head: "Lucy, this is not good." She frowned, looked past King, out the window. Across the river, the Eye was slowly revolving. *Need to finish this. Find the antidote. Right fucking now. But Clapham's buggered off, Orange Trainers is gone, Helen Cox has an alibi. And Hurst? Wouldn't steal the antidote, would he, practically his anyway, and besides...the crucifix? A CEO, doing that? Doesn't feel right.*

But maybe he knows something?

A taxi horn blared. The Toyota slowed to a stop.

"Christ," said King. "More fucking traffic."

Lucy looked out her window. They were by the Salt-and-Pepper Shakers: the Monuments, Old and New, rising up side by side. The old limestone column, grey in the cold morning light, looked faded next to its new black granite twin. She remembered climbing Old Monument with Simon once, back before, when it was just *the* Monument. All those steps, easy for her but hard for him—*never could get you to train, Si, could I?*—up to the caged-in top beneath the fake gold flame. Looked out at the city spread beneath them. Ours, he'd said. She'd kissed him. Now you couldn't climb it any more, too risky, too close to the real flame on New Monument, the one that burned day and night: an eternal reminder to Londoners. *Reminding us, the ones who don't need reminding.*

Next to her, King sighed.

Looks knackered, she thought, as she rubbed her own puffy eyes. *He was tired yesterday, worse today.* "All right?" she asked. *Can't have you crumbling on me now, Ed.*

"Yeah." A quick glance at her, then he looked away, across the road to the entrance of an old church. "Just, couldn't sleep. Well, I did, hour maybe, but then I dreamed about her. My daughter.

Tina." Another sigh. Half to himself: "Awful dream. She was an adult. Looked like she would've, if only...well. On her forehead, she had this red X, like it was cut by a knife. Fucking awful." He shrugged. "Couldn't sleep after that. Probably the run-in with Clapham made me think of it."

Bet you think about it every night, though, don't you? Poor guy.

She held out her Coke bottle.

King waved it off. Began to tap the steering wheel with his thumbs. Two cars ahead, a cabbie held his arm out the window, palm up: the fuck is going on here? King checked his watch again. "Unbelievable. Can't even turn around. Never make it." Big exhale. Looked at Lucy. "Look," he said, "we're stuck. And I told you I'd tell you about it. My daughter. Do you mind? It's just...it helps me, somehow. Talking."

She shrugged. He looked pretty bad. "Sure, yeah."

You do you, Ed. Just don't expect a story back. Not some fucking Arabian Nights thing here.

"Right. Thanks. Yeah." He looked away, eyes back on the church. Took a deep breath, launched in. "So. It was early days. Just after Waterloo. Tina was living down in London with my wife. Bromley, her parents'. We were living apart then. Anyway. They did the tests. Tina popped black. I told my wife I'd come get her, just to be safe. Wouldn't hear of it. Don't be daft, we're fine, Ed. Knew she'd never give in. Decided I'd buy Tina a Boost. All gone, from the chemists anyway, but word was you could get them on the street if you knew where to look. Four k a jab, they said. Still early on, not like later, ten grand or whatever it was, but still...fuck of a lot of money for a cop."

Lucy nodded. *Fuck of a lot, yes.* Thought of her own box of Boosts, the one Melanie filled.

"Went round my bank the next day. Pulled the money. Three thousand, seven-hundred forty-three pounds, sixteen pence. Figured, close enough. Had them put it in an old black briefcase,

127

coins and all. Remember thinking, glad I've got those sixteen p. *That'll* make all the difference, right?"

He laughed. A dry laugh. The traffic inched forward, stopped again.

"Drove around all day," he continued. "All the likelies. Dealers, dodgy massage parlours, guys owed me a favour. Every fucking lead, everywhere. Nothing. Wasn't there. Birmingham was tapped out. Couldn't buy a Boost, not for love or money. Down in London, maybe, but up in Brum we had fuck all."

Yeah, well, we had our own problems down here, Ed. Trust me.

"Thing is," he said, "there was this one moment. Down by the river, headed towards this piece-of-shit traphouse, someone said maybe there, try there. So I did. Went down. Had the briefcase. Had it in my hand. And I looked down at it, and just for a second—one fucking second—I had this thought. This awful, terrible fucking thought. I thought..." He exhaled. Stared out the window. His hands were shaking, Lucy noticed. "I thought...*is it worth it*? *Am* I just being daft? Because it was a lot of money. All that cash, down to the sixteen fucking pence, just...in case? Then I pushed it away, told myself, yes, God, yes, of course. Buy it for in her a heartbeat, just give me the fucking chance." Paused. "But that's the thing. I never got the chance. Next day, there was an attack. Drone over Bromley."

A tear slid down his stubbly cheek.

"So how can I ever really *know*?"

Lucy looked at him, at his tired green eyes, the strong, Jack-like jaw. Caught a whiff of aftershave. *It's okay. You're good, Ed. Deep-down good, I can tell. You are. Not like me.* Thought about what to say. "Oh," she began. "Well." Felt something stir, maybe just sympathy but no, her stomach was twisting. Something more. She shoved it away. *Mustn't.* "Ed..."

His mobile rang.

"King," he answered. "Uh-huh." A sniffle, then his voice snapped back to business mode. "Oh, good. Yeah. Stepney, right? Fine. As soon as. Cheers."

Stepney?

"What's up?" she asked, but she already knew the answer.

Have to go to Stepney.

To go...there.

"Fucking Hurst," King said. "Heard that the interview team was coming to the Cox Labs HQ to do some of the low-levels, so he decided, fuck it, he'd pop over. Make it a party. So now we need to head over to Stepney."

"Right," she said. "Stepney." Looked out the window, but her stare was blank now. *It's okay*, she told herself. *It's fine. You can do this.*

"Be there in a few," he said.

"Mmm."

Knew this would happen, sooner or later. Their HQ now, course you'd have to go. Course.

They sped up. She began to rub her tattoo. Watched as they swooped past the Tower, past Tower Bridge with the giant black poppies hung from the middle bit like they'd once hung the Olympic rings, years ago now. Past boarded-up pubs, battered council flats. Vacant lots filled with rubble, buildings fired in the body removal riots. Flipped up her hood, fuck what King thinks, just did it, pulled the strings, closed off the world. All the while, thinking: *It's okay. Just a building. A fucking car park. You'll be fine. You can do this.*

And then, stronger, much: *I can't do it. Fuck me. Just can't.*

They turned a corner. She shut her eyes. Felt her hands begin to shake, jammed them into the hoodie pockets. *Inhale, exhale.* Her stomach burned: Coke and coffee, bile chaser.

Hurst may know something, she told herself. *Must find out.*

Do it for the Debt.

You have to.

Felt the Toyota slow, knew they were there.

"Lucy?" King's voice, muffled by the hood: "You all right, Lucy? Stone?"

You have to do this. Now. Do it.

Look.

She took a breath. Opened her eyes, pulled back the hood.

Lucy stared out the Toyota window at a big brick building with five chimneys.

CHAPTER ELEVEN
London, 2027

Lucy stared out the cab window at a big brick building with five chimneys.

"Close as I get," said the cabbie. He pulled to a stop at the edge of the car park, waved towards the Iso Centre entrance. "You can walk it from here." Glanced at her in his rear-view as Simon pulled fifty quid from his wallet: special fare, pre-agreed. Hazard pay. "Heard it's like Hell in there."

She shrugged, opened the door. Got out.

Guess I'm going to Hell, then.

"Finally," said Simon, as the taxi pulled away. "Took ages."

Lucy nodded. They'd left Goswell Road two hours ago. Cabbie after cabbie had rolled down his window, heard their destination, pissed right off. *Sorry, mate, on my way home now, wrong way.* Only one actually said it: *Iso Centre? What, the Stepney Death House? One near St Dunstan's, like? Fuck's sake, not going there, guv.* And when they finally did find a taker, half the East End was blocked off. Removal riots had been bad in Hackney, Shadwell, Whitechapel. Body wagons attacked. Whole streets burnt. A haze still hung in the air; she'd noticed it as they snaked through the maze of army trucks and rubble. He took them through Bethnal Green and she'd turned away as they passed Dad's shop. Couldn't bear to see it, see the big red X on the door that she'd warned him would come, a dead cert, couldn't he just be *reasonable* for once and take the bloody drugs? But no. Not stubborn Joe Stone. *And now I'm off to see you in Hell. Fucking Christ, Dad.*

She took a deep breath. Looked at the Iso Centre, its five brick chimneys.

"I'm going in," she told Simon. "Stay here."

Started walking across the car park towards the visitor checkpoint. Jammed her hands in her pockets, wished she'd worn a jacket over the Max Mara suit. It was crowded. Soldiers in camo, nurses in scrubs. Family members hugging, weeping. Every few seconds, someone would stumble out of the visitor exit, their eyes wide, staring.

Lucy pushed through the crowd, made her way to the chain-link fence that led to the checkpoint queue. Every hundred feet, a notice was cable-tied to the links:

All Isolation Centre Visitors Must Present
Certificates of Non-Vulnerability

And below, in all caps:

NO VULNERABLE VISITORS

She fingered the fake cert in her suit pocket. Prayed it would work. Bought it from a fat bloke she knew in Camden Town, dodgy boxing promoter with a line in fakies, one of Jack's old mates. *Lemme get this straight,* he'd said when she explained. *A Vulnerable? Trying to get* INTO *a Death House?* Knocked off a hundred quid, just for the sheer fucking insanity of the thing.

Now, from behind her, Simon's voice: "Wait up, Luce."

Fuck's sake, Si. We talked about this.

"I want to come," he said, as he fell into step beside her. "Really. I insist. Please."

"No." She shook her head. Sped up. "Too risky."

"But if *you* can do it…" She'd boosted in the cab, an extra to be safe. Tried not to think about the fact that a Boost was worth a month's salary, maybe more now, fucking crazy. "Look," he said, reaching for her shoulder, "I've got my emergency, right? I'll go around the corner and shoot it. Just hang on a tick and—"

She stopped. Turned, eyes blazing. In a whisper: "There's still a risk. That much Black in the air? We don't really know for sure, you don't, no one does. Now *stay*."

"I'll take the risk." He pointed at her ring. "I'm your fiancé, right?"

A few feet away, a short soldier with a big nose and a neck-beard stopped pacing and looked at them.

Christ, Si. Keep it down. Get me fucking nicked.

She grabbed his wrist, marched him through the crowd, over to the kerb. "I need to do this," she told him. "Just let me do this. Hard enough as it is, yeah?"

A pout. "I want to be there for you."

Stop trying to make up for Melanie. Don't need a goddamn martyr. She ran fingers through her hair, frowned. Dad was impossible, had been ever since Jack. But with Simon in the mix? Total fucking nightmare. Never got along: butcher and veggie, chalk and cheese. Guaranteed shit-show, Simon knew it as well as she did. "Please, Si. You know what would happen."

"Yeah, well…but still…"

Fuck's sake. "Simon." Stared at him. Her fiercest stare, armour-piercing, the one that made him say, Jesus, Luce, and leave the room. "I need to say goodbye. Wait. Here. Yeah?"

"Luce—"

She turned and walked away.

As she joined the checkpoint queue, she noticed that Neckbeard was staring at her again. Turned her head, hoped he was just checking her out. *I need to get inside.* She was dreading it, knew it would be bad in there, but she had to do it, owed Dad that much. Sighed. *Should've forced him to boost, jabbed him myself, come by every day if I had to, I mean he would fight it yeah but why didn't I try, maybe I should've tried harder…*

133

The queue shuffled forward. At the front, a soldier held up a cert, squinted at the hologram.

Her stomach hurt.

Fuck. Better fucking work. Caught with a fakie? Christ. Be my badge, yeah? Rules are strict. A fine, prison even, well and truly fucked...

An Iso Patrol wagon pulled into the car park, lights flashing, siren blaring. She watched it screech to a stop. Imagined Dad in the back of one; tried not to, couldn't help it. They'd had to sedate him. She'd heard it from Benny the shop boy when he rang up: picked him up inside Smithfield the day after an East End drone attack. He was buying black pudding, arguing. Couldn't show a cert. LB test on the spot: positive. Told them to sod off. It got ugly, the boy said. *Bet it did. Dammit, Dad...*

Raised voices in front of her. A man with a little girl in a grubby pink coat was yelling at one of the soldiers. Lucy caught snippets: "...and *I'm* saying, she's not Vulnerable...got the papers, everything." He waved a tiny plastic wallet, pink with a sparkly unicorn. "See, just look...her cert..."

The soldier pointed to a notice above the checkpoint:

No Visitors Under Ten Years Old

"But...it's her mother. For God's sake..."

The girl began to cry. She was young: three, maybe. The man looked down at her, back at the soldier, then swore and led her away. Lucy heard her wail as they disappeared into the car park crowd. A memory flashed: a florist shop in Bethnal, the one where her mum had worked. Suddenly she wanted to run after them, do something, poor girl, her mother...

Ahead, a soldier called out: "Next."

Her turn.

She let the girl go, took a breath. Walked up, pulled out the cert. Handed it over.

Please. Please fucking work.

He took it without looking up. "Gooner, eh?" The fat boxing promoter had stuck the cert in an Arsenal passport holder. She'd just left it. "United, me." He glanced at the photo, then down at her. Frowned. Checked it again. Turned to his buddy. Pointed to the cert, to her. Low voices.

Fuck.

She kept a straight face, felt like vomiting.

Fuck fuck fuck…

The soldier cleared his throat.

"Funny," he said. Paused. "You look just like…"

Oh, thank Christ. The Actor. She nodded, forced a smile. "Get that sometimes." *But it's just me, DC Lucy Stone, extremely legal holder of an extremely not-fake Non-Vulnerable Cert. Nothing to see here.*

And PS, I don't look like her.

He took one more look. Shrugged.

Waved her through.

She pocketed the cert, walked through the checkpoint gate. Exhaled.

Made it.

Arrows pointed around a corner. She followed them, thinking now about what to say, damn him for not just taking the fucking drugs. Rounded the bend. Looked up.

Stopped.

A giant hazard sign hung above a steel door. Yellow and black, six feet high, red stripes around the edges. Big bold letters:

DANGER—RISK OF DEATH

Her skin prickled. She thought of Simon injecting her in the back of the moving taxi as she looked out the window at the

135

barbed wire and broken windows, at the bloodstained hazmat suit hanging from a traffic signal.

Heard her own voice, minutes ago: *There's still a risk. That much Black in the air?*

She shut her eyes. Thought about Jack. About what Jack would do.

Fuck it.

Opened her eyes, walked to the door, pushed through.

Gasped.

The cabbie was right.

She was in Hell.

‡ ‡ ‡

Oh Jesus Christ.

The lobby was a shambles. Dirty. Hazy. Chemicals in the air: bleach, so thick she could taste it. She rubbed her eyes, coughed. Looked around for a nurse, an orderly, someone to tell her where to go. Saw no one. Just families, visitors, slumped, sprawled. Red-eyed, sobbing. Somewhere in the haze, a woman wailed: *Oh God, oh God, oh God.* It was a nightmare. A death watch. They all knew it, may as well be one of the all-caps notices taped to the wall: NO ONE GOES TO A DEATH HOUSE TO GET BETTER.

God fucking dammit, Dad.

Damn you for bringing me here. For being such a stubborn old bastard.

She spotted a door across the lobby marked *Entrances* and made for it, sticking close to the windowed left-hand wall to avoid the crowds. Someone had leaned sheets of plywood against it, blocking the view to the other side. Looked like shit, she thought, half-arse job, but then they'd done it all practically overnight: found the buildings and stripped them down, set up wards, beds, equipment. And not just Stepney. Another in Vincent Square. Soho. Posh one up in Marylebone. Others, too, she forgot where exactly, hard to remember, everything happened so fast now. *Two weeks. Two fucking weeks. Only two weeks since Waterloo, since the attacks started and the army rolled in, and the Iso laws and the drones and—*

OH SHIT.

She leapt back.

Through a gap in the plywood: a face. Pressed up against the glass, mouth open, screaming for help. A man, eyes wide, ruby-red: not from crying, from blood. Skin blistered. Peeling. He banged on the glass, thump thump thump, then turned, shoved away an orderly. She watched as two more tackled him and he went down, writhing, screaming as they dragged him off to a ward.

"Patient intake," said a man at her elbow. "Put the plywood up yesterday."

She nodded, exhaled. Rubbed her tattoo.

Christ…

Moved away from the wall, pushed through the crowds to the entrance door. It branched in two, male and female, and she followed the female sign to a makeshift changing room: battered metal lockers, benches. A heavyset nurse stood behind a counter, handing out disposable hospital gowns and crap gauze slippers. Much less crowded here, Lucy noticed. Almost empty, just an old woman, hair wet from the decon shower, struggling into a black dress. *All those people out there, they want to be close, but no one wants to actually see…*Grabbed a gown, walked to a locker, plunked a pound coin into the slot. Thought of the risk as she stripped. *So many patients. All of them toxic, shooting out bits of it each time they breathe. What if the extra Boost wasn't enough? No one knows, not like they've done tests. Could be me in there. My face. I get it, then Simon* *gets it, and that's us then, blood and skin and dying in this fucking place…*

Shook her head.

Focus. Need to think about Dad now. Poor Dad…

She walked through an exit marked TO THE WARDS. It led to a long corridor. Brick walls, a string of grey metal doors on one side. Sellotaped above the doors were signs with numbers on them, just sheets of plain white A4 with the numbers drawn by hand. Cold here, freezing in the thin gown. She held her arms to her chest as she looked around.

Now where…?

A nurse passed by, blue tunic soaked in blood. Glassy-eyed stare.

"Sorry," Lucy began, but the nurse ignored her. Just kept walking, like Lucy hadn't spoken, wasn't even there.

Christ. Even the nurses are in shock.

One of the metal doors clanged open. A tall man in green scrubs came out. Oval face, hooked nose, heavy stubble. Wide-set eyes, dark bags. She glanced at his name badge: Dr Hodges. "Doctor…" He tried to blow past but she turned, fell into step beside him. "I'm looking for someone. My dad. Can you please…?"

"Postcode?"

Huh?

Hodges stopped walking. "Where's he from? Current address?" Swayed on his feet, she noticed. "We tried triage first. Early stage, late stage. Waste of bloody time. Everyone died anyway." Said it bluntly, just a fact. "Switched to postcodes. Easier."

She nodded. "Bethnal Green. E2."

"Five. Try ward five." He pointed to a door, then left her.

Right.

Lucy walked to the grey metal door. Pushed through, into a small corridor. An exhaust fan whirred overhead. A door at the other end, this one bright orange, with a sign:

She let the grey door shut with a click. Heard muffled noises coming from the ward, sounded like voices crying out.

No one wants to see this…

Took a breath. Prepared herself.

You're a homicide cop. See death every day. Terrible shit. You can deal, yeah?

Go see Dad.

She pushed the door open.

It was fucking awful.

The room was huge. Orange air vents on the ceiling, plastic-lined walls. A hundred beds, more maybe, rows and rows, all full. Patients were screaming at each other, at the nurses, at the ceiling. Waving bloody arms, yanking IV drips. Blood was everywhere, soaking through bed sheets, dripping onto the floor. It smelt like blood and shit and death.

She ran her fingers through her hair. Looked around. *Fuck. So many of them.* Began winding through the maze of beds, scanning the faces, searching for Dad. Her gears spun as she glanced from face to face, the Party Trick always on, like it or not; even here, even with faces that were hardly faces any more, just jet-black eyes and giant blood blisters and sheets of peeling skin. *Barista. Waiter. Postie.* Wanted to stop, vomit, run, run as fast as she could from this place, fucking Hell on Earth. But: *Dad… where are you, Dad?*

He saw her first.

"The hell are *you* doing here?"

His face wasn't bad: eyes just starting to bleed, skin only spotting. Early stages. She stared at him, thought: *You're ANGRY?* Wanted to punch him. Hug him and punch him all at once.

"Dad…I heard, Benny called. I'm so sorry, Dad—"

"Get out of here," he said. "Don't want you here. You leave. Right now." Said it like he always said everything: This is it, done, don't waste time arguing. *Top round's a bargain. This guy can't fight. Don't even want to see you on my deathbed, Lucy.* "Leave."

She crossed her arms. *Risking my fucking life for this and you don't want me here?* "Dad—"

"Go on. Go." Voice rising. "Right now. Don't want you here. Hear me, Lucy?"

Lucy didn't move.

Came for you, all this way, and it's just like always, like I'm not even your daughter...

"*Now.*" He tried to get up, couldn't. "Run along, go. Goddamn it, go back to your uni and your Met, your posh little suits..." Coughed, kept going, choking out the words. "*Go.* Now. Piss off."

A tear. She wiped it. "No," she said.

Not like this, Dad...please...just be happy to see me, just for once...

"Don't you hear me?" He stared at her, frowning, furious. "What do I have to say? I...I wish Jack were here." Yelling now, raspy from blood in his throat. "Wish he were here, not you, understand? Just go, go on, right now, get the fuck out of here."

Oh, Dad...

But she didn't go, just stood there, trying not to cry.

"Christ," he said. "Make me say it? I'll say it if I have to, if you won't go." Paused.

Then:

"Should've been you that died."

Fuck you.

Fuck. You.

She stared down at him, shaking now. Saw bitterness, pain, same as always, all her life. Knew that he was thinking of Jack, of Mum, but not her, never her, never little leftover Lucy. *Fuck you Dad and fuck me and I'm fucking out of here, go bleed, go on, melt into the fucking sheets for all I care...*

Lucy ran, crap slippers leaving bloody footprints on the cold ward floor.

‡ ‡ ‡

She was naked now.

Naked, alone in the decon shower, crying. Shaking. A thick yellow haze: chemicals everywhere, raining down, stinging her bare skin. Her eyes burned. She rubbed them. Covered her face. Deep breaths, control herself, stop it but it hurt, so fucking hurtful, why the fuck would you say that? and could you believe it, really? *Oh yes I can, course I can. Same old shit, he just fucking said it this time. Should be glad he actually said it for once and now you know, know what you always knew, deep down knew.* Felt angry, like she wanted to just explode into a million billion pieces of fucked-off Lucy Stone. *Goddamn it, you miserable, awful old man...*

Water now. Cold. It washed over her, rinsing away the chemicals, the tears. She pulled her arms close to her chest. Exhaled. *Breathe.* Stared down at the floor, watched the water pool. Fell into her old fantasy: *not my Dad, never were. It was someone else, some stranger and that's why, that's why you hate me, can't stand to look at me. Not my fault, it's not my fault, so just go to hell.*

Hell with you.

The water stopped.

She took a deep breath. Another. A third.

Get out of here...

Shook her head, walked to the shower exit. Grabbed a paper-thin towel from the heavyset nurse. Opened her locker. The pound coin fell out, hit the floor, rolled away but fuck it, leave it. *Getting out of this place, right fucking now.* Tugged on her clothes, the posh suit, yes it was, so what? She *liked* it. Into her shoes, they were nice too. See, even her boss liked her, took her shopping, not unlovable at all. *Very lovable, actually, and I even have a fiancé now, a real man who loves me, handsome too, not perfect but he loves me…*

She walked out of the changing room and into the lobby.

Saw Simon.

Oh, for fuck's sake, Si…

He was standing by the gap in the plywood. Looked horrified: skin pale, sky blue eyes wide. She pushed her way over to him, heels clicking on the floor. He saw her coming, turned to her as she reached him.

"Luce—"

"Come on," she said. "We're leaving. Now." Grabbed his elbow, pulled him along as she stormed towards the exit.

"I'm sorry…"

Yeah? Sorry for what? For coming in, when I told you to stay put? Practically fucking begged you? Or sorry because my dad's a vicious old bastard and you know it, knew just what he'd say?

She kept walking, head down, ignoring his apologies. Even more crowded now. A group of large men in tracksuits blocked her way but she shoved through, reached the exit, popped out into the cold air.

It was nearly dark already.

Her eyes adjusted as she moved past the checkpoint, past the people waving their certs, the weary soldiers. Spotted Neckbeard, still patrolling the chain-link fence, sub-machine gun slung across his chest. Simon followed in her wake, puffing hard.

"Luce," he said, as they arrived at the edge of the car park. "Hold up a tick."

She stopped. Took a breath, turned to him.

"What?"

"You saw him, then?"

Lucy nodded. Said nothing, looked away.

"Ah," he said. "Yeah. Well. I'm so sorry, babe."

142

Don't be. He's an arse. Waste of time, this whole thing.

"Listen, I can guess what you're feeling…"

She frowned at him. *Oh, really?*

"And you mustn't feel guilty," he continued. "Believe me. You tried. I was there. You did everything you possibly could. Tried to give him half your Boosts, it was…amazing, really, like a scene from some old film or something. Really, Luce. Don't."

"Yeah," she said. "Well. Thanks." Started moving again, across the car park towards the road. Tried to push it all away, shove it down, just be practical now. *How do we get home? Never find a black cab. No Tube, no car services.*

"So," he said as they walked, "I heard…erm, I heard people are surviving it."

Only half-listening: "Yeah?" *Long walk, but could do. Just not through fucking Bethnal…*

"Bloke inside there was telling me. Starting to sort it out. Reckon as many as five, ten per cent pull through now. Said it's still bad, their faces, all scarred, horrible…" Shuddered, then realized what he was saying, pressed on. "But anyway, there's a chance, that's the main thing."

"Huh."

Hear that, Dad?

A chance for you. Great. Hope you make it. Can't fucking help it, care about you even though you don't give a shit about me, can't be arsed to see me, don't want me…

Stopped. *Wait.*

Remembered his words. His exact words.

Don't want you…here.

Get out of…here.

Here.

Realized: he knew. He knew the risk, her risk, of course he did. He knew about her Boosts. Knew she could be exposed. That's what he was doing. He was getting her out of *there,* out of danger, fast as he could. Any way he could, even if it hurt.

In his own bloody-minded, fucked-up Dad way, he was protecting her.

Her, his damn Vulnerable leftover of a daughter.

Oh God, Dad.

Turned around, started running back across the car park, back towards him. Crying. She wiped the tears as they fell but there were too many, she was raining tears and running and—

Dad...wait...

And then the building exploded.

CHAPTER TWELVE

London, 2029

She took a breath. Stepped out of the Toyota, into the car park. Into the past.

And it's then, then is now, and I see the flash and we're all down, everyone is down on the ground, car park gravel scraping my hands and heat on my back and I look up, the building is burning. Flames. Flames shooting up, smoke, haze. Get up and Simon's up and it's the rear, he says, pointing, look, rear of the building's burning and oh God Dad, coming Dad, here I come…

A step. Another one.

Moved towards the brick building. Big breaths, shaking.

Told herself she could do this. Needed to do this.

…and then the people, wave of people, the visitors, families, all of them running at me, past the fence and past the soldiers and crashing into me, screaming, a crush. I'm fighting through, pushing, shoving, they knock me back but I keep going, don't stop, can't stop, coming Dad and I'm through them now…

Halfway. Halfway to the door.

Wanted to stop. To curl up, run away, anything but this, fuck me, anything.

Rubbed her tattoo. Felt the Debt crushing her.

Kept going.

…and then the patients. So many, hundreds, thousands, bloody, screaming. Running, running from the fire and blood everywhere and faces, screaming faces, peeling, blood, and they reach me, hit me, a wall, feels like a hundred punches all at once and down, I'm down, hard gravel and wait, Dad, I'm coming Dad but they're everywhere and I can't get up and…

Almost there now.

Shaking. Just a few steps more.

Just keep…fucking…going.

…then the noise, I hear it, rat-tat-tat, rat-tat-tat and I look up and see the soldiers, they're firing, fucking firing and oh God oh Jesus fucking help me Jack, they're shooting the fucking patients now, patients falling all around, and I see them hit the ground thump thump, mouths open, eyes open, blood streaming and I'm screaming, screaming for Dad and how could I not see it, see what he was doing, not just run away and where are you Dad and bodies and a grubby pink jacket and everyone's dying, all fucking dying, screaming and dying and…

She reached the door. Grabbed it, pulled. Went inside.

Exhaled.

And suddenly, it was now again.

Made it, she thought.

I fucking made it.

Lucy stood in the Cox Labs lobby, tear-stained, panting. Ran her fingers through her hair. Felt exhausted, beat up, like when she first joined Jack's training sessions and wound up with her head in a bucket, puking in the corner of the ratty gym. *But I got back up, finished it. I did it. And I did it now, I made it, walked through a fucking nightmare, so look out Orange Trainers and Clapham and whoever else is behind all this. Here I fucking come.*

"You all right there, Miss?" asked the receptionist.

Lucy looked up at her. A deep breath. Smiled. *Brilliant, actually.* Wiped a tear, then flashed her badge. "Here for an interview," she said. "Geoff Hurst."

As the receptionist picked up her phone, Lucy glanced around the lobby. It looked different. Unrecognizable. Total overhaul, no more plywood or crap plastic benches. Everything gleamed: black granite, marble, chrome. A memorial on the far wall, names etched into the stone, hundreds and hundreds of them. Big gold letters at the top:

In Memory. Stepney Isolation Centre
Bombing. 19th November 2027.

She let her eyes drift down the names, and there it was.

There *he* was: *Joseph Stone, Jr.*

Made it, Dad.

"Lucy?" King appeared from around a corner, walked over to her. "You all right? Thought we decided you were heading back?" He looked concerned, but she couldn't tell if he was thinking about her or just worried about another Veronica Cox scene. "You were shaking pretty hard there in the car."

She shrugged. Held up her hand: just a tiny tremble. "Fine."

Just glad that it's back to now, Ed.

"Good," he said. "Great. Well, we're around the corner. Just kicking off. In with Hurst now. Salford's brought along five other DCs for the low-level interviews." Paused. "Sure you're okay?"

Lucy nodded.

Stop asking and let's do this.

"Right," he said. "Come on, then."

She followed him across the lobby, grimy trainers squeaking on the polished floor. Around a bend, past a giant framed photograph of Flinders Cox, into a wood-lined conference room. A few Cox Labs employees stood, fiddling with their name tags, waiting. In the corner, a tall man in a pinstripe suit and bright red necktie was holding court beneath a bronze memorial to the bombing first responders. Salford and the other DCs were gathered around, nodding, eating it up. Red Necktie was handsome in a rugged, craggy way: square jaw, carefully parted salt-and-pepper hair, big white teeth set off by a deep tan. Charming smile.

Hello, Geoff Hurst, Lucy thought.

She squinted at him, felt her gears turning.

And I know I've seen you someplace else before, too. Know it. But where?

"Just amongst ourselves," Hurst was saying, "it *was* a stroke of genius." A cheeky grin. The DCs grinned right back, nudged each other: *worth billions, mate, and here he is chatting to us like we're mates.* "Terrorists explode the rear, the toxic patients stampede, scatter out the front, and presto—biological dirty bomb, made of people. Genius." A little chuckle. "Quick thinking by the soldiers, really, firing to stop them from spreading the agent…"

Lucy's eyes blazed.

I'll fucking drop you…

Started towards him through the crowd of DCs, but King was too quick. He grabbed her shoulder, held her back. "No," he whispered. Stared down at her, a meaningful stare: *Goddamn it, Lucy, be cool.*

She glared back at him. *Oh, you're Mr Cool now? How about back there with Facer? But fuck it. Sure, Ed. I can wait.* Shook off his hand, smoothed her hoodie. *But Geoff Hurst, I don't like you. Not one fucking bit.*

So beware.

"Oh, hello," said Hurst, who had just noticed Lucy's arrival. Huge smile. "Geoff Hurst. And you are?" He reached through the DCs, extended his hand to her. Gold rings twinkled.

She crossed her arms. Frowned. "DI Stone."

Hurst was unfazed. "Well, welcome to Cox Labs, DI Stone." Another big grin, and—

Was that a fucking wink?

Wanker.

"As I was telling your colleagues," Hurst continued, "we're very proud of our new headquarters. Like to think our being here—on such a historic site—symbolizes London's triumph over London Black." *Reckon you've said that a million times,* Lucy thought. "Now, we have a room all set up for interviews, but before we do that, I thought perhaps a quick tour of our labs?"

Might be nice, actually. See where all those Boosts come from.

A lanky brown-haired man in a green tie cleared his throat.

"Ah," said Hurst. "Sorry. Lawyers. Our General Counsel is reminding me…assume no one here is Vulnerable, correct?"

She thought of her fakie in its little Arsenal wallet. Gone now, burned somewhere out there in the car park. Incident response team orders: everything goes. A man in a blue hazmat suit had handed her a burn bag and she'd thrown it in, right on top of the Max Mara. Stood, naked under her Mylar blanket, watching from the yellow emergency decon tent as the men with flame-throwers moved in.

"Yes?" the GC prompted. "Anyone?"

King glanced down at her. She said nothing, stared straight ahead.

Nothing to see here.

"Brilliant. Then we just need to do a quick finger prick test to confirm. Right this way…"

King elbowed her. She shrugged—*What, Ed? Worth a try*—and raised her hand. "I am," she said. "But I've got this." Flashed her warrant card at the lawyer. *Want to test it instead?*

"Very sorry," he said, "but with all due respect, we still can't allow you into the hot areas. Violates our public health licence, not to mention our insurance policies. Unless, of course, you have a search warrant that specifies you personally, DI Stone…?"

"It's okay," King told him. Pulled Lucy aside. "We'll meet back in the interview room."

She frowned. "Just don't start on him without me, yeah?"

"Sure. Of course." He shrugged. "Relax."

Didn't walk through a nightmare just to relax, Ed.

Hurst was already headed out the door. "Gentlemen," he said, "right this way." The DCs followed on his heels, still nudging one another: *billions!* King met her stare, gave a tiny nod—*don't worry, Lucy*—and joined them.

"DI Stone?" The GC waved at her. "I'll show you to the interview room. This way, please."

Lucy followed him down one carpeted corridor after another. Windowless offices, copy machines, indoor plants. Security cameras hung from ceiling tiles. She tried to work out where they were in relation to the old Iso Centre layout, but couldn't. *All so different now. Everything here is gleaming. Back then, nothing gleamed.*

They turned a corner, passed a bustling meeting room: a half-dozen men in white shirts, rooting through boxes of files. At the back, a bald man with thick black eyebrows and a yellow leather jacket stood looking on, arms crossed. He glanced up as Lucy passed. Followed her with hard-looking eyes.

Another man frowned and shut the blinds.

Well, then. Bit creepy.

Two minutes later, they arrived. The GC showed her into a large conference room. Dim daylight shone through a long window at the far end. In the centre, pads of paper and pens were laid out on a mahogany table. "Tea and coffee," he said, pointing to a cart. "A few fizzy drinks…"

Lucy ignored him. She walked past the table, across the room. Stood at the window, arms crossed, looking out at an old church surrounded by a large green churchyard.

"St Dunstan," the GC told her. "After the bombing, that's where the aid groups—"

"I know," she said. *Trust me.* Remembered standing in the medieval nave, holding a paper beaker of tea with both hands, grateful for the warmth. Still dazed, still shaking. Wondering whether Dad was still alive, possibly, a chance? Knowing, deep down, he wasn't. *Probably already burnt by then. Just another pile of ash in the bottom of the big emergency burn pit. Out there now, under that churchyard, him and all those others, hundreds, thousands…*

Behind her, the door clicked shut as the GC left.

She stood for a moment. Let a tear run down her cheeks. *You did save my life, Dad. Not how you thought, but you did.* Bowed her head, thought about everything that came after the bombing, the rest of the Scourge. All of it, right up to The Thing.

And look at what I fucking did with it.

Then she exhaled, walked to the beverage cart and grabbed a Coke and the pot of filter coffee from the hot plate. Mixed a drink. *Focus.* Turned her thoughts to the group of cops making their way around the laboratories.

Bit funny, that.

Five DCs, plus Salford is six. King, a DI.

Zero Commissioners, Assistant Commissioners, Chief Supers. Not even Wilkes.

So what's your game, Hurst? CEO of a billion pound business drops everything to give a tour to a bunch of homicide rank-and-file? The fuck is that?

She took a sip of her drink. Felt exhausted. Hadn't slept in three days, she realized.

Must be something you're worried about. Something you don't want us to see. Dodgy. Just like Clapham, and Facer, and Helen Cox and Orange Trainers and fuck, so fucking knackered, need to fight it, need to push through but fuck, fading, so fucking tired…

Her mobile vibrated. She blinked. Pulled it from her jeans.

It was a text from King:

"Stay where you are. Do not leave the room. Trust me."

‡ ‡ ‡

The fuck does THAT mean, Ed? What the hell's up?

As Lucy stared down at her mobile, she heard the conference room door click open. A Cox Labs employee in a yellow tie stuck his head in, smiled at her. "Right this way, gents," he said. The DCs filed in behind him, chattering: *Can you fucking believe it, told us he might buy a Premier League side, asked us our thoughts like we were mates?* "Help yourselves to drinks," said the employee. "I'll send your first interview in."

Lucy grabbed Salford.

"What's going on?" she asked.

Salford shrugged as he inspected the beverage cart. "Finished the tour. Didn't miss much. Test tubes, chemicals in big glass bottles. Load of boffins in lab coats banging on about drugs, bit technical." He took a Coke, cracked it open. "Hurst talking about buying a football club, actually, not the time if you ask me, but—"

"But no emergency? Nothing's, I don't know, leaking or something?"

A blank stare. "I...no, don't think so, why? Feeling all right, Lucy?"

Do I look like I'm feeling all right, Salford?

The fuck is going on?

"Where's King? And where in blazes is Hurst?"

Salford took a sip of his Coke, shrugged again. "Went off together. Back to Hurst's office, I reckon. Took a fancy to King. Wanted to show him something." Smoothed his tie, then looked around, frowned. "What, no biscuits?"

God fucking dammit, Ed.

She turned away, typed out a text to King: "?!?!? >:("

Hit send.

A minute passed. Two. No response.

Lucy sighed, sat back down in her chair. Tugged on her hoodie drawstrings. Wondered what King was on about, why he'd just taken Hurst and buggered off, fuck you, Lucy, have fun sitting round with six DCs doing fuck all. *Trust you, Ed? Why? You don't trust me. Think I can't handle myself with this wanker Hurst, that I'll lose it, mouth off? Christ. I want to be there. Want to grill Hurst myself, strong lead, can't fuck it up and I fucking need this, God fucking dammit...*A big exhale. "Rats," she said out loud.

The door opened.

"Afternoon, Officers." A yellow-haired spotty man in his early twenties entered and slid into a chair. He wore jeans and a black quarter-zip jumper. "Richard Banks. VP, Market Research. Believe I'm your first victim?"

His grin faded as seven cops stared back at him.

"The first victim," said a fat DC, "was Flinders Cox. Any others we should know about?"

Two hours passed.

A parade of low-level Cox Labs employees rolled in, said absolutely nothing of interest, left.

Lucy spent the time frowning at her mobile and wishing there were more Cokes. Salford had nicked the last one, bit of a dick move, knew she wanted it. *Fuck's sake, Salford.* She switched to straight coffee, refilling as each new interviewee sat down. They began to blend:

COFFEE NO. 1: Flinders Cox was a truly great man. Everyone here admired him...

COFFEE NO. 2: ...and felt proud to be working for his company. He was a brilliant...

COFFEE NO. 3: ...biochemist, and his death is a loss to London Black research...

COFFEE NO. 4: ...worldwide. What's that? Antidote? No, years away, I'm afraid, but...

COFFEE NO. 5: ...in the meantime, we're working on something called Elemidox Ultra...

COFFEE NO. 6: ...which ought to be ready in about a year, touch wood.

She thought of her monitor. She'd checked it after King's text: down to 6.7 already.

Christ. Need to find this antidote. Find it right fucking now.

Not just for the Debt, for me.

It was nearly three. Lucy glanced outside. Dim, just a few yellow lights shining from the windows of the old church. She checked her mobile. BTP still working on pulling the Orange Trainers CCTV footage. Nothing from King. Sent him another text: "grrrr". Thought, *Wait 'til I get my hands on you, Ed King…*

"By the way," Coffee No. 6 said, as he rose to his feet, "the coffee in here is crap. There's a Nero down the road, I'd send someone if I were you…"

Lucy watched him stand. Decided: *Hell with this.*

May as well get something useful out of this nonsense.

"Hold up," she said. "Not done yet." Took a last sip from her mug as Coffee No. 6 sat back down. Said: "Geoff Hurst. Your CEO." Paused. "What's *he* like, then?"

The DCs stared at her as one: *Hurst? Legend! Might buy a football club…*

"Mr Hurst?" Coffee No. 6 shifted in his seat. "He's…erm, a great leader."

Lucy said nothing. Just arched an eyebrow.

"Very…inspirational," he continued. "We're in great hands. Truly."

She leaned towards him across the table. Voice low: "Are you *lying* to me?"

He began to fiddle with the zip on his navy jumper.

Across the room, Salford shot her a look: *Lucy, what the fuck?*

Lucy ignored him. *Piss off, Coke thief.* Coffee No. 6's foot was tapping, she noticed. *Come on, then. Out with it.* "Bad idea," she told him. "Truly. Lying to a homicide detective, not very clever. Get yourself done for that." She crossed her arms. "Care to have another go?"

He frowned. Thought about it. Shrugged, then: "Nightmare. Total bloody nightmare. Constant mixed messages, firings, all that. No grasp of toxicology, not even the basics. Wouldn't know an antidote from his Auntie Vera." *Bet they love that one in the lab*, Lucy thought. "Everyone hates him."

"Oh?"

Coffee No. 6 nodded a head covered in curly orange hair. "Bullied an executive assistant so badly she had to be hospitalized. Breakdown."

Thought as much. She glanced over at the DCs. *There's your new pal, lads.*

"So how come he's the CEO, then?" she asked.

Another shrug. "He and Mr Cox were old school friends. Mr Cox, he only cared about the science. Needed someone to handle the business end. Hurst was the best he could do, I expect. And since Mr Cox was practically a saint, Hurst just does what he pleases. But, yeah. Five years ago, the man was running some crap letting agency in Shadwell."

"I see," Lucy said.

She took one last glance at her mobile: still nothing from King. Made up her mind.

Enough of this. Not playing your crap little game, Ed. Here I come.

"Come with me," she told Coffee No. 6 as she stood and walked to the door. Salford started to get up, but she sat him back down with a stare. *Enjoy the fizzy drinks, Salford. On my own now.* Coffee No. 6 followed her out of the room. As the door clicked shut behind them, Lucy asked: "Which way is Geoff Hurst's office?"

He pointed. "Around the bend there. Left, then right. Keep going. Can't miss it."

She nodded. Took off, hands in her hoodie pockets.

The first turn took her past the room with the creepy bald man. Blinds still shut. Kept on walking, past offices, loos, an empty kitchen. CCTV really was everywhere, she noticed: every fifth ceiling tile had a drop-down camera with a blinking red light. *Bit extreme, yeah?* Turned right. This corridor was empty, just vacant offices and indoor plants. She followed it to the end, then stopped. Stood, staring.

Coffee No. 6 was right. There was no missing it.

Hurst's office was the size of her flat. Larger. The wall facing the corridor was glass, so she could see it all: two Chesterfields, art on the wall, gilded frames. Dark wood, leather. The desk chair looked like it was lifted from a Ferrari. *Fuck's sake. Reckon there are worse people to know than Auntie Vera.*

The lights were off.

Lucy sighed. Pulled a hand from her hoodie pocket, ran it through her hair. Thought about King's text: so cryptic, so fucking annoying. *Where'd you scarper off to, then, Ed? Not here, so where are you? And why couldn't I come, too?*

She turned, headed back to the conference room. As she passed the bald man's room, she noticed that the blinds were open now. She stopped. Looked in. It was empty: no men in ties, no bald man. Not even his yellow leather jacket, just a stack of file boxes shoved up against a wall. *Just gone three o'clock, bit early to bunk off, not even Sykes would…*

Her monitor beeped.

Again?

She reached for her mobile, swiped under her hoodie: *6.0.*

Christ. It's dropping so fast.

Thought of the laboratories on the other side of the building. Of all the London Black swirling around over there. Remembered the Iso Centre ward, the peeling faces. The blood. Decided fuck it, no point taking chances, may as well top up. But then she heard Doctor Hodges's voice in her head: *Anything beyond the first Boost of the day is meaningless.*

Lucy frowned.

Let's test that theory.

Can't hurt. And a Boost's only what, five quid these days, anyway.

She doubled back, made for the lav. Thought about the Cox

Labs GC as she marched along. *Wouldn't let me in here if it wasn't safe, yeah? They test it, must do, reckon it's fine…but then, what about King's text? What if there was some leak, if Salford just didn't know? If it was in the air?* Sped up as she turned the corner. The women's was on the left. She opened the door, went inside, ducked into a cubicle. Sat down. Reached into her special hoodie pocket.

Fuck.

It was empty.

She remembered now. Used her emergency Boost last night. Alone in the MIT19 loo, shoulder aching, still fuming from the Orange Trainers attack. *Right. Well, we're here at the source, plenty of Boosts, must be a way to score a box, yeah? Reckon Coffee No. 6 would know.* She stood, pushed open the cubicle door, in the mirror the bald man and *wait, what—*

Felt his hand over her mouth.

‡ ‡ ‡

"Shhh," the bald man said.

She frowned.

Then—

Grabbed his hand, twisted. *Bastard.* Behind him now, pulled up on his arm, harder, *harder*, fuck are you *thinking*, mate, grabbing *me*? Over to the wall, slammed him, *like that?*, another slam. *Wanker.* One more slam. Spun him round, hand on his neck, fist raised.

"I hate. Being. *Shushed*," Lucy said.

Watched as blood trickled from his nose.

"Please," gasped the bald man. "Let…go…"

She glanced at his wrist: no tattoo.

Not Orange Trainers.

So, who the fuck? Fuck are you doing, grabbing me in the loo?

Lucy kept her fist raised. Said: "Talk."

"Can't…breathe…"

She thought about it. Decided, fuck it, he tries something, she could take him. Shoved him away, took a step back. Stood, fists up, ready. *Better be good.*

"*Fuck*," he said. Coughed. Touched his nose, stared at the blood. "Sorry. Sorry, I'm not…it's just…" He took a deep breath. "Didn't mean to frighten…I just thought, soon as you saw me in here, you'd scream…"

Scream? Me? I'd fucking drop you, is what.

"Keep going," she said.

"Well…you're a cop, right?"

She narrowed her eyes. *And?*

"I'm an auditor," he said. "An accountant."

Lucy looked at his yellow leather jacket, now speckled with blood. His black jeans, big black boots. Frowned. *The fuck you are.* "What, dressed like *that*? Taking the mick?"

"Business casual," he said. Shrugged. "What? You're dressed like *that*…" Gestured with his chin at her baggy black hoodie. *Fair.*

"So why are you grabbing me in the bloody loo?"

The blood from his nose was beginning to drip onto the tile floor. "Heard you were here, needed to talk. Can't be seen with you. Too risky. Only place I could think of. CCTV everywhere else."

She remembered all the hallway ceiling cameras. *True.*

The bald man cupped his hand to catch the blood. Pointed at a box of tissues by the sink. "May I?" Waited for her nod, then shuffled over, took one, started cleaning himself up. "A month ago," he said, jamming a bit of tissue in his left nostril, "Flinders Cox ordered a special audit of the company. Called in external auditors. Us. Worried about some charitable donations, thought something smelt a bit whiffy." Cleared his throat, spat blood in the sink.

"And?"

"And the charity checked out, but we found something bigger. Someone's skimming. Routing payments from a Cox Labs sub in Mauritius to some shell company in Panama." Stuck a tissue in the other nostril as well. "Fake invoices, dodgy bank accounts. Proper financial crime." Paused. "Millions."

Lucy thought about it as he washed his hands. *Right, embezzlement, then. Interesting. Motive? Thief wouldn't want Mr Cox to find out, so there's that. But the murder didn't stop anything, hasn't stopped Bloody Tissues here, which, seriously, grabbing me in the fucking loo, the fuck were you thinking, mate? Terrible idea, Christ. Any event, though, the real question is—*

"Who?" she asked.

"Still dotting the i's. But with the murder…" His voice dropped to a whisper. "A fair few people have the access and authority. Any of the Directors, the CFO, some others. But only one would gain by killing Cox. See, the way the corporate by-laws work…"

Let's cut to the chase. It's the wanker, yeah?

"Geoff Hurst?"

The bald man exhaled. Nodded. "Think so. Only the Chairman of the Board can call off an audit. That was Flinders. Now, it's Hurst. Anyone else, murder wouldn't matter, really. But if it's Hurst? Now he can shut it down. Looks too dodgy straight away, but there's a Board meeting in a week. Reckon he'll do it then, find some excuse."

Like I said. The wanker.

"Does he know you know?"

He shook his head. "Told him we're weeks away. I lied. We'll have it all sorted by today, tomorrow latest. Just waiting on something from the Panamanian registry. But if Hurst finds out we've spoken…I mean, what he did to Flinders…"

Relax, Bloody Tissues.

"You'll be fine," she said. "Soon as it's set, call me. Straight away. Here." She pulled out her mobile, showed him the number. "And yours?"

A sniffle. The tissues were fully crimson. "Here you go." He reached into the breast pocket of the yellow leather jacket, pulled out a card. Thick ivory stock. Handed it to her. It read: Bartholomew L. Huffington-Burleigh, CFA.

Bloody Tissues it is.

"Right," she said, pushing the card into her padded hoodie pocket. "I'll leave first. Give it a few minutes, then you." She nodded at him, turned, walked to the door. Over her shoulder: "And stay out of the women's, yeah?"

Such a fucking terrible idea. Do like the jacket, though.

Lucy flew along the corridor towards the interview room. Head down, thinking. Felt good, definitely, this was a lead, no question. Proper motive. But still: fair bit left for her to sort. Wondered about the forensics. Hurst had no blood on him, she needed to work that out. *And then, the antidote. Must tie to the antidote, somehow. Because I know it exists, must do, need it to pay the Debt, don't I?, and finding it has to be—*

"Lucy?"

She looked up. King was running towards her.

"There you are," he said, panting. "Fuck's sake. Looking all over. Salford, everyone. Where the hell *were* you?"

Are you fucking kidding me, Ed?

"I was in the loo," she said. Glared at him. "And what about—"

"Come on." He turned, started walking the other way, back towards the building lobby.

"Wait," she said, as she caught up. "Stop. Where is he? Hurst?" King shrugged. "Gone."

Gone? God fucking dammit…

"We need to talk to him," she said. "I do. Stop, Ed, listen—"

"Tell me on the way. Enoch Clapham called. He wants to talk."

160

CHAPTER THIRTEEN

"Just saying, who the fuck *does* that?" King asked. "Just pisses off and never comes back?"

Lucy glared at him from the passenger seat.

She'd told him about Bloody Tissues as soon as she'd made it out, easier leaving, thank God. Skipped over the fight bit. But the skimming, she told King all about *that*. That Hurst had a motive, a proper one. That she needed to grill him, right bloody now, but a bit tricky to do when *someone* left her to rot in a Coke-less conference room, then went and lost the bloody suspect, yeah? *He took you to look at his fucking car, Ed. Told you to wait there while he took a call. And you just waited? Standing in the car park, staring at the Lambo Maybach whatever the fuck while I'm stuck listening to Coffees Nos 1 to 6 witter on and anyway I should've been there, not your call, such fucking bullshit…*She snorted, went back to staring out the window.

He slowed the Toyota to a stop at a red light. Nearly sunset now. A sign to their left:

Advance Warning, Road Closure, Remembrance Wreath Procession

London Strong Week banners hung from the street lights.

"Point is," he said, accelerating again, "I asked him everything. Helen Cox? Admitted it straight away—sure, few times, she wanted it, why not? Couldn't give a toss what Flinders thought. Secret lab? Didn't notice. Antidote? News to him, and if it does exist, it's company property, so please fucking find it."

"Still." Lucy turned back to him, narrowed her eyes. "It was *wrong*."

King sighed.

"I told you," he said. "Second you left, he started banging on about you. Lads' talk, what he would do, all that. Filthy. Trust me. Said he could pull you, just reach out and *grab* you, do it right there in the conference room, and—"

"Left up there," she said. Pointed. "By the church."

Don't need your fucking protection, Ed. Just ask Bloody Tissues.

"Ta," he said. Turned off The Highway, into Wapping. "Any event, we'll find him again. Meantime, let's hear what our friend Clapham is so keen to tell us." Steered the car over a red metal bridge. Flashes of skyscrapers on either side: Canary Wharf left, City right. Slowed, then parked in front of an ancient-looking three-storey pub. "And here we are."

They got out.

"Proper old boozer," King said. He eyed a sign hung on the yellow brick: London's Oldest Riverside Inn, circa 1520. "Been in before?"

Lucy nodded as she pushed through the door. Dark inside. Felt old: worn stone floor, dark wood, timbered ceiling. Bits and bobs on shelves, model ships and bottles. Remembered Simon dragging her here, back before Boosts, before two sips of beer left her with her head in the toilet. *Such a Si spot. Wouldn't leave off about it for days after.* "The history, Luce." *Fair enough, Si, but lager at a Spoons just as wet and a pound cheaper, yeah?* "Just once," she told King. "Did Clapham say where in here?"

He shook his head. "Only that we'd best hurry."

And we came running. Hmm.

They walked through the ground floor, scanning the punters' faces. Quiet, even for a Tuesday. Few tourists. Pretty woman in a pleather jacket laughing with a prematurely grey bloke. *Seen her before, below me in school.* No sign of Clapham.

162

"Don't see him," said King.

"There's an upstairs," she said. Doubled back, led King up a creaky staircase. Turned right at the top, into a small square room. Tables of drinkers, low chatter. She remembered this place. Simon's Aussie baritone in her head: *Used to use it as a bare-knuckle boxing ring. Thought you'd like that, Luce.* She looked around.

A faint voice from behind her: "Officers?"

Clapham was at a corner table, drinking ale. Looked even thinner than before: skin and bones, a skeleton with a pint glass. No sign of the cassock with the double-barred cross, just a suit and the croc leather loafers. Lucy frowned at him.

There you are.

She walked over, sat down. King followed.

"Quite fond of this pub," Clapham said, taking a sip of his drink. "Worked round here, once." He raised his glass, smiled at King. "Join me for a pint, Officer?" To Lucy: "Or, perhaps a soft drink?"

Cute. Reckon you've done your homework on me, yeah?

You don't know the half of it.

"Talk," she said. "Why are we here?"

King, at the same time: "Where'd you go last night?"

Christ, Ed, let me do the talking. Don't need you to bollocks this up, too.

Clapham looked from one DI to the other. Another smile. He reached into a leather satchel at his feet, drew out a paper folder with the letters *MLF* in spidery scrawl on the tab. Pushed it across the table to Lucy. "I bring gifts," he said. Watched as she opened it, began flipping.

It was a dossier: lists of names, bios, head shots. All Survivors. She pulled out a page, began to read out loud: "John Johnson." The photograph clipped to the paper was blurry, just a red oval face and two black eyes. "Founder of the..." Saw the next words, stopped speaking.

Founder of the Meat Liberation Force.

She thought of the sign she'd seen earlier, sitting in traffic on the Embankment: THE MLF IS COMING. The Survivor holding it had been screaming at a man in a Hand of God T-shirt. They looked ready to tear each other apart.

"You won't have heard of them," said Clapham. "Not yet."

King looked over her shoulder. "Who?"

"Devils," Clapham told him. "A band of devils. Call themselves the MLF. The paramilitary wing of the SRA, in fact. Radicals. Violent. Dangerous."

Lucy watched him take another sip of ale. *Funny. That's just what I heard about your lot.*

"So what?" asked King.

Clapham turned to Lucy. "You said Flinders Cox was working on an antidote, yes?"

She nodded. Noticed he was wearing a metal chain beneath his white collared shirt. *Probably that medallion. One you couldn't stop stroking yesterday, all those letters, looks like Orange Trainers's tattoo.*

"These," he tapped on the folder, "*these* are sworn enemies of God *and* man. And they want to multiply. They want the world to follow in their sin, for everyone to look as they look, suffer as they suffer." Paused. "An antidote for London Black? The MLF would see that as a catastrophe."

"So would you," Lucy said.

Clapham chuckled. "Me? No. I know the Truth, Officer."

You know something, anyway. That's a dead fucking cert.

"Yeah? Tell me."

The preacher leaned forward. "The Truth is, London Black is God's own arrow. And no antidote can slacken His bowstring." Long pale fingers crept to his chest, to the shirt-covered crucifix. "We bury the past in a sepulchre of oblivion, but we forget at our peril. Someday His arrows will fly once more, just as they always have. More bodies, more pits, ash and—"

"Enough," Lucy said. Glared at him.

Don't have time for this shit.

"I don't get it, Clapham." King was flipping through the dossier. "Why give us this? Why now?"

"Just yesterday you filed a complaint," Lucy added.

Clapham looked at her. Frowned. "Someone is lying," he said. "I made no complaint." Turned to King. "But as for your question, this isn't the first time. Three times I went to the police with my concerns about the MLF. Brought this very folder." A shrug. "Ignored. But you…" He stared at Lucy. "I thought perhaps you would understand."

She stared back at him.

You look so mild now, Clapham. Thought of him in the old church, at the front of his congregation: shaking, screeching, eyes blazing. *It's fucking terrifying.*

"Well," he said. Shrugged. "Perhaps not." Took a last sip of his ale, placed the empty glass on the table. "Afraid I must be going. My ministry is a busy one and my children need me. Thank you for your indulgence, Officers." He stood, took a black felt coat from his chair back, began pulling it on.

Not yet, Clapham.

"Geoff Hurst," Lucy said. "What do you know?"

She watched as he stopped moving.

"Who?" A frown. "Sorry, Officer, don't think I know the name…"

Yeah, you fucking do.

"The CEO of Cox Labs," said King.

Clapham shook his head. Buttoned his coat, picked up his satchel. "Perhaps if I saw his face. Evening."

Lucy didn't turn around as he walked past. Just sat, staring at the wall, listening to his footsteps on the old wooden floor.

Suddenly felt hot. Stuffy in here. Old books on shelves and men in big wigs frowning down from antique picture frames: Simon things. *Need some air.* She stood, threaded through the tables to a door that led outside. Pushed her way out, onto a little wooden balcony overlooking the Thames. Breathed in the cold night air.

Better.

But as she stood, staring out at the sun setting over the river: a surge of guilt.

The Debt was rising up.

I'm so close, though. I know it. She ran her fingers through her hair. Exhaled. Thought of Hurst, leering. Had to be him, must be, perfect motive, plus just the type. But then, why take the antidote? And no blood on him, she knew that. King had told her. Forensics. *So you had someone do it for you, yeah? That it? You tell Clapham, Clapham sends Orange Trainers, and as he kills Cox he spots an antidote you don't know about. Pinches it.*

Yes. Could be.

But then how do Hurst and Clapham connect?

King opened the door, joined her. "What a wanker," he said. Waggled the folder. "Waste of fucking time. Probably laughing at us right now. My pet coppers, come running when I sneeze."

"He's important," Lucy said. "Just need to tie him to Hurst."

"Hurst? Why?"

"The antidote."

King shook his head. Softly: "There is no antidote, Lucy."

She looked away, out to the river.

Has to be an antidote, Ed. I need it. Antidote pays the Debt. I need to pay the Debt.

Or…

For a moment, she thought of her monitor. Of Doctor Hodges, tenting his fingers.

Or do you just want it for yourself, Lucy?

"Forget about that," he said. "Please. Just focus on the murder."

She tugged on her hoodie strings, stared down into the dark water. *It could all work. Hurst and Clapham, need them both, two parts to the puzzle. Just need to tie them together, work out how they fit, then—*

And then she remembered something Coffee No. 6 had said.

That's it.

That's fucking it.

"Ed? Clapham just said he worked around here, yeah?"

King nodded.

"But he wasn't Clapham then. He was Morley. Gavin Morley, the dodgy letting agent."

Another nod. "And?"

Her voice was rising. "D'you know who ran a letting agents in Shadwell? Just up across The Highway?" She pulled her mobile from her hoodie pocket, started to type. Smiled as images flashed on her screen. "Look," she said, "it's cached." Showed him: an old bio page, Clapham's skeletal face at the top. It read:

Gavin Morley, Agent. Hurst Properties Ltd.

"It all fits," she said. "Clapham, Hurst. Antidote, murder. We need Geoff Hurst. Right bloody now. His EA. Call her…"

She tapped her foot as King dialled, spoke, rang off.

He turned to her, eyes wide.

"Hurst is about to board his private jet at City Airport."

And that's why Clapham called us.

A distraction.

"He's running," said Lucy.

‡ ‡ ‡

Faster, Ed. Fucking faster.

Lucy beat her thumb on the passenger window. *Come on, come on, come on.* The Toyota was on blues and twos, pushing through traffic towards City Airport. Beside her, King hunched over the wheel, frowning at the red tail lights ahead.

"Fucking *look* at this," he said. Waved a brawny hand. "The traffic in this town…" To the painter's van in front of them: "See the blue lights? You can see them, yeah? Then *move*, for fuck's sake…"

Their estimated arrival flashed on the dashboard GPS: twenty minutes.

She checked her mobile. It was 4:20. Hurst's flight was at half four.

Ten minutes.

We have ten fucking minutes.

And all this traffic…

"Christ," said King. "*Go.*" He laid on the horn.

"It's the Wreath Procession," she told him. "A13's completely shut, everything's re-routed." Pointed at a blockaded turn-off up ahead. "See?"

He nodded.

She watched the painter's van inch to the side. Frowned. Remembered last year's Procession, catching a glimpse on the kitchen telly as she made coffee. Aerial shots: big black cars, a line of them, heading down the empty A13, out to the burn-site memorials. Sunset. Crowds. Children with banners. She'd looked away. Bunch of Non-Vulnerables with black poppy wreaths, the fuck good does any of it do anyway? *None. Fuck all. And now? Now I need to get to the airport and I can't, it's all fucked, just so the royals can wave and the PM can smile and give some crap speech and nine minutes now, nine, God fucking dammit, Ed, drive faster, fucking faster…*

Her mobile rang.

She looked down: Wilkes.

Tell me, Ma'am. Please. Tell me you grounded him.

She hit the speakerphone button. Held the mobile out for King to hear.

"Ma'am?"

Silence. Then: "I tried, Lucy."

Fuck.

"Please, Ma'am," she said. "We can't let him take off. He'll vanish. I know it."

Wilkes sighed. "Airport police won't step in. Not terrorism, not smuggling. Saying they won't cause an air traffic incident just so we can do an interview."

An interview?

"An arrest, Ma'am. I'm arresting him."

Another sigh. "About that. You can't. Sorry. Not enough yet."

"But—"

"No." Paused. "Chief Super's call."

Chief Super?

The fuck, Ma'am? You brought it to the Chief Super? Hurst's old school chum, course he'd say no, no chance, zero. Why would you DO that?

She glanced at the dashboard clock.

Eight minutes.

King, to the phone: "Marie? It's Ed." He swerved the Toyota around a delivery scooter. "We're in traffic. It's awful. There's really nothing?"

"I'm on with Interpol in five. If we get proof by the time he lands, proper rock-solid proof, local authorities in Monaco will grab him."

Local authorities? Really? Ma'am, if he hits Monaco, he's gone. End of.

"Right," King said.

Lucy said nothing. Just rang off, felt her heart pounding. *No, Ed. Not "Right". We need to do something. Right fucking now.*

169

"A diversion," she said. "We need another route, a side road, something, somehow…" Her thumb beat on the window, *thump thump thump thump*.

He glanced at the GPS. Shrugged. "There's nothing. Look. There's a river in the way."

They squeezed past a bus. The siren wailed.

We're not going to make it.

Fuck.

She tugged on her hoodie strings. Looked at the GPS. Saw King was right, this was it. And with no A13 it was either this or go up to Bow, and that's another fifteen minutes, fucking Christ. *He's getting away, getting away and I need this, need to stop him or he's gone, fuck me and—*

And then she realized:

The A13.

The A13 was clear.

"*There*," she told King. Pointed to the blockade. "There, turn there."

"No, that's the procession route…look…" A parked patrol wagon, Special Constable standing in front, sipping coffee.

Seven minutes.

"Turn. *There*."

"We can't just jump onto a locked-down parade route, it's mental, and—"

"Look at me, Ed."

He glanced over. She stared back at him. Black bags, no sleep. Pain.

"I *need* this," she said. "Do it. *Now*."

For me, Ed.

A pause.

And then he took a breath, swore, spun the wheel. The SC dropped his coffee as they roared past. Shot up an on-ramp, around another blockade, then out onto the A13. It was empty.

Four lanes, no traffic, just crowds behind barriers, black paper poppies everywhere.

Thank you, Ed.

Now drive.

He hit the gas and they raced ahead.

Hurry.

Blew down the road, fast, faster. Flying now. Blurring windows. Trees signs buildings streaking past them, all a blur, moving fast into the darkness, so fast...

Six minutes.

Come on, come on...

A line of black cars appeared ahead.

They'd caught the Procession.

"Fuck," said King. "Now what?"

Their car radio cracked. A female voice: "All units. This is Mike Whiskey. Stand by for information. Situation developing, location London Motorway A13, possible incident. Over."

King glanced over. "They know we're cops, right? The lights..."

She frowned.

Thought of the AFO at Westminster Station: *London Strong Week, everyone's a bit on edge.*

"Anyone can buy lights," she said.

Ahead, an escort wagon left the procession, dropped back. Movement in its rear window: an AFO. Watching them.

Through a rifle sight.

Christ...

Lucy grabbed her phone, punched the Airwave button. "Stone. Location, London Motorway A13. Eastbound. Grey Toyota. Advise, we are police. Over."

Static back.

"Repeat. This is Stone. Location, A13. Over."

"Don't fucking shoot us," King yelled.

More static. Then: "Stone, say again your location. Over."

They were nearly even with the escort now. She could see the rifle, tracking them.

Inhale, exhale.

Five minutes.

"Lucy?" King's massive knuckles were turning white. "Think we need to drop back."

She shook her head. "No."

He glanced over but she kept staring ahead.

The rifle was pointing straight at her. A red dot from its laser sight appeared on her hoodie.

"Ed?"

"Yes?"

She felt the Debt, rising up, sky high and—

"*Punch it,*" she said.

And they were flying now, *oh God oh Jack* and she held her breath as they blew past the escort, past the black cars and the wreaths and *Evening Your Majesty* and swerved back around them all, *clear, fucking clear,* then faster, faster still until they swung right down an exit, past the blockade, tires squealing, siren blaring.

Ahead, in the distance: the airport.

King swore as they burned down a connecting road, wove through taxis, cars, vans.

Please be there. Please God.

Inhale, exhale.

Watched a jet take off, too big, not him, can't be but fucking *hurry*.

Four minutes.

They roared around a bend. Saw the sign: *Private Terminal.* Hit a roundabout, a turn, *up there,* another turn, *almost there,* blasted down a straightaway and turned and—

A thin metal fence.

No one at the guard post.

Fuck, no time, Christ fucking dammit…

"Hang on," King said.

Floored it.

Oh shit…

‡ ‡ ‡

A screech as the car tore through the metal fence.

Lucy felt the seatbelt chafe against her neck. Smiled.

Nice one, Ed.

They raced onto the airport apron. Nearly dark now. She scanned the tarmac ahead. Saw luggage carts, tractors, dollies: everything in motion, vehicles everywhere. Ground crew in high-vis. Jets parked, refuelling, preparing to taxi. Chaos.

Now where are you, Hurst?

Behind them, a burst of siren. Blue lights flashed as an airport cop car left its spot by the terminal, raced towards them. King sped up, swerved around a trolley, kept driving.

"Where, Lucy?" Glanced in his rear-view. "Where am I going? *Lucy?*"

"Looking." She stared ahead, scanning frantically. *Must be here. Must be.*

The airport cop's siren blared.

"Stone?"

"*Looking.*" Frowned. So many jets, too many, Christ. *Where…
…fuck…*

…FUCK…

"There!" She pointed to the end of the apron. Hurst was climbing the steps of a small grey jet, leather holdall slung over his shoulder. "See?"

King nodded. Mashed the accelerator. They flew across the tarmac, straight for him, past ground crew, passengers, everyone diving and bags everywhere. *Look out, Hurst, here we fucking come…*

They squealed to a stop in front of the jet.

Hurst stopped climbing. Stood, looking down at them.

Lucy stared back through the windscreen.

You're mine now.

Opened her door. Got out. Her mobile rang: Wilkes. She tossed it to King. "Mind? And…that lot, too?" Pointed to the airport cops, scrambling out of their car, guns raised. "Ta." *I've got something to do.* Marched across the tarmac, chin down, eyes up. Reached the foot of the stairway. Looked up.

Hurst was grinning.

"You," he said. A flash of over-white teeth. "Hoping I'd see you again." To King: "Hey, Ed. Told you she fancied me." He stared down at Lucy. "Heading to Monaco. Care to join?"

Behind him, the sun dropped beneath the horizon.

"You're nicked," she said. "Murder of Flinders Cox."

He laughed.

Right. Laugh, you wanker. But I've got you, and you'll lead me to the antidote.

"Love to have you," he said. "Join, that is. Truly. Yacht's waiting."

She ignored him. Began the caution: "You do not have to say anything…"

"No need to pack."

"…but it may harm your defence…"

"In fact, clothing optional."

She stopped. Glared up at Hurst. Thought of him, praising the Iso Centre bombers. Of Flinders Cox, throat slit, crucifix in his eye. Of the Debt. *I don't like you, Geoff Hurst. And that's a problem for you, big one, because I'll tear you apart, break you down, fact when I'm through with you—*

"Lucy?"

King was running towards her, waving her mobile.

Not now, Ed.

She said: "Tell Wilkes—"

"Not Wilkes," he said. "Huffington-Burleigh."

She frowned. *Huffington…?*

Oh. Right. Bloody Tissues.

What do you want?

Took the phone.

"Stone," she said.

Bloody Tissues's voice was faint. He said something, but the jets were too loud. Every third word dropped. Lucy frowned, covered her free ear: "…received the…from Panama and…. turns out…*not* Hurst…"

Wait…no…

Then: "…Helen Cox."

"*What?*" She stared at the phone. Felt the world collapsing around her, the Debt laughing as it rose up to the skies.

"Helen Cox," said Bloody Tissues. "And some solicitor. Skimming. Have been…"

Lucy looked up. Hurst was walking down the stairs, heading towards her. Smirking.

But…I know it's you…I was sure…

He was a foot away. She could smell his cologne. Smelt like whiskey.

"So, about Monaco." Another grin. His sunglasses were big black circles: Survivor eyes, but menacing, terrifying. Tan skin, perfect hair. A black rubber London Strong bracelet peeked out from beneath his shirt cuff. Voice low: "I know you want to…"

He reached for her.

She tried to duck, to slip him, but his arms were too long. His fingers grazed her stomach.

Images began to flash. Her vision tunnelled. Then red, a red mist covering everything, and she saw his lips move but heard nothing, just watched him sneer as he reached again and she didn't run, just stood, glaring, felt her fists ball, and *red, red, it's all red...*

And then:

Lucy fucking dropped him.

CHAPTER FOURTEEN

Screamers will be bad tonight.

Lucy tossed her empty Boost syringe into the sharps bin. Exhaled. Stood, staring into her cobweb-cracked bathroom mirror. The gash on her jaw still hurt. She touched it, felt a burst of pain. Wondered which of the airport cops tackled her. *Fat one? Tall one? Reckon it was the tall one. Fat one too slow, I'd slip him, must have been the tall.* Tried again to remember what happened after she punched Hurst but it was red, all red, only a few shards of memory: dirty tarmac, inches from her nose; the smell of petrol; an airport cop's knee in her back, pinning her down. Not King's knee, she knew that. *Because I remember you, Ed. You pulling them off me. Flash of stubble, whiff of aftershave, I remember that.*

When the red fog finally lifted, she'd found herself at MIT19. In Wilkes's office. A lecture. Sound back by then, so she'd heard every word, heard the disappointment in Wilkes's voice: *Suspension. Official, yes. Misconduct hearing. Expect dismissal, Lucy.* No point arguing. She'd just pulled her badge and warrant card from her hoodie pocket, slid them across the desk. Watched Wilkes shake her head.

I didn't mean it, Ma'am.

Well…fine. A bit. Fucking Hurst, handsy wanker…

But what do I do now?

She'd taken a black cab home. Cardboard box on her lap, few bits and bobs from her crap little desk. Wilkes's suggestion: never know when they'll clean out your desk. As the taxi whipped through darkened city streets, she'd stared out the window into the black, wondering what would happen next, how she could pay the Debt, how she would cope.

And now here she was.

In her bathroom. After midnight. Shattered.

Still wondering.

She frowned at the Lucys in the mirror. Touched the gash again. Pain. Thought, fuck it. Let it hurt. Had worse in the ring, yeah, and anyway doesn't matter, it's like the Boosts, same thing, really. *You deserve it, Lucy. You do. Boosts, shoulder, this. What you did two years ago?*

Rubbed the gash, hard. Felt it burn.

You deserve the fucking pain.

One more deep breath, then she left the bathroom, walked to her desk. Grabbed her phone. They let her keep that for now, thank God. Swiped it across her stomach. Looked down at the number on the screen.

8.2.

8.2, right after a Boost?

Fuck.

Maybe I deserve this, too.

Her head began to spin. Tired. *So fucking tired.* She walked into the kitchen, bare feet cold on the tile. Didn't bother flicking on the light. Opened the fridge door, but she already knew: no more coffees, no more Cokes. Said, "Rats," but it didn't really matter, anyway. She hadn't slept in sixty hours. Caffeine could only do so much.

Screamers will be bad tonight. I know it.

And there's fuck all I can do.

Lucy shut the fridge. Stared out the grubby kitchen window, down to the deserted car park behind the flat. Rubbish everywhere. Rough sleeper camped next to the skip. She ran her fingers through her hair, thought about two years ago. About running past that car park, down Goswell Road, into the darkness. Panting. Chasing.

Thought about raising the gun.

And then everything after, all of it, just a row of jet-black dominoes, falling, one after another, *clack clack clack*, all the way up to the end, up to the Thing. The Thing that caused the Debt, the Debt she could never pay, not now, not even a proper cop any more, *fuck*.

Enoch Clapham's voice in her head: "We forget at our peril." *Yeah, well, we remember at our peril, too...*

Her eyelids began to close. Forced them open, but she was dizzy now. Nauseous. Sleep was coming. Almost here. She knew it, knew all sleep's moves, every feint and dip and jab. She shook her head. *Not yet.* Padded back into the bedroom, past the stack of empty drink cans and the pull-up bar, to the centre of the room, the spot where the bed had once been. Sat down cross-legged on the threadbare carpet. Stared at the black wall in front of her. Felt her mind drifting, but she tucked her chin, gritted her teeth.

Not going down easy.

Forced herself to fight it, to think—think about something, anything.

Think about the case. Mustn't let it go. Pay the Debt, only chance. A deep breath.

Think about Orange Trainers. Out there. I'll fucking find you. Her head wobbled.

Clapham. Vile. Know you're in it, dodgy as fuck, figure it out... Straining.

Mr Cox. Found an antidote and...I'll find it and...

Her eyes were slits but she fought it, focused on Cox, on Cox's body. *Blood. Blood on the floor, arms out, tiny room, room like this, bare, bare walls...*Slipping now. *Bed. Desk, books. Red books, a photo...*Eyes closing. *Photo? Odd, something...odd. A photo. One. Photo. And...photo not Veronica. No. Not Helen...*

So odd...

Photo a man...so...

Lucy slumped over, head on the carpet, eyes shut. Black. Last thought:

Who?

And then the Screamers started.

‡ ‡ ‡

Lucy sat in the Brompton caff, staring down at her half-eaten veggie fry-up.

She took a sip of her drink. Rubbed her eyes. She'd been right. Nightmares last night were horrific. When the last one ended, when she screamed herself awake for good, she found she'd crawled into the space under her desk and was balled up, knees to chest, rocking. Panting. Drenched in sweat, cheeks tear-stained.

Her first thought: *I'm in Hell.*

The memory of Cox's photo had come back in the shower. It popped into her mind as she was rinsing her hair, and seconds later she was out, grabbing her phone, dripping water on the tile floor as she tapped out a text to King: "Must speak. Asap. Lead. Caff. Meet me. Bring files. PS phone dying."

Felt a twinge of guilt at the last bit. A lie: her phone was charged.

But I need you here, Ed. Face-to-face. Call won't work. Too easy to get the lead then drop me, thanks Lucy, nice one, now piss off. And you wouldn't just leave me sitting here forever, phone dead, would you, Ed?

Or would you?

Lucy pushed a cold mushroom around her plate. It was nine now. She'd left the flat at quarter to six, been at the caff since seven. King read the text at eight, started typing something, but then the ellipses disappeared. No reply. She pulled her phone from her hoodie pocket, checked for the thirtieth time. Still nothing. Took a deep breath. *He'll show up. Dead cert. Needs a lead. And I need to stay in it, need to help, else it doesn't really count towards the Debt, does it? And besides, he doesn't believe in the antidote, really, no one does, so without me—*

A tinkle as the caff door swung open. King walked in. Olive rain jacket, plain black rucksack slung over one shoulder. He sat down across from her. Frowned.

"You're fucking radioactive," he said. "You know that, yeah?"

Well, good morning to you, too.

She shrugged. "Wilkes threw a bit of a wobbly last night, but I reckon—"

"Wilkes? It's not just Wilkes, Lucy." He put his big forearms on the table, leaned towards her. "Tried to tell you. Listen. The lab tour. The one yesterday, remember?"

A nod. *Course I fucking remember, Ed. It was yesterday. This a lecture? Because only Ma'am gets to lecture…*

"Right," he said. "Well, I watched Hurst. Carefully. Actually sort of charming in an alpha-male, cheeky-bugger sort of way, but something about him just felt *off*. Little things. Took credit for *everything*: science stuff, stuff he didn't even seem to understand. Anyone else tried to speak, he bulldozed them. Some poor sod in a lab coat tried to correct him once, Hurst bit his fucking head off. The DCs lapped it all up, but I knew straight away. Knew what he was." Paused. "Man's a total fucking narcissist."

No shit.

"Clearly…" she said.

"Right, 'clearly', fine, but I mean, the real deal. Clinical. I'm positive. Had a DCI once, same thing. Fucking nightmare. Literally didn't give a single solitary shit about anyone else. Problem was, Hurst had his eye on you. Told you that. And I knew the second he saw you again, he'd try it on. And of course, you'd tell him to bugger off."

And you wanted to protect me, I know, and I don't fucking need it, so…

King kept talking. "So, fine. Let him try. You can handle yourself, yeah? Not like you need protecting, think *that* was pretty clear even before you practically broke the man's fucking jaw."

Oh.

"Thing is," he said, "bloke like that? True narcissist? Deep down, he's insecure. You say no, it bursts his little bubble. So then he has to destroy you. Tear you to shreds, prove you're rubbish, never wanted you anyway. Not the best atmosphere for questioning, yeah? Why I tried to keep you apart." He sighed. Rubbed his jaw. "And that's if you turn him down the normal way."

Oh fuck.

"So if I deck him?"

"See for yourself," he said. "Mind?" Pointed at her phone. She nodded, pushed it across the table. "Here," he said, tapping. "If you deck him, Lucy, you get *this*." Showed her.

The article's headline read: Cox CEO slams "disgraceful" Met.

She started reading. Stopped, looked up, eyes wide. "He went after the *Commissioner*?"

"Keep going. Mayor, too. *And* he tweets. Nasty ones. Five so far today."

Fuck fuck fuck.

"*Rats*," she said.

"Yes. Rats. So right now? You? You're a fucking leper."

He sat back. Crossed his arms.

Fuck.

Geoff Hurst, you may not be a killer, but you're a world-class wanker. And as for you, Ed…

She put the phone down. Exhaled. Stared across the table at King, at his stubble, his green eyes. For a second, she wanted to tell him. All of it, everything, about the Thing and the Debt and her monitor levels dropping, why she needed this, he'd understand, knew he would. *But I can't. No sharing. Not how it works, not for me. But then again…I do need this. Truly.*

And you need my lead.

So…

Afraid this is going to get uncomfortable for you, Ed.

"May be a leper," she said. Paused. "But I'm a leper with a lead."

"You said. And I'm here. So tell me."

She shook her head. "Not that simple. I need to stay involved."

"Christ." He chuckled. "Didn't I just tell you? Radioactive, remember? Can you imagine if Wilkes found out? What she'd think? Or the Chief Super?"

Lucy pushed her plate aside. Leaned forward, stared at him. "But what do *you* think, Ed?"

Come on. I need you on board.

And you need me.

He turned away. She watched him knit his brow and stare at the grubby caff wallpaper. Noticed he wasn't wearing his aftershave today. Wondered why not, then wondered why she was disappointed. Felt the guilt surge. *Stop. Come on, Lucy. Focus.*

King took a deep breath, then:

"What I think is, Hurst's a wanker. Deserved it. Nice cross, by the way." A tiny grin, then serious again. "And I think you need help, Lucy. Real help. Just like I did. There's no shame."

She frowned. *No lectures.*

"And I do need a lead."

Yes, Ed. Yes, you do.

"But," he said, "most importantly, I think you're stubborn as fuck, and that you're going to do whatever you want anyway. Which means I cave, or I wind up slapping bracelets on you. And I don't want to get punched, so…yeah. Fuck it. You stay involved. *Unofficially.*" A pause. "Now tell me the lead."

*Well…*She pulled her hoodie strings. *Are you playing me, Ed?* Wanted to believe him, but tricky, barely knew him, needed to be sure. "Prove it," she said.

He laughed. "Christ, you're…I wouldn't lie, Lucy. I believe in openness, remember?" Thought about it, then tapped the table twice and stood up. "Fine. I'll prove it. Wait a tick. And PS…your battery's full."

Whoops.

She turned in her seat and watched as he walked up to the till. Ordered something from the man in the greasy apron, paid. A moment later he slid back into his seat, holding a large glass of frothy brown liquid. "Your drink," he said. "Cheers." Swallowed a big mouthful. Coughed.

Lucy smiled at him. *Not bad, yeah?*

Another cough. "Right. Well. Burns a bit, but not bad, actually."

Told you.

"So," he said, "believe me now? I'm with you. Keep you involved, best I can. Okay?"

She thought about it.

Don't have much choice, really, do I? So fine.

Let's do this.

"Cox had a framed photo on his desk," she told him. "Man, twenties. Brown hair, blue eyes, high cheekbones."

He rolled his eyes. "I drank this for *that*?"

Lucy frowned. *Said you liked it. And, anyway, don't you see?* "That room was bare, yeah? Little monastic cell. Your words. Room like that? Every single thing in there had meaning to him. Must have done."

A shrug. "If you say so."

"I do." *Trust me, Ed. I know all about bare rooms.* "So why *that* photo? Not Helen. Not Veronica. To be honest, didn't think anything of it at the time. Reckoned it was a son. Brother, maybe. But Cox didn't have either. Checked." Her eyes were shining. "So, who?"

"I don't know," said King. "Tell me. Who?"

"I don't know either. But we need to find out. Listen. Cox developed an antidote—"

"No, Lucy—"

"He *did*. I know it. And he kept it secret. But *someone* knew. Who? How about that man? The man who was so bloody important that Cox kept his photograph, *only* his, in a tiny little bare room like that?" She smiled at King. *Admit it, Ed. It's a lead.* "Here, I'll show you. You brought the files? Have the scene photos?"

He nodded. Reached into the black rucksack at his feet, pulled out a paper folder. "Fine. Have a go." Slid it across the table to her.

Perf. Lucy dug through the folder, pulled out a photograph. Plunked it down next to her plate. "See, right..." Frowned. "Hang on." Pulled out a second photograph. Another frown. "I don't understand," she said. Started to flip through the entire stack.

"What?" asked King.

Lucy stared up at him.

"The photo," she said. "The one I saw. It's gone."

‡ ‡ ‡

"This is fucking insane," said King. "You know that, right?"

The Toyota was parked in a grimy Westminster alley. It was raining. Lucy took a sip from her Coke bottle, stared out the window at the building across the street. Three storeys, brick, dirty white placard with small black letters, easily missed:

METROPOLITAN POLICE, SPECIAL IDENTIFICATION UNIT

A big steel door.

She hated that door.

Hated walking through it back when this was her unit, her first one, before Wilkes and homicide and MIT19. Back when work meant another day of sitting, staring at faces on a screen, feeling her gears turn over and over and over until her eyes burned and her head ached. *When I was nothing but the Party Trick. And now I'm back, welcome home, Lucy, and fuck me because I'm a leper and official suspension and because what I need most in the entire fucking world is stuck behind that goddamn fucking door.* She took a breath. "It's the only way," she said.

"You're sure?"

A nod. *You know another database with 40,000,000 faces, we can try that one instead.*

King frowned. Took a last sip of coffee, then glanced down at his cheap watch.

It was half ten. They'd spent another hour at the caff, King on his mobile, Lucy listening in. Tried Veronica Cox: *A photo? In Dad's study? Never really went in, sorry.* Salford was sent to lock-up to ask Helen. Nothing. King found out there was an hour window between when they'd left Cox's body and when the techs took the crime scene shots. The uniform guarding the front door to the flat had bunked off by then. Anyone could've nicked the desk photo. *Could've been a cop,* King had said. *Could've been the killer,* Lucy told him. *Could've come back for it. Might even be his photo, yeah? I saw the face. Can match it to a name, no probs, know just where to go.*

And now here they were.

King sighed. "It's just, it's chock full of people with your… you know…"

Abnormal fusiform face area?

"Super Recognizers," she said.

"Right. Super Recognizers. An entire fucking unit. Must be what, twenty in there? Thirty?" His big paw crumpled the empty

Costa cup. "And every one of them can ID you instantly? Christ." A sigh. "And we can't be seen together because you're—"

"Radioactive?" *Said it like five times now, Ed. Want to go for six? No?*

She flipped up her hood.

Then time to get cracking.

Lucy opened her door, got out. Raining hard now. Big drops soaked her hoodie as she marched across the alley towards the brick building. Beside her, King's voice, muffled through the hoodie: "Remember, they catch you, you're done. Dismissed, no warning. Gone."

Relax, Ed. We'll be fine.

I hope.

They reached the big steel door. She grabbed the handle, then glanced over at him. "Just do like I told you, yeah?" Watched him nod. *Right. Then here we go.* Took a deep breath.

They went inside.

The SIU lobby was quiet. No furniture, bare white walls. An electronic gate blocked their way. Next to it, a receptionist with wire-rimmed specs frowned at a Sudoku puzzle. Lucy turned away. Receptionists weren't Supers, hadn't been in her day, anyway, but no point taking chances. She held her breath and listened as King stepped forward. *Come on, Ed. Just like I told you. Flash your badge, scribble in the little black logbook, nod at me and say—*

"Homicide vic's sister." King's voice was even. "Helped ID the killers. Signs of Super ability. Bringing her in for testing." A pause, then: "Cheers."

The gate slid open.

See, Ed? Told you it would work.

"Easy enough," he whispered, as they walked through. "But the next bit…"

She ignored him. Stared straight down, focused on her grimy black trainers as they squeaked along the corridor. It was simple, really. Risky, but simple. She'd told him everything as they'd driven in from Brompton: *Super sees me dead on? Bang. Instant ID. But from the side? Different story. Doesn't work in profile. Don't know why to be honest, just doesn't. So if I flip my hood and stare at the floor, reckon we should be fine. Just can't look up.*

But if someone notices? he'd asked. *Stops us?*

She'd shrugged. *Then we bloody run.*

They turned right. Another corridor, this one busy, full of chattering Supers. Voices everywhere. Lucy jammed her hands into her hoodie pockets, felt her pulse racing. *Keep calm. Must keep calm.* Forced herself to think about the lead. Good lead, great actually, she should be happy; might be the killer himself, yeah? *Just, no one fucking stop us now. Please.*

"So far, so good," King said, voice low. "Nearly there."

She kept her head down. Tried to picture where they were on the map she'd drawn for him as they sat in his car. *Right, that must be the grotty little kitchen then, still smells like cabbage. Which means, now we turn left. Past the testing rooms, all those fucking tests, Christ. Left again. Go through a door, brill, then straight away it starts getting darker and then—*

"Oh fuck," King said.

Here we are, then.

She didn't need to look up. Saw it in her mind's eye: a huge room, lights dimmed. No windows. Rows and rows of desks, a hundred, more, each with a set of twinned monitors on top. And each with a Super staring at grainy CCTV footage as it flickered on the screens. Lucy sniffed. It smelt like eye drops. *Christ, I hated this fucking place.*

"So many," he whispered. "You didn't say…"

Well, then you wouldn't have agreed, would you?

And I need this. So focus, Ed.

They kept walking. She held her breath. Knew they were in the thick of it now, that any one of the hundred Supers around them might be staring at her right this moment. Might be walking up, reaching out to tap her and then it would all be up, end of, game fucking over.

Hurry, Ed. Please?

She heard his rain jacket rustle as he looked around the room. She'd told him exactly what to look for: big cubicle in the rear, high walls, set back from the desks. *Looks like a giant black phone box, no windows, can't miss it. So how are you missing it, Ed? Ed? Come on, how the fuck are you—*

"There," he said.

Finally. She followed him as he threaded through desks, past Super after Super until the mouse clicks grew faint. Turned right, and there it was: the LFR terminal. One old monitor, one crap keyboard, 40,000,000 fully indexed faces. And no one could see her work.

"Perf," she said. Slid into the seat, clicked the mouse. The monitor flashed on. At the top of the screen: PND Live Facial Recognition Database. Lucy smiled.

King stood behind her, just outside the cubicle. "How long do you reckon this takes, then?"

"Oh, well…" She took a deep breath, began to do the maths. *Filter for gender, race, eyes, hair, Survivor. Then the face ratios, nose types, all that. Down to maybe…three k? Then two per second, fast but I can do it, that's, what?* "Thirty minutes?"

"Fine," he said. "I'll just wait over there and—"

Suddenly, from somewhere across the room: "*Oi. King? That you?*"

Fuck.

She knew that voice.

Fucking Sykes. Here?

"I'll handle him," King whispered. "Hurry."

Hurry? Lucy clicked into the database and began to type. She could hear King talking. He'd stopped Sykes, but they couldn't be more than twenty feet away. *Hold him, Ed. Somehow.* Finished filling in the fields, blinked hard, hit return. Faces began to flash across the screen, two per second. She felt the Party Trick working: *Not you. Not you. Not you.*

Meanwhile, in the background, she heard their voices:

King: Andy? What're you doing here?

Sykes: BTP sent the Tube footage. We get six of these freaks to help.

King: Tube footage? Thought that was Salford?

Sykes: Well...

She tried to block out Sykes's voice, focus on the faces streaming across the monitor—*not you, not you, not you*—but words kept slipping through: "See...bird in the corner there... last Christmas...blowie in the loo...thought maybe..." Voices getting louder, closer. *Fuck. Go away.* Sykes again: "Waste of time...Meat's a Meat, all look the same..." She tugged her hoodie strings, stared at the screen. *Need to go faster...*

She clicked the mouse: *Five per second.*

The faces sped up.

No. No. No. No.

Sykes: So, what've you got there, then?

King: Nothing. Lead. Looks crap...

Go away, Sykes.

No. No. No. No.

Sykes: Lead? What, more CCTV?

King: Nah, it's shit, really...

Sykes: Mind if I...

Fuck. Clicked again. Faster.

No no no no no...

Sykes: Come on, just a squiz...

King: Waste of time...

Eyes burning. Screen a blur.

No no no no no....

Sykes: The fuck, Ed? Just wanna see…

No no no no no….

King: No, listen, stop…Andy…*don't…*

No no no no no…WAIT.

THERE.

She clicked the mouse. *Rewind, come on, come on.* And there, on the screen: the face. *Got you! But…Sykes sees me, I'm fucked…* She heard them getting closer and closer, *can't run, fuck,* Sykes louder, *trapped,* almost on her now, *oh fuck oh fuck* and then:

King: Andy, come on, how about a swift one?

A pause.

Then she heard Sykes laughing, and King said something she couldn't catch, and their voices began to fade away. She took a deep breath. Exhaled. *Nice one, Ed.* Steadied herself, then looked back at the face on the screen. Smiled.

You. It's you.

The face from the photograph.

A twenty-something man stared out from the monitor. Brown hair, blue eyes, high cheekbones. *Definitely you. I recognize that face. But who the fuck ARE you?* Her eyes flitted down the screen. Robert Jordan Cates, DOB 13/05/99. *Right. Hiya, Rob. Murdered anyone recently?* Checked the employer field: Cox Laboratories Pty Ltd. *Interesting. Very.* And then she frowned. Pushed back the hoodie, ran fingers through her short brown hair.

Oh.

Rob Cates wasn't the killer.

He wasn't Orange Trainers, hadn't swiped the photo.

Rob Cates was dead.

CHAPTER FIFTEEN

"It'll work," Lucy told King an hour later. "Just focus on your bit and…oh, brill, he's here."

She rang off and watched as Coffee No. 6 stormed into the Caffè Nero. He was sopping wet. Didn't bother to wipe his feet on the mat, just marched straight to the back of the queue and stood, panting, fiddling with the zip on his rain-slicked jacket. Looked upset, she thought. *Fair enough. Someone calls, says she's a barista at your coffee shop. Says she found your wallet, course it's yours, mate, don't be silly, got eight credit cards in your name and your contact details inside.*

But your wallet's in your pocket.

Reckon it's only natural you'd be a bit nervy, yeah?

He reached the front of the queue. Only got a few words out before the barista stopped him. Pointed across the shop, to where Lucy was sitting in the corner, sipping her drink.

She waved her Coke bottle.

Hiya, Coffee No. 6.

A frown, then he recognized her. Headed over. She nodded at a chair and he sat down, jacket still on, rain dripping from his mop of curly orange hair. "Officer?" he said. "What, you? I don't understand…" His fingers crept back to the zip. "Listen, someone called. Barista, twenty minutes ago, said they found—"

"There is no wallet."

He stared at her.

"Rob Cates," she said. "Worked at Cox Labs? Remember him?"

"Cates, yeah, sure…" Another frown. "Sorry, did you just say there *is* no wallet? Because I practically ran here from the lab. My mum had her identity stolen last year, nasty business, still getting rung up at all hours by debt collectors swearing at her in Russian, and I thought—"

Focus, Coffee No. 6.

"No," she said. "Sorry. Just needed you here, straight away. It's important."

"Important?" Still catching his breath. "Right, fine, but... look, I don't understand. Why the wallet bit, then? Just call and ask. Or come by the lab, whichever, but why scare me, make me bloody sprint over to Caffè Nero when it's pissing down and... *oh.* Oh. Wait, hang on. Think I get it." A slow grin. "Yes. That's brilliant." Slapped the tabletop, big laugh. "Fucking brilliant. It was *you*, wasn't it?"

Hmm.

"I rang you, yes. Not the coffee shop."

Bit thicker than I thought...

"No, no. I mean, yes, of course, but...I know why you didn't just come to the lab. You *couldn't.* Not allowed, right? Because *you're* the cop that dropped Geoff Hurst."

Lucy sat up in her chair. Hurst hadn't mentioned the punch itself to the papers, not exactly. Police misconduct, yes. Truly awful, scandalous, Met should be ashamed. But being decked by a woman? That bit, specifically? Not something he seemed keen to get out there.

So how do YOU know, Coffee No. 6?

"Hurst's PA," he said, reading her stare. "Watching from the jet window. Hates him, of course. Told his executive assistant, the one with all the nervous breakdowns. *She* told half the lab. Spread like wildfire—some little female cop knocked out Geoff bloody Hurst with one punch? Best goss *ever.*"

Little?

"Tell me about Cates," she said.

"Well." He put his elbows on the table. "Thing is, our GC pinged an email round this morning. All police inquiries go

through him, no exceptions. But for you? The Hurst Slayer?"
Another chuckle. "Sure, fine, yeah. Fuck it. Rob Cates. What
can I tell you?"

That's more like it.

"What do you know?" she asked.

"About Cates? Well..."

The woman at the next table coughed.

He glanced over. Frowned. Reached into the pocket of
his jacket, pulled out a tiny bottle of hand sanitizer. As he
squeezed it onto his palm, the woman coughed again. "Perhaps
we could...," he began. Looked around for another table, but
the coffee shop was full. "Sorry," he said, "but would you mind
terribly if we walked?"

One more cough.

Lucy shrugged. "Fine." Watched him rub his hands together.
*You work in a lab with enough nerve agent to kill every Vulnerable in
London three times over. And you're scared of a cold?* She drained
her Coke bottle, looked over to the espresso machines. "Just a
tick, actually. Want anything?"

Five minutes later, they were walking north across St Dunstan's
churchyard.

Still raining, but lighter now, a drizzle. She could see the five
chimneys of Cox Labs HQ rising up in the distance, towering
over the old stone church. Coming at it from the rear this
time, so no car park, thank Christ, no attacks or flashbacks.
But still: memories flickered. Lucy wished she could flip up
her hood.

Beside her, Coffee No. 6 was apologizing.

"Know I seem like a nutter," he said. "But it happens. Common
in my field, actually. Read one too many epidemiological articles
in the biochem journals, suddenly every time someone coughs
you...*Jesus.*" He watched, horrified, as Lucy made her drink.
"Really? Christ, you must have a stomach of iron."

She let the foam rise to the top of the bottle. Binned the empty paper cup, then took a sip. "Bit sensitive, actually," she said. *Ask your boss.* "So. Cates. Tell me."

"Right." He paused, and they walked a few steps in silence. "Sorry, just trying to remember everything. Been awhile now, is all. He left the lab a few years back. Just sort of vanished. Very like him, actually."

"Like him how?"

"Mysterious, I mean. Bit of an odd duck, Cates. Loner, all that. Intense. Genius, though. Least, that was the word round the lab. Young, late twenties, only a few years out of grad school. Sort of Flinders's little protégé."

Protégé? Hmm. Is protégé enough to get your photo on a desk?

"And what exactly did he do?"

A shrug. "Not sure, to be honest. Never worked with him. No one did, actually. Had his own little lab, reported directly to Flinders. Rob Cates, Director of Special Projects. I remember the title because it caused a bit of a bunfight. Twenty-something Director? Some noses out of joint at that one, believe you me."

She nodded. *Try making DI at twenty-nine.* "Any noses in particular?"

"Well…" He thought about it. "No, not especially. Just a bit of whinging here and there."

Lucy made a mental note: Rob Cates had enemies.

Interesting.

"So," she said, "who else at Cox Labs might know what Cates was working on?"

"No one, really. Worked solo. Not even a lab tech."

"No reports, circulars, nothing like that?"

He shook his head. Rain dribbled down his forehead. "Don't think so," he said. "None that I ever saw. Not really the culture. Still fairly small until two years ago, remember. Flinders liked to run things like an academic lab. Group meetings, let's all go round the table and give updates." A shrug. "And Cates never said a word."

They passed a few old gravestones, inscriptions worn away. Lucy took a sip of her drink.

So Cates has a secret lab, then hey, presto, dead.

Mr Cox has a secret lab. Dead.

Not a coincidence…

"Right," said Coffee No. 6, as they reached the church. "Afraid that's all I know about Rob Cates, really." He waved towards the Cox Labs building. "And my lunch break's long gone. So…mind if I head back?" Waited for her to nod. She exhaled: not happy about it, clearly, but what could she do? Gave the nod. "Cheers," he said. "And, nice punch. If I think of anything…"

Lucy watched him walk away.

Fuck.

She tugged her hoodie strings, thought about her monitor: down to 6.9 when she'd checked it in the manky Caffè Nero toilet, barely noon, fucking terrifying. *Boosts might stop working soon. Any day now. Any minute, really, no way to know exactly when.* She took a breath. Focused. *Cates is still a good lead, though. Secret lab? Brilliant. Might've been working on anything in there, antidote research, something that connects. But how do I find out what? No reports, Cox dead, Cates dead, everyone fucking dead, and unless I can figure it out, sort it some way, then it's another dead fucking end and—*

Coffee No. 6 stopped walking.

He turned around, came back. Smiled at her.

"Lab notebooks," he said.

Yes! Brilliant. Perf.

And those are…?

"We keep lab notebooks," he told her. "Everyone does, have to; it's how you document your experiments. Even Cates must have done. There's a whole room full of them, going back to the start, back when we were just researching pesticides. Can't

196

remove them, I'm afraid, but I can get access. Just give me a few days."

She frowned. "Don't have a few days."

"Well, okay, but—"

"Now. Has to be. And I want to see for myself."

Can't risk it. You change your mind, go running to Hurst, I'm fucked.

He shook his head. "No way. Look, I'm sorry, but if Hurst sees you, or anyone else—"

"Who else would even know I'm a cop?"

"Still. Sorry. No. Not even for the Hurst Slayer."

She pulled out her mobile. Sighed. *Didn't want to do this, truly, seems a good enough bloke.* Then she thought of Dad, ashes in a pit nearby. Of all the Vulnerables buried here, hundreds, thousands even. *There's an antidote. I know it. And that means no more deaths, no more copycat attacks, fuck you, London Black, but clock's ticking so apologies, Coffee No. 6. Needs must.* Tapped the phone, then started to read out loud:

"Nightmare. Total bloody nightmare…no grasp of toxicology…ah, best bit. Wouldn't know an antidote from his Auntie Vera." Stopped. Looked at him. "Remember?"

Remember saying all that?

He shrugged—*yeah, and?*—then it hit him. "No. No, you can't." Stared at her: shock, disgust. "You wouldn't, surely. I don't believe it." He turned, tried walking away, but she caught up. "I told you that in confidence," he said. "I was helping you, remember? So now you'd what, tell Hurst? Grass? Tell that wanker, get me sacked, just because I won't put my job on the line, for fuck's sake, that *can't* be legal…"

Lucy grabbed his arm. Looked him in the eye.

I need this.

"It's happening," she said. "So come on. We need to hurry."

‡   ‡   ‡

197

Open. Come on. Fucking OPEN.

Lucy frowned at the red metal door. She was standing outside the Cox Labs building. A side entrance: grim little courtyard, fag ends everywhere, overflowing skip. Smelt like chemicals, wasn't sure which. *Si would know.* No one around. She checked her mobile. Two. Thirty minutes since Coffee No. 6 left to go let her in.

Better not have grassed on me, Coffee No. 6.

She'd already rung King back. Told him she had a lead, good one, any luck finding out how Cates died? *Not much*, he'd said. *Rough going, actually.* Sighed. *Cates died during the Scourge. Know that much, death registered, but no cause listed. Records complete crap. Fucking useless. System was just so over-whelmed then.* Another sigh; Lucy pictured him sitting in the Toyota, cracking his big knuckles. *Might've been London Black, but he's not in the memorial list. Ditto the Iso Centre rolls. So I'm thinking, Lucy—if you wanted to kill someone, the Scourge wasn't such a bad time to do it...*

She'd told him, yes, her thought too, question is *why*. Why kill Rob Cates? Told him it must've been Cates's work with Cox, dead cert, just needed to find out what that work *was*, exactly.

And now here she was. At Cox Labs.

Ready to find out.

If this fucking thing would just—

The door cracked open.

Coffee No. 6 stuck his head out. "Coming?"

Lucy stepped inside, pulled the door shut. Glared at him: *About time, thought you'd pissed off.* Looked around. They were at one end of a short corridor, nothing ahead but a big set of metal doors. Chilly inside, air con in winter. She shoved her hands into her hoodie pockets as they walked. *Don't you get scared of catching cold, Coffee No. 6?*

They reached the metal doors. "Here," he said. "Take this." Tossed her a lanyard with an ID pouch. The card inside read: VISITOR. "Had a spare in my desk, should do the trick."

She slipped it on over her hoodie.

"And if anyone talks to you," he told her, "don't say *anything*. Nothing. Too easy to get caught out. Just look to me, I'll handle it." Paused. "You're a mute, got it?"

Lucy nodded.

Lucky you told me. Do tend to witter on...

The doors led to a small lobby. She followed as he turned right down a busy corridor, then jogged up three flights of an internal stairwell. Popped out, turned left, left, then right again. Everything white: floors, walls, ceiling. Spotless. CCTV cameras everywhere, she noticed. Didn't bother turning away, just looked straight ahead, focused on oncoming traffic. *No way some bloke in a video room spots me. But someone from yesterday? Want to see them coming.*

"Getting close now," said Coffee No. 6, voice low, as they sped past a kitchen. "Around this next corner, there's a door. Locked. Your pass won't work, but I'll tap us through. Stick close." He nodded to a passing lab tech. "Hiya, Bill." Back to her, quietly again: "Meant to be one person through at a time, and the system's fiddly. Don't want it to close on you."

"Got it."

Nearly there. Brill. She thought about Rob Cates's notebook as they rounded the corner. Felt excited, might be anything in there, really, early antidote studies, formulas. Anything. *And once I know what he was working on, I can work out who would nick his photo, and then from there all I need is—*

Oh fuck.

The door in front of them was an airlock.

In the middle, all caps:

"Bit of a short cut through the hot side," he said. "Avoids the hallway where Hurst sits."

She took a breath. *Right, okay, fine.* Tried to work out what her levels were, hadn't checked since the coffee shop toilet. *So, heard three beeps outside, that's 6.5. But not down to 6 yet, ways to go before 5, reckon it's fine. It'll be fine, has to be.*

"Keep close," he said. Glanced around, then pulled an ID from his trouser pocket. Tapped it on a grey sensor next to the door. Green lights flashed. A click: the door slid open. He walked through, turned, waved her in. "Hurry. Before someone sees."

Lucy ran fingers through her hair. Thought about Cox. The Debt. The antidote.

Decided, fuck it.

She stepped through.

Another click as the airlock door slid shut behind her.

It'll be fine. She exhaled, rubbed her tattoo. *Just watch out for me, Jack.*

"Come on," Coffee No. 6 said. They were in a long corridor now, big windows on one side, whitewashed brick on the other. He pointed to a window. "Have a quick look down there. Great view."

Lucy moved closer. Looked through the thick glass, down into a giant room, fifty feet below. High glass walls divided it into a string of sealed-off workspaces, five of them, airlocks in between. Five toxicology labs, each filled with blinking machines, chemicals, dozens of scientists in green hazmat suits and face shields. Coiled red air hoses hung from orange ceiling vents.

"Those are our main research labs."

"Oh," she said, then froze. Realized: *I know that place.* Remembered it from two years ago, walls lined in plastic, filled with rows and rows of beds, screaming patients, IV drips. Blood.

Saw herself, running, furious, leaving a trail of bloody footprints as she stormed away from Dad.

Ward five.

A tear welled up. She turned away, wiped it. Took a breath. Focused.

"It's brilliant," she said.

He didn't notice the catch in her voice, just kept talking as they walked along. "That's where Cox gate sniffers were invented," he told her, waving at a lab with an orange floor. The floor in each lab was a different colour, she saw: orange on the far right, then green, blue, grey, black. "Those three are all Ultra research. Have a few employees using prototypes now, hoping it helps speed up the launch."

She nodded.

U for Ultra. Hurry up, lads.

"And that," he said, pointing to the lab with the black floor, "is the Black Lab. Like the dog, but *not* friendly. Team in there is working with new LB compounds. Nasty stuff. Horrible. Just trying to stay ahead of the curve, really. Never know what terrorists will cook up next, but it won't be pleasant."

Another nod. She thought of Simon, scribbling on his prescription pad: *It's* not *tear gas.*

They kept walking.

"How about antidotes?" she asked. "Is that in Orange, or...?"

Coffee No. 6 shrugged. "Not a core area for us, to be honest," he said. "Shedload of academics focused on antidotes, not as much in the industrial space. All years away, from what I've read. For the time being, we're focusing on prophylactics and detection, which are the main things, really, but—"

RRRRRRRRING—

An alarm blared. Lights flashed.

She stopped. Looked around, eyes wide.

Fuck. Fucking cameras. Spotted me.

Can't get caught here. Mustn't. Go, go, get the fuck out...
RRRRRRRRING—

As she started to run, Coffee No. 6 grabbed her arm.

"No," he hissed. "Stop."

The fuck?

What, a trap? You?

She twisted, pushed him away, started to run back but remembered:

The door was locked.

Fuck fuck fuck.

She stared at Coffee No. 6.

"*Stop*," he said. Voice louder.

He has a key. Could take it, need to, only way, do it—

RRRRRRRRING—

Raised her fists. Tucked her chin, moved towards him.

"Look," he yelled. "Just, please, *look*."

He pointed to the room below. She gave a quick glance over—*another trap? Tricking me?*—then stopped. Realized what was happening. Took a deep breath, lowered her hands.

"*See?*"

She saw. Downstairs, giant steel gates were slamming shut, one after another, blocking the airlocks and sealing off the individual labs. The hazmat-suited scientists were still working away, ignoring the chaos.

"For fuck's sake," he gasped. "Calm down. It's just a fucking test. The lockdown system, in case there's a spill. Test it daily."

Oh.

The alarm stopped.

"Right," she said.

"Jesus," said Coffee No. 6, "you were really ready to fight me, weren't you?" He shook his head. A lock of damp orange hair fell down over one eye. "Going to get me sacked *and* beat me up? Pfft. Starting to see Hurst's point of view."

Lucy frowned at him.

No need to get sarky, now.

"If I'm caught here," she told him, "it's bad. Very."

"Yeah, well, it's not great for me, either. So let's get this fucking over with."

Couldn't have put it better.

The end of the corridor fed into a small room with multiple exits. She smiled to herself as he tapped through another airlock, back out to the cold side. *Better.* The decor changed as they walked: less like a lab, more like the corporate headquarters she'd seen the day before. Offices, copy machines, carpets. As they passed a meeting room, she spotted Coffee No. 2—*long nose, flat cheekbones, pointy jaw*—but turned away before he could see her.

Two minutes later, Coffee No. 6 slowed to a stop in front of a wooden door.

"Here we are," he said.

Overhead lights turned on automatically as they entered. A small, musty room: doorway at the rear, low wooden table in the middle, bookcases lining the walls to the right and left. Prim rows of leather-bound binders filled one bookcase. The shelves of the other sagged with the weight of hundreds of pressboard-covered notebooks.

"Corporate records," said Coffee No. 6, pointing to the leather binders. Walked over to the notebooks, crouched down. "And *these* are what we're after. Lab notebooks. Use electronic ones now, but two years ago, all paper." He pulled one from the shelf, stared at the cover. Slid it back. "Chronological. So, let's see, Cates…say, mid-2027…" Another notebook was pulled out, checked, returned. "Hmm. Bit later…"

Lucy watched him search.

Somewhere in that bookshelf is the key to this case…

"Ah," he said. "Here."

She smiled.

He grabbed a notebook, turned, plunked it down on the table. "Right. Let's see." Spread it open. "Should be at the back…" Lucy walked over, looked at it upside down as he flipped. Page after page of quadrille paper was filled with numbers, charts, graphs. Coffee No. 6 muttered to himself as he read. Finally: "That's odd." He tapped a finger on a table of figures. "See this bit right here? Thing about that is…" He stopped. Looked up, over her shoulder.

Lucy turned around.

Oh, fuck.

The Cox Labs GC was standing in the doorway.

‡ ‡ ‡

Don't recognize me. Please, God, don't recognize me.

Lucy held her breath as the GC squinted at her. He tilted his head. Frowned.

"Wait," he said, "aren't you…?"

Fuck.

Coffee No. 6 stood up straight. "She's a visitor," he said. "Academic, from UCL."

The GC ignored him. Stared at Lucy. "No," he said, "I remember you. Yesterday, walked you to the room, right? You're a cop. Not dressed like one, but you bloody well are." A snort. "Incredible. Wasn't I clear enough with the Chief Superintendent this morning? Thought I was. Fucking crystal, actually." Voice rising. "Going forward, *all* police requests come to me, personally, *in writing*, and that most certainly includes whatever the hell it is you're doing in here."

She said nothing.

Just took a step backwards, towards the table. Another. Glanced down at the notebook.

There's something in there.

"You need to leave, Officer. Right now. I insist. Actually, wait, no…"

Something important. Know it.

"…no, actually, *don't* leave. Stay. Don't move. I'm calling security. Security escort. Stay right *there*." He pointed to a chair. "Right there, don't move." Turned, left the room.

Another glance at the notebook.

I leave it here, word gets around, killer hears. It vanishes. Gone. Can't let that happen.

"Fuck," said Coffee No. 6. "I'm so fucked."

Lucy looked at him.

Sorry, No. 6. Truly, I am.

But—

She reached over, grabbed the notebook.

"Wait," he cried, but she was gone. Running out the door, down the hall, flying past doorways, offices, people. Eyes up, searching.

Exit, need an exit…where the fuck is the exit…

She hit a junction.

Looked left. Right.

Somewhere behind her, a voice: "*Stop!*"

Fuck…

Saw an exit sign.

There.

Dashed towards it. Pushed through a door, into a stairwell. Down three flights, spiralling, footsteps ringing out: *chunk chunk chunk*. Shouts from above as she reached the bottom, *thump*, shot out the door, into a corridor. Stopped.

Another junction. No signs.

Right? Left? Right?

Went left.

Ran around a corner. Up ahead: the lobby. Gleaming. Granite, chrome. She sped up.

Almost there…

"*Oi!* You!"

Saw two security guards running towards her.

Crap.

Spun around, tore back up the hall. Another guard popped out of the stairwell, but she slipped him, kept going, *where the fuck is that exit*, turned left, *fuck me*, right, *fucking maze*, down a long hallway…

More guards appeared ahead.

Blocked.

Looked back. Two others, trailing her.

Trapped.

On her right, a beep: an airlock door slid open. A tech came through. She ran for it, blew past him, *ta*, through the door and sprinting now, fast, *faster*, a blur, past signs, hazmat suits, masks, *must be an exit*, around a corner…

Skidded to a stop.

Oh fuck.

The labs.

A massive chemical weapons symbol hung above the entrance to a decon shower. Warning signs everywhere, yellow and black. On the other side of the glass, a scientist in a blue hazmat suit noticed her. Frowned at her through his face shield. Shook his head, said something.

For a second, they stared at each other.

Then she turned, but it was too late. Footsteps headed towards her. She could hear someone running, getting closer, closer, *fuck fuck fuck*…

And:

It was Coffee No. 6.

"Hey!" he shouted. "Come on."

No. 6? You?

"*Hurry.*" He waved frantically.

She nodded, ran towards him.

"This way." He took off, Lucy on his heels. Ducked through a door, then another, twisting through corridor after corridor. Around a bend, the metal doors appeared. *There you are.* She pushed through them, kept on through the last red door, burst out into the rain.

Oh thank Christ.

She shoved the notebook under her hoodie. Took a breath, then tore down the street, heading east, past a row of terraced houses, big blocks of council flats, a school. Glanced over her shoulder: nothing, no guards, just Coffee No. 6, struggling to keep pace. Two minutes later, she reached a small bridge over a canal and slowed. Still no guards. Waited a moment for Coffee No. 6 to catch up, then turned off the road, down a dirt path to the canal. Doubled back beneath the bridge. Stopped.

Safe.

A moment later he joined her and they stood, hands on knees, panting.

He spoke first. "That went well."

His voice echoed off the graffitied walls. A canal boat floated past.

Lucy exhaled. Ran fingers through her hair. Thought about the GC's face: furious. Knew he'd call the Chief Super, describe her—*female, hoodie, looks a little like...*—and then that was it, she'd be finished, well and truly. *Goodbye, DI Stone. Farewell. Just Lucy now. Fuck me. But...at least I have this.* She reached under her hoodie, pulled out the notebook. It was battered, its black tape binding frayed. Turned it over in her hands, then passed it to Coffee No. 6.

"Show me," she said. "It's why you helped me, yeah?"

It's important. I know it. An antidote?

Tell me it's an antidote.

He nodded. "Saw it straight away." Took the notebook, flipped through. "Look," he said. "See this?" Showed her a page filled with symbols and arrows. "Know what this is?"

Lucy shrugged.

Tell me, No. 6.

"This is the synthesis for Elemidox. How it's made. All the steps, the full process, start to finish. But it isn't the original version." He shook his head. "The original synthesis, the one Flinders Cox developed three years ago, used a different reagent in this step, right here." Pointed to a red arrow. "That one step alone took thirty-five days. It's what caused the Elemidox shortage during the Scourge. We simply couldn't make Boosts fast enough."

She nodded. *One arrow. All those lives…*

"But this?" He tapped the notebook page with his fingers. "*This* is the improved synthesis. Developed later. Cut production time from forty days down to two."

Okay, so…

"Now look at the date," he said. Pointed to the top of the page. In crabbed writing: *7 Nov 2027.*

Lucy frowned. "That's…"

"Yes," he said. "Three days after Waterloo. And look here. Same day, last entry in the notebook." Read it out loud: "*Spoke with FC. Appraised results. Advised urgent adoption of new reagent.*" Paused. "But that didn't happen. Not for weeks. Not until after the Scourge was over." He looked up at her, eyes wide beneath his shaggy orange brows. "Do you realize what this means?"

Oh, Christ.

She nodded.

Pictured Flinders Cox lying on the floor of his tiny study, bathed in blood. Spartan room, blank walls, crap furniture. She knew what a room like that meant. Meant guilt. Guilt, rising up, crushing him like it crushed her, a black tidal wave pounding,

pounding, pounding away until someone finally came along and jammed a fucking cross in his eye. And now she knew why.

Oh, Jesus fucking Christ.

She shut her eyes.

The Boost shortage was artificial.

Remembered the prices rocketing up, day after day. Thousands, tens of thousands a jab.

And someone getting very, very rich.

Her eyes opened.

"It means Flinders Cox wasn't a saint," she said.

He was a fucking monster.

CHAPTER SIXTEEN

"Just saying," said King, "could've done a curry if you'd wanted."

Lucy shrugged. Looked down at her orange polystyrene tray of chips.

What? Don't like chips, Ed?

They were standing in a chip shop behind Angel Tube. Proper chippy, old one, no frills. Cracked tile floor, jar of pickled eggs. Grease. Plastic clock on the wall: half six. She'd called King hours ago, from beneath the canal bridge. Told him about Cox, needed to plan next steps, when could he meet? *Stuck at HQ for a bit*, he'd said. *But six-ish? Over food? Not bothered about what, really, your choice.*

She'd chosen chips.

"So," King said, as he handed the man behind the till a twenty pound note, "don't eat fish, then? Strict veggie?" Took his change. She'd already paid for hers, wrinkled fiver pulled from the bottom of her damp jeans pocket.

"No fish," Lucy told him. Squirted brown sauce on the chips. Faintest hint of a smile. Chips were her favourite, always had been. Ate them with Jack, their little tradition: special treat, day after he fought. She remembered him grinning, rubbing her hair, can't train *all* the time, Luce, can we? Need chips every now and then, yeah? *Like when you find out, oh, know your hero Flinders Cox? Proper fucking villain, actually, world's worst, turns out up is down and black is white and white is fucking black.*

Definitely need chips then.

King picked up his box of cod. Looked around. No tables, just a ledge. He pointed to two stools. "Yeah?" She nodded, grabbed her chips and can of Coke and sat down. He put his black rucksack on the ledge, dropped onto the stool beside her. Loosened the tie from his bull neck. Exhaled. "So."

"So," she said, "next steps."

"Right." He speared a chip from beneath his fish. "Actually, wait, no." Glanced over at her. A cheeky grin. "Listen. How about we eat first? Give the shop talk a rest for a few?" Paused. "It's been so full on. Just need a bit of a breather, is all."

Lucy frowned. Watched his eyes scan her face.

Need a breather, yeah? Or, you think that I do? Because I don't, Ed. What I need is to find the fucking antidote.

"Come on, Stone, just humour me. Few minutes, normal chat." Forked another chip, ate it. "So…know you're a boxer, too. Who's your favourite fighter, then?"

She shrugged.

Leave it out, Ed. Work to do.

He kept pushing. "Come on. Easy question. Favourite fighter, must have one. Every boxer does. Or…" Eyes twinkled. "Maybe I'm wrong about you? Boxing's just a bit of a laugh, then, good way to keep fit? Maybe do a bit of hot yoga, too? Pilates, that's big, or barre or—"

Fuck it.

"Lennox Lewis," she said.

So there.

"Ah." He grinned. Took a swig of his Irn-Bru. "The Lion. A heavyweight. I see." He cut into his cod. The wooden fork looked tiny in his huge hands. "Why Mr Pugilist Specialist, then?"

Lucy ate a chip. Thought about it, about the tatty old poster: Lennox Lewis, gloves up, Big Ben in the background. The one Sellotaped to the wall of her old bedroom, hers and Jack's. Jack liked Lennox Lewis so she did too, course she did, loved when Jack would show her old fights online, explain everything, stances, punches. *Felt happy then.* She shrugged. "Hard puncher. Great against taller opponents."

He chuckled. "They say he had a weak chin."

"*What?* Because of McCall? Rubbish." A dismissive wave of her chip fork. "Got back up, didn't he? Just, ref stopped it early. *Clearly.* I mean, Lennox was the champ, wasn't he? Deserved more time, and anyway he avenged that, yeah?" Her eyes blazed. "Had McCall *crying*, for heaven's sake, and avenged Rahman, too, both of them and…what? *What?*"

King was laughing.

"Nothing," he said. "Only…you're actually smiling."

Well…

Maybe a bit.

"Just saying," she said. Ate another chip. *So good, chips.* "Who's yours, then?"

"Old-timer. Kid Berg. Fought in the thirties. Grew up hearing stories from my Grandad. Nickname was—"

"The Whitechapel Windmill," Lucy said. She grinned at him.

King dropped his fork in mock surprise.

"You know Kid Berg? Wow, proper historian here. How about Jimmy Wilde?"

Come on, Ed. Seriously?

"Course. Legend. Greatest flyweight ever. The Mighty Atom, barely a hundred pounds but he knocked out bantams, yeah? Of course I know Jimmy bloody Wilde."

"Of course." Another laugh. "So, what, did you read about these guys growing up?"

Lucy shrugged. A flicker of memory: framed black-and-white photos of boxers, rows of them, hanging on the back wall of Dad's shop. Simon, standing next to her as she tried to show him, to explain—*you'll like it, Si, it's history, sort of*—but he'd just nodded, bored. She glanced at King. He smiled, a big, wide smile. She smiled back. *Interesting.* Felt a twinge of something, a light feeling, felt nice, *like this guy*—but then the guilt struck, a hard shot, right to the gut, and she frowned, turned her head. Looked away. A deep breath.

Enough.

That's enough.

She closed her tray of chips. Stood up, walked over to the bin, shoved it in. *No chips. Not now, not for you. You owe a Debt, Lucy, and you need to fucking pay it.*

King stared at her.

"Break's over," she told him. Nodded at the door. "Let's go."

‡ ‡ ‡

Outside, the rain had stopped.

The Toyota was parked up by Islington Green, five minutes away. They headed towards it, King sipping his Irn-Bru, Lucy walking beside him, hands in her hoodie pockets. It was dark. Not yet seven: restaurants quiet, pubs already packed. She listened to his update as they wove through a crowd of punters vaping on the pavement.

"Tube CCTV finally showed up," he told her. "BTP sent it to Salford. Today's tie looks like a Quality Street tin, by the way. Christ. Anyway, he's got a team looking for your friend with the orange trainers. Checking footage from every station, see if we can track him. They're using Supers."

She nodded. "Sykes said. At SIU, remember?" *That wanker.*

"Right. Forgot. Christ, Sykes. Did I tell you? Just drank the pint I bought him then pissed right off, the bastard, didn't even offer one back." A disgusted snort. "Not that I wanted it, but still, principle of the thing. And the worst of it is—"

Focus, Ed.

"Any more on Cates's death?"

213

He shrugged. "Nothing. Records from the Scourge are rubbish. Everything was a shambles then." Drained the Irn-Bru, lobbed the can into a passing bin. "Few DCs digging into it, maybe we get lucky. But to be honest? What you found is better. Much. Motive for half of London. The real question is, who else knew? *That's* what we need to sort out."

"No." *Come on, Ed, think about it…* Started to shake her head, but felt dizzy. Tried to remember her last drink, proper one with espresso, not just a Coke. *Need a quick top-up.* Spotted a Starbucks across the street and made for it, King following as she wove through traffic. "No," she told him, as she pushed through the door, "that's *not* it. Killer *didn't* know about what Cox did. Couldn't have done. Else he would've told the world. Why keep it a secret?" Grabbed a Coke from the fridge, ordered, paid. Back to King: "It's all about Cates."

"Well, but think what Cox did, what you found…"

Don't you see?

"Flinders Cox murdered Rob Cates."

He stared. "You reckon?"

Lucy nodded. Took the espresso, *ta*, into the Coke bottle, big sip. Sighed. *Better.* "Cates knew what Cox did, yeah? Cox couldn't chance him talking, so he killed him. Burnt the body. Cates's foot in the kiln, must be." Another sip as she led King back outside. "But someone found out."

"Revenge, then."

"Exactly." Thought of Cox's body. Of the crucifix. "Eye for an eye." *See, Ed?*

They arrived at Islington Green: a little triangle of grass, a few leafless plane trees dotted about. "Other side," King told her. They began to cut across. She noticed a man in a dirty white Survivor mask sleeping rough on a bench. Bent down, put a pound coin in his cup. "So," King said, as he added another, "what next?"

Good question.

"Been thinking," she told him. "You said Cates's death was registered. Body can't register itself, can it? Wasn't a hospital or coroner, they'd list the cause. But it must have been *someone*. Someone knew Cates died, cared enough to register him. So... who?" Pointed to King's rucksack. "Is the death cert in there?"

"No, but..." He pulled out his mobile, began to tap. "I've got it in my inbox, hang on."

"Should say who registered. Look for informant."

She watched him scroll.

Come on...

"Here," he said. "Name of informant...John Johnson."

Johnson? Now where did I...

She frowned, then it hit her.

Brilliant.

"The folder," she said. "One Clapham gave us. At the pub, remember? Still have it?"

King unzipped the rucksack, rooted around. Pulled out the folder. "Here..."

"Perf," she said. Took it, started to flip through. "John Johnson. Look." Showed him. "Founder of the MLF. Location unknown. And somehow connected to Rob Cates." Lucy stared down at the photograph clipped to the file. Two jet-black eyes stared back. "Remember what Enoch Clapham said about them?" she asked. "Violent, dangerous?"

"Clapham's a bellend."

Stay with me, Ed.

"Fair, but he also said the MLF would hate an antidote. What if he's right?" Her husky voice rose. "Then it's simple, yeah? Johnson learns Cox killed Cates, wants revenge, murders him, spots the antidote, nicks it, end of." She looked at King. Smiled.

It all fits. It all fucking fits, know it's right, has to be. Now I just need to find Johnson. And if I take this to Wilkes, maybe she listens. Helps me. She's always helped me...

"Ed," she said, "I think we should tell Wilkes."

"Hmm." King frowned. "Well, about that."

About what?

"Was about to tell you before," he said. Dug his hands into his trouser pockets. "This Hurst kerfuffle, all the press...word is, Wilkes is about to be reduced a rank. Knocked back to DI. There'll be a new DCI."

Oh, fuck no.

Lucy ran her fingers through her hair. Fucking Met politics, she hated it, all just nonsense really. Ignored Wilkes when she tried to talk about it, worse than interior design even, Christ. *But you love it, Ma'am. Good at it. And now someone's making a run at you, some muppet wants your window and thinks, yeah, whole Hurst thing, Wilkes is weak, time to make a play.* "Who? Who's being made up?"

"Well, thing is..." He looked down at his shoes. Took a deep breath. "Bit awkward..."

You?

It's you, Ed? Really? That's what you're like then, is it? Come down from Brum, hi chaps, bang on about openness and trust and lovely green eyes and actually you're just a fucking snake, stabbing Ma'am in the back and—

"Andy Sykes."

Oh.

Oh God fucking bitch shit wanker.

"Rats," she said. Stomped her trainer on the ground. "No. No, no, *no.*" *Fucking fuck.* "Sykes? Bloody *Sykes*? How is that *possible*? That bone-idle, fedora-wearing, stupid...*bleeder*..."

He shook his head sadly. "Bone-idle bleeder with the Chief Super's ear, apparently."

Oh, for fuck's sake.

She tugged on her hoodie strings. Felt like punching

something. Fucking Sykes, *course* it was him, Christ. *And it's all my fault, decking Hurst, all the press, and now Ma'am is out and...*

No.

Took a deep breath. Another. Set her jaw.

No. No, can't let it happen. Has to be a way.

Asked King: "Not official yet, is it?"

"Well—"

His mobile rang. A shrill two-tone: Code Zero, emergency message.

"The fuck?" He checked it, frowned. "Christ." Looked up at Lucy, eyes wide. "Copycat attacks," he told her. "Men spraying aerosols. All central. Soho, Barbican, Mayfair. One outside the Tower." Kept reading. "And more expected tonight. Could be a dozen."

Uh-oh.

She pulled out her phone. Turned away, swiped her monitor.

5.2.

Fuck.

"I need to go," she told him. "Now." Flipped up her hood. "I'll ring you. Need to chat about Wilkes. Ping me a copy of that Johnson file, yeah?" Turned, started to walk away.

"Lucy," he called after her. "Hey, wait a tick. I'll drop you. Can't take the Tube now, not safe, not all the way out to Brompton."

Never said I live in Brompton, Ed.

"No." She shook her head. Goswell Road was only ten minutes, quick walk. No one came to her flat. Not allowed. Just her and the Debt and four black walls. *And certainly not Ed King.* "I'll be fine," she said.

I hope.

Lucy walked off into the night.

‡ ‡ ‡

It started to rain again as she reached Goswell Road.

Pissing down, hard. The hood kept her dry. Fat droplets struck her shoulders, thump thump thump, but she hardly noticed, too busy thinking about copycat attacks. *Mayfair, Soho and…where again? Barbican? Fuck. Close.* Told herself not to worry. Above 5, all good, but she still tensed up. Felt queasy. Nervy, almost like back then, when every other day brought a new attack: yes, they had Boosts, two full boxes, but a drone could pop up anywhere, fucking *anywhere*, and you just never fucking knew…

But it's not then.

It's now. And you're fine. Have a lead. John Johnson, brilliant.

Just get home.

Lucy crossed to her side of the road. Eyes up, alert. Passed three men smoking outside a pub, huddled under the awning. Half-drunk pint glasses. Survivor masks pulled down around their necks, she noticed. Not Survivors, though. Normal eyes, no scars. Masks just for solidarity. Or fashion, more likely, knew that was a thing now: Survivor chic, Christ. *And we can't drink lager with our fucking fashion statement on, now can we?*

One of them had on a black wristband. He turned to watch her walk, said something.

Sorry, mate.

Afraid I'm not an officially licensed London Strong Week accessory.

Nearly home now, just two streets away. Half the shops in this stretch were boarded up, victims of the aftermath: the Big Slump, the Dollar Peg, the Deval, all that. Quieter here. Unlikely place for an copycat attack. She exhaled, rolled her shoulders, let her thoughts flit back to Flinders Cox, to the same question that had nagged at her all afternoon. She'd walked back from Stepney, fuck the rain, two hours of just following the canal path, head down, hood up, thinking. Frowning. Wondering: if Flinders Cox was truly a monster, which he *was*, proper fucking villain, then…what about the antidote? Could a man that bad

218

still do good? Or was she wrong, was A just U after all? *No, no, can't be wrong…*

She turned off Goswell Road, onto her side street.

…Cox felt guilt, know he did. That room? Come on, he did, dead cert. And, thing is…

Walked past the corner pub, shuttered. Quiet.

…a debt like that doesn't get paid off with a few SRA dinner parties…

Past the back alley that led to the dirty, dead-end car park.

…not even three mil to rebuild a cathedral. But an antidote? Cox might think an antidote would pay it off. Might do. Reckon he would, actually, wouldn't know for sure, that's the problem with debts like that, but reckon he'd try it, all he can do, and that means—

CRACK!

A blow. Hard one, back of her head, *the fuck?*, and then she felt a hand over her mouth, rough hand, grabbing her. Shook her head, *mmmf*, squirmed, but too strong, *can't shake him, fuck.* Threw an elbow, *wanker*, but he had her arm now, twisting, hard, harder, *fuck, hurts*, pushing her, marching her back into the alley, to the car park, *oh fuck*, deserted, *fuck fuck fuck…*

Glimpse of his feet. Orange.

You…

Deep breath and she tried another elbow, another, kept trying, *fuck you fuck you fuck*—and then: a hit. He grunted. Grip loosened. She shook, pulled free and ran, stumbling, *just go*, one step, two steps, *fucking go*, sprinting, but then she realized:

Wrong way.

She was in the car park. A dead end.

Turned around and there he was: Orange Trainers. Black jumper, Survivor mask. Coming for her, knife out, growling.

And my stabby's damaged, fuck, fuck…

No. Breathe. You know this, trained for this. Pulled off the hoodie, *quick now*, wound it round her left hand, held a sleeve in her right, *here he comes…* He lunged but she blocked it, wrapped the sleeve, *perf*, pulled, twisted, *please work…*

The knife flew out of his hand, clattered beneath a skip.

She shoved him back and he stumbled. Caught himself. Stood.

For a moment, they stared at each other.

"Johnson," she called out. "John Johnson."

It's you, right? Has to be…

He said nothing. Silence. Rain. The car park behind her, the alley ahead: all quiet.

"Police." Voice firm as she could make it. "You're nicked. Assault. Murder. You do not have to say anything…"

He started towards her.

Right, then.

She put her fists up. Tucked her chin.

Bring it.

He swung but she ducked, threw a jab. Another. Pawing, finding range. Bouncing, jabbing, keeping him back. *Can't let him close, too big.* He kept reaching for her and she jabbed, fending him off, left, left, feinting, right.

Inhale, exhale. Inhale, exhale.

Incoming—

He threw, hard. She rolled, popped him, nice one, ribs. *Like that?* He roared. Backed up, stared at her. *Black eyes.* Wound up, big haymaker, huge but she slipped it, *perf*, closed in and *watch me now, Jack—*

Jab.

Cross.

HOOK.

Landed one more cross and he was down, on the ground. Dropped. Sprawled on his back, arms spread, mask on but eyes shut, out. Done. She stood over him, panting, triumphant.

Like that, yeah?

Whack, whack, whack, motherf—
Wha—

Someone from behind: a hood thrown over her head, *dark*, yanked back, *can't breathe*, tried to scream but it was muffled, gasping, *mmfh*. A blow: her temple. Saw stars. Felt herself fall. Hit the ground, *oof*, dazed, felt her arm grabbed, pulled back. Metal on her wrist, a handcuff. Heard a click.

No...

She reached out for her hoodie. *The Boost.* Nails scraped the wet pavement, stretching, clawing, *need the Boost, Boost's in the hoodie, I need it*, and then he had that wrist too, *no, no, fuck...* She rolled on her back, kicked, but he yanked her wrists together. Cold metal. Click.

Fuck fuck FUCK—

And they were pulling her, both of them now, dragging her body across the car park. She heard the car engine, pop of the boot. *No, need the Boost, fucking need it...* Kicked frantically, hard as she could but they had her, hauled her up, punch to the gut, threw her in, *no no no*, another punch then:

Slam.

She was trapped.

Oh God, oh Jesus, no...

Trapped, trapped like back then, felt like she was back then, it was then—

Focus. Must focus. It's now, need to focus, stay here, fuck's sake, stay here...

Stay now...

Please, God, stay now...

CHAPTER SEVENTEEN
London, 2027

"It's going to be fine, Luce," Simon told her. "Don't panic."

Panic?

She frowned as she pulled a jar of pickle down from the shelf. *Not fucking panicking. Called being sensible.*

The grotty little corner shop on Goswell Road was nearly empty. Just the two of them, plus the bearded bloke slumped behind the till, reading something, looked like manga maybe. Lucy scanned the shelves: odd to see so much missing. No fizzy water, soup tins, HP. Only the crap crisp flavours left. All across London, Vulnerables were stockpiling, holing up. Hoping the stories weren't true, the ones about how easily London Black could float into ventilation systems, under doors, through cracks in windows. The ones that meant nowhere was safe. *But they are true. Terribly, horribly true. Which is why we need to leave London, right fucking now.* She reached into the fridge for a packet of cheddar.

"It's been four days," Simon said. Voice booming, like this was one of his walking tours, Jack the Ripper or Haunted London or something, and she was actually fifteen Yanks wearing those outdoorsy trousers with the zips round the knees. Not that there were tours these days. "Four days, no drones. Nothing. And the *Guardian* says it's probably over…"

At least there was bread. She grabbed a loaf.

"…maybe one or two more attacks, worst case…"

Worst case?

"…and we still have a full box left—"

"*Si*," she said. Motioned: *Quietly, for fuck's sake.* She glanced around, but there was no one to hear, just Manga, ignoring them, reading. *Still. Christ.* Need to be careful, what with Boosts going for she didn't even know how much any more, fucking fortune in a syringe. "Later, yeah?"

He rolled his sky blue eyes: *No one else here, Luce.*

Behind them, an electric bell sounded. The shop door swung open. She turned to look.

Oh, Christ.

A Vulnerable.

The man who entered was tall and thin. About all she could tell, the rest was covered. A gas mask hung from his neck, the visor shield covering his nose and mouth. Wrong type of mask, she saw. Designed for paint fumes or tear gas, do precisely fuck all in a drone attack. He wore a wax jacket, blue boiler suit tucked into olive wellies. The boiler suit was torn in the rear. *Reckon it's single use. But not much choice when everything's sold out and death could rain down from above every time you pop out for a tin of beans.*

She elbowed Simon.

See?

Tell that guy not to fucking panic.

The man didn't say anything. Just walked to the till, pulled three twenty-quid notes from a jacket pocket, fanned them out on the counter. Butyl rubber gloves, she noticed, must have got a pair early on. Manga looked up. Nodded, then ducked below the till. Resurfaced with a roll of clear plastic sheeting. He held it out.

"No," said the man, voice muffled. "We agreed. The thick kind. Six mils."

He put his gloved hand down on top of the twenties.

Manga shrugged. Pulled another roll from beneath the counter, this one black. The man nodded, took it, marched to the door. Lucy watched his torn boiler suit disappear into the night.

We so need to fucking leave.

223

Five minutes later, they were walking home down Goswell Road, rucksack of food slung over Lucy's shoulder. Half ten, dark. A drizzle. They walked in silence for a few, then Simon started back in.

"Just saying. Yes, it's scary, I know, but it's ending."

Scary?

It's fucking terrifying, Si.

"Not here," she told him. "Almost home."

They turned onto their side street. Up ahead, she saw a crowd of people moving towards them down the road. Frowned. *Strange.* Then she spotted the flashing lights behind the mob and realized: it was a removal team, taking a body to the biscuit factory. Some poor attack victim who'd managed to die in their own bed, corpse now headed for the ash-pits. The crowd was massing in front of the body wagon, trying to block it. Banging on the windows, on the bonnet, shouting, screaming. Somewhere in the crush, a woman wailed: *Oh! Dead, dead, dead.*

Lucy's skin prickled.

Could get ugly.

She grabbed Simon's elbow. "Back way. Hurry." Led him up the alley, into the car park. A whiff of piss as they passed the overfull skip. She unlocked the rear door, trotted up three flights of metal stairs, then stood at the end of their hallway as he struggled to catch up.

In the distance, klaxons blared.

Very ugly. Could be another removal riot.

She opened the grimy hallway window and looked out. Craned her neck, but no view of the street from here, just the car park and the skip. Thought about the crowd. She'd recognized someone, a man from the dry cleaners around the corner. He'd been pounding on the side of the van, screaming. Looked ready to tear off the door, drag the driver into the street, off with his hazmat suit, kill the fucking bastard.

Like it was his fault, like he created London Black.

Their flat was cold inside: gas supplies low in the building. She kept her hoodie on. Dodged a stack of Simon's books, walked into the kitchen. Simon leaned against the countertop as she began to pull the groceries from the rucksack.

"Like I was saying," he said, "it's almost over. We'll be fine. Trust me."

Trust you?

She took out the jar of pickle, put it down on the table. Looked at him. Remembered how scared he was that first night. Only three weeks ago, Christ. And then they got those two precious boxes, and after that, it was just, don't worry, Luce, all sorted. *Why aren't you more scared, Si?* "We should go," she told him. "We should."

"Truly, it's fine."

It's not fine, Si, it's so fucking far from fine that I don't see how—

The alarm on her mobile chirped.

Fuck. Shift time already?

Lucy pulled out her phone, turned away. She hadn't told anyone at the Met she was Vulnerable, not even Wilkes. Didn't want questions. Not because it was awkward; just that she couldn't take the risk. They might work out that she had Boosts, and who knew what some random DC might do for that much fucking dosh? *Need to tell them if I'm leaving London, though. Plenty of holiday left, Wilkes would understand. But can't go in, not this second. Need to stay here, get Simon focused, sort this.*

She sighed.

Ducked into the bedroom. Tried Wilkes: no answer. Thought about Salford. He'd covered for her once already: the day she'd gone to Stepney to visit Dad, *that* day. *And he's a good enough sort, Salford. Well, ambitious, anyway.* She dialled his number, told him, sorry, personal matter, bit unexpected, any chance of another cover? As she talked, Simon trailed in and began to check his reflection in the mirrored cupboard. Dapper as always: navy jacket, chinos, brogues. Designer leather belt, the one with the big metal buckle. She watched as he snapped out five pull-ups, then disappeared into the bathroom. Meanwhile, Salford was telling her, no worries, on it, owe me a pint, yeah?, cheers.

As she rang off, Simon returned. "See?" He was holding the box of Boosts. "Right here. And it's basically over. We're fine."

Stop saying that.

"Come on, Luce. You're the Brit. Blitz spirit, right? Keep calm. And even the people who fled at first are starting to come back, actually, so I don't see why—"

Christ.

She fixed him with her fiercest stare.

"If we're short," she said, "even by one single day, we could be dead. Just one." Crossed her arms. "I don't trust some bloody *Guardian* article. The terrorists are still out there. And they won't stop, not ever, not until it's total chaos and everyone's dead and London's a burning bloody ruin."

"Come on, Luce, bit dramatic."

A glare.

Don't you see, Si?

Don't you fucking see?

"I was staying for Dad," she said. "That's why. And now Dad's gone. All gone, nothing left, just ash in a bloody churchyard." She felt a tear well, ignored it. "So now? Now we run. We pack our things, buy a train ticket. Cornwall or Devon or wherever, doesn't matter, really, we just go, the two of us, right now, we leave and—"

CRACK!

The door flew open.

From the doorway, Manga pointed a gun at her face.

‡ ‡ ‡

226

"Don't fucking move," Manga told her.

He entered, gun up. Kept it pointed at Lucy. A second man followed him in: ugly, beard, Spurs hat. No gun. Spurs shut the door. "The Boosts," Manga said. Russian accent, thick one. "Where are they? *Where?*"

Lucy stared at him.

Felt her pulse spike. Started to panic, fuck me, *fuck*, then fought it off. Kept calm. Glared.

Fuck you, Manga.

"Boosts?" Simon had his hands raised. "Mate, think maybe there's been a—"

"No." Manga turned, pointed the gun at his head. Took a step closer. "No mistake. Heard you say it. Said you had a whole fucking box." Lucy watched him scan the room. The Boosts were on the window ledge, behind Simon's back, blocked from sight. She stared at the gun as Manga checked the bed, the desk, the floor. Tried to work it out: if she leapt, grabbed his wrist, timed it…? *No. Too far. Fuck.*

Spurs kicked over a stack of London tour guide books.

Simon, still playing dumb: "Mate, come on, now…"

"*Where?*" Manga marched across the room, gun high and sideways. Shoved it up against Simon's forehead. "No fucking games, Aussie. Where the *fuck* is it?"

"I don't…" Simon stammered. "I…"

Keep calm, Si.

Maybe I can reach his knees…no…

"Fucking *tell* me," Manga shouted. "*Now.*"

Noises from the bathroom as Spurs rifled through the cupboard. She heard him swear: a London accent. Watched as he stormed back to the bedroom, started tearing drawers from the desk, dumping them out onto the floor. Shit flew everywhere: pens, papers, a highlighter.

Grab him, he's a shield, then…no, can't, then Manga shoots Si…

A crash as Spurs threw down the last drawer. He looked up at Manga, shrugged, then froze. His eyes widened. "*Oi*," he said. "Mate." Pointed to the ledge. "There, back of him. See it?"

Oh, fuck.

Manga waved Simon away with his gun. Smirked. Lucy watched as he grabbed the box, tucked it under his arm. Started to back up, gun still raised. To Spurs: "Come on."

Fuck, fuck, fuck.

Spurs nodded, followed him towards the door, then stopped. Looked at Lucy, like he was seeing her for the first time. A vile little grin. She felt his eyes run over her body. Knew what he was thinking, seen that look before: age thirteen, out late, some thug, fought him off. She raised her fists. *Fucking kill you first. Fuck you and the fucking gun, try it and I'll find a way, you—*

"Come *on*," said Manga. "Now."

Spurs shrugged. "Fuck it." He spat, big gob on the carpet, then turned, pissed off into the hallway. Manga followed, backing away slowly, gun still up. Lucy watched the barrel as it disappeared through the doorway.

And then they were gone.

With the Boosts.

Fuck.

She looked over at Simon. His head was down. Hands on knees, shaking.

Need the Boosts.

If Si won't leave London, if we stay, then we need them.

Lucy rubbed her tattoo.

Deep breath.

So—

She took off. Heard Simon—*No, wait, Luce, don't*—but no chance, she was gone. Out the door, into the hallway, here I fucking come. Knew they'd take the back stairs so she went left, main stairwell, bombing down the steps, three at a time, four, hit the ground floor and burst through the door into the street.

Dark. Quiet.

In the distance: a siren.

Where?

No sign of them.

Right, beat them down then, must've, so they'll pop out up there…

Started running towards the alleyway.

There.

Up ahead: Spurs and Manga appeared, walking quickly. Didn't look back, just turned out of the alley, headed for Goswell Road. *Perf.* She sped up. Faster, flying. Knew Manga had everything: gun, Boosts. Streaked towards his back, trainers quiet, *don't turn, don't turn,* almost there, braced herself and leapt and—

SMASH!

She hit him hard. They went down in a heap, him on bottom, her on top, and she heard the gun clatter to the ground. Scrambled to her feet, *need the Boosts,* but it was too late. Spurs picked them up and started running towards Goswell Road.

Get back here.

She reached down for the gun. Grabbed it, and she was after him, sprinting, and—

Wha—

Manga grabbed her foot and she tripped, fell, landed hard on the wet street. Felt her ankle turn, *fuck,* a bolt of pain as she shook him loose, *fuck you,* staggered to her feet. Still had the gun, but Spurs was moving fast. He turned the corner. Disappeared.

Christ…

She grit her teeth, tore after him. Around the bend, up the road, mind racing.

Keep going, keep going…

But he was fast and she was hurt.

Faster, come on…

Faster…

She was losing ground. Shooting pain in her ankle, fuck, *hurts.*

Turned a corner.

Fuck.

Ahead: a crowd.

Riots. The body wagon from earlier was still pushing its way along, but there were more people now, a mob, shaking the wagon, trying to stop it, flip it. Hundreds of people, spilling out of alleys and blocks of flats, from shuttered shops and boarded pubs. Angry people everywhere.

Spurs headed for the throng.

Getting away…

She was trying, digging, but her ankle was on fire now.

Can't catch him. Fuck me. Can't.

Almost out of sight.

Only one chance.

She pulled to a stop. Raised the gun. Aimed.

One chance…

Gritted her teeth, aimed again, then—

Can't.

Can't do it.

Lucy lowered the gun.

Fuck fuck FUCK…

Limped after him, but it was too late. He was gone.

Vanished.

And then, in the distance, she heard a noise:

It was the buzzing of a drone.

‡ ‡ ‡

Lucy flew through her flat's battered door.

Inside was a shambles. Shit everywhere. Manga's sour BO still hung in the air. Simon was kneeling on the carpet, rummaging through the desk drawer wreckage. He looked up. "Oh, Luce, thank God—"

"Drone," she said. "Heard it. Need to leave. *Now*."

He shook his head. Kept digging through papers.

Lucy stared at him.

What the fuck, Si?

"*Simon*." She put the gun down, limped towards him, around the bed. "Listen to me. We're still boosted. It's eleven. Another hour." Reached down, grabbed his shoulder. "We can run, get away, decon before the Boosts wear off. But we need to go, right bloody now…"

He pulled out his mobile, handed it up to her. "Look."

She took it. On the screen was a map of London: a BBC real-time attack update.

There were drone symbols everywhere.

The screen was filled with them, tiny dots scattered all across the city: Wembley to Stratford, Enfield to Croydon. Everywhere she looked, London Black was raining down from the sky.

"Sixty," he said. "Maybe more now. Swarms. Nowhere to run."

Oh, fuck.

Images flashed in her head: the Iso Centre. Dad's ward. Rickety metal camp beds, rows and rows of them, all filled with people. Screaming, terrified, watching in horror as their skin sloughed off in sheets. Blood. Death. Her fingers crept to her tattoo.

Not like that. Oh God, please, not like that.

Simon tossed aside a piece of splintered wood. "Now, where in blazes…"

She let the phone fall to the carpet.

Took a breath.

Right.

So stay here? A glance around. *Can't. Impossible.* They'd need seals on the windows, masks, supplies. And even then, it never worked, something went wrong. Always a hole in the plastic or a tear in your clothes, a mask filter that wears out. London Black would get you. Always. *Bloke at the store? Boiler suit? Dead man walking, never fucking make it. Not without Boosts.*

And we have none. Not any more.

Which means…

"We're dead." A sharp tug on her hoodie strings, then she looked at Simon.

He was smiling.

"I have to go," he told her. She watched, confused, as he stood, grabbed his overcoat, threw it on. "It'll be fine. Promise. You have to stay here. But trust me, it'll be fine."

Fine? She shook her head. "Simon?" He was already moving, tried to blow right past her but she was too quick, grabbed his wrist, held him back. "What is it, Si? *What?* Tell me."

"No, look, I need to—"

"Simon…"

"Luce." A sigh. "Fine. Don't get upset," he said, "but there's more."

More?

Wait, what?

"Four more boxes. I…look, remember when I tried to get us all those boxes and Mel made me put four back? Well, I didn't. Not exactly." His blue eyes shone. "I hid them. Stashed them in a dusty corner, behind the meds no one ever wants. And then the next day, the hospital was evac'ed."

She gaped at him.

Holy shit.

"Didn't need to risk it while we had our box, but they're still there. Must be."

She shook her head, tried to process. Felt like kissing him and punching him, both at once. *Brilliant. Fucking brilliant, let's go, right now. But—you were hoarding it, then? Letting it sit in a storeroom while people died? Christ, Si—*

"Anyway," he said, "I'm getting them." Held up his employee ID. "Needed this but I found it, so…" He started to move again but she held onto his wrist.

"I'm coming."

"Luce…"

The fuck I'm letting you do this without me.

"Too dangerous," he told her. "And it's completely locked down, remember? Troops. Reckon I can get through myself, employee, but you…"

Lucy shook her head. "I'm going. Cop. It'll help."

"No, Luce."

A death stare. "Yes." Reached for her mobile. Realized it was gone, must have fallen out when she tackled Manga. "We've got an hour." *An hour until the Boosts wear off and we're stuck, exposed. So let's get out of here and…*She took a step. Felt a burst of pain. *Fucking ankle.* "Hang on a tick," she told him. Nodded to the toilet. "Just one second." Frowned. "Don't you dare leave."

She did her best to hide her limp as she shuffled into the bathroom.

It was messy, worse than the bedroom. Spurs had tossed it, thrown things everywhere, cracking the mirror as an added fuck-you. She looked around. Somewhere there was a wrap, big roll of thick tan gauze, used it on her wrists sometimes after bag work. *Now where the fuck…*Dug through the sink, shoving aside tiny soaps, packets of floss. *Stupid thing.* Bent down to the floor. Swept aside a box of plasters and a half-dozen Lemsips, then spotted it: hidden in the corner behind the toilet. *There.* She grabbed the roll, sat down, tugged off her shoe and—

The door slammed shut.

Oh, fucking hell.

"Si? Simon?"

"Sorry, babe." His voice was muffled by the wood. "Can't let you take the risk."

God fucking dammit, Si. She grabbed the door handle, shook it. Locked. *Fuck.* Heard a screeching sound, metal on wood. Realized: he was barricading her inside. *Oh Christ. Jesus. No you fucking don't.* She banged on the door. "*Simon?* Let me out. Hear me? Right bloody now."

"Can't…"

Then I'll break out…

She backed up a step, then ran, slammed her shoulder against the door. *Thump.* Bounced off. Tried again. *Thump.* "Si?" Voice loud, frantic. "Si, I'm stuck in here…no mobile…if you don't come back…don't, Si, please…"

"Don't worry."

"It'll get in, I'll be exposed, *please…*"

"It'll be fine." His voice was moving away. "Be back with Boosts. It'll be okay…"

Oh God oh Jesus. Stuck, fucking stuck, trapped, can't be, fuck. She reared back, threw herself against the door, crashing into it over and over, pounding, furious, *fuck fuck fuck…*

The front door slammed.

Trapped…

Lucy screamed.

CHAPTER EIGHTEEN
London, 2029

It's now. Stay now.

For fuck's sake, stay now.

She exhaled into the hood. It was coarse cloth, hessian maybe. Itchy. Smelt like sick. Her breath warmed her face. Wished she could warm her arms, bare now without her hoodie. Cold in here, wherever the fuck *here* was. Still London, knew that. Had to be. Only spent a few minutes in the boot, thrashing, screaming in the darkness, before the car stopped and she was pulled out, made to stand, marched into a building. A punch to the chin, *wankers*, then they threw her into a room. This room. Slammed the door. Left her, hooded and handcuffed, monitor beeping. Panting. Terrified.

Focus. Need to focus.

They'll come back.

Her body ached: ribs, shoulder, chin. Sore as fuck. But sore was fine. She knew sore, *hiya, mate*, felt like after a fight. Sore was better than the blackness. Much. The blackness, that was the worst bit. Maddening. *Fucking hood. Christ, this fucking hood.* She shook her head, tugged at it with her cuffed hands, but it was fastened in the back and she couldn't get it off. No light any more, just black. Just this thick fucking fabric, covering her eyes, muffling her screams.

From her torso: *BEEEP*.

It was nine o'clock. Or midnight. Or six in the morning, she couldn't tell. There was no time now, just the monitor, beeping over and over and over, faster, louder, *BEEEP*, reminding her that this was a nightmare, a Screamer come to life: trapped, levels dropping, stuck in a room, in a London where Black was in the air. *It's out there. Could be in here, no way to know, could be too late, fuck, fuck me…*

BEEEP.

Calm calm calm…

Tried to fight off the terror, but it was rising up, and she was exposed, below 5, no Boosts, no hoodie, and she was back there, back then, trapped in her bathroom, then was now and *BEEEP,* fucking stop it, couldn't hit the switch to stop it, make it stop, just *BEEEP* not stopping *BEEEP* not ever just…

BEEEEEP.

And that was it.

Too much, all too much, it pushed her over and she felt herself come apart, a million Lucys, screaming *screaming* screaming and she let herself go. *Anywhere, fucking anywhere. Just not here, just not now,* she shut her eyes and screamed and—

She was fifteen.

At home, in her bedroom, hers and Jack's. Hadn't touched his things. Not yet, only been five days, still didn't believe it, not real. She was sitting on the bottom bunk. Three cops with her: two fat blokes and a woman, tall, well-dressed, leaning up against the Lennox Lewis poster. Lucy had long hair then. Brushed it back from her face as she stared down at the photo in her hand. Grainy image, CCTV capture: a man's face. Ugly. One of the fat cops tapped it, sausage forefinger. *Know him?* She nodded. Another photo, another tap. *This one?* Yeah. Knew him too. *Your brother's mates, then? Boxed with them? Or the drugs, mixed up in that…?* She'd looked up, eyes blazing. Jack? Drugs? Bog off, cop. *How, then? Suspects in your brother's death, need to speak with them, urgent like, trying to locate them but we don't know…* So she told them. Garage in Limehouse, manky one by the rail station, know it, yeah? They worked there. *And you know this how? Hang out there, friends, or…?* She'd shrugged, explained: in there once last year, bought oil for Dad's van, saw them in the back. Remembered.

Watched them stare at each other. At her.

Wait, you saw them once? Just once? But how…

I recognize faces, she'd told them. Another shrug. Don't know how. Just do.

BEEEP.

And then a month had passed, and she was in another room. Dark, no windows. On the table in front of her: a deck of photo cards, smiling children. Celeb childhood photos. Two men with matching specs and clipboards watching her as she ripped through, calling out names, no pauses, *bang bang bang*. Forty-nine out of fifty, only missed some bloody footballer, who's he then?

BEEEP.

Six years later. Constable Lucy Stone now. A coffee shop: the Starbucks on Palmer Street, the one next to SIU, next to the big steel door she'd spent the past year fucking hating. Across the table was a female cop. The same one from years before: tall, well-dressed. Lucy sipped her tea. Thanked the older woman for coming, out of the blue, grateful. Told her how she'd joined the Met after uni. Wanted homicide, all she bloody wanted, because of her brother, Jack, you remember his case, yeah? But something went wrong. A note in a file, a mark by her name. Those face tests, years before. She was sent to SIU, no choice, bloody awful, hated it, all day just staring at bloody screens, eye drops, boring. Tried everything: formal requests, contacts, pulling strings. Nothing worked. Despair. About to quit. Then she'd remembered the tall cop who'd leaned against the Lennox Lewis poster, the one who'd worked Jack's case, solved it. Thought perhaps, maybe, something you could do, Ma'am, anything at all, forever grateful…

Think that can be arranged, Marie Wilkes had told her.

BEEEP.

And then it was now again, and she was back in the hood, still cuffed. On the floor, shaking. Thinking about Wilkes. About the one person she still had left, someone who had helped her, cared about her. And what had she done, how had she repaid her? With guilt trips. Lies. A broken fucking window. Remembered King frowning, digging hands into his pockets, saying, *Well, about that* and *reduced a rank* and *Andy Sykes.* All her fault, yes it fucking was, and now here she was again, trapped, below 5, stuck in a room, *fuck, fuck me,* and she screamed—

A click.

She heard the door open.

‡ ‡ ‡

You're going to get hit now, Lucy.

She stopped screaming. Took a breath and held it, body still shaking. Heard footsteps: trainers on concrete, coming towards her. She exhaled, pushed the panic away. Focused. Easier now that he was here, actually. Felt familiar, sort of, like a fight. Like this cold, hard floor was her corner, and she was sitting on her stool, tapping her worn black Lonsdales together, watching the other girl climb through the ropes. Staring at her across the ring, sizing her up.

So come on, then. Bring it, you Orange Trainers wanker.

The door clanged shut.

Or is it your friend? Cheap Shot man, the one who caught me from behind? No way to tell which, not in the blackness. Didn't matter. Either way, she knew what was coming. Knew they wanted something from her, some information. Reason she was still alive, had to be. And as soon as she gave it up, whatever the fuck *it* was, she was done. *Goodbye, Lucy.* So: that was the game, then. Give up nothing. Zero. Fuck all. She needed to keep her mouth shut, no matter what happened next.

And what happens next is going to fucking hurt.

Lucy closed her eyes. Listened to the footsteps get closer.

Heard Jack's voice in her head, a memory: at the gym, night of her first fight, talking to her as he wrapped her hands. *Remember now, Luce, you're going to get hit. Happens. Always. Don't be scared of it. What counts is how you take it, yeah? How you respond. Rhythm. Timing.* He'd ruffled her hair with his big hand. *Strong chin, now, Champ. Strong chin.*

She nodded to herself, set her jaw.

Strong chin.

A sudden noise next to her: metal striking concrete.

"Sit."

His voice was raspy. Survivor's voice. Harsh, guttural. Larynx scarred like the rest of him.

She reached out with cuffed hands, felt the round leg of a metal chair. Knew what he was doing: easier to strike her if she was sitting. Teeing her head up like a golf ball, not that she ever watched golf, fucking deadly, worse than football even. She shook her head. Snorted. "No."

Offering your seat to the lady? Come on, mate. Chivalry's dead.

He kicked her. Hard one, square in the ribs. She gasped. Pain.

"Sit."

Well, if you insist.

Pulled herself up. Sat, staring into the blackness. Knew he was standing there, somewhere. Two steps away, maybe. Three, four. Couldn't say for sure, goddamn fucking hood, made it impossible to find range. *And I need to find range, need to work out where he is, how far he is.*

"Who did you tell?" he asked.

She thought about it. *Tell what? About Johnson? Cates? What Cox did?* Decided best not to ask. *Give up nothing.*

"So," she said, "how's your jaw, then?"

His fist crunched her temple and she went down, off the chair, onto the floor. *Fuck.* She tasted blood. Wished she could spit, but the hood already smelt like sick. She let the blood

239

dribble out of her mouth, down her chin. *So it IS you, Orange Trainers.*

Jack's voice: *What counts is how you respond…*

She shook her head. Exhaled.

Climbed back onto the chair.

Kept her cuffed hands down, wrists on knees. No point trying to cover up. He'd just change his punches, vary his attack, and that wasn't what she wanted. Not at all.

"Now," he growled, "*talk*. Who else did you tell?"

"Because I got you good, I reckon, and—"

Another punch. Harder. Down again, gasping. Saw stars.

Jack: *Rhythm…*

Lucy took a breath. Sat up. Smiled at him under the hood, a little fuck-you grin she wished he could see. *Strong chin, yeah? And you punch like a fucking pin-weight.* She shook her head, grabbed the seat of the chair. Pulled herself up, must do, fuck the pain. Sat, swaying.

"Told?"

"About Cates," he said. "Who else knows?"

"Well," she said, "thing is." Paused. "Bog off."

Timing.

He threw another punch but she timed it, ducked, then she was up off the chair, launching herself at him, cuffed hands out, attacking. Bowled him over and she was on top of him now, knees pressing down, hands together, chopping down on his head, *fuck you.* He caught her hands but she kneed his groin, *like that?*, shook him off, then started in with an elbow, slamming it down on his face, over and over. *Fuck. You. Fuck. You.* Heard him howl but she kept going, *asked for it*, another elbow, *tried to kill me*, one more. *Bastard.*

He stopped moving.

She hit him one last time then rolled off. Sat, panting.

And stay down.

Now then…

A deep breath. Everything was still black. *Need to see. So where's that little knife of yours?* Patted him down, hands still cuffed, fingers digging through his pockets. *There.* She felt it, pulled it out, flicked it open. *Carefully now.* Put the blade up to the corner of the hood, holding the handle between her clasped hands. Pushed.

The blade slipped off the surface.

Come on.

She tried it again. Dug the blade in deeper this time, until she could feel it pricking her temple. *Right.* Knew she had to hurry. Cheap Shot might be around, could show up any second. Steadied her hands, then pushed.

Please.

Heard the fabric tear. A dot of light shone through. *Brill.* Kept going, working the blade, until the dot was a hole and the hole was a gash, and then she put the knife down and grabbed hold of the hood. Turned her head, quick twist. Heard the fabric rip. Light flooded in.

Thank fucking God.

She stood up. Looked around. A big room. Knew exactly what it was: an abandoned pub. Taps and glassware gone, walls stripped, but the long wooden bar was unmistakable. Windows boarded. Rubbish all over the floor. Old newspapers, cream canisters, broken spirit bottles. *Rough sleepers. Or kids, maybe.* No furniture except for the single metal chair. And at her feet, a man lay sprawled, blood gushing from the mouth hole of his Survivor mask.

On his feet: orange trainers.

He groaned. Eyelids fluttered. Lucy stared down at him.

Wanker. Bringing you in, but first—

Her monitor beeped.

First, I need a Boost.

Right fucking now.

Lucy bent down, dropped the knife and began to search his pockets again, this time for the handcuff key. *Not there. Not there.* Moved down to his jeans, then stopped: a noise. She turned, looked up.

A man in a blue Survivor mask was standing at the far end of the bar.

Crap. No time for a fight, so…

She sprang to her feet, took off running. Blew through the door, out into a corridor. Turned a bend and hit the main entrance. Tried the door handle: locked. *Come on.* She backed up, then ran forward, hurled herself against the door. *Thud.* Bounced off. Tried again. *Thud.* A third time, everything she had, *come on, come on*, and—

The door flew open. She burst outside, into morning light.

Stopped. Stared.

Oh, fuck me.

‡ ‡ ‡

It's here. In the air.

She was in Mayfair. Saw an ancient black-and-white house wedged between brick flats, knew it instantly. Knew this street. This pub, even: been in before, years back, super posh. Boarded up since the Scourge. This was MIT19 territory, her ground. And last night, somewhere nearby, there was a copycat attack. King's voice: *Men spraying aerosols. Soho, Barbican. Mayfair.*

Mayfair. Where she was standing now.

Breathing the air.

Exposed.

Fuck.

Need a Boost. Need it right fucking now.

She took off. Glanced back, saw Cheap Shot barrel out of the pub. Sped up. Hard to run with hands cuffed but she pulled them close to her chest, kept her balance, kept moving. Tore down the street, thoughts racing.

Pharmacy, pharmacy, now where the fuck—

Remembered one. *Audley Street.* Turned right, down an alley, to a garden. Shot across, trainers flying. Tried to keep calm but Black could be anywhere, in the air, floating, hanging. Waiting for her to run past, breathe it in, catch it, Christ…

Need a Boost. Need it now.

Quick look back. Cheap Shot still chasing. She reached the north side, *nearly there*, blew through a gate, *almost*, hit Mount Street.

Stopped. Eyes wide.

The restaurant in front of her was covered in clear plastic sheeting. Yellow tape everywhere. Hazard signs. Men in green suits and face shields sprayed chemicals on windows, waved testing wands, burned linens.

The attack site.

She took a breath, held it. *In the air. It's in the air. Don't breathe, mustn't breathe.* Spun around. Cheap Shot was running towards her across the gardens, so she swung right, made for the west exit. Running hard, flying past benches, signs, trees. Legs pumping, lungs burning, *don't breathe, hold it, hold it, fucking hold it…*

Saw the exit ahead. Big iron grate, red phone booths either side.

Hold it…

Shot through the gate. Down a street, hit a junction, turned right. In the distance: the pharmacy's green cross, blinking. Realized she didn't know the time, could be six, eight, ten. *Be open, please God.* People on the pavement so she hopped down, into the street, sprinting past taxis, cycles, cars. Looked back. Cheap Shot struggling, losing ground.

Need to hurry…

Her eyes watered. Dying for a breath but she couldn't risk it, had to keep running, get away, far away, not safe, it floats, carries…

It's in the air…

Reached the pharmacy. *Open. Brill.* Pushed through the door. Exhaled. *Phew.* Stood, gasping. Looked around. Posh. Thick carpet. Wooden shelves, products behind glass: perfumes, combs, shaving brushes. A glass case filled with real sponges. She spotted a sign in the back, gold lettering: *Prescriptions.* Ran to it, rapped her handcuffs on the glass countertop.

The pharmacist appeared. Bald, thick specs.

"*Boost,*" she told him. Her eyes blazed. "Need a Boost."

He gaped at her. The specs slid down his nose.

"Do you have…that is, I mean, it's prescription, and…"

Christ.

"Cop." She shook her cuffs at him. "I need. Elemidox. *Now.* Yeah?"

A stare, then he nodded. Started to pull out drawers, dig through boxes, bottles, tubes.

Come on…

"Ah." He pulled out a box. Set it down on the glass. Smiled at her. "Elemidox. 30 mils."

Oh, for fuck's sake.

She held up her cuffs. "Need you to open it." *Christ.* "Prep it. Please, hurry…" She watched him fiddle with the box, pull out the syringe. Shake it, tap the side.

Come on, come on—

The door slammed. She looked up.

Cheap Shot stood in the doorway.

Oh, goddamn it.

She glanced back at the Boost but the pharmacist was still removing the seal, priming the needle. *Fucking hurry.* Wanted to grab it, inject herself, but she couldn't, not enough time, not with Cheap Shot running towards her across the thick green carpet.

Right. You first, then.

She put up her cuffed hands. Kept them high, close to her cheeks, guarding her face.

Peek-a-boo style. Jack taught me. Wanna see?

He took a huge swing. She ducked it. Ducked another. *Too slow.* A third. Bobbing, weaving. He threw one more punch and she jabbed, met it with the steel cuffs, clang. *Peek-a-boo!* Watched as he howled in pain, backed up. Shook his hand. Swore.

Want more, yeah?

He did. Rushed at her. Not punching now, trying to grab her. She darted away, kept moving. Couldn't grapple, not like this, not in cuffs. Just kept circling, thinking, trying to work out how to fend him off, inject the Boost.

Need that Boost.

Quickest of glances back at the counter but he noticed, charged in, grabbed her shoulders. Started to shake her so she headbutted him, good one, knocked him staggering into the glass case, *crash.* Sponges rolled. She reached back for the Boost, *hurry, need to inject,* but he was already up, charging again, lunging. Tried to sidestep but he caught her, whirled, flung her against the shelves, *fuck,* glass shattering.

Ugh…

He grabbed her again. She tried to punch, hit his chin but it was weak, *fucking cuffs.* He caught her neck with one hand, then the other. *Fuck.* Squeezed. She pushed his chest away, tried to shake him, but he was too strong. Backing her up, *can't breathe,* back towards the counter, back, *need air,* and she stared into his eyes, *normal eyes?,* up against the counter now, felt herself slipping, fading, blackness…

No.

Kneed him in the groin.

He let go, staggered back. She gasped in air, *thank God*, then watched as he snarled, charged, threw a massive punch but she ducked it, grabbed the Boost, turned and—

Heya—

Jabbed it into his fucking neck.

Peek-a-boo.

He screamed.

Grabbed the syringe, pulled it out. Blood sprayed all over the thick carpet, crimson on green. The pharmacist shrieked. Cheap Shot reached down, took a sponge, pressed it to his neck as he lurched away, dripping red, towards the door, into the street.

Lucy watched him go.

Thought about chasing. Wanted to, but she couldn't, not now. *Need to boost.*

To the pharmacist, still huddled behind the counter: "Another." She watched as he prepared the syringe, then grabbed it. "Ta." Lifted her vest. Aimed the needle. Injected.

Christ, it fucking hurts.

As the liquid disappeared into her body, she shut her eyes. Took a breath. Another. Thought about everything, what she'd done two years ago, all of it. The Thing. Gasped with pain. And then swore to herself that she wasn't done yet, that she was going to find the antidote, pay the Debt.

Fuck you Orange Trainers and Cheap Shot, Johnson and Enoch Clapham and everyone else, fuck you all. I'm still here. Still alive.

And you wankers are mine now.

CHAPTER NINETEEN

Lucy stared up at the giant stone column.

So fucking old. She remembered Simon pointing it out on a walk, years ago: *Bit out of place, Luce, don't you think? Ancient Egyptian monument, here, by the Thames?* But she'd been impressed. Oldest thing she'd ever seen. Well, Stonehenge, that was older maybe. Not sure, Si would know. *Proper old, anyway.* It was sixty feet high, sides all covered in carved beetles and owls, pointy tip jabbing the afternoon sky. *Like a massive stone Boost. But no such thing as a nerve agent back then.*

She looked around. Quiet here, by the river. Empty benches. A few tourists stopped, took selfies, pissed off again; otherwise, no one. Good meeting spot. Five minutes' walk from New Scotland Yard. Hidden from Embankment traffic. Perfect for meeting an MIT19 detective when you don't want to be seen.

Or when they don't want to be seen meeting you…

She checked her phone. Half one.

Late. Fifteen minutes.

Please, don't ditch me.

Took a sip from her Coke bottle. Her head throbbed. All those punches, probably, but at least she had caffeine in her system now. Practically the first thing she'd done, right after buying an LB insta-test from the pharmacy, holding her breath until the green dot flashed. *All clear. Not dead yet.* Tubed it home from Mayfair, Jubilee Line to Circle. Searched the car park. Found her hoodie on the ground, bit damp from the drizzle but fuck it, just get rained on anyway, yeah? And then she'd set up this meeting.

She checked her mobile again.

Sixteen minutes late.

Please show. Please...

A circular on the ground caught her eye. She reached down, grabbed it. Black poppy border, bold letters at the top:

Official London Strong Week Programme of Events

She frowned. Today was what, Thursday? Week nearly over, thank Christ. Couldn't take much more. She scanned the schedule. Another wreath ceremony today, minute of silence tomorrow night, then bang, done. *And all the Non-Vulnerables can stop it, stop pretending like they actually give a fuck, and I get a break, full year without seeing any more black poppies or goddamn wristbands or commemorative fucking knitwear and—*

"Cleopatra's Needle."

Huh?

Lucy looked up. Marie Wilkes was standing behind her, staring at the column. "That's its name," she said. Well-dressed as always. Suit, heels, navy scarf with the logo that was all Cs or Gs, both maybe, Lucy didn't know. "Your text said to meet by the 'old Egyptian wotsit'. I mean, I knew where you *meant*, but just so you—oh, Christ, Lucy. Your eye..."

What?

Her left eye was purple. Not just bags beneath, but all over purple. She touched it, felt the swelling, shrugged. *Proper shiner, Ma'am. Happens. Wrists hurt more, actually, stupid fucking cuffs.* "It's fine," she said. "Had worse."

"Right..." Wilkes sounded unconvinced but she shrugged, sat down on the bench. "Expect I can guess why you asked me here. John Johnson, right? Ed told me." Clasped her hands. No watch, Lucy noticed. "You want some help, and—"

"No, Ma'am." She shook her head. "Not it."

"Really?" Genuine surprise. "Well, what then?"

A deep breath.

"Here to apologize, Ma'am."

Wilkes stared. "Apologize? For…?"

Everything, really. Lucy tugged her hoodie strings. Remembered what Wilkes had done for her, all of it. Then thought of the watch. Of the guilt trip. Crap thing to do, really, knew it at the time. But then again, to be fair, she had no choice, did she? Needed the case to pay the Debt, and Wilkes was saying no, so… *Well, okay, fine. Hurst, then.* She'd punched Hurst. Caused a shit-storm, and *that* was what Wilkes was getting done for. Knocked back down a rank, fucking Sykes as DCI, all her fault, no question. *But Hurst was a wanker. Deserved it, yeah? Fuck's sake, deck him again if I could, the bastard. So…*She sighed. Stared out at the river. Finally: "Your window, Ma'am." Looked over at Wilkes. "I'm sorry I broke your window. Never said it, but I am. Truly. You deserved it, really you did, and I broke it."

Wilkes nodded. Hint of a smile.

"Well, thank you, Lucy."

Lucy shrugged. *Welcome, Ma'am.* Took a sip of her drink, then looked across the river. Watched the Eye as it spun. Started to think about next steps. *Need to ring King back. Have a lead, Johnson, but it's a bit complicated because—*

Wilkes cleared her throat.

"So," she said, "about John Johnson. Meant to tell you. I've had an idea."

Lucy looked over. "Ma'am?"

"To help you. But…the men who took you. You think Johnson was one of them?"

"No." Lucy shook her head. She'd changed her mind. Thought about it for the past few hours, staring out the window as she rode the Tube from her flat out to Brompton, frowning over a veggie fry-up. *Orange Trainers isn't Johnson. Can't be.* Militant Survivor with Hand of God ink? Not fucking likely, she had to admit. And then: Cheap Shot's eyes. She'd seen them, stared into them as he choked her. *Normal eyes. Not a Survivor, not Johnson, not MLF.* "I don't think so, Ma'am."

"So Johnson wouldn't recognize you by sight?"

A shrug. "Can't say, really."

"But you still want to meet him?"

She thought of the text King had sent overnight, the one she'd read when she pulled her mobile from the damp hoodie pocket in the car park: "Cates and Johnson were half-brothers." Nodded. "Yes, Ma'am. Very keen." *Still think Johnson killed Cox. Revenge for his brother. Not sure how the pieces fit together, exactly, but yes.*

Yes, I want to meet John Johnson.

"Well, as I say, I've had an idea. *But,*" she said, as Lucy started to smile, "it wasn't just me alone. I've asked Ed to join us. You don't mind, do you? That's him now."

She pointed.

Lucy turned around, looked out from behind the column. Watched as King crossed the Embankment, dodging nimbly between black cabs. *Light on his feet for such a big bloke. Good footwork, I reckon.*

"Wife left him for a solicitor," Wilkes said. "Did I tell you?"

Lucy shook her head. *So that's why he lost it with Facer, then.*

"Shame. But you two seem to get on." A meaningful glance. "And he *is* a bit of a dish…"

Not thinking about it, Ma'am.

King slipped past a cycle, then hopped onto the pavement, trotted down the steps, joined them by the bench. Suit, loosened tie, olive rain jacket. Stubble gone, Lucy noticed. She sniffed. *Aftershave again.* He looked down at Lucy, pointed to her eye. "Nice mouse." Grinned. "Get some ice on that."

"You should see the other lot."

A laugh. "I bet."

"How was your meeting?" Wilkes asked him. "Are we a go, then?"

He nodded. To Lucy: "Marie's idea. Clever one, must admit."

"Not just me to thank," said Wilkes.

"Fair enough. Veronica Cox, too. Had a meeting with her earlier. Very helpful. She has good contacts in the MLF."

Lucy pictured Nurse Jowlsey, smiling as she handed out a cheese and pickle. *Kind of you.*

"Not Johnson himself, I'm afraid, but his lieutenant. Winter's his name. Tommy. Hard man, long stretch in the Ville before he joined up MLF. Veronica's set up a meeting with him tonight." Glanced at Wilkes, then back at Lucy. "Just you in there though, Lucy, only way it would work. You meet Winter, and touch wood, you can use him to get to Johnson."

She beamed. *Brilliant. Love it.*

"Thing is," he said, "MLF don't like police, so you'll have a cover story. Survivors' rights thing."

Wilkes nodded. "And if you're wrong, and the MLF is behind your kidnapping last night, then they'll know you straight away and..." Her voice trailed off.

You'll never see me again.

King: "And that's not all. One more thing." He grimaced. Looked at Wilkes. "You tell her."

Tell me what?

What?

Wilkes sighed. "There's one more thing, Lucy..."

‡ ‡ ‡

Don't like this. Not one fucking bit.

Lucy frowned as she walked down the alley. It was dark. Deserted. Which was fair enough, no reason for anyone else to be in this grim bit of Lambeth, not this late. Nothing here but crumbling brick warehouses with broken windows, some niffy puddles. Empty cream chargers, heaps of them. She kicked one, heard it clink. Thought about the plan. About King, sitting in the Toyota near Vauxhall station, five minutes away.

It's the only way, he'd told her on the drive over. *Look, you needed a cover story to meet Johnson. Now you have one. Just bang on about Survivors' rights for a few, then you're in.* She'd turned away, stared out the window, but he kept talking. *Listen. The cover is important. This lot work out you're a cop? They'll kill you, Lucy. Right fucking there.*

So here she was.

Still suspended. Wilkes was clear: this was all unofficial, off the books.

But now, she was undercover, too.

Which, right, fine, only…this cover story? No way it works, no fucking way.

Her mobile flickered and she glanced down. Almost there now. Veronica Cox had sent her GPS coordinates, along with Winter's rules: *Just her. Alone. And don't expect any fucking masks.* She was dreading that bit, seeing the faces. Knew the guilt would hit her. Always did. Told herself it was fine, no worries, handled it at SRA headquarters, yeah? *So you can do it again. Need to for the cover, no choice, really, because—*

She stopped.

Up ahead, in the shadows: a rustle.

Her skin prickled.

"Hello?"

No response.

Another rustle.

"Someone there?"

A fox darted out from behind a bin. She watched it run.

Oh—

And for a second she was back then, on Goswell Road. Midnight. Just after the last attack, the big one, when everything fell to shit, no more body wagons and people dropped dead in the street and the city was black with burnings, black as night, fucking hell. Coming from a food handout, walking home, alone. Turned a corner. Saw a fox, running towards her, something in its mouth. Odd shape. She frowned. Squinted. Realized:

A hand.

Oh Christ, it's a hand, a child's hand, oh...

And then it was now again, and she was bent over, hands on knees, gasping.

Christ...

Took a deep breath. Exhaled, straightened up. *Come on. Focus.* Another breath, then she set her jaw, started moving again. *It's not then, it's now, and you need to do this. Fucking need to.* Walked down the alley, straight through the puddles, splash. Kicked through spent chargers, trainers wet, until the blue dot on her mobile was directly on top of the GPS pin.

Here.

She looked up.

In front of her was a door. No number, just a side entrance to one of the warehouses. Big one, yellow brick, old. Graffiti. Looked empty: windows mostly boarded, or else dark. A faded paper notice was taped to the door, something about seizure, impossible to read because the ink had run in the rain.

Here?

She knocked. Listened.

Nothing.

King's voice in her head: *They'll kill you. Right fucking there.*

Another knock.

"Hiya? Anyone?"

A pause, and then the door opened a crack.

Here we go.

"Get inside," hissed a voice. "Hurry."

She nodded, pushed her way in. Dark inside. No lights, just a dim camping lantern held by the man standing in front of her. He was a giant. Larger than King. Larger than Salad Cream, even. Dressed in camo trousers and a hoodie, navy or black, she couldn't tell in the darkness. His face was hidden in shadow.

The door creaked shut.

"Dutton," said the man. Deep voice, scratchy like all Survivors. He held out a massive hand, seamed with red and white scars. Lucy shook it. "Pleasure," he said. "Truly. Sorry for the dark." Bobbed the lantern. "No electricity just now. We're here... unofficially."

Funny. Me, too.

She looked around. A long, narrow room, too big for her to see the far wall in the darkness. Dank. Industrial. Steel girders overhead, thick chains dangling down. Floor covered in glass, cardboard, bits of broken tile. She sniffed, smelt mould.

In the distance: a faint banging, metal on metal.

"Follow me." Dutton waved a giant paw, turned away, started walking. "Mind your step. Turn an ankle in this bloody place." She followed him though a doorway, into a maze of empty rooms. Kept track of their path in her head as they walked: *right, left, left.* "Bit of a heap, this." He coughed, a dry, hacking cough. "Textile factory. Reckon it'll be converted soon. Flats. Or they'll just knock it down, build some rubbish fucking office block."

"Mmm," said Lucy.

Right, left, left, right...or was it right, right, left, right? Fuck...

"And here we are," he said, leading her into a square room with another door in the far wall and an empty cable spool in the centre. "MLF HQ. For a few days, anyway." He put the lantern down on the spool, motioned to a rusted metal chair. "Please, sit. Tommy's finishing up on something, so it's just us for a tick. Sorry to disappoint." Walked to the ledge of a boarded window. Stood, back to her, fiddling with something. "I'm Head of Security, by the way. Look out for Tommy and the rest of command. Keep 'em safe. On high alert, actually. Need to be careful just now. Can't trust anyone."

"Ah," said Lucy.

More clanging noises in the background. Louder here.

"Lager?" He turned back to her, can in hand. Cracked it open.

"Oh," she said, "thanks, but I can't. Boosts." Regretted it as soon as she said it. *Fuck. Was that bad? Remind him of back then, that he couldn't get Boosts, and that's why…?* But he just shrugged, took a swig himself. Sat down across from her, chair squeaking under his weight.

Phew.

"So," he said. "Before you meet Tommy. Something you need to tell me." His voice changed: serious. He folded his arms, looked at her. A hard stare. Deep, like the look Jack would give her when she was small and he was trying to work out whether she was lying. Half of his face was still in shadow, but she could see the other half. Scars: heavy, red. Wanted to turn away, but she pushed the guilt aside, *not now, Christ.* "If you don't mind, of course."

Lucy nodded.

King's voice: *Kill you, Lucy. Right fucking there.*

Dutton took another gulp of the beer. Leaned forward. Frowned.

"Which of your films is your favourite?"

Oh, for fuck's sake.

"I mean, do you watch any of them, just for enjoyment? Or can't you? Is it too odd, seeing yourself? Sorry, must get it all the time, I'm sure, but I just…"

King's voice again: *It's the only way. You need a cover story.*

So now I'm the Actor.

She shifted in her chair. Faked a smile. "I love all my films." Voice as chipper as she could make it. "They're like…

my children." *Can't believe I just said that, fuck. Never go for it, never.*

He nodded. "Fair enough."

Worked? That fucking worked?

She leaned forward, towards the camping lantern.

Dutton gasped. "Oh, poor thing…"

What?

Oh. Right. Shiner. Umm…"Hurt it shooting," she told him. A firm nod. "Fight scene."

Plausible, yeah?

See, you can do this. Not so bad, acting, reckon I could—

"I thought you were working on a Jane Austen film?"

She stared at him. *Calm. Keep calm.* "It's a gritty reboot."

He frowned, but before he could say anything, the door in front of her opened and another man walked in. "Sorry I'm late," he said. "Tommy Winter." He was average height. Bulky, muscle turned to fat. A tattoo covered one scarred hand, giant letters: MLF. *Reckon that hurt.* Face worse than Dutton's, but she didn't let herself flinch. Just shoved away the guilt, *fuck's sake, I'm trying,* shook his hand.

"Hiya," she said.

"Pleasure," Winter said. "Bit of a fan, actually."

I don't. Look. Like her.

But thank you.

He kept talking. "So. Veronica Cox said you were interested in the MLF. How can I help?"

She smiled, a real one. *Finally.* "I'm working on a project. Biopic, actually. Producing it. Early stages, but very exciting. It's meant to be about John Johnson. His story." Watched him frown. "We've tried to get hold of him, but…"

"John Johnson is a very private man."

"Right." She gave her best pleading look. "Veronica hoped you might help with that."

"Hmm." Winter stood, walked over to the window ledge. She heard glasses clinking. "Not really kitted out for hospitality here, I'm afraid," he told her, "but can I offer you a drink?"

"Water would be lovely."

A laugh. "We don't drink water here. Lager? Some whiskey? Bit shit, if I'm honest, but…"

"No, kind of you but I'm fine, really."

Dutton, from behind her: "She can't, Tommy. Vulnerable. Boosts."

Winter stopped pouring his drink. Frowned. "Odd." Shook his head. "Never heard that before…" He thought for a moment, then to Lucy: "No, I remember. You were in London then, right? Had to be, had tickets to see you at the Old Vic, actually, me and the missus, well, the ex, meant to be a few weeks after the big attack. *Spotlight*, remember? With the bloke from that show, blond one?" He frowned at Dutton. "So she *was* in London then. And she's not one of the Sixty-Two, seen *that* list." Back to Lucy: "Right?"

Fuck.

"Really, water's fine…or a Coke…"

Her monitor beeped.

Fuck fuck fuck…

Winter grabbed the lantern off the table, held it out. Stared at her. Frowned.

"You aren't her," he said slowly. "Dead ringer, but no. Chin's *just* a bit different."

Come on, act…

Lucy stood up. Eyes blazing. Indignant. "How *dare* you…"

He pulled a knife.

She felt Dutton's hand grip her shoulder, force her down into the chair.

Winter leaned close, black eyes wide, scarred face inches from hers.

"You aren't," he said. "I know it. So—who the fuck *are* you?"

‡ ‡ ‡

Calm. Keep calm.

Winter sneered at her. "One of Clapham's, are we?"

His blade glinted in the lantern light.

Clapham? That wanker? She shook her head. "No."

"No? Oh, right, well then." To Dutton: "She says, no…" Back to Lucy: "But I don't fucking believe her." A scowl. "You lot disgust me. Filth. All your spying? Fucking sick of it. And now *this*?" He waggled the knife. "What d'you reckon, Tony? What should we do, then?"

Dutton grunted. His giant hand squeezed Lucy's sore shoulder.

Christ, hurts…

Winter kept talking. "Fucking Hand of God, yeah? Cut off your hands, then, shouldn't I? So keen on God's fucking hands, you can bloody well use those. Or, wait. I know." He pointed the knife at her face. "I'll cut that rubbish cross into your fucking forehead, see how *you* like it, yeah? Everyone staring at you, pointing. *Whispering*." Cupped his hand to his mouth, a whisper: *psst psst psst psst*. Grinned. Again: *psst psst psst psst*. Right in Lucy's face now. "How 'bout that? Like that?"

She frowned. Deep breath.

Could do.

Or—

Grabbed the lantern, threw it down, hard floor, *smash*. Black. She heard him lunge, dodged the knife, *missed me*, Dutton howled and she shook free. Spun, scrambling, pushing, *go*, running back through the door, headed to the alley, fast, *faster*, another door, another, another…

And now—

258

She cut left, hard. Stopped.

Pressed her back up against the wall. *Quiet.* Pitch black, heart pounding.

Don't breathe.

And then they blew by, ran right past her, and she watched as they stumbled through the darkness, swearing, headed back through the maze of rooms, back to the alley.

She took a breath. Exhaled.

Right.

Quietly now.

Doubled back through the doorway, trainers padding past heaps of debris. Reached the room with the cable spool, kept going. *Another exit, must be.* Crept through a string of small rooms, all dark, empty, dirty.

Her monitor beeped.

Christ. She froze. Listened: only the metal clanging, somewhere ahead. Reached down, fingered the monitor. Knew she was at 6.5, must be, checked when she left the Toyota. The late Boost had reset her clock, but she was still dropping quickly. *And right now? Best be quiet.* Pulled the disc away from her skin, shoved it into her pocket. Grabbed her phone, shot King a text—"blown come now don't call shhh"—then kept moving.

Quietly.

Picked her way forward, treading softly. Only two directions, forward or back. *And those two are behind, so…*Ahead, the clanging grew louder. She saw a faint light. Reached a doorway. Hid herself behind the frame, looked in.

A big room, biggest so far. High ceiling, rusted girders criss-crossing below. Rubbish everywhere. To her right, by the wall, five camping lanterns were placed in a ring. In the middle was a car-sized object, hidden under a black tarp. Next to it, two men were talking, backs to her. Survivor voices, raspy. One was thin, dressed in a camo smock and trousers; the other held a large hammer.

Lucy squinted into the darkness. At the far end of the room: an open door.

She turned around. Listened. Heard shouting in the distance, getting louder.

They're coming back.

Fuck.

"Still not working," Camo was telling Hammer. "Give it another tonk, right there." He pointed.

Lucy looked across the big room to the open door.

Might make it. Backs to me. But if they turn around…

"Tried that already," said Hammer. "But, fine…" He gave it a whack. The clang echoed off the walls. "See?"

No choice.

Fuck it.

She crept into the room. *Carefully, carefully.* Kept her eyes on the ground, squinting into the darkness, looking for obstacles. *Mustn't stumble.* Lifting her foot, checking, planting. *One. Step. At. A. Time.*

Across the room, Hammer bent down. Another swing.

"Fucking rubbish," he said. "The Ukrainian fucked us."

Camo waved something. "When I hit this," he said, "it needs to work."

Lucy held her breath as she tiptoed.

Halfway there.

Please don't turn around…

Hammer: "Yeah? Like to see *you* fix it, then, mate."

Camo: "Like to see you do your fucking job for once."

The doorway was only a few steps ahead.

Almost there…

Hammer: "Doing my fucking best. How 'bout you piss off now, John?"

John?

She turned her head, looked back.

John Johnson?

Her foot landed on a tile. A crack. Echoes.

Fuck...

Camo looked up.

She saw his face, red and scarred. Felt her gears turn.

Her eyes widened.

Wait—

"*Oi,*" shouted Hammer. "The fuck are you doing here?"

She bolted for the door. Blew through it, into a corridor, another, a junction. Lost now, just guessing, *right, left,* skidding over rubbish, leaping, *keep going, run.* Saw a big door, ran to it, turned the handle, *please God,* and it opened and she burst outside into the night.

She was on a quiet side street.

Behind her: "Hey, you, get back here..."

Looked ahead, saw the Toyota race right past. She sprinted after it, watched as it turned away, towards the GPS coordinates.

Fuck...

"Ed!" She ran after him, waving her arms. "Wait! I'm here!"

Glanced back. Hammer flew out the door after her.

"*Ed!*"

Come back...

Please...

Brake lights.

The car stopped. Reversed. Lucy ran to it, jumped in, slammed the door, and they were off, pulling away, gone.

"Oh," she gasped. "That was...I mean..." Exhaled. "Bloody close one..."

"All right?" He glanced over. Frowned. "Lucy?"

She nodded, panting. Turned in her seat and watched as Hammer disappeared into the darkness. *Bye.* Said nothing for a moment, just stared out the rear window, caught her breath.

They sped over Lambeth Bridge.

"Did you see Winter?" he asked.

Did better than that. She turned to him. "I saw John Johnson. Saw his face." Paused. Deep breath. "And, Ed...he's *not* John Johnson."

"Sorry, what?"

She shook her head.

"That man? In there? MLF's founder? He's not Johnson. Not really."

He stared at her.

"But then—"

"The man in there? That's Rob Cates."

CHAPTER TWENTY

"Gone four already," King said, as he checked his battered watch. "Thought you'd want to meet first thing in the morning." A grin. "Having a cheeky lie-in, were you?"

Lucy frowned at him. *Not in the mood.* Not after all that work, hardly stopped since arriving back at her flat last night after Lambeth. Passed out for an hour at half three. Screamed herself awake, wiped the tears, then straight back at it. Boost at seven. Brompton at eight. And then more work, calling and reading and thinking, right up until she left to meet King here, now, at four. Knackered. "No," she said. Took a sip from her Coke bottle.

No, Ed, I was not having a cheeky lie-in.

I was solving the fucking case.

They were standing behind St Paul's. South side, facing the river. Wobbly Bridge in the distance, Tate smokestack beyond. Crowded here. Nearly dark already, fucking winter. She looked down to the Thames. Remembered something Simon had said once, watching the sun disappear at four o'clock: *London in winter, Luce? It's just LDN. Long. Dark. Nights.*

King pointed at the Coke bottle. "Thought we were meant to get a coffee?"

She shrugged. *Didn't say that. Said we were going to a coffee shop. But fair enough, let's get cracking.* "This way," she said. Started walking down the pedestrian path, pushing past tourists, prams, men in suits. He fell into step beside her. "So," she said, "tell me about the warehouse."

"Nothing." A sigh. "Cleared out. Took the magistrate until noon to swear out the warrant. By then they'd scarpered. And still no joy on the Tube CCTV. Salford's cracking the whip, really working the Supers, but they can't seem to spot your man anywhere. Trying to pull cameras from where you were captured, by the way." He glanced over at her, green eyes questioning. "Mount Mills, was it? Off Goswell Road?"

Lucy looked away.

Why are you asking, Ed? Because you think I live near Brompton? Because that's where we meet, the Brompton caff? And so you're wondering, what was I doing there, some shit car park in Clerkenwell? Or did you ask Wilkes, and she told you, Oh, no, Lucy lives in Clerkenwell, so then you wondered, why Brompton?

She sniffed: no aftershave. Felt disappointed, then caught herself, pushed it away.

You don't get to know why Brompton, Ed. I never asked you about Facer.

And come on, Lucy. Stop.

Fucking focus.

"Still no word from Clapham?" she asked.

He dodged a bicycle. "No. Tried last night, this morning, an hour ago, just like you asked. Voicemail. Told him we needed to speak about the MLF straight away. Nothing. Odd, yeah? Few days ago he couldn't wait to hand over that folder, now he can't be arsed to ring me back?"

A nod. *It is odd.*

"Anyway," he said, "you said you had something."

Lucy stopped walking. They were in front of a modern office block, halfway to the river. Businessmen were pushing through the revolving glass door. She looked at him, nodded.

"The man I saw last night. Not Johnson, Cates. He killed Cox. I know it now. Dead cert."

"Right, about that." He frowned. "Look, I know you said you thought it was Cates, but you only saw his face for a second, and—"

Really? You've seen the Party Trick before. "All I need, a second. Not even."

"Right, but…he's a Survivor. Are you sure—"

"Yes." She stared at him. Felt exhausted, so fucking tired. "It works with Survivors."

Trust me, Ed.

Trust me on this.

"If you say so. Right, you thought Cox killed Cates. But now, you think…Cates killed Cox?"

"Know he did."

"*Know?*"

She nodded. *Know.* She'd figured it out this morning, eating her veggie fry-up, thinking about last night's Screamer. Had it before, scores of times: running over Westminster bridge, crowds of people, everyone exposed, hands grabbing, skin peeling. But this time, it was different. This time, everyone had Rob Cates's face. All of them, hundreds. She'd thought about that as she speared a mushroom. And then, suddenly, she knew what to do.

"I called the caterer," she told King.

"What?" He laughed. "Come on. We did that, first thing. Twelve caterers, no masks. Checked their backgrounds. Interviews, full on, the works. *And* we checked the background of the owner, his family, and every single other employee. Nothing. Fuck all." He spread his big hands. "So, what'd you ask him, then?"

She stared at him. "Whether anyone had quit just *before* Cox's party."

And no one had asked him that, Ed.

King said nothing.

"Said yes, actually, now that you mention it. Some bloke. Rocked up the week before, interview, work papers, the lot. Then he just pissed off." She took a sip of her drink. "And he kept the uniform."

"So, what, you think…"

Come on, Ed.

"Not twelve caterers. Thirteen." She knew it, just like Rob Cates knew it. Knew no one would ever notice, not a single fucking one of them. Not the guests, not even the other caterers, because no one notices Survivor faces. They just turn their heads. Look away. Or if they do look, all they see is *Survivor*. See scars. Horror. A memory of something awful, something they want to shove away, push down, bury. Just that. Just like the Screamer: hundreds of Survivor faces, all of them the same. *All of them Rob Cates.*

A voice in her head, and it was Sykes, fucking Sykes: *A Meat is a Meat.*

And Cates fucking knew it.

Knew it because—that's his life now.

Invisible.

King frowned. "But how do you even know it was Cates? Could've been anyone, yeah? Some plonker signed up, changed his mind, got a better job, decided fuck it, keep the togs, can't be arsed to give them back." She watched him try to fight it. "Must have given a name, right? Don't tell me it's Cates? Or Johnson?"

She shook her head. *No, he wouldn't use his real name.*

"Rudy Peters."

"Well, then, there you go, just some poor sod who—"

She pulled her mobile from her hoodie pocket. Tapped, handed it to him. "Meet Sir Rudoph Peters," she told him. "Died, 1982." Watched as he scrolled down. "Biochemist." He looked up at her. Stared. She nodded, took a sip of her drink. "Developed the antidote for a chemical weapon called Lewisite during World War II."

Clever Rob Cates.

Bit too clever, yeah?

"Christ," said King. He handed back her mobile, tiny in his huge hand. "That's...but...look, we thought Johnson was avenging Cates. But if Johnson *is* Cates, then where's the real Johnson? And why would Cates kill Cox?"

A tiny grin. "What I want to ask Cates. Which is why we're here."

"Cates is coming *here*?"

She shook her head. *Not Cates.* Checked her mobile: quarter past. *Perfect. And now…*She looked up. Smiled. Pointed. "Him."

Enoch Clapham pushed his way through the revolving glass door.

‡ ‡ ‡

Right on time, you horrid fucking skeleton.

Clapham emerged from the door and stepped onto the pedestrian path. Striped suit, red tie, croc loafers: a businessman. No sign of the big metal cross, but Lucy guessed it was there, hidden under his shirt. He straightened the tie, slung a leather satchel over his bony shoulder, then turned left, towards the river.

"That wanker," King growled. "Couldn't be bothered to ring me back?"

He started to follow, but Lucy held up a hand. "Give it a tick." *Don't want Clapham scuttling back into his little hole.* She stood, watching, as the preacher reached the end of the office block and turned left down a side street. "Now," she said. Started walking after him.

"I don't understand," King told her, as they rounded the corner. "Where's he—"

"Business meeting. Coffee shop." She pointed up ahead. "Just there."

"How do you know?"

"Rang his office." She'd worked it out this morning, after King texted to tell her Clapham wasn't returning calls. Remembered something she'd seen doing research. Went online and there it was, in every single Hand of God video, bottom of the screen, tiny letters: © Divine Sword Ltd. *Clapham's company*. And once she had that, the rest was a snap. The Companies House website gave her everything she needed. Registered office? Right next to St Paul's. *Easy-peasy*. "Called a few hours ago."

"And they just told you when and where he was having a business meeting?"

She shrugged. *Something like that.* "I can be persuasive."

Ahead, Clapham checked his watch. Sped up. Passed another office block, a car park, a Pret. At the end of the street, a spire rose high above the modern glass and concrete buildings: an old church, soot-blackened, mossy. Lucy watched as he trotted up the church steps and entered.

King frowned. "You said a coffee shop…"

Trust me, Ed.

She climbed the steps, pushed through the church door. Bright inside: white walls, high ceilings. Stained glass windows, big ones. A pulpit. But no pews, just square tables filled with people drinking coffee, eating, chatting. Remembered Simon taking her here, banging on about the old coat of arms on the wall, a Charles or a James, forgot which, whatever. *Just wanted to drink my espresso, Si.* "See?" she told King. "Coffee shop."

He nodded. "Not exactly your little local caff."

Local? Never said I lived in Brompton, Ed.

She looked around, spotted Clapham at a table in the corner, fiddling with something in his satchel. Had his back to her. "Come on," she told King. Wove through the coffee drinkers, walked up to Clapham's table. Pulled out a chair, sat. "Sorry I'm late," she said. "But thanks for taking the time."

Clapham stared at her. "Officer?" Glanced at King, then back to Lucy. A skeletal smile, but she saw a flicker of something else in his eyes. *Anger? Fear?* "A pleasure to see you both, but afraid I'm here to meet—"

"Advertising exec, woman? Rung up a few hours back? Wants to put adverts in your videos, companies all lined up, big money?" She grinned. *I could hear you drooling over the phone. Practically begged me to meet.* "Not so keen on the business bit any more. Sorry." Shrugged. "Did say the coffee was on me, though, so…" Nodded at the barista. "If you'd like something, by all means, my shout."

Out the corner of her eye, she caught King looking at her. *What? Told you I called his office.*

"Thank you," said Clapham, "but afraid I must be leaving." He began to pack up his satchel. "My children depend on me, and—"

"Johnson," she said. Leaned forward. "The man you call John Johnson. Need to find him."

Clapham stopped packing. "I wouldn't know how to begin…"

Lucy watched his fingers steal towards the hidden metal cross. Thought about Tom Winter, pointing a blade in her face, telling her how sick he was of Hand of God spies: so fucking sick, ready to mutilate her just to make the point. *You know, Clapham. May not know where he rests his head, exactly, but you sure as fuck know how to get to him.*

So spill.

"You have spies," she said. "Know you do. Just tell me. How do I find him?"

"Spies?" He shrugged again. "We must know our enemy, and the devils are enemies of God and man. But caution is always called for. Mistakes are made. Even those men sent by Moses into Canaan brought back a false report, and for it they faced God's arrow and—"

Don't have time for this shit.

Cates is the killer, he has the antidote, I need it. End of.

So fucking tell me.

"Where?"

"Afraid I would need a few days."

She sat back in her chair. Crossed her arms, glared. Thought about King's question: *Few days back, you were dying to point us to the MLF. Ought to be delighted to have us after them. Over the fucking moon. So why suddenly shtum?*

King was staring at her now, but she ignored him. Kept thinking.

Know you're awful, Clapham. Vile.

So what's the worst possible explanation?

Ran fingers through her hair. Thought about Hammer, whacking away at something. Something big, something hidden. About Cates: *When I hit this…*About the both of them, working away in the middle of the night, something so secret that they had to hide it in an old abandoned warehouse in Lambeth…

And then she knew.

"An attack," she said.

Clapham flinched, and she knew she was right.

"Not just the usual copycat attacks," she told him. "Bigger, right?" Watched him squirm. "And *you* don't want us to stop it." Tugged her hoodie strings. *You want it to happen, you fucking horror. Because it fits perfectly with your vile message, yeah? Survivors are evil, Survivors are the enemy. And if a few of them do something awful, well then, you'll get more page views, won't you? More fucking sheep, sell more fucking Hand of God T-shirts.* "It's why you've been avoiding us."

King chimed in. "Could've rung me back, arsehole."

Clapham said nothing, just stared down at the table. Around them, cups clinked, people laughed.

Finally: "If something happens, it is God's plan. Who am I to interfere?"

God's plan? For fuck's sake.

King balled a huge fist. "A terrorist attack? Are you fucking mental?"

"What God wills, must be right." A maddening smile spread across Clapham's face. "Because it is He who so wills it, you see? If the devils were to do a thing, whatever that may be, it is because our Father in His awful, wondrous, incomprehensible—"

Lucy pounded the table.

Enough.

She stood. Stared down at Clapham, eyes blazing. "If you know something," she said, "you tell me. Right. Bloody. *Now.*" Paused. "Or else I *will* find a way to make you pay. Yeah?"

Fucking try me.

He took a breath. Looked at her, then away. Finally, voice faint: "Might have heard something. My sources, they aren't clear, you understand? But I *may* have overheard something about, perhaps, say, an explosion—"

"*Where?*"

"The Eye." Startled to chuckle; tried to hold it, couldn't. "Which is perfect. Because, you see, the eye is the Devil's doorway, and—"

"*When?*"

He grinned. "The moment of silence."

Oh fuck.

King grabbed her shoulder, green eyes wide.

"Lucy…that's in fifteen minutes."

‡ ‡ ‡

"Hold on tight," King told her.

The Toyota tore over Waterloo Bridge.

Lucy held her breath. Checked her phone. *Five minutes, fuck.* Looked out the window, saw the Eye, getting closer, *hurry, fucking hurry.* They were on blues and twos now, blowing past buses, cars, vans. Saw blue lights on the Embankment, other cops: too far away, never make it. *But we can, hope we can, faster, come on, faster, fucking faster...*

"Fuck," said King. "Fucking Clapham. If he'd just told us sooner..."

Drive, Ed.

The car radio was crackling: "...all units...Code Zero... repeat, London Eye..."

Come on, come on.

King slammed the brakes. A van, black one, blocking them.

"*Move*," he yelled. Hit the horn. "Fuck's sake, come on."

Her thumb beat on the window, *thump thump thump.*

Hurry.

King: "Fucking *move*..."

Come on...

Then it moved and they were flying over the bridge, Eye on their right. King swung them round a roundabout, *hang on*, wheel spinning, tyres squealing, *four minutes*. Past Waterloo and then down the street, people staring, lights flashing, siren blaring, *almost*...

Squealed to a stop in front of the Eye.

A cabbie's voice, two years back, that first night: *Mind if I set you down here?*

"Come on," she said. Grabbed the door handle, jumped out, looked up. The Eye was lit, a ring of white light cutting a circle in the black sky. Not rotating: stopped. She ran towards it, trainers flying, legs pumping, *three minutes* and she needed to find Cates, *where the fuck, must be here, must be...*

"Look," cried King.

She looked, saw tourists, down on the ground, hands over heads. Half-dozen armed Survivors standing over them, guns drawn. Scanned their faces as she ran, looking for Cates, find Cates, must find Cates...

Not you, not you, not you...

Saw Dutton, huge. Winter, scowling.

No Cates.

Fuck.

King: "Where do we—"

"*Cates.* Cates has the trigger."

"But how…they all look the same…"

Fuck fuck fuck…

Saw Hammer. Off to the side, staring at something attached to a capsule. Something big, bulky, car-sized. Saw more of them, two more, attached to other capsules. Big long tube like a cable strung between them. Watched him as he turned, shouted something to someone. Looked to see who and—

Cates.

She pointed. "*There.*"

There, up by the boarding platform, near an open capsule: Rob Cates.

He was holding his phone.

King ran for him but she was faster, sprinting ahead, top speed, a blur. Over a railing, another, onto the entrance ramp, almost on him but Hammer spotted her, shouted. Cates froze. Looked around, trapped. Nearly there but he turned, ran to a capsule, and it was moving now, the Eye was moving, his door was closing and she sped down the platform fast *faster* closing *fuck* but she caught it, leapt inside.

The capsule door clicked shut behind her.

She looked up. Rob Cates was staring at her, phone in his left hand.

"Stay back," he said.

Lucy took a breath. *Inhale, exhale.* One step towards him.

"You don't want to do this, Rob."

The capsule jolted and they were rising up, floating into the jet-black sky.

"Of course I do."

His face was scarred, badly, worse than most, but she knew it was him. Saw the photo from the SIU database in her mind. *Same face. It's you.*

"No," she said. "No, please."

"*Yes.* I need to. It needs to be done. They need to *see.*"

She glanced out the window. Saw the capsules with the bulky black objects dangling from them, the long black tube. Rubbed her tattoo, tried not to think about what was inside, what would happen. *Focus. Focus on Cates.*

"They all need to see." A sigh. "Wanted to watch this from the ground, but so be it…"

Right. No choice then.

She raised her fists. Another step towards him. Chin tucked, eyes up.

Asking for it…

He pulled a gun.

A memory flashed: her flat, two years ago. Manga's gun, pointed at her face.

Fuck…

Felt her pulse spike. Started to panic, fuck me, *fuck*, then fought it off.

Calm.

"I know you killed Cox," she told him. "Know why. What he did. Holding back Boosts."

She stared at his mobile as she talked.

If I leap…time it just right, grab his wrist…no, too far, fuck…

Cates laughed.

"Everyone loved him," he said. "Flinders Cox, England's hero. Oh, what a great man. Money for churches. Survivors' rights. Christ." He spat, big gob on the metal floor. "But *I* knew. Knew what he did. And so yes, I killed him. Killed him before he could get his glory, jammed a cross in his fucking eye." A grin. "Know why? Why the cross?"

274

She shook her head.

Took a half-step forward.

Little bit closer…just a little…

"From the Bible. Matthew. Know the one? *You hypocrite, first take the plank out of your own eye…*Goddamn hypocrite. What he was. Posh SRA dinners, fundraisers, disgusting." The capsule kept rising, higher and higher. "He created Survivors. We're his children, he made us, caused us to be, it's unspeakable…"

Another step.

Almost…

"Stay *back*." He held the gun up.

The Thames below them was black. Coal-black.

Cates kept talking. "Know the worst bit? He didn't even recognize me. Didn't even *see* me. Just saw this." Ran fingers over his scarred skin. "A Meat. A Meat is a Meat is a Meat."

Another jolt. The capsule stopped. They were at the top of the circle, high above London.

So close…

Quick glance down at the other capsules. He noticed. Frowned.

"Don't look down *there*," he told her. "That's nothing. Look *there*."

He pointed across the river.

Towards Big Ben: a giant needle, jabbing the sky.

Oh.

Oh fuck.

And she realized: *He's going to blow up Parliament, too.*

Cates smiled. "You don't understand," he told her. "How could you?"

"I understand. I do, Rob, I swear…"

Oh God, I do…

A laugh, loud one. Gun still raised. "How can you *possibly* understand?"

275

She stared at him. Eyes dark, bagged, purple.

Took a breath.

"Because I lost someone," she said.

Then she leapt.

Caught his wrist, pulled him down. He held onto the phone but the gun clanged on the floor and she reached for it, *must get it*, straining, *almost*, but he grabbed her. Long arms, strong. Pulled her back. Her fingers scraped the floor but he was too strong, she was sliding, slipping backwards and then he had her, arm back, *fuck*, trapped. He pulled her up, pushed her face against the glass.

In the distance, a bell rang, once.

Oh God oh Jack…

"Look," he said. "*Look.* I want you to *look*."

It was the moment of silence.

No.

No no no fuck FUCK…

"Now," he said.

And then he pressed the button.

CHAPTER TWENTY-ONE

Oh God oh Jack…

…?

A moment passed.

Lucy opened an eye.

Did it…? Am I…?

The fuck?

Felt Cates relax his grip. Shook loose, dove for the gun, grabbed it. Pointed it at his back. "*Hands,*" she said. "Raise them. Do it. *Now.*"

He ignored her. Just stood, staring across the river.

"Look," he said.

She looked. Quick glance, then another, longer, a stare.

Giant beams of light cut the night sky. Searchlights, slicing upward from Lambeth embankment: eight, nine, ten, she lost count. All of them were pointed at Big Ben.

Lighting it? But…

"Now," he said. "Watch."

At the top of the clock dials: movement. She squinted. Something falling, unfolding: giant banners, red and black, dropping down over the dials, covering them. They billowed for a moment, and then she saw what they were.

Oh—

Survivor faces.

Enormous red scarred faces, their great black eyes staring out at London.

She shook her head. *But…the bombs? Clapham said…?*

"Now they'll see us," Cates said. Voice calm. "They all will. Can't look away, not from this. No masks, no little Hand of God stickers blotting us out." He glanced down at his mobile, tapped, then smiled. "Here." Turned to her, waved the phone. "Can't see this one from here. Have a look."

She kept the gun raised but reached, grabbed the mobile. Looked down at the screen.

Below them, the Eye's great circle was covered. Another banner: a Survivor eye, huge and black, hanging down from a giant black tube. It was lit from the side by lights dangling from the capsules. Bulky, car-sized lights.

Oh…

Clapham's voice: *My sources, they aren't clear, you understand?*

She lowered the gun.

Took a breath.

Stared out at Big Ben. At the Survivor faces, faces she'd spent two years avoiding, dodging, slipping like punches because that's what they were: a punch in the gut, hard one, guilt working her bruised body over and over, *whack whack whack*. She felt herself tear up. Tried to stop it, hold it back but she couldn't so fuck it, crying now. Crying because she didn't understand, couldn't work it out, never could: *I'm still here, alive, breathing, not blown to bits, ash in the Thames…but why?*

Why am I still here, Si?

Why am I still here, and you're not?

She shut her eyes.

Heard a screech. Thought it was the Eye moving but no, not that, it was a different screech, a screech in her mind. And she was back then, two years ago, in the bathroom, on the floor, had been for hours now, knees to chest, rocking. Then the screech, again: metal on wood, furniture moving. The door clicked open. Just a crack, just enough for a Boost to roll through. It hit her foot. Stopped. Simon's voice: *Inject it, Luce.* So she did, right there, and then she opened the door, rushed out, saw him. Fear in his eyes. On the bed: four boxes, stacked.

Think I'm okay, he said. *Exposed at the end, just a bit, but think I'm okay.*

It's okay, Luce.

Hours later, tightness in his chest. Could just be imagining it, Luce, but she knew, they both knew. Then the drooling. Pinpoint pupils. And then it was a blur, all a blur and she was at an Iso Centre, grim nurses, doctors with clipboards, orderly pushing her back, thick arms, raspy voice: *Time to go, Miss, don't make me...* Then she was on the floor, the cold, dirty lobby floor, fingering her ring as women wailed and families sobbed and she was in Hell again, a death watch, they all knew what was coming, all of them, no one goes to a Death House to get better, *oh God, Si...*

And it was now again.

Eyes still closed, but she was now. Here. *And I shouldn't be, shouldn't, no, because it was my fault, Si, mine, and I should be gone and you should be here Si and I don't fucking understand...*

In the distance, a bell rang.

Lucy opened her eyes.

Exhaled. Looked out.

Across the river, banners fell to earth. Spotlights shut. The sky above the river was black.

"It's done," Cates said. Took a deep breath, then turned to her. "I'm all yours now. Had to see this through, else I would've turned myself in a week ago, still soaked in Flinders's blood." Reached into his black jacket, chuckled as she raised the gun. "Shoot me for this?" Pulled out a fag packet and a lighter. "Bit excessive, no?" Offered, shrugged, put one in his mouth. "Disabled the smoke alarms," he told her. "Had to, release mechanism would've triggered them, stopped the wheel."

She watched him light up. Wiped a tear. Frowned.

Ought to be happy.

Have the killer, there he is. Caught him. You did, Lucy. You.

A jolt as the Eye began to move again.

Cates sat down on the bench in the centre of the capsule. Blew a cloud of smoke. "In my defence," he said, "Flinders tried to kill me first. Did you know that?"

Lucy shook her head, but she was only half-listening now. Just standing by the window, arms crossed, staring down into the blackness of the Thames below.

Caught the killer, but it doesn't feel like it matters any more, does it? Doesn't feel like it pays the Debt...

"He did," Cates said. "Tried two years ago." Took another drag. "I went to him, start of the Scourge, showed him the new reagent. He agreed with my findings. Promised we'd make the switch, roll out the new process. Boosts for all." A chuckle. "Went home to the miserable little flat John and I were sharing in Shepherd Market. Remember thinking I'd get John to make omelettes. Best omelettes, John's. Old girlfriend taught him. Bit of a lush but she made a great fucking omelette..."

Point was always that Cox is a hero, the man who stopped London Black.

Cates took the cigarette out of his mouth. "And then I noticed my pupils. Pinpoint. John's, too. Knew what that meant. Must have been a night-time attack, or else we walked through it, touched something, who knows? Too late for Boosts. Fucked. Fuck hospitals, knew we were toxic, just spread it. So we locked ourselves up. Waited to die." Rolled the cig between his fingers, stared down at it. A sigh. "Only thing to do, really."

They were moving down, down into the blackness.

But if Cox was a monster...

He kept talking. "Mine came with high fever. Delirious. John's, I don't know." A shrug. "Bit of a blur for a week or so. And then it was over, and I was alive. And John was not. Found him in his room. Blood everywhere. Skin. Christ." He paused. Deep breath. "Cleaned him up, thought about what to do next. Took two seconds on my phone to realize there was a Boost shortage, world had gone to complete shit. Rang Flinders. Said he wanted to speak with me, had to explain. Could I meet him?"

If Cox was a monster, then catching his killer doesn't pay the Debt, does it?

"On my way, I was attacked. Knife. Fled home. They followed. Pounded on the door. John's body was there, so I put my jacket on him. My hat. Didn't look much like me, John. We looked like our fathers, not Mum. But now? Well…" Another shrug. "Pushed him up against the door, sort of how you would be if you were trying to stop a break-in. And then I hid. In a wardrobe, like a fucking child. Heard the door come down. Stayed there, two minutes, five, ten. When I came out, I saw the door down, blood on the floor. John's body was gone. Thought they'd killed me. And they had, in a way." Took a last drag, exhaled, rubbed the butt out on the wooden bench. "No more Rob Cates. Too risky, they'd just try again. Filed a police report, and that was it. I was John now."

Lucy stared down into the Thames: a giant black pit, gaping, ready to swallow her up.

Only one thing can pay the Debt now.

Only one thing, and it must be real, must be, please God, please be real…

She turned to Cates.

"So you let him live because of the antidote?"

Please…please, God…

"Of course," he said. "Why else?"

Oh, thank you. She smiled. Big smile, first in years, her cheek squeezing her black eye shut. Felt like laughing and crying, both, fuck, fucking amazing, it was happening, finally fucking happening, she could pay the Debt. *Oh, God, thank you…*

He nodded. "Hated Flinders, but I respected him as a scientist. He promised us an antidote. I believed him. Spent two years waiting. Watching. D'you know, he actually used my old lab to do the work? Tiny little lab built into a railway arch…"

I was right, the secret lab, the antidote, all of it, oh, thank you…

She smiled again. "So it's—"

"It's beautiful," he said. "Better than just a normal antidote. Works prophylactically, too. One jab, that's it. Vulnerable no more. Fucking genius. And to think that someone so evil could do that, make something so brilliant, so good…"

Lucy stared at his face, looking at him, drinking it in. A red face, completely red: ragged red forehead, crimson nose, cheeks lumpy. Scars everywhere: red chin, red neck, red hands. And then, in the middle of his chest, a bright red dot.

She frowned.

Wait—

Started to move, but it was too late. Heard glass breaking behind her, and Cates was down, sprawled on the floor, blood gushing from the gunshot wound, wetting her hands as she tried to stop it, *fuck*, pressing down, *oh fuck…*

"Doesn't matter," he gasped. "It's done."

No, no, wait…I need the antidote, you have the antidote…

She leant over him, pleading: "Where *is* it? Who has it? Did you hide it? *Where?*"

Can't lose it, not now, oh fuck…

He looked up at her, black eyes wide.

"What? The antidote?" He coughed, sprayed blood. "But…"

But what?

Eyes closed. A last gasp.

"…but I left it…on Flinders' desk…"

CHAPTER TWENTY-TWO

"You need to tell me where we're going," King said. "I'm driving, for fuck's sake."

"Left." The respirator muffled Lucy's voice. It was her best mask, the black one with two 40mm filters. Reusable. Bought it online after the Scourge ended: never know, just in case. *And this is as "case" as it fucking gets, yeah?* "There." She pointed a butyl rubber-gloved finger. "Left there." Watched him frown.

Not telling you where we're going, Ed.

You'd never take me if I did.

King spun the wheel. "Then at least tell me why you're…you know." He waved a big hand in front of his own face: *wearing a fucking gas mask.*

She shrugged. Said nothing, just stared out the window as they passed Charterhouse Square. Everything looked blue. Foggy. *Fucking lens inserts, can't see a thing, shittest bit of kit.* The mask pinched her ears, too. She pulled on the rubber strap, thought about last night. Six o'clock by the time she'd finished the post-shooting trauma debrief—*why yes, Mr Occupational Health Advisor, I have heard of PTSD before, actually*—and cabbed it back to her flat. Her levels dropped from 6.2 to 5.6 in the taxi. Just fell off a cliff, fucking terrifying. And as she'd stood at her bathroom sink, scrubbing the last of Rob Cates's blood from her hands, the monitor started to shriek again.

The drop from 5.6 to 4.9 took sixty seconds.

She knew what *that* meant.

Means this is it. Today was her last day out, she could feel it. Could be six hours, four, two. And then she was finished. Done. Emergency kit would do for this car ride, maybe, but give it a week or two, the usual copycat attacks? No chance. Too easy to fuck up: a tear, a slip, all it took. No, she'd be trapped in the flat, alone with her thoughts and the Debt and the bare black walls, a real-live, never-ending, fuck-you-Lucy Screamer. *One more day to find the antidote. All I've got.*

No more tomorrows.

She sighed. Looked over at King. "Clapham. Do we have him yet?"

"Three DCs looking. But once we find him, I still don't understand what you mean to—"

She waved a glove. *Don't need to understand, Ed. Just fucking find him.* "And the rifle?"

"Still checking."

They passed Smithfield Market. For a split second she thought she saw Dad, a blue-tinted ghost, wandering alone among the pig heads and hanging carcasses, searching for his discount black pudding. She blinked: gone. Turned back to King. "But it *was* a police rifle, yeah?"

A nod. "Chief Super just finished a presser. Official stance is, yes, the bullet that killed Rob Cates was Met-issued, investigation ongoing, but by the way we just solved Flinders Cox's murder, thank you very much, so how about you lot fuck off and let us do our job for a change?" He grinned. "Bit more media-friendly, perhaps, but that was the thrust." Sped up to beat a red light. "And behind the scenes, it's already being written off. Dozen AFOs watched Cates point a gun at you just minutes before. Everyone nervy. A finger slipped. Accident."

Accident?

Come on, Ed.

"Another left," she said. Looked out the window as the Toyota turned onto the Embankment. Remembered Rob Cates, smile stretching his scarred skin when he'd told her about the antidote. *Beautiful. Said it was beautiful. One jab, no longer Vulnerable.*

But fuck that, who cares, point is it pays the Debt, yeah? That's what counts. All that counts. Or... She tugged her hoodie strings with purple fingers. Frowned. *Or do I just want it for myself? That it, Lucy? Levels dropping so you need a way out? Just saving yourself, really, doing the selfish fucking thing after all and that's why it should've been you, you not him and you'll never pay it off, never, and—*

King cleared his throat.

"I have a confession," he said. "Sorry. Can't hold it any longer."

She looked over. Deep breath. Nodded.

Go on, then.

"Brompton," he said. "I worked it out." Paused. "Didn't mean to. None of my business, I know. But then you texted this morning, gave an address." Nodded behind them, towards Goswell Road. "Said 'at my flat'. But...that's half an hour away from Brompton."

Whoops.

"And then I just couldn't help it. Tried, but I'm a detective, for Christ's sake, it was going to fucking kill me. So I pulled up a map, and there it was. Your little caff, one with the veggie fry-ups, spot we always meet." He glanced over. "Bang next to Brompton Cemetery."

The car raced down the Embankment.

Lucy said nothing.

Turned away. Closed her eyes, thought about the cemetery. Big iron gates, gravel paths that crunched beneath her trainers. Simon had taken her there once, prep for a new tour. Fucking loved it. *This is London, Luce. Right here. Can't you feel it? All these Londoners, hundreds of years of history and people and stories. Brilliant, yeah?* So that's where she'd chosen. Picked out the gravestone: old one, skull at the top, spidery writing. What he'd want. Bottom covered now, half-buried in tiny black discs: her Boost caps. Saved them, brought them, one at a time, over and over. Every morning, dark out, Tube all the way from Goswell Road. Hundreds of them now, stacks and stacks, spilling onto the cold ground. Her tokens. Promises.

The gas mask muffled a sigh.

Don't want to talk about it.

"I told you about my daughter," he said. Softly: "I know you lost someone, too."

You think you know, Ed. Reckon you've got it all worked out.

But you don't.

Not all of it.

Because you don't know about The Thing. You can't, no one does…

She started to run gloved fingers through her hair but stopped, mustn't, fuck up the seal.

"I just can't help it," King told her. "I see you and think of me…" Kept talking, *openness* and *helped me* and the T-word, but she was ignoring him now. Eyes open again, staring straight ahead as they passed Waterloo Bridge, the old Egyptian needle, Embankment Station.

Right. Close enough.

Go time.

"I need the antidote," she said.

King stopped talking about therapy. Glanced over, frowned. "Yeah," he said, "I know, you keep saying you want to find it. But honestly, Lucy, are you *sure* you heard Cates right? Because it still seems so fucking unlikely…"

You're not listening, Ed.

"Boosts aren't working any more." A pause. "Not for me."

She watched through her mask as he connected the dots.

"Wait, so that's why all the…"

Yes. That's why all the fucking kit.

She reached into her hoodie pocket. Took out the Boost. Uncapped it, held it up. "The second I jab this, my clock is ticking, yeah?" Turned away from him, pulled up the hoodie. Her entire stomach was purple: bruises from Boosts, from Orange Trainers's punches, all the same, really. "So I'll need to move fast. Fast as I bloody can." She took a breath. Jabbed, pressed the plunger, gasped. Watched as the drug disappeared into her body, as her hand started to shake. *You deserve it, deserve the pain, oh Christ it fucking hurts.* Pulled the syringe away. Capped it. Exhaled, then turned back to King: "Now pull over. Here."

He frowned.

"*Here?*"

Yes, Ed.

Of course, here. Where the fuck else?

She looked out the window as he turned the wheel.

They were pulling into New Scotland Yard.

‡ ‡ ‡

Lucy got out of the Toyota. Slammed the door. Started walking.

"Wait, Lucy…"

She heard King calling after her. Ignored him, kept marching down the pavement towards New Scotland Yard. It was raining. Grey. Better than blue, at least, fucking lens inserts, she hated those things. Left the mask in the car. Gloves, too. *Don't need them. Not just yet. One more day, just one left, need to hurry, fucking hurry—*

"Look," said King, as he caught up and fell into step beside her, "you can't just storm in…"

"No?"

"No." He shook his head. "Right, fine, you figured out Cates, well done you, but it doesn't *matter*. Not for this. Rules and regs, that's the game, right? And as of now, you're still formally suspended, still—"

Lucy cut him off with a glare.

Radioactive?

So get a lead apron, Ed.

I'm going the fuck inside.

She shot through the revolving door, into the gleaming lobby. "Someone's dirty," she told him as she pushed through a crowd of milling reporters. "Must be. Else, who nicked that photo?"

He lowered his voice.

"Well, Cates might've…"

Come on. "No." She shook her head. Sped up. "Might've missed it. Or, might've seen it and left it." Blew right past the intake desk, fuck signing in. "But he *definitely* didn't see it, leave it, then change his bloody mind and stomp back to the scene of his carefully planned murder, yeah? No one bloody would." *And definitely not clever Rob Cates.*

Two uniforms sauntered towards them. Lucy blazed right through, sending coffees flying.

"But why?" King was struggling to keep pace. "Why would a cop take that photo?"

"Don't know yet." A frown. "But it's *there.* I see it. The photo, Cates's shooting. It's everywhere. A giant, cop-shaped hole." She hit the end of a corridor, turned left. "Look. Who would want to steal the antidote? Clapham." *Vile fucking skeleton.* "But how would Clapham know it's there? Who tells him, Cox? Cates? Not bloody likely." Another left, speeding down a hallway, whizzing past secretaries, uniforms, suits. "But what about a cop? A cop who follows Clapham? Told us himself, cops in his little flock."

"So, what, Cates kills Cox…"

"And then a cop spots the antidote, realizes what it is, nicks it for his precious Father Enoch."

She stopped.

They were outside MIT19. A blue plastic tarp covered the missing window.

King frowned as she reached for the door. "You can't go in there. You go in, still working, blatantly violating your suspension, and—"

"There's a dirty cop," she said. "And I know who. Look."

She dug into her jeans pocket, pulled out her mobile. Started tapping. Her head felt light from staying up all night in her little black flat, working. Searching. Watching every fucking Hand of God video ever posted, two years' worth, gears turning, looking for a link. Actors in all the recent videos. But as she'd dug deeper, scrolling back through time, the actors fell away and she began to see the beginning, the real Hand of God. Small meetings, manky little basements. Men, angry ones. Men who stared, grinning, listening as Clapham screeched. Who screeched right back, writhing, shaking, drinking in the hatred. *So fucking terrifying.* And as she'd stared at her mobile, eyes weary, blackness all around, the Party Trick worked its magic: *Bouncer. Boxer. Teacher.*

And one dirty fucking cop.

She handed the phone to King.

See, Ed?

On the screen, dressed in a white robe, face caught mid-shriek— DCI-to-be Andy Sykes.

‡ ‡ ‡

"Oh fuck," King said.

Lucy nodded. *Oh fuck indeed.* "With me now?" Didn't wait for an answer, just pushed past, through the door, into the squad room.

It was packed.

"All-hands," King told her from the doorway. "Chief Super's orders. After that presser, he wants the Cox murder done and dusted. Final reports, straight away. So everyone's in."

Everyone? Perf. She looked around. Sniffed. It smelt like BO. A dozen DCs sat in cubicles, jackets off, sleeves rolled. One nodded to her but she ignored him, just took off marching across the room. *Here I come, Sykes.* Stormed past her crap little desk, over to the window office Sykes had managed to bag, never knew how, probably fucking blackmailed someone. *Fucking Sykes.* The door was shut. She pulled it open.

Empty.

Now where is he?

"When you find him," King asked behind her, "what then?"

"I have a plan." She turned, dodged a fat DS—*look out, coming through*—and started down the hallway, ducking into conference rooms as she went. "Sure everyone's in?" she asked King, ignoring the glares from the budget meeting she'd just bombed into. "*Everyone?* Dead positive?"

"Meant to be." He shrugged. "Chief Super emails round, that's a three-line whip, right?"

Right. So, where'd you scarper off to, Sykes?

Fuck, no time for this shit.

She kept moving, blazing down the corridor, past Wilkes's office—*hiya, Ma'am*—checking every room as she raced along. Pulled a door: a cluttered room filled with laptops, Media Review stacking chairs. *No.* She tried another door. *No.* Another. *No, Christ.* Almost at the end of the hallway now, *where the fuck*, nearly running, *fuck me*, reached the kitchen and—

There you are.

Sykes was standing next to the kettle, huddled over his mobile with a skinny DC. She watched them snicker. Sykes pointed at the screen, sneered, muttered something she couldn't quite hear.

You're mine now, you wanker.

"Sykes," she said.

He looked up. Did a double take.

"The fuck are *you* doing here?"

"I know about you," she told him. Crossed her arms. "The Hand of God. The antidote."

Sykes waved the skinny DC away: "Swifty later, mate." Stared at Lucy. "Don't know what you're on about, Stone." To King, towering behind her: "And I'm surprised at *you*, new man. Seem clever enough." Pointed his mobile at Lucy. "Really want to hitch yourself to this fucking nutter?"

King held up Lucy's phone.

"That's not you, then, Andy?"

Sykes frowned, then leaned forward. Peered at the screen. "Yeah, well…" Shrugged. "Fuck it. So what if it is?" A smug grin. "Not illegal, yeah? Can't tell me how to worship my god."

Worship? God?

You're a walking fucking hate crime, Sykes.

He waggled his mobile at her. "Not even against the Code now, is it?"

"Maybe not," she said. "But swiping something from a murder scene bloody well is."

Sykes smirked. To King: "See? Mental, this one."

She ignored him. "Night of Cox's murder. Saw you by the staircase." *You were acting like a right fucking wanker. Hard for you to remember, I know, since that's all the time.* "I went upstairs after. Examined the scene. Where'd *you* go, then? Rest of the night, where?"

A snort. "You taking the piss? That's personal."

Lucy said nothing, just stared. Watched his eyes move. Knew he was coming up with a story, dead cert, seen it a million times before. *I'm a fucking pro, Sykes. Lie to me and I'll know.*

"Fine," he said. Gave an exaggerated shrug. "Really want to know? I went to check on Veronica Cox. Family liaison, yeah? Doing my fucking job. Drove her home. May have stayed on a bit." He winked at King. "Liaised."

So fucking vile.

Nurse Jowlsey would never.

King's eyes flashed and he scowled, crossed his giant forearms.

Sykes: "And after that, had a fag, headed back to mine. Why?"

She took a step towards him. "You're lying, Sykes." Another step. "You disgusting muppet." Close to him now, close enough to smell his breath, smelt like stale beer. *Don't have time for this shit.* "You're lying and I can prove it."

"Oh, yeah?" Another waggle of his phone. "Really?"

She looked down at the mobile.

Really. Watch me.

Grabbed it.

"Oi," cried Sykes, but he was too late. She was on the move, flying back down the hallway, towards the squad room. Pulled out the paperclip she'd tucked into her jeans pocket, straightened it as she marched. Thought of her plan. *Step one: get his mobile, check.* "Hold up," shouted Sykes, from somewhere behind her, "that's my fucking phone, you crazy bint, you can't just *do* that..." But she did. Jammed the clip into the mobile, pulled out the SIM card. Tossed the phone over her shoulder. *Want it? All yours.* Reached a corner desk, where a tablet-sized device was hooked to a laptop. *Hello, old friend.* Sat down, shoved the SIM card into the device.

*Step two: geotracking data. Now...*She clicked the mouse. *Date?* Another click. *Time?*

"Fucking mental," Sykes said. "I swear by Christ..."

He lunged at her, but King reached out, held him back. "Let her."

She kept clicking.

Now I hit this, bang, and then—

A map flashed onto the screen, video controls beneath.

Brilliant.

"So," she said. "Night of the murder." Pulled the slider to midnight.

A blue dot appeared on the map: Mayfair.

"Cox's flat. Now, then, let's see where you *really* went..."

She clicked the play button.

Dots began to pop, one after another. Three more on Cox's flat, then they began to move east. Lucy watched as they crossed London: past Soho, up Charing Cross Road, down Theobalds Road. Reached Clerkenwell, then stopped.

"There," said King. Pointed. "That's Veronica's."

Lucy clicked pause. "Right." Turned in her seat, eyed Sykes. "Now, where do you live? May as well tell me. Find out in two ticks, must be in here, somewhere…"

He scowled. Spat it out: "Epping."

"Brill," she said. "Epping. Right. North then, yeah?"

So let's see…

She clicked the mouse.

"Stop this," Sykes told her. "Right fucking now."

The dots began to move again.

They headed west, back towards Mayfair.

See, Ed? Now watch this…

The dots marched along, up Theobalds Road, down Charing Cross Road.

Reached Soho.

Stopped.

Huh?

Lucy frowned at the screen. *What, did you stop for a pint, then? Or…?* Pushed the slider forward: one o'clock. Half one. Two. *The fuck?* Three, half three, four o'clock. *Can't be…*

No movement. Just dot after dot, all on the same spot in Soho. *I don't understand…*

"Where *is* that?" King asked. Pointed at the dots.

She zoomed in. Read the name: "The Velvet Rope."

Oh.

Oh fuck.

A fucking strip club.

But—

"Happy now, Stone?" She didn't turn around, couldn't bear to see the look on Sykes's face. "Said it was personal, but you just don't listen, do you?" A little chuckle. "You're done, you are. Throwing fucking chairs, now this nonsense." Paused. "Stay there. Right there. Both of you. I'm off to have a word with the Chief Super."

Fuck. Fuck fuck fuck...

"Fuck," said King.

"*Rats*," said Lucy.

She shut her eyes. Felt like vomiting. *But it has to be Sykes. Fucking has to be, else what? Who? Clapham, yes, but there needs to be a cop for it to make sense...* Ran fingers through her hair. *And there's no time, no more fucking time.*

She took a deep breath. Let it out.

Calm. Need to focus.

Tugged her hoodie strings. Wished she hadn't just done that, but fuck it, nothing she could do about it now. *So what next?* There was last night, Cates's shooting, but that would be tricky, she knew. Dark, everyone scrambling, easy to swap out a rifle. *No.* She shook her head. *No, must be something else, another lead, something I missed. Something I haven't seen...*

Oh.

Opened her eyes, turned back to King.

"CCTV," she said. "Still finishing that up, yeah?"

He shrugged. "About finished, I think. Why?"

Why? Because someone missed something. Must have done. "Where?" She stood, started walking back across the squad room, towards the hallway. *Must be in one of those rooms.* Sped up as she hit the corridor. "Where'd Salford set it up?" *Not over at SIU, can't be, because Sykes went to fetch the Supers, bring them back here, so...*

King caught up with her. "The room Jenkins was in."

"Jenkins?"

"You just saw him…specs, dark hair, shortish. Seen him bring you coffee before…"

Oh, Media Review. Right. So, here…

She pulled open a door. Inside, Media Review was finishing his chair stacking. The room was filled with desks: twenty, maybe. Laptops scattered everywhere, all of them closed.

"The CCTV footage," Lucy said. "Where are we?"

Media Review stared at her for a moment.

Come on, out with it.

"Done," he finally said. "We're done." To King: "Thought I told you we were nearly there?" Back to Lucy: "Supers just left. Few hours ago. Checked every Tube station, every single camera. No joy." He pointed to the chairs. "Just tidying up now."

She shook her head. *Can't be done.* "What about the rest? Anything from where I was held? Mayfair, the pub?"

"Sorry, Ma'am." Media Review shrugged. "Don't know anything about that."

Christ. So don't have time for this.

And I'm not Ma'am. Ma'am is Ma'am, I'm Stone.

"Where's Salford?" she asked. "Need him." *He'll know, Salford will.*

Another shrug. "Haven't seen him at all today."

"What, not at all? Did he call, or…?"

Media Review shook his head. "Last couple of days he's seemed a bit poorly, to be honest. Then today, nothing. No call. Just didn't show."

Huh. Odd.

She turned to King: "You said it was all-hands today, though, yeah?"

He nodded. "Not the day to skive off."

And not like Salford. Not a bit. In fact…

A memory from two years ago flashed: three weeks into the Scourge. The night of the stolen Boosts, *that* night. Just home from Manga's corner shop. Standing in her bedroom, on the phone, watching as Simon tugged on his designer belt, one with the big metal buckle. Salford's voice in her ear: *no worries, on it, owe me a pint.*

Lucy frowned.

The times I skived off, Salford covered for me.

Wait...

Her eyes widened. "Ed? Need you. Come on." She turned, sped out the door, raced back down the hall. Crossed the squad room, stopped at King's messy desk. Tapped her thumb on the desktop as he reached her, Media Review tagging along behind. "Log in," she told King. "Hurry. Before Sykes gets back." *And before my levels drop.*

He shrugged. "Okay..." Squeezed himself into the office chair, began to type. Hit return, looked up. "Right. Logged in. Now what? What is this, Lucy? I don't—"

"When was Rob Cates killed?"

He stared at her, alarmed. "I mean, surely, you...that was just last night..."

"No, no." She waved her hand. *Come on.* "I mean, the first time. Two years ago. Swapped out his brother's body at their flat in Shepherd Market, reported it as Cates. That. When was *that*?"

"Erm..." A series of clicks. "19th November 2027."

Night of the Stepney Iso Centre bombing.

"Now check the active duty roster. Who was intake that night?"

He clicked. Looked up. Frowned.

"You were, Lucy."

"But I wasn't," she told him. "I skived off."

"Okay, so..."

"Look, Cates told me he filed a police report. Called in his own murder. But you found nothing, right? Just a registration of death, that's what, the GRO? Not us. No police record at all."

A shrug. "Yeah, but I told you. Records were shambolic then."
Come on, Ed.

"Skinny reports, errors? Knackered cops bodging their work? Fine, okay. But absolutely nothing? Zero? Sweet Fanny Adams, on any of our systems?" She shook her head. "No bloody way. That's not shambolic, that's a cover-up."

And if a cop was covering up Cates's death, he might want to nick his photo too…

"I don't know, Lucy." King spread his huge hands. "It's just, how does *that* connect back to Clapham? And your antidote? I don't understand."

Lucy shrugged. *Don't know. Not yet. But it must.*

Don't believe me?

Watch this, Ed.

She turned to Media Review.

"You said Salford was poorly, yeah?"

A nod. "Moving slowly. Seemed a bit beat up. Thought maybe a cold…"

"How was he *dressed*? Anything unusual? At all?"

"Well…"

Please, please, be right…

He shrugged. "Thing is, Salford always wears those ties, right? Always. But the past two days, he's had on a roll-neck jumper. Seemed a bit odd. New one, too, left the tag on for a bit. Marks and Sparks…"

Lucy smiled.

Brilliant.

A roll-neck jumper.

To cover his neck.

To cover the spot where I jabbed a needle into his dirty fucking neck.

She stared up at King.

"It's not Sykes," she said. "It's Salford."

"*Salford?*"

She nodded. *Salford is Cheap Shot, that bastard.* Tugged her hoodie strings, felt her mind racing. *Starting to make sense now.* "The Tube CCTV. Remember how slow BTP was? Thing is, they weren't. Sent it all to Salford, yeah? *That* was the hold-up. He was just holding it back, waiting until he could get it all sorted on his end."

"Well—"

Her voice was getting louder. To Media Review: "Salford divided the footage up amongst the Supers, right? But I bet he kept something for himself. Said he was pitching in, doing his bit. Sound right?"

He nodded.

"One station," he said. "Aldgate."

Bingo.

And that's where Orange Trainers was going after he attacked me.

"Fine, so what, we just…," King began, but Lucy was already up, headed for the door.

"Come on," she said, over her shoulder. "Let's go."

We're going to Aldgate, Ed.

And we need to fucking hurry.

CHAPTER TWENTY-THREE

"He's headed up the stairs," said King. "What's next?"

They were standing in the Aldgate Station ticket hall. Lucy frowned as she stared down at her mobile. The map Media Review had sent her was rubbish: 132 CCTV camera locations squeezed onto a single PDF page, fucking nightmare to read on a phone. *Right, so, stairwell cam was RY734, which means...* She looked back up, scanned the ceiling. Spotted a camera. "Tell him, RZ829 next."

"Right."

She watched King relay the message into his phone. Tapped her foot, took a sip from her Coke bottle: watery, ugh. Wished she had proper espresso, none of this filter nonsense, but filter was all the station kiosk had and it wasn't like she had five spare minutes to duck into a Costa. *No spare minutes. None. Down to 7.2 already, only boosted an hour ago, fuck.* "And tell him, hurry."

Come on, Media Review, work that CCTV footage.

Fucking dying here.

"Okay," King said into his phone. Nodded. "Got it." To Lucy: "We have him tapping through the ticket barriers. Timestamp 23:09. Still wearing his mask."

Right. So, next up...

She walked across the ticket hall, towards the station entrance. Spotted two cameras hanging from the entrance canopy. Glanced down at her screen. *And your names are...* "RX492 and RZ166," she told King. Checked the camera angles: one pointed left down Aldgate High Street; the other, right. A smile. *Brill. Covered whichever way he went. And then we can see*

299

where he turned off, pull that street camera, keep tracking. Or maybe he went into a building straight away, be brilliant, fucking amazing, actually, because then we'd just—

"I'll tell her." King rang off. Turned to Lucy, frowned.

Tell me what, Ed?

"Nothing on that one." He waved at the camera facing left. "Which means, he turned right out of the station. Must have done. But *that* camera?" Pointed at RZ166. "Wonky. Tape is just black. So…"

Fuck.

King shrugged. "Only option is to just start pulling all of the street cameras. Check them, one at a time. Eventually we'll work out where he turned off."

She shook her head.

No time, Ed.

Need to find another way. Fast.

"Quick recce," she said. Finished her drink, binned it, then headed outside, into the rain. Flipped her hood as she sped down the pavement, eyes up, searching for clues. For something, anything. *Need to find you, Orange Trainers. Right fucking now.* Made it a hundred feet, then stopped. Looked around. Modern office blocks, a church, handful of sandwich shops. Big skyscrapers above her: Gherkin, Walkie Talkie, Cheesegrater. Streets branched in all directions.

A million billion places for him to go.

No way to check them all.

No fucking time, fuck…

She took a deep breath, fought off the panic. *Okay, right, work it out, then. Why Aldgate? Must be a reason.* Turned to King, who had just caught up. "Say you try to kill someone. Doing it for someone else. You bodge the job. Where do you go?"

A shrug. "Apologize to your boss? Give him the bad news straight away?" He looked around. "What, reckon he had a meet-up with Clapham in the diary? One of these office blocks, maybe—"

"No." *Clapham wouldn't meet. Too risky. He'd just call.* "Don't think so."

"Maybe he was heading home, then?"

"Here? Lives in an office?"

"Well…" Another shrug. "To be honest? I'd go down the pub, myself."

Hmm. She pulled out her mobile, started tapping. *Pubs near Aldgate…*Hit the button. A dozen dots popped up on her map. *Christ. So many.* She tugged on her hoodie strings. Closed her eyes. Thought about Orange Trainers, rocking up to the bar at some crowded boozer, ordering a pint, chatting up the barmaid.

Shook her head.

A pub? Ed King would go to a pub. Yes.

But if you're Orange Trainers? Hand of God, killing because Enoch fucking Clapham told you it was God's plan? Because you think God himself wanted me to fall a hundred feet, splat, big bloody puddle on the Tube station floor, and it didn't happen because you cocked it up? Wouldn't go to a pub. And you wouldn't go apologize to Clapham.

She opened her eyes. Looked over at the church: old one, red brick, tiny gated churchyard.

An image of Orange Trainers's cross tattoo flashed in her mind.

You'd go apologize to God, yeah?

"Come on," she told King. "Think I know." Marched down the pavement, through the gate, up a few steps to the green church door. Knocked. No response. "Police," she called out. "Hello?"

Her monitor beeped.

Fuck. That'll be 7.0.

Need to hurry.

She knocked again, louder.

Come on…

The door swung open. An elderly man, wearing rimless specs and a moth-eaten cardigan, squinted out at them. "I'm terribly sorry," he said, "but I'm afraid the church is closed. Saturday, you see." He coughed into his elbow. "Although, to be honest, if you've just come for a look round, I'd be more than happy to give you a quick—"

"Police," Lucy said. *-ish.* "Need to come in."

"Oh, right, well…" Cardigan began, but she had already pushed past him, into the entrance. Dark inside. Stuffy. An old monument hung on the wall, a man's bust: long white beard, a two-pointer, flowing over a frilly collar. His hands were folded on top of a grinning skull. "That's Robbie," Cardigan told her, following her eyes. "Robert Dow. Splendid effigy, isn't it? He died in 1612, but it wasn't until 1623 that the Merchant Taylors had this wonderful—"

No time, Cardy.

"Seen him?" She held out her mobile, showed him the screen-grab Media Review had sent. "Survivor. About your height." *Likes sharp objects, hitting people in handcuffs.* "Think he comes here to pray."

Cardigan lifted his glasses, peered at the screen.

Come on…

"Well," he said, "afraid I can't see much from this angle. You say he's part of the congregation?" Another wheezing cough. "Perhaps if you were to ask the rector…"

Lucy frowned. "That's not you?"

"Oh, dear, no," Cardigan said. He looked shocked. "Just the sexton, I'm afraid. I look after maintenance, repairs, that sort of thing." Pulled a yellowed handkerchief from a pocket, began to polish his specs. "But I *do* know quite a fair bit about the church's history, bits and bobs I've managed to pick up along the way, and so—"

"Dead sure?" Lucy held up the phone again. "Take another look. Wears orange trainers. Tattoo on his wrist, wonky-looking cross with an extra set of arms."

Cardigan stopped polishing.

"Double-barred?" he asked.

What I said, yeah? She nodded. Watched as he looked down, began to finger a moth hole in his cardigan. *That rang a bell...*

"Well, perhaps...but he's not a worshipper, exactly, so to be honest I couldn't be—"

"Who?"

Spill it, Cardy.

He sighed. Slid his specs back on. "My assistant. Lucas. Been with us for two years now, helps with the more physical bits of the job. Lucas is a Survivor, and he has a double-barred cross tattoo on his wrist. I've noticed it when he works on the grounds." He looked from Lucy to King, then back. "Very... *reserved* young man, Lucas. Quiet. Good worker, though. Taken quite a fancy to the churchyard." A frown. "I trust he hasn't done anything too...that is, I mean, his paperwork is all in order, and I'd *hate* to think that..."

King stepped in. "Do you have his contact details? Address, mobile number..."

Cardigan shrugged. "He lives here, actually. Downstairs."

"*Here?*"

"In the crypt. We ran it as a shelter for rough sleepers, but had to close shop a few years back. Pity. It was just being used as storage, so when Lucas arrived, I thought perhaps—"

Brilliant.

"Show us," Lucy said.

"Is he here?" King asked.

Cardigan shrugged at King. "I don't think so. Haven't seen him today. But to be honest, I wasn't particularly looking. It's his day off." To Lucy: "Follow me. And I expect you'll enjoy seeing the interior, it really is quite something…" Led them through a double door, into the nave, down a side aisle, wittering on about church history as he went: "…married here in 1683… rebuilt in Georgian…archaeological dig in 1980, and if you like I could…"

Lucy smiled as she walked.

Coming for you, Orange Trainers.

They stopped in front of a red door, halfway up the side aisle. "The stairs down to the crypt are just through here," Cardigan said. "Go, if you like." He opened the door. It creaked. "Lucas's space is at the far end. Not much more than a bed, really. No doors down there, so I try not to venture down too often. Bit of privacy for him, you understand. Mind the steps, it's a touch dark…"

"Thanks," said King.

Lucy said nothing, just nodded, marched down the steps into the blackness. Cardigan's voice floated behind her: "…and I'll have a quick look round for that excavation report…" She reached the bottom. Felt around on the wall for a light switch. Found one, flicked it.

Overhead, a bare bulb fizzed on.

"Christ," said King, as he took the last step down. "Grim."

She glanced around. *It's like an old tunnel.* Grimy brick walls on either side of her curved up to a low arched ceiling. Smelt dank: old earth, mould. Clammy. No furniture, just cobwebs, dirt. The space behind them was bricked up. *Only one way to go, then.* She stared ahead into the darkness.

"Careful," whispered King. "He might be here."

Hoping he is, Ed.

Stick close if you're scared.

She reached into her jeans pocket, pulled out her mobile. Hit the torch button. Took a breath, then started walking, King at her heels. Cold down here: her skin prickled. The light behind them grew dimmer as they went. She played the mobile beam off the cracked tile floor. Thought of her levels dropping, *fuck*, then pushed it aside, kept walking, staring into the darkness ahead. *Come on, must be here, please God, fucking need this…*

They reached the end of the corridor, turned the corner, and— *Found you.*

‡ ‡ ‡

"Reckon this is it," King said.

Lucy stared through the darkness at the tiny room in front of her. Not even a room, really, just a recess in the crypt wall, barely larger than the bathroom in her little black flat. It reeked: something dead, rotting. She squinted, saw a crumbling chest of drawers, half a dozen melted candles on top. A camp bed, unmade, heap of clothing piled on the rumpled sheet. And mounted to the grimy brick wall: a giant double-barred cross.

Found you, Orange Trainers. Your little lair.

"Dead cert," she said.

"Might need a warrant to open those drawers."

A shrug. *Might not need them. Let's see what other prizes we've won, shall we?* She stepped closer to the camp bed. *Hmm, nothing special.* Played her mobile beam around, spotted a stack of boxes on the ground. Frowned. *The fuck?* "Look," she told King. "The boxes. See?"

"Yes, but aren't those…?"

She nodded. "Boosts."

"But he's a Survivor, I thought? Certain they're Boosts?"

Of course I'm sure, Ed. She looked down at the boxes. Glossy white cardboard, big Cox Labs logo on the flap. *Trust me, I know these fucking boxes. But…here?* She tugged her hoodie strings, thought about Orange Trainers. She'd seen his eyes: big black

Survivor eyes. *No question.* And his voice was raspy, proper Survivor voice. *But then again, why the fuck would a Survivor be Hand of God? Never made sense, not really...*

"Christ," King said. "Have a glance at *that.*" He pointed to something sitting on top of the chest of drawers. "Not looking great for Salford."

She looked. It was Salford's warrant card. The leather wallet glistened under the mobile's beam. She leaned closer: blood. Lots of it. *Fuck.* Stood in silence for a minute, processing. *Is Salford dead? Did Orange Trainers kill him? Was it the Cates shooting? Clapham figures, we're bound to trace the rifle, not worth the risk Salford grasses, so fuck it, farewell, my faithful pet cop?*

Salford, you poor sod.

"Need to call this in," King said. "No service down here. Be right back." Handed back her mobile, turned towards the stairs. Disappeared into the darkness, but kept talking. "And while I'm up there, I'll get the full details from the sexton. Put out an APW, and then we can start to—"

CRACK!

She heard King hit the ground.

The fuck—

Pointed the phone: a glimpse of Orange Trainers, running away.

"Hey!"

She took off after him.

Leapt over King. Flew down the hallway, up the steps, trainers pounding, thunk thunk thunk. Reached the top, through the door, into the nave.

There...

He was streaking down the aisle, heading for the double doors leading out.

Beyond, Cardigan stood in the entrance, arms full of papers.

"Shut the doors," she screamed.

Orange Trainers sped up.

Cardigan just stared.

"Shut them!"

Fuck—

And then Cardigan, suddenly in motion: dropping his papers, grabbing the doors, slamming them shut just in time. *Brilliant.* Orange Trainers lunged, grabbed the doorknobs, rattled them: locked. Pounded the doors with his fists, once, twice, then stopped. Muttered something.

Turned to face Lucy.

She walked down the side aisle towards him.

And now you're mine.

"Hiya," she said. Grinned. "Coming quietly?"

He raised his fists.

Right.

She kept walking. Passed a pew, another. Reached the end of the side aisle, turned the corner towards him. "Last chance," she said. "Avoid a thumping."

He snarled.

Lucy raised her fists, tucked her chin. *Well, you asked for it, yeah?* Took a step towards him. Another. Almost to him now, felt adrenaline surge, fight thoughts take over: *Careful of his reach, he comes out fast, need to jab, keep him off balance, remember rhythm, timing, and then—*

He took off down the main aisle.

God dammit…

She turned, raced after him. Up the side aisle, trainers flying, tried to cut him off but he was too fast, streaking down the nave, turning right, out a door.

Get back here…

She flew through the door, burst outside, into the rear churchyard. Tall iron fences, all sides. Saw him, sprinting across, aiming for the far fence.

He's going to climb it.

Tore after him, legs pumping, lungs burning. He reached the fence, started climbing.

Hurry, faster, come on, come on…

Nearly over the fence now.

Almost there…

She sped up, reached the fence, leapt. Grabbed his jumper. *Got you, you shit.* He struggled, tried to hoist himself over but her arms were strong, all those fucking pull-ups and she pulled on him, hard, *harder*, felt him let go and they tumbled back, falling, down onto the hard earth, *oof.*

Need to hold him…

He tried to stumble to his feet but she caught his legs, pulled him down, rolled on top. Grabbed his wrist, tried to pin him down but he was writhing, twisting, kicking. *Hold…on…*Hit her in the face, *fuck*, another, but she held on, *mustn't let go*, taking blows, reaching for his other wrist, *so close*, stretching, *come on—*

And then she had it. Had both wrists, and he was trapped, pinned beneath her knees.

She stared down into his black eyes. Took a breath.

Smiled.

Got you.

"You're nicked," she said. Read him the caution, blood dripping from her nose, trickling down her chin. To her left, the church door opened and King burst out, ran towards them.

'Bout time, Ed. Look what I found.

"Fucking cheap shot," King growled. His jaw was already beginning to swell. "Just when it was starting to feel better." Rubbed it, grimaced. To Orange Trainers: "You bellend…" Pulled bracelets from beneath his rain jacket, bent down, snapped them onto Orange Trainers's wrists. "Ought to give you a crack, see how you like it."

Lucy rolled off. Stood up, hands on knees, panting.

"His mask," she said. "Grab it."

Let's see if we've crossed paths before.

King nodded. "Take it off," he told Orange Trainers. "Giving you the chance to do it yourself if you like." Paused. "No? Well then…" Reached down, pulled the zip, tugged the mask away.

Gasped.

Lucy stared down at Orange Trainers's face.

What the fuck?

‡ ‡ ‡

"Never seen anything like it," Doctor Hodges said. He mumbled something Lucy couldn't hear.

She frowned. Pressed the mobile to her ear: crap signal in this church, God knows why, not like Aldgate wasn't bang in the middle of London, for fuck's sake. And Hodges was pissed as a newt; she could tell the second he slurred his hello. *Christ, Doc, sloshed at half ten? Know you've been through Hell, but still…* She glanced across the nave. Saw Orange Trainers, still slumped in the corner pew, head bent over his cuffed hands. Still silent. *Need to get him talking, right fucking now. So come on, Doc. Stay with me.* "Say again? Not seen this before, but…?"

"Said, possible. Theoretically." Hodges paused. "What you sent…it's real? Really real?"

"Took it myself," she said. Thought about the photo she'd sent. Knew it looked fake, some half-arsed clickbait Photoshop, but still, there it was: Orange Trainers's face, unmasked. A normal face, mostly, Survivor eyes aside. Square jaw, bulbous nose. Big brow. But then, starting at his left temple, strips of seamy, scarred skin stretched across his cheek, worming their way down to his lips. And then they stopped. *But London Black doesn't just stop. Never, ever. Scars you everywhere, head to toe, always. Which is why I need you to tell me what the fuck I'm looking at, Doc.* She nodded. "It's real."

Now step away from the fucking bottle.

Running out of time here.

"Right. Course. Mmm." Lucy heard a glass clink. "Well, never seen that. Or heard of it. But…possible. Yes. Need a weaker version of the compound. Much weaker. Then Elemidox, stonking big dose, straight away." She imagined him tenting his fingers next to a half-drained bottle of sherry. "But, thing is…not easy to do. Need lab prep. Difficult. And has to be exposure, then Boost. Bang, bang. Need knowledge. Specialist." Slurred it: *specialish.* "Not a doctor, is he? Researcher, maybe?"

"Works at a church." *And as a henchman for a lunatic con-man preacher. Bit of both, really.*

"Then…" He sighed. "Someone did this to him." Another clink. "Someone terrible."

Lucy pictured Enoch Clapham, shrieking to his followers.

Funny. I know someone terrible.

But why, Clapham? Why do this?

She rang off, walked over to the old wooden pulpit. King was leaning up against it, texting with one hand, holding a bag of frozen peas to his swollen jaw with the other. He didn't look up, just kept tapping. "Heard from Jenkins," he told her. "Record check's done."

"And?"

"Fuck all. Here." Handed her his phone.

She scanned the screen. *Lucas Benjamin. Born 4 Apr 1998, London. Parents, Walter P. and Patience G., both deceased, 2007. No criminal history. No cautions. No citations.*

"Orphan," she said. *Interesting.* Gave his mobile back.

"Yeah, well, not exactly Oliver Twist, is he?" King fingered his jaw, winced. "Cheap shot wanker is what he is. Oh, and we found Clapham. He's in Wapping, eating brekkie. Fry-up, I'm told." Hint of a grin. "No word on whether it's veggie."

Lucy smiled. *Brilliant.* "Pull him."

"For what? Just being evil isn't an arrestable offence."

Should be. She sighed. Looked over at Orange Trainers, still bowing his head. *Finally learnt to keep your chin tucked, yeah?* "Then we need him to grass on Clapham. Only way." *So let's get cracking.* She started to move, but he grabbed her shoulder, held her back.

Hey, what the fuck?

"Looks bad in the record if it's you doing the grilling," he said. "Suspended, no authority…" He let go. "Hey, just the messenger. You know it's true. Here." Tossed her his bag of frozen peas. "Stay here. I'll get him talking."

Lucy frowned at him.

Better not bollocks this up, Ed. No time left.

And hold your own fucking peas.

As he walked across the aisle, she lobbed the peas into a pew. Took a deep breath, tugged her hoodie strings, stared up at the church ceiling. It was sky blue and white. Looked like a cake, she thought, all icing and roses, giant plaster angels with big flapping wings. *Could use a fucking angel right about now.* She rubbed her tattoo, thumb still cold from the peas. *Know it's not exactly not your line, Jack, but this guy needs to talk, so any help…*

King reached Orange Trainers. Bent down, tapped him on the shoulder. "All right, Chummy?"

No reply.

"You decked me. Twice. Which means, now we talk. Who do you work for?"

Orange Trainers looked up. "I obey my father," he said. Said it so softly that Lucy could barely hear from her spot next to the pulpit. She inched closer.

"Your father's dead," King said. Frowned, then followed Orange Trainers's gaze to the stained glass window above the altar. "Oh, what, you mean *God*? Right, well, *that's* good to hear. Thing is, you also stabbed Detective Stone in the chest. Tried to toss her off a fucking escalator. Naughty." He tutted. "Trying to splat a cop? That's an awful long stretch, Lucas, doesn't matter how well you get on with the Invisible Bloke Upstairs." He cracked a giant knuckle. "So you need to start fucking talking. Tell me who you work for."

A whisper: "I obey my father."

His hands were trembling, Lucy noticed.

Scared. But not of you, Ed. There's something else…

"And then there's Salford," King continued. "For a moment, I thought you two were mates." Another knuckle: *crack*. "But guess not, because you fucking killed him, too, didn't you? Shedloads of blood down there, forensics will love you. So that's, what, one homicide, two attempts, bit of assault mixed in? Life. No parole." *Crack.* "Or you can start talking. Like, right fucking now."

"I obey my father."

Lucy frowned.

So don't have time for this shit.

She marched over, grabbed King's shoulder, pulled him back to the pulpit. "It's not working. The threats. Look at him." Nodded at Orange Trainers, who had lowered his head again. "He doesn't mean God, he's talking about Clapham. Know he is. Clapham calls them his little children, yeah? But he needs to bloody *say* it. You need another angle." *Quickly.*

"Yeah, well—"

King's mobile chirped. He checked it. Frowned.

"Wilkes," he told her. "Be right back."

"No, wait," she said, but he was already walking back to the entrance way, phone to his ear.

Fuck.

She pulled out her mobile. Swiped her stomach. Checked it. *6.7.*

Could start plunging any minute now.

Looked over at Orange Trainers.

He was staring up at the stained glass window, hands clasped, rocking. Muttering to himself. She watched his lips move: *I obey my father.* Closed her eyes, ran fingers through her hair. Thought about two years ago, everything she'd done, all of it, down to the very end, to The Thing. *Worse than you, Orange Trainers. In a way, I'm worse than you, just no one knows. None of them.* Thought about Wilkes. All those fucking PTSD leaflets, the ones she crumpled, binned without reading. About King, banging on about therapy and how it saved him, all *trust* and *transparency* and fucking *openness*. She exhaled. Opened her eyes.

Well, fuck it, then.

Let's try some fucking openness.

Marched over to the corner pew. Stood in front of Orange Trainers, blocking his view of the stained glass. *You look at* ME *now, yeah?* Crouched down. Stared at him, eyes bagged. Purple.

Took a breath.

"It will *swallow* you," she said.

He said nothing, but she saw motion in his all-black eyes: pupils focusing.

"If you don't talk? If you don't open up, talk, confess? It will swallow you whole. It *will.*"

One orange trainer began to tap on the mosaic floor.

"You look scared," she said. "You should be. Bloody *terrified.* Because unless you start talking, unless you do that, what you've done will *own* you, yeah?" His foot sped up, *tap tap tap.* "Everything you did will just *own* you, the guilt will crush you and you'll be a prisoner, you understand? A prisoner, no way out, trapped, stuck with yourself, nothing but long dark nights, forever and ever and ever." Paused. "Trust me, Lucas."

Trust me, and talk.

He sighed. It came out as a wheeze, air whistling through his scarred larynx.

"Once," he whispered. "I disobeyed him, once."

She nodded.

Good. A start. Now keep going, give me something...

"It was *then*. The Scourge. God's arrows. I knew I could get it. I was...scared."

He spoke slowly, labouring over each word.

"And then Father, he rang me. Out of the blue. Said, *Come*." Lucy pictured Clapham, stretching out a bony finger, beckoning. "Father, he'd never rang me before, never ever. So I went. And he asked me, do I believe in the Hand of God, the teachings? So I said, Yes. Yes, Father, yes, I do." He paused. "He said that was good. And then he gave me a Boost. But he said, don't use it. Mustn't. Must trust in God. Said I had to obey him, what God said, in the Scriptures." Mechanically: "Obey your father in everything, for this pleases God." Another pause. "But..."

He trailed off. Looked down at his trainers.

"Go on," Lucy said.

Another whistling sigh, then: "But I was scared. So I gave in. Used it. And God knew, He knew I'd disobeyed Father, so straight away...this." He ran fingers down his scarred cheek. "I ran back to Father, fell on the floor, said, So sorry, Father, I'll obey. He gave me another Boost, and said, God forgave me, God would heal me, but I must never, *ever* do it again. Never disobey. And if I do, *it* will come back. And now, I don't know..."

She stared at him.

So that's how Enoch Clapham made you his little henchman.

Right. I can work with that.

Softly: "Lucas? It was a trick."

He looked up.

314

She kept talking. "He tricked you. That Boost, the one you used?" A shrug. "Not a Boost. That was London Black. He tricked you, you understand? Manipulated you, so that you'd do what he said, all the time."

"No. Father wouldn't…" He shook his head.

Keep going, push him just a bit more…

"Yes, Lucas. He would. I spoke with a doctor, an expert. Showed him your photo. It's the only way you'd have scars like that." She waved her mobile. "I can ring him again if you like."

"No…"

He started rocking. Frowned: angry.

Little bit more, almost there…

"Awful, isn't it? Vile? The man you call your father, the man you obey, what he did to you?"

And now—

"So what do you think *now* about your beloved Father Clapham, do you *really* want to…"

She trailed off. The look on his face changed. It wasn't anger any more.

It was confusion.

"Did you say…Father *Clapham*?"

She heard a rustle behind her: King, back from his call. He cleared his throat but she waved him off. *Not now, Ed.* "I know it, Lucas," she said. "Enoch Clapham, the man who—"

"No."

No?

The fuck?

What the fucking fuck?

Orange Trainers shook his head. "Father knows that I follow the Hand of God. It's good, he says. But he doesn't even *like* Father Clapham, know he doesn't, not any more, because of the black…" He stopped. Scowled at her. "You don't know anything, do you?"

But—

King grabbed her arm, pulled her back to the pulpit. "Transport van on its way. Here in five."

"No." She frowned. "Tell them no, Ed. He's denying it, I need more time—"

"Fine, well, why don't *you* try, then?" He threw up his hands. "Because as for me, *I'm* fucking suspended."

Oh shit. "Blimey."

"Yes, Stone, blimey." He snorted. "It was Sykes. Went to the Chief Super, just like he fucking said he would. Effective immediately."

Lucy watched him grab the bag of peas, press it to his jaw, turn away.

"*Rats,*" she said.

So I've got five minutes.

Five minutes, and then Orange Trainers is gone, and no one else believes in the antidote so it'll all just go straight to hell, Christ…

She took a breath.

Looked over at Orange Trainers. *Why are you lying? You must be lying, has to be Clapham, must be.* Stared as his face: like nothing she'd ever seen before. And *he* was no one she'd ever seen, either, she knew it. Party Trick said no. *And yet…*She felt something nagging. Tugged her hoodie strings, tried to think. Something still felt familiar, like she'd seen bits of him, somehow. *The nose? Could be the nose. Or the jaw, maybe, but it doesn't make sense, Party Trick's not wrong, never, so how—*

And then it hit her.

What if…?

She started tapping on her mobile.

Maybe. Could be. Please, God, be right…

Marched over to Orange Trainers. Shoved the phone in front of his face.

"That's him, isn't it? Your father? Your real, biological father?"

Held her breath.

Come on, come on…

He glanced at the screen, then looked away. Didn't say anything, but didn't need to. She knew instantly: she was right.

Oh fuck yes.

Should've known it all along.

Lucy smiled.

On her screen was a photo of Geoff Hurst.

CHAPTER TWENTY-FOUR

Look out, Hurst. Here I fucking come.

The Toyota raced down Aldgate High Street. Wipers on, full-bore: really chucking it down now. Lucy watched office blocks whizz past. She took a breath, exhaled, pulled her hoodie zip halfway down. Her heart was pounding. Only a few streets from the church to the car but she'd done it full throttle, a dead sprint, took off running the moment the van arrived for Orange Trainers. *No time to lose, none, not a single fucking second.*

Beside her, King was still panting. He glanced over. "So it's Hurst, then? Not Clapham?"

"Left up here," she told him. Pointed.

Just drive, Ed.

"Liked Clapham for it, if I'm honest." He spun the wheel, whipped them around the corner. "So fucking evil." A pedestrian dove for the pavement. "But if Chummy back there is Hurst's kid, then that means...what, a right up there? By the light?... then that means, it was still Cates that killed Cox." Another sharp turn. "But the rest of it? It's all Hurst, not Clapham?" He just missed a cyclist. Horns blared.

Right, fine, I'll talk, you drive.

"Not *Cox*," she said. "It was Hurst, not *Cox*." Took a breath. *Only saying this once, Ed, so listen up.* "Cates made his break-through, yeah? Told Cox. Then, Cox told Hurst. He must've. Needed to, Hurst handled the business bit, operations and that, remember? Reckon Cox told Hurst to make the switch, then bumbled off to his lab, started in on an antidote." She pictured Flinders Cox, middle of the night, green hazmat suit on, hunched over a test tube. *Never dreamed he would do something that evil, did you, Mr Cox? Didn't see him for what he was.* Heard Helen Cox's heroin-slurred voice in her head: *Flinders? Flinders doesn't pay attention to humans. Just his precious little chemicals.* "But Hurst does bugger all, lets the shortage happen, then just trousers the black market millions."

The car shot beneath a railway arch.

King glanced over again. "Right, so then, Cates told Cox about his brainwave, but then he's exposed. Fever, delirious. Finally wakes up…"

Eyes on the road, Ed.

"Cates wakes up, rings Cox. Cox rings Hurst, probably confused as Cates. Now Hurst needs to cover his tracks, silence Cates. Sends Lucas, Lucas bodges it, wrong brother. Salford catches the case, Hurst bends him. Bullies Cox into keeping quiet." She shrugged. "Bob's your uncle."

Now hurry the fuck up, yeah?

Have a stop to make.

King swerved around a bend. Ahead, the Tower popped into view, then Tower Bridge. Lucy watched tourists scurry from their spray as they spun around the roundabout, onto The Highway, headed towards Wapping.

"But," King said, "then why're we still running after Clapham…?"

Trust me, Ed. "Need Clapham to get to Hurst." *And that reminds me.* She pulled out her mobile, started tapping. Hit the call button, held the phone to her ear. *Come on, pick up, pick up…*

"Hello?" Bloody Tissues sounded groggy. "Is this—"

"Am I right?"

A sigh. "You only texted ten bloody minutes ago. It's Saturday morning, for fuck's sake…"

So? "Need to know. *Now.*"

The Toyota zoomed down The Highway.

Another sigh. "Yes," he said. "I checked. You're spot on. But…"

But what?

Bloody Tissues cleared his throat. "I'm only telling you informally. Best I can do. And those docs you asked for? Can't send those. Can't send anything, no emails, too risky. Client confidentiality, get me struck off. Need a formal request, maybe a warrant, and even then—"

He cut off.

"Bloody Tissues..."

King glanced over. "Just once," he said. "Just say 'fuck' one fucking time, I *promise* you'll feel so much better..."

She ignored him. Stared down at her phone. The screen was black.

Battery? Can't be, just charged it, so...

Oh fuck.

Fucking Sykes.

"Ed? Your phone. Mind if I...?" She grabbed it from the console, tapped the screen. Nothing happened. Kept tapping, then frowned, tossed it back. "Rats." *That goddamn bone-idle, fedora-wearing tosspot.*

"What?"

"Met property." She frowned. "They've bricked them. Remotely."

He stared at her, green eyes wide. "That bastard. Erm...my own phone's at home. You?"

Lucy shrugged. "Just have this."

Who would I call?

"Fuck," he said. "No phones, then." Slammed on the brake, then cut across oncoming traffic into Wapping. A cabbie laid on his horn. "Thing is...what if Clapham moves? Still eating breakfast when we left, but now I can't check with the DC doing the obbo..."

Sykes, you twat. She watched a row of luxury flats flash past. Tugged her hoodie strings, tried to work out her level. Knew it was 6.7 back in the church, been what, twenty minutes, so down to 6.6, maybe? *Or 6.5, no way to know without the phone, not until it beeps again at 6.0 and by then it could be plunging, falling off a fucking cliff, Christ...*She turned to King. "Drive. Faster."

"Right." He hit the gas and they were blowing through Wapping now, swerving, flying over the cobbles, *thump-thump-thump*, old warehouses and yellow brick blurring fucking *fast*.

Please still be there...

"Left," she said. Grabbed the oh-shit handle, hung on as he spun the wheel, blazed down a side street. Fenced green square on the left, old church on the right. "*There.*" Pointed ahead. "See it? Coffee shop, old pub building?"

They squealed to a stop.

Okay, Clapham, now be here...

Lucy opened the door, leapt out into the rain. Sprinted through puddles to the shop, pushed her way inside.

Where...?

She looked around. Saw parents sipping tea; children eating, playing. *Come on. Be here, damn you.* In the corner, a man sat hidden behind a newspaper. She marched over, grabbed it, pulled it down. *No. Fuck.* "Hey," the man said, but she was already moving, checking the tables again, each one, hoping, praying, *please...*

No sign of Clapham.

Fuck.

The door squeaked open: King. He made eye contact. She shook her head: *Gone.* He frowned, grabbed a waiter, started in. "Looking for a bloke, skinny, looks like death. Just eating breakfast, a fry-up..."

Lucy turned away.

Crossed her arms, stared out the window, into the driving rain. Felt like vomiting. *Need Clapham. Plan would work, know it*

*would, figured it all out but I need him, no other way. Because Hurst's
connected, old school chums with the brass for fuck's sake, and anyway
we're suspended, official, can't do shit, don't have fucking phones even
and out of time and—*

There.

There you are.

Across the street, Enoch Clapham was walking into the
fenced green square.

‡ ‡ ‡

Lucy ran.

Didn't wait for King, just bolted. Full-on sprint: out the door,
across the street, into the square. *Get back here, Clapham.* Pulled
to a stop next to the spiky iron gate and looked around, panting.
Quiet. Bare twisting trees, empty benches. Saw Clapham up
ahead, walking away, following a path that snaked across the
dead grass. The collar of his long black overcoat was turned up
against the rain.

"Clapham!"

He turned. Stared at her, then kept walking.

Can't just skulk away from me, Enoch.

She made straight for him, fuck the path, trainers squelching
through thick black mud. Caught up halfway across the square.
Fell into step, breathing hard.

"Call Geoff Hurst," she said. "Need you to. Now."

He kept moving, eyes straight ahead. Said nothing for a
moment, then, calmly: "Did you know, Officer, Wapping was a
dangerous place, once? A slum. Notorious. Disease-riddled."

She frowned.

Don't care. "Hurst. Call him. Do it."

"But now?" A smile stretched his waxy skin. "Warehouse con-
versions. Multimillion-pound flats, all around us." He chuckled.

322

"Imagine it, can you? People actually dying to live here, right where we're standing, when back then…"

No time for this shit.

She sped up, stepped in front of him. Mud from her trainers splashed onto a spotless croc loafer. Reached into her hoodie for her warrant card but it was gone, fuck, fucking Hurst, Sykes, whole parade of wankers, so she just held up her hands, palms out: *stop.* "Call. Hurst." She glared. "Right bloody now."

He looked down at the loafer. Scowled. "Afraid I don't know who that is," he said. "So if you don't mind…" Sidestepped her, kept walking.

Oh yeah?

"Course you do," she called out. "You're blackmailing him."

Clapham stopped.

Turned.

Lucy watched as the meek façade crumbled and his eyes lit up, blazing like they had when he was pounding his pulpit, shrieking to a writhing mob in white robes. "How *dare* you," he spat. "*You*, accusing *me*? Me, emissary of our Great Father of Nations, the Lord God? You're making a mistake, a grave mistake, Officer, crossing the one He has put upon this Earth to spread His Word…"

She smiled.

There you are at last. The real Enoch Clapham.

A rustle behind her as King joined them, panting.

Look who I found, Ed. Thinks he's scary.

But I'm the scary one, Clapham.

She marched up to the preacher. Leaned in close, face inches from his, bagged eyes staring him down. "Already told me you don't know Hurst," she said. Voice low, hard. "Said it back at that old pub. But you do. Worked for his dodgy letting agency, one with the corporate tax fraud that got you put away." A shrug. "So I wondered, why lie? Odd, yeah? Man's worth a mint, buying a bloody football club, expect a muppet like you'd be shouting your bloody head off about it."

"I have friends," Clapham hissed. "Police friends…"

"And then I got a bit of a helper from one of your precious little children."

Heard Orange Trainers's raspy voice in her head: *He doesn't even like Father Clapham…not any more, because of the black…*She smiled. Almost missed it, so focused on solving the mystery of Orange Trainers that it nearly slipped right past her. But she'd caught it a few minutes later, as she stood in the rear of the Aldgate church, eyes closed, trying to sort out how in the fuck she was ever going to get to Geoff Hurst. Suddenly realized what Orange Trainers was about to say:

Because of the blackmail.

"Cox Labs is being audited," she told Clapham. "Had a word with the auditor. Company gives money once a quarter to Divine Sword Ltd. Authorized by Geoff Hurst himself. What triggered the audit in the first place, actually. Flinders Cox noticed, thought it smelt whiffy."

A sneer. "Those are charitable donations, Officer, disgraceful that you'd—"

She cut him off. *No time for your bollocks.* "Thing is, before Divine Sword, before your little sham Hand of God outfit was set up? Same quarterly payments, same exact amount, but back then it went straight to a certain Gavin Morley. You. Called a consulting fee. Which seemed, don't know, a bit odd, yeah?" She grinned. "Given you were sitting in the nick at the time."

His fingers reached for the hidden double-barred cross.

"The Hand of God is *not* a sham," he said. A fierce scowl. "The money is used to spread the Word. And the people are listening, thirsty for God's sacred truth." He spread his bony arms. "Our videos have gone *viral*, thousands and thousands of streams, and

I am with my children all the time now, every minute of every day, in their homes, their cars, their phones…"

Lucy stared at him. Crossed her arms.

Can't tell. Still can't.

Just an act? A front to launder dirty money and flog crap T-shirts? Or do you actually believe the vile filth you're spreading, infecting people's minds, preying on our worst instincts?

She took a breath.

"Doesn't matter," she told him. "What you do with it doesn't matter. Still blackmail. Still illegal, get you nicked, everything seized, poof." A shrug. "Or? You call Hurst. Say you know he's got an antidote. Know he's hiding it, holding it back. You have proof, got it from his son. One of your precious little children." She watched as his hand moved from his chest to his coat pocket. "Tell him you'll tell the whole bloody world, put it in one of your videos, unless he ponies up. You want a meet, soon as. Want to talk terms, face to face."

All around them, the rain poured down.

He pulled out his mobile.

"And, Clapham? The meet?" She paused. "It has to be right bloody now."

No time to lose. Not a single fucking second.

He glared. "Who's blackmailing whom now, Officer?" Turned away. Started dialling.

King pulled her aside. His eyes were wide.

Follow all that, Ed?

He glanced over at Clapham. Whispered: "What's he black-mailing Hurst *for*?"

Who cares? She shrugged. "Reckon it's to do with that tax fraud knock. Hurst stitched him up, now he's getting his own back, maybe." Wiped the rain off her face, really pissing down now. "Or could be something else. Expect Hurst's done plenty." *The fucking bastard.* "Doesn't matter, really, does it?"

"Well, but are you really willing to just turn your head on the blackmail? Let that arsehole walk, let him keep spreading his awful rubbish?"

She held up a finger, listened to Clapham's conversation for a moment. He was playing it rough: *No, I'll tell you, Geoff...now you listen to me...*She grinned. *Go get him, Enoch.* Back to King: "Course not. Don't be daft. Already pinged Media Review back at the church, told him to call Bloody Tissues, get the details, then refer it on."

He tilted his head.

What, Ed?

"Done." Clapham turned back to them, slipped his phone into his overcoat pocket.

"And?"

"He'll meet. He's at their offices in Stepney. Said he can do it in fifteen minutes, but after that he's headed to the airport and it would need to be next week. I told him I could make it."

She nodded. *Brilliant. Fifteen minutes, perf, should be fine. Only, can't tell for certain, actually, levels could start dropping any second, so we need to go, get moving, right fucking now.* To King: "Come on." She turned, started to run towards the Toyota.

Clapham called after her. "*Officer?* Think you should know..."

She stopped. Looked back at him. "Know what?"

The rain was sideways now. Hard drops stung her face.

"He told me, no terms. Not a negotiation. He won't pay anything, not a brass farthing." He grinned, a vile little grin. "He just wants me there to watch."

To watch?

Watch what?

"There's only one dose of the antidote. And he's going to destroy it."

‡ ‡ ‡

Her monitor beeped as the Toyota sped down Wapping High Street.

Lucy felt her heart pound. *Six. Down to 6, must be plunging now, fuck.* Looked out the window, saw buildings flash past, shops, flats, *faster*, rain blurring, *fucking hurry*. Siren blaring, blues and twos. Held her breath, there in five, just hang the fuck on. *Few more minutes, almost over, come on, faster, fucking faster...*

King glanced over.

"So there is an antidote," he said. "It's really real."

Course. Told you. A not U.

Drive faster.

They flew past the old pub, over a red metal bridge. "Hang on," he said. Gripped the wheel, spun it hard, whipped them out onto The Highway. "But why would Hurst take it? Belongs to his own company." Sped up, swerved around a bus, past a cab. Lucy held her breath. "And why..." He mashed the gas, blew through a light, then swung left. "Why *destroy* it? Worth a fucking fortune..."

Come on, Ed. Don't you see?

The car shot over the A13.

"He's doing it again," she said.

"It?"

Keep driving. Just listen. "Fortune to others, maybe. But to him?" She shook her head. Stared through the windscreen as they zipped down the street, *hurry*. "Millions worldwide, all boosting. Boost a day, every day. Forever." Grabbed the door handle as they cornered. "Plus monitors, Cox gates, testing strips. All Cox Labs. All of it." Paused. "All gone if there's an antidote, if one jab can make someone not Vulnerable."

"Christ."

No, Ed.

More like, Anti.

They were getting close now. Into Stepney, blowing past boarded-up pubs, battered council flats. Burned-out buildings, fired in the riots. Red X's on doors. She heard a beep. *Fuck. 5.9. But so close, hang on, please, almost there...*

King cleared his throat.

"When we get there..." He glanced at her. "Need to go in the front. Are you...?"

Lucy nodded. "Fine." But her hands had already begun to shake. She shoved them into her damp hoodie pockets. Told herself to be strong, fight it, need to pay the fucking Debt so that's it, end of. *Just a fucking car park. Did it before. Do it again. Just breathe.*

Inhale, exhale.

The Toyota swung around a bend and there they were: the five chimneys of Cox Labs HQ.

No choice. You can do it.

Need to do it.

Kept her hoodie down, fuck hiding: *look out, past.* Watched the car park appear. Nearly empty, just one lone silver car. Her heart was pounding. They turned in, *almost there*, flew over the speed humps, *get ready*, slowed down, *steady*, stopped.

Here I fucking come.

She leapt out.

Her trainers hit the ground and she was off, running, sprinting through her past now. Kept her eyes open, saw images flashing: the explosion, thick black smoke, flames licking dark sky. Saw herself fall to the ground up ahead, gravel on her hands and Simon's down and she was running past herself now, tearing ahead, pushing, harder, *faster...*

It's now, it's now, stay now...

Felt the heat. The crush of people running into her, surging, slamming into her like body blows, another, another, another, *ugh*, and she was pushing past them, fighting her way through, can't stop, mustn't stop...

Halfway…

Heard the soldiers' guns, rat-tat-tat. People screaming: patients, children. Bodies thumped the ground around her. Somewhere, sometime, a woman mourning, wailing, piercing shrieks: *Oh! Dead, dead, dead…*

But she kept running.

Keep going, must keep going…

Need to…

And then she slammed through the lobby door.

Skidded to a stop.

Made it.

Stood, panting, hair rain-slicked. Wiped a tear. Looked around.

At the other end of the lobby: Geoff Hurst.

Tall, tanned, perfect hair. Crisp white shirt, red chinos. She felt her gears turn, seen him before somewhere, knew it, so fucking frustrating but it didn't matter now. There he was, right there.

Hiya, Geoff. Remember me?

He stared at her for a second.

Then he turned and ran.

Oh no you fucking don't.

She heard King calling out from somewhere behind her, but there was no time, she was faster anyway, *come on, Ed, follow me.* Lungs burning, legs aching, but she couldn't stop, couldn't wait, must keep running. Chased him down a corridor, down the stairs, *no one here*, turning left, another left, no lights, empty, just their footsteps echoing off dark walls.

He'll destroy it. Need to catch him.

He was fast but she was faster. Gaining on him now. Tearing past signs, hazmat suits, masks, *come on, almost*, around a corner, another, and then—

Fuck.

The labs.

Saw the chem weapons symbol, the warning signs but there was no doubt, he was headed right for them, going in. *Course there, chemicals, destroy it there, need to stop him.* She kept going, *need to,* blew through the decon shower, the airlock. No people but equipment everywhere. He knocked a chair over and she leapt it, dodged a machine, another, ran past dangling red air hoses, airlock after airlock, through the labs, orange, green, blue.

Almost…so close…

Into the grey lab but he kept running, towards the last airlock. *The Black Lab.*

No exit there. Knew it, seen it from above. A dead-end, *perf,* and she blew through the final airlock, into the lab, *got you now,* saw him stop, *mine,* and—

Wha—

Her foot caught on something and she tripped, fell, landed hard on the black floor. Heard her ankle pop, *fuck,* then a huge crash, *oh Jesus,* and her ankles were throbbing, both of them, felt like they were on fucking fire. *Hurts, Christ.* Tried to scramble to her feet but she couldn't, couldn't move her legs, stuck.

Looked down: a big steel freezer, crushing her ankles, pinning her down.

Oh…

Her cheek burned too and she touched it, felt a tiny piece of glass. *The fuck?* Turned her head. Saw a vial, smashed on the floor. Labels: skull, crossbones, **TOXIC — LB**.

Fuck fuck fuck…

RRRRRRRRING—

An alarm blared. All around her, lights flashed.

A memory: staring down at the labs from above, watching the lockdown test.

Black in the air…

Behind her, a giant steel gate slammed shut, blocking the airlock.

RRRRRRRING—

She reached down, grabbed her legs, tugged, *fucking hurts*. Another tug. Nothing. Trapped, she was trapped, needed to get up, chase Hurst but she couldn't, fucking nailed to the floor, monitor beeping and another tug, *harder*, and hurts, goddamn it, must get up but—

The alarm stopped.

Silence.

And then, from the other end of the lab, Hurst's voice, an annoying singsong:

"Oops-a-daisy."

CHAPTER TWENTY-FIVE

"This is all your fault, you know."

Lucy heard him chuckle. *A trap. Fucking trapped me.* Wanted to punch him, deck him like she had at the airport but it was impossible, no way, pinned down, *fuck. Hurts so fucking much.* She gritted her teeth. Pushed herself up on her elbows, looked around. Couldn't see Hurst, crap in the way: tables, equipment, thick red air hoses hanging down from an orange ceiling vent. She reached out, *hurts*, grabbed the hoses, pulled them aside. *There you are, you fuck.* He was leaning up against the far wall, grinning, metal racks of lab kit behind him: microscopes, test tubes, big glass jars of chemicals. She tried her legs again, felt a blast of pain.

Need to get up...

"Your fault, using Clapham," he said. "Dirty little shit rang me back the second you left. Should've seen that coming, you and your pet giant over there." He turned his head. She knew he was looking through the window at King, trapped back in another lab, no help at all. And no phones, no backup, Black in the air, *Christ, so fucking fucked...*

She fought the panic, pushed it away.

Focus.

"And besides," Hurst said, "you're a cop. Ought to be doing your job. Catching people that, you know, actually *break* the law." Smirked, pulled something small from the pocket of his chinos, turned it over in his hands. "What laws did *I* break? Two years ago? Made a business call. Optimized the timing for implementing production improvements. Perfectly legal. Didn't even lie to Flinders. Told him I'd make the switch, and I did." A tiny grin. "Just never said *when*, exactly."

The pain was unbearable. She felt herself fading.

Heard Jack's voice in her head: *Get up, Champ.*

But I can't, Jack...

Hurst kept talking. "And then, the murder? Went upstairs to speak with my business partner about corporate strategy. Found him dead." A shrug. He fiddled with whatever was in his hands. "Noticed a piece of company property on his desk, so as a good corporate fiduciary, I reclaimed it. Doing my duty. Might be valuable someday. See?" He held it up: a syringe, capped, bright green liquid inside.

Lucy stared.

Antidote.

A for antidote, oh God, there it is.

Need to save it, need to, must be a way...

"And as for my old EA's brat, the half-Meat..."

She looked around, left, right, searching for something, anything: a weapon, a tool, a lever to move the freezer. *Fuck. Nothing.* Tried to block Hurst out, focus, but snatches slipped through: "...bitch should've just kept quiet, husband would never...damn kid harassed me for years...finally made him useful..." Felt like screaming, but no point, the room was perfectly sealed. Glass walls ran all the way up to the high tiled ceiling with its goddamn orange vent, no one to hear her, no way in or out and—

Wait.

She looked up at the vent.

It was hanging from a wire brace fixed to the ceiling tiles, thirty feet above the far side of the lab. Air hoses dangled down from its side, five or six of them, thick red coils like giant Slinkys.

She could reach two.

What if...

Her monitor beeped.

"...and I *told* him not to touch that syringe," Hurst said. "Warned him." As he spoke, he stared down at the antidote, twirling it like a biro in his fingers. "Grown man, made his own decision. Just like *you* made yours." Another chuckle. "First attacking me at the airport, *completely* unprovoked, now chasing me in here. You knew better. Specifically warned you not to enter the hot side when you came onsite. Ten witnesses. But you just couldn't let go…"

She stretched out, grabbed the hoses.

Her ankles burned.

If I pull…?

Gave a tug. The coils went taut.

Heavy. So fucking heavy. And even if I can pull the vent loose, it could fall anywhere. On him, on me, in between. Total shot in the dark. And then the tiles, they may come down too, the whole fucking ceiling…

"No," he said, eyes still focused on the antidote, "you just *had* to chase me back here. And then that cable you tripped over? Clumsy, clumsy." He tutted. "We do tell the techs to take care but, well, accidents happen." An exaggerated shrug. "Experimental types of London Black here, too. Nasty. One you just so *happened* to knock over? Choke to death on your own blood, so they say."

Her skin prickled.

Another beep.

"Well, expect you're just obsessed with me," he said. Sighed. "Wouldn't be the first."

She watched him grin.

You're disgusting, Hurst.

Took a breath, started to pull. Her ankles throbbed but she ignored the pain, pulled hard, *harder*, hard as she could. Felt her shoulders burn. Remembered pull-ups in her little black flat, late at night, doing them over and over until the tears streamed down and her mind burned because of the Thing, the Thing, always the fucking Thing, pull-up after pull-up until she crumpled to the floor, gasping, shaking, drowning in guilt.

Oh God oh Jack, help me now, fuck, fucking PULL…

The vent brace began to shake.

"Funny." Hurst was checking his reflection in the fume-hood window. "Salford said you had this bizarre *guilt* thing. A complex." He laughed, a sarky little titter. "Christ, haven't you *heard*? Guilt is dead. Do what's best for you, everyone else bloody well will…"

She pulled as hard as she fucking could.

A bolt popped loose.

The vent was teetering now.

"Shame, really." He turned back to her. "Would've loved to have you in Monaco." Grinned. "You know what they say about the crazy ones…"

"Hey," she called out. "Hurst."

Stared at his perfect white teeth. Thought of his massive office, the Chesterfields, the Ferrari desk chair. Then the Scourge. All of it, the Boost shortage, people crying, screaming, bodies burning in the streets, riots and blood and death.

And Lucy said:

"Fuck. *You.*"

Then she pulled, one last pull, *here it fucking comes.* Felt the hoses go slack. Covered her head and shut her eyes and heard the vent crash down, everything crashing at once, all around her, blows to her body, her head, *fuck*, pain shooting from her ankles, *fucking hurts*, then a horrible piercing shriek, sounded like an animal screaming, screeching in pain…

Then: silence.

She took a breath.

Another.

Uncovered her head. Looked around.

The lab was a shambles. Shit everywhere. Ceiling tiles, broken glass. Hazy. She sniffed, smelled rotten eggs. Glanced down and saw the freezer had shifted. *Maybe…?* Her ankles still throbbed but she reached down, tugged her legs. They slid free.

Oh, thank Christ.

Now…

She started to crawl.

Felt dizzy, knew it was the blow to her head. Her vision blurred. She shoved aside a stool and pulled herself forward, hands gripping the cold black floor, feet dragging behind.

Her monitor beeped.

5.6? Or 5.5, could be, dropping so fast.

Simon's voice: *Five alive, Luce…*

She crawled around a machine that had been knocked down by a ceiling tile. Her head was throbbing, she was fading and for a second, it was two years ago, this room was still an Iso Centre ward and she was crawling through rows of camp beds, past blood and skin and sick, patients screaming and Dad somewhere and—

Focus.

Shook her head. Snapped back to now. Shoved aside a chair and there he was: Geoff Hurst, lying face down in a big red puddle. He was still. All around him, glass from shattered chemical jars sparkled.

The antidote…now where…

She spotted it, a few feet away from Hurst's outstretched fingers.

There.

The red puddle was slowly spreading, oozing towards the syringe.

Could be acid, fuck…

She took a breath, then started crawling. Glass everywhere but she had no choice, no time, the hoodie protected her arms but she could feel tiny slivers cutting into her hands, wrists, *fucking hurts, Christ.* Looked up. Fumes: her eyes watered. Saw that the puddle was almost there now, almost to the syringe so she sped up, crawling as fast as she could, whole body burning, ankles, head, wrists, *come on, faster…*

She reached out.

Grabbed it.

Got you.

Pulled it back, held it close. Smiled. *Safe.*

Then her monitor beeped.

5.4.

And she remembered: the Black.

Tiny, invisible particles, suspended in the air. In her lungs already, all over her, face, hands, everywhere, and her levels plummeting, Boost nearly gone. She closed her eyes. Remembered faces she'd seen, patients dying, their skin peeling away, blood pouring from their eyes, noses, mouths.

Oh, please, not that way.

Don't want to go that way…

Heard Hurst's voice in her head: *Do what's best for you, everyone else bloody well will.*

She took a deep breath.

Looked down at the syringe.

No one would know.

Tried to push the thought away, but she couldn't. It was true. Knew it was, knew no one else even believed in the antidote, never had, not really. *Told them, told King, Wilkes, but no one listened.* Ran fingers through her hair, blood from her wrists smearing her face. *And isn't this what you wanted all along, really, Lucy? What this was all about, deep down? Always knew it. Tried to tell yourself it wasn't but it was, had to be. Not the Debt, not really, just about a way out, a way to live, not your fault, genetics and bad luck and not your fucking fault…*

BEEEEEEEP.

The needle glinted.

One jab.

One jab, and you live.

She took a breath. Her vision was blurred again. She felt dizzy.

What do I do, Jack?

And everything was spinning now, and she felt herself fading, slipping away like it was the middle of the night and she hadn't slept for days, like she was sitting in her little black flat, legs crossed, feeling the darkness come, trying to fight it off, fuck you sleep…

Focus, fucking focus, need to—

She slumped to the ground.

Her eyes closed: black.

‡ ‡ ‡

I'm in Hell now.

Hell is an Iso Centre lobby floor. Cold, dirty. I'm sitting, slumped, eyes red. Tired, so fucking tired. Fifth day. No leaving, can't leave, mustn't, just sitting, fingering my ring, crying, watching as the orderlies come and call out names and women wail and Oh! Dead, dead, dead. Know Si's in there, somewhere, lying on a crap camp bed, skin peeling and he's bleeding, dying, fucking dying because he saved me, saved my life and now he's in there and I'm here and—

Someone says my name, and I look up.

And it's him.

He's standing. Si, oh God, it's Si, he's standing right there, oh thank you and I hear the doctor say Survivor and I'm leaping up, running to him, holding him. And he's wearing a mask, crap white gauze, and I know what's happened, what's under there but fuck it, doesn't matter, didn't lose him, still here and it's okay, oh thank fucking God, okay. Kissing him, hard as I can but he's turning away…

And then we're home.

We're home in our little flat and it's December now. Dark, night, cold. Kitchen table. His whiskey bottle is a quarter gone, drinking lots now, fuck else can he do? Hospital's told him, sorry, not his fault, nothing personal but patients don't like it, hard for them, he understands of course? Tour guide instructor took him aside, word of advice, there's a good chap. And he's frowning at me, mask on but I can still tell, tell what he's thinking too: about me, what he did for me, what he gave.

And now it's January.

Cold, only three o'clock but it's dark and his vodka's half gone, and I see him looking at me, scowling, know he's thinking it: you. Because of you. I'm like this because of you. It's there now, all the time, hanging in the air, thick, a fucking haze, and I'm smiling at him, trying, trying fucking everything but nothing works, he's turning away, another drink, another.

And February now.

Gin bottle's empty. Dark out, window black. He's staring at me across the table, black eyes burning, hating me and it's awful, awful all the time now, so fuck it, enough. And I'm standing up, crying, saying it one more time: It's me, Si. It's me, and I see you. See your same face, doesn't matter to me, young, old, red, scarred, none of it because I always know it's you, your face, how the Party Trick works, yeah? I'm the girl that sees faces and I still. See. You.

And then he throws the bottle.

Smash. Hits the wall, behind my head. A million pieces of glass on the table, the floor, my clothes. Tiny sparkling jewels everywhere.

And now I'm staring at him.

Taking off the ring.

Putting it down.

I'm walking out, and he's saying, Stop, no Luce, didn't mean it, please. Reaching for me, and I try to slip him, dodge him like a punch but his fingers graze my stomach and I feel them, feel his touch on my bruises, bruises from the Boosts, his Boosts but still I keep going, out the door, down the hall. Off to the pub, shit pub, the usual, Harry.

And I'm thinking about it, fuck was I thinking, know him, know how he is. Starting to worry.

Texting him, but nothing.

Calling.

And something's wrong, very wrong, know it is, can feel it so I'm off, back to Goswell Road. Running now. Down the street, dodging cars, running hard, so fucking hard and how the fuck could I do it and please God and I'm turning the corner, outside the flat and I see her, oh God oh Jesus, a paramedic, pretty blonde long neck and she sees me, tries to stop me but I push past and I'm up the stairs now, sprinting down the hall, pushing through the red door and I'm there and I see the belt, his belt, oh God Si, and it's stretched out, fuck me Christ it's wrapped round the pull-up bar and I see his feet dangling and I'm screaming, screaming in the mirror and I see myself screaming and it's The Thing, The Thing That Happened, is Happening and I scream, fucking SCREAM and—

‡ ‡ ‡

Her eyes opened.

And she knew.

Know what I need to do.

I'm paying the fucking Debt.

Lucy pulled off her hoodie. Opened the special padded pocket, the one she'd had custom sewn. Took a last look at the antidote—*so beautiful*—then pushed it inside. Closed the pocket. Thought about what happened back then. What she'd done. One more time, everything, all of it, start to finish, right up to The Thing. A tear plunked to the black lab floor. Then she balled the hoodie up, threw it as far as she could, up on a rack, out of reach, safe.

There.

Her monitor beeped.

5.1.

She pulled up her vest. Looked down at the little disc, a white circle in the middle of the angry purple bruises. Read the logo: Cox Labs. *Done with this.* Grabbed it, pulled the sensor needles away from her skin, threw the monitor into the puddle. Heard it fizz. *No more beeps.*

Took a breath.

Inhale, exhale.

Felt the guilt fall away.

All gone now. Debt paid in full, big black mountain crumbling into ash.

Finished.

It's fucking finished.

She looked down at her wrist. Saw her tattoo, smeared with blood. Rubbed it with her thumb, then closed her eyes. *Look out, Jack. Here I come. Coming, be there soon, maybe we can spar, find me some gloves, yeah?* A big smile. *It's okay, it's all okay, truly, better than okay, actually because I did it, paid the Debt at last, and I'm not scared, not scared at all now, and here I come and—*

Wait.

She felt her gears turning.

Felt the Party Trick working.

And then she finally remembered where she'd seen Geoff Hurst before: just once, two years ago. Reading a magazine in a small room. Horrid taupe wallpaper, fake palm trees. *Doctor Hodges's waiting room. Which means...* Her eyes popped open. *Which means, Hurst's Vulnerable. Must be. And he was in London during the big attack, know he was, which means Boosts aren't working for him either, can't be. But he was in here, right here, not scared of Black, so...*

Heard Coffee No. 6's voice: *There are a few employees using Ultra prototypes.*

She looked over at Hurst's body. Started crawling. Fast as she could, through the glass, *hurts*, no time, *hurry*, skirted the puddle, *fucking hurry*. Reached his waist. Grabbed his red chinos, rolled him over onto his back. Pulled herself up, crawling onto his body, a raft in the big red puddle. Glanced at his face, but he had no face now, just a red mess, smelt awful, *Christ*. Patted him down, hands flying, fingers digging through his pockets. *Come on, come on*. Checked the chinos, the shirt. *Please*. Felt the jacket, *no*, outside pockets, *fuck*, the liner and—*there*. She felt something. Thin, hard. Pulled it out. Held it up: a syringe. Read the label: COX LABS—ELEMIDOX ULTRA ©—25mL.

Ultra.

U not A.

She ripped off the cap. Prepped the needle, pulled up her vest, picked a spot.

Took a breath.

Spoke out loud, the pain making each word come out as a gasp:

"You. Deserve. This."

And then Lucy injected.

CHAPTER TWENTY-SIX

Three Weeks Later

"But I thought you were sleeping better now?"

Wilkes eyed the Coke bottle as it foamed.

Lucy crumpled her empty espresso cup, tossed it in the overflowing Starbucks bin. Shrugged. She *was* sleeping better. Five sessions in, and the Screamers were down to every other night. Even had a bed now, proper one from Ikea, put it together herself straight away after she finished painting the flat. *So, yes, Ma'am. Sleeping better.* She took a sip from the bottle. *Still a fab fucking drink, though.*

They sat down at a window table.

"It's official, then?" Lucy asked.

Wilkes nodded. "Official, I'm afraid."

Sad, in a way.

"Well," Lucy said, "the new DCI won't hold a candle to you, Ma'am. Whoever it is." Took another sip, then smiled. "But you'll be a brilliant Chief Superintendent."

Wilkes laughed. "Funny, isn't it? Turns out being old school chums with Geoff Hurst might not be the best thing for your career after all." She toyed with her tea bag, then drank. Her lipstick left a dark red smudge on the cup. "And since you mention the new DCI…"

Lucy shrugged. "To be honest, Ma'am? Just glad it's not Sykes." *Fucking Sykes.* Wished like hell she'd been there to see it: Sykes slapped in the face by a TV reporter. On camera, live, standing outside Cox Labs HQ. Media Review told her that the red mark was still there the next day.

Now that's the Hand of God.

"Andy Sykes?" Wilkes waved him away. "Pfft. Never would have allowed it, even if he hadn't been knocked all the way down to DC. Honestly? Expect he'll be gone once the dust settles on his court case. What a twat." She grinned. Took a sip of tea, fingered her gold watch. Thought for a moment, then: "Thing is, Lucy, as of today, you're officially back."

A nod. Lucy fingered her warrant card, safe in her hoodie pocket.

I am.

Thank fucking Christ.

"And so I thought, well, you made DI at twenty-nine." A smile. "So…what do you say to DCI at thirty?" She noticed a drop of white paint on Lucy's hoodie sleeve, frowned at it. "Might need to make a quick trip to Max Mara, though…"

Lucy stared at her for a moment, speechless.

Then she burst into a grin.

"Be brilliant, Ma'am. Truly. Thank you very much, Ma'am."

Might still wear the hoodie, though.

"Fuck's sake," Wilkes groaned. "Ma'am, *still*? You *really* need to start calling me Marie…"

Oh. Well…

Lucy looked down at her Coke bottle.

For a moment, she thought of a florist in Bethnal Green, three doors down from Dad's shop. Tried to picture the woman who'd worked there so many years ago. The one face the Party Trick couldn't recall, that she could never *quite* remember…but then again, how could she, really? Only three when it happened. When the cancer sneaked in, snatched her Mum away. *But she looked like me. Everyone said. Jack. Dad, even. Who I look like, really, not the Actor, not anyone else. I look like her.*

She sighed.

Glanced back up, watched Wilkes take a last sip of tea. Thought about her, now: the tall, well-dressed cop who'd saved her, taken her in from awful SIU, welcomed her into MIT 19 with open arms. About the shopping trips, the late-night chats. And all those leaflets, two full years of them. Didn't matter that she'd binned them, just kept showing up on her crap little desk, over and over, day after day. *Only family I've got, really. The only one who helped me, who actually gave a toss about me.*

You, Ma'am.

Lucy shrugged. Gave a tiny smile.

"Just like calling you Ma'am," she said. "Ma'am."

‡ ‡ ‡

Two hours later, she walked through the gate at Brompton Cemetery.

It was quiet. Bit parky: stiff December wind. She shoved her hands into her hoodie pockets as she walked. No ankle pain. *Bloody miracle,* the doctor had told her. *Should've taken two months. Fast healer, you are.* She'd just shrugged. Tugged on her socks, her grimy black trainers. Gone back to thinking about how the fuck to heal the rest of her.

And now here she was, in Brompton again.

Second crossing, turn right at the red marble tomb…

She passed an old gravestone, lettering worn smooth. A memory: Simon, pointing out a green square in the City, telling her it was a burial ground once, Luce, believe that? Three hundred years old, more maybe, she didn't remember. Wondered if that would happen here in Brompton someday, if all these crosses and vaults would be gone, dragged away, and this would just be an empty green field, a stop on a walking tour maybe, someplace for a cute Aussie guide to give a cheeky grin and say, Know what you're walking on, mate?

Now a left at the angel, then down three plots and…

She stopped.

There it was: Simon's gravestone. Skull at the top, spidery writing. She looked at the stacks of black Boost caps, hundreds of them, covering the stone's base. A stack had fallen over and scattered on the ground. Lucy knelt, started picking them up. Her fingers still hurt: all that glass, cuts everywhere, and then the acid had burnt the tips where she'd touched Hurst's red chinos. But she did it anyway, grabbed every last cap, stacked them back up and then stood.

Took a breath.

Right. Now then...

She closed her eyes, thought about The Thing That Happened.

It was tragic. So fucking awful, heartbreaking, Christ. Knew she'd never be done with it, not all the way done. Never. It would be there always, in the back of her dreams, a splinter stuck in her mind that she couldn't shake free. But she could talk about it now, and talking helped. King had been right. Five sessions in, shedloads more to go but fuck it, the time for this bit had come.

She pictured Simon, his high cheekbones, sky blue eyes.

I loved you, Si. Still do, if I'm honest.

But...you tricked me.

A frown.

You tricked me. Trapped me. Didn't ask for a martyr, never wanted that, not fair to throw it in my face, over and over and over. And then, a bottle? Fuck's sake, Si. Glass everywhere, bits in my clothes, could've hurt me. Might've, next time. Why I left, why I did what I did, every right to.

So...

Yes. Yes, Si, I needed to pay the Debt.

Needed to pay it, because only now, now that I've paid, can I finally see.

Lucy opened her eyes. Knelt down, stared at the gravestone.

Felt a tear wet her cheek.

Now I can see the truth.

Then she said it out loud, voice firm, to him, to Simon:

"There never really was a Debt at all."

The wind picked up.

She flipped her hood, tugged on the strings. Stood. Looked down at the piles of tiny black discs. "Clinical trials started yesterday," she said. A little smile. "I went first." Reached into her hoodie, pulled out another disc: white. "Saved it. For you, Si." She put it down on the headstone, then took a breath, leaned over. Gave the stone a kiss.

And then Lucy turned and walked away.

‡ ‡ ‡

She finally caught King outside the MIT 19 toilets.

She'd been looking for him off and on all afternoon. Started searching as soon as she was back from Brompton, but he was always busy, always with someone. She wanted him alone. No Media Review, no Wilkes, no HR reps barging in with stacks of bumf for her to sign. *Just Ed King.* And now, finally, here he was, all six foot three of him, clean-shaven, toying with his battered watch.

"Ed?"

He looked up. She smelt his aftershave.

Wearing it again.

And he knew it was my first day back…

Lucy smiled at him. "Wanted to tell you something," she said.

"Sure." A glance at the watch. "But…it's getting on. Anything important?"

She thought about it. About all the times over the past three weeks she'd rehearsed this, the million ways she'd tried to say it. It always came out the same somehow. *Remember when we met, Ed? And I said I recognized you from Bristol, the coffee queue? And then Sykes was awful, course he bloody was, and said, Oh, Lucy, Super*

*Recognizer? Well…not true. Not exactly. I mean, yes, Party Trick would've worked, always does, but actually, with you? Didn't need it. Thing is, Ed, I remembered you because…I thought you were cute. And, now that I can drink again, wondered if you maybe wanted to drop by the Carpenters? Pint, dinner after? Doesn't have to be chips, promise…*She nodded. "Yes. Important." Glanced at the toilet doors. *Not the most romantic, maybe, but fuck it. I tried, yeah?*

He shrugged. "In that case? To be honest, I've got something important to tell you, too."

She tried to hide her grin. Couldn't.

Knew it.

Fucking knew it.

"But," he said, "you first."

She shook her head. *Come on, Ed. Chivalry's dead.* "You."

"Right, well, fair enough." He took a deep breath. Looked her in the eyes.

It's okay. Out with it.

King said: "Remember back at SRA headquarters? Your attack? I'm the one that grassed on you to Wilkes. Not Sykes. It was me."

Lucy stared at him.

The fuck?

He kept talking. "Now that you're getting better, I wanted to tell you." A sigh. "Felt awful about it, but honestly, thought it was the right thing. Knew you needed help. I mean, it was just so clear, and I didn't know if Wilkes was ignoring it, or what." He spread his big hands. "Really, Lucy. I had your best interests at heart…"

She frowned.

Well, suppose that's okay. I mean, good intentions, true, but—

"And also," he said, "if I'm honest? Really honest, openness and transparency? There was another reason, too."

Yes?

348

Yes, Ed?

"Thing is, I'd just finished interviewing Veronica for the first time, and, well, sounds silly, I realize, I'd only just met her, but already I was thinking that, I don't know, maybe—"

Behind him, the door of the women's opened.

Veronica Cox stepped out.

Huh?

She didn't notice Lucy. Just walked up behind King, frowning, fiddling with a posh-looking earring. "Sorry, Ed," she said, "just had to fix this bloody thing, such a faff, but I'll give the restaurant a ring and—" She saw Lucy. Stopped.

The two women stared at each other.

Oh.

And then it all made sense: why the aftershave on some days, but not others. *Wore it when you knew you would see her, yeah? Returning my red SRA water bottle, setting up the Lambeth meeting. For fuck's sake, and here I thought…*She glanced away. Felt like a punch to the gut, worse even, because she hadn't covered up in the slightest. Left herself wide fucking open, poor tactics, Lucy. She looked back at him. Saw the big jaw, green eyes. Reminded her a bit of Jack, boxer even, Christ, really liked this guy, and it hurt, felt sick, such a blow but then suddenly she realized: she wasn't having an attack. *Hang on a tick. That's Veronica Cox. Ex-paramedic, pretty blonde, long neck. She's right fucking there, staring at you, and you aren't losing your shit, flashing back, sprinting off to scream in the fucking loo. So…that's brilliant, right?* She took a breath. Turned to Veronica. "Hiya," she said.

"Hiya," Veronica said. Glanced at King, then back to Lucy. Awkward smile. "Erm…"

"Thank you for the cheese and pickle," Lucy said.

"Oh," said Veronica. "Well. *So* glad. Ed said you were veggie, so I just thought…"

Lucy nodded. "Nice one," she said. "Truly." To King: "Right, well, Ed, it's getting on and you should probably…"

"Thanks," he said. "Really. I feel better." Smiled at her, then looked at Veronica. "Let's?"

Veronica nodded, slipped her arm through King's, and together they strolled away.

Lucy watched them walk down the corridor.

Took a deep breath. Another.

Thought for a moment, then decided:

It's fine, actually.

It is.

In fact, it's better than fine, because it's Tuesday. And Tuesday's spar night. And she remembered two years ago, the last time she tried to go to spar night. Back before everything happened. Before the little black rectangle, before her world fell to shit. Remembered lying on the floor, under the bed, reaching out for a boxing glove that had been shoved behind a stack of Simon's London books: hidden away, left to rot. She nodded to herself, ran her fingers through her short brown hair. *It's fine, really it is. Don't need Ed King. Fact, I don't need anyone now, not just yet. I'm free. Free from the Debt, from Si, from everything. I can go to spar night, eat my chips and drink my drink and fuck it, I can be happy.*

At the end of the corridor, Veronica glanced back over her shoulder.

Lucy gave a little wave to the pretty blonde with the long neck.

Then she looked down.

Smiled.

Her hands weren't shaking.

Her hands were rock fucking solid.

ACKNOWLEDGEMENTS

I owe thanks to many more people than I can list here, but especially—

To Craig Taylor, for whose teaching, mentorship and enthusiastic support I'm forever grateful. Thank you, Craig.

To Laurence King and Amanda Saint, amazing teachers both.

This book was written on a Jericho Writers novel-writing course designed by Craig and Amanda, and simply would not exist without it. Many thanks to the helpful and inspiring crew at Jericho, including Harry Bingham, Esther Vincent, Maria Pace, Polly Peraza-Brown and especially Rachael Cooper, whose dedication made all the difference.

To my wonderful agent, Jordan Lees at The Blair Partnership, who believed in this book from the first time he read it and worked tirelessly to help it on its way. Massive thanks, Jordan.

To Harriet Wade at Pushkin, whose enthusiasm blew me away from the start. To Liz Woabank, for her insight and patience. To everyone else at Pushkin, especially India Edwards, Kirsten Chapman, Elise Jackson, Tara McEvoy, Poppy Luckett and Jo Walker (whose cover I love). And to Lin Vasey, who made copyediting a pleasure.

To my friends and colleagues (and especially those who are both).

To the authors and musicians, actors and filmmakers who provided inspiration along the way. To Ernest B. Gilman, whose work fascinated me. To London and Londoners, past, present and future. And to Rikki Harden, we did it and I hope you like your cameo.

To Lucy, for teaching me to just keep…fucking…going.

And most of all, to my family, especially my father, Bob, and brother, Dave; my mother-in-law, Betsy, who helped enormously during this book's early days; my mother, Barbara, who provided unending support and was the first person to read these pages; my wonderful wife, Emily, who was first to hear about Lucy and who was by my side every step of the long journey to publication; and my daughter, Mia, who fills every day with joy and love.